"I can help you," he said before he could let himself think about it, and he thrust out his hand. **"Massimo Valtieri. If you're ready to go, I can give you a lift to Siena now."**

He pronounced it Mah-*see*-mo, long and slow and drawn out, his Italian accent coming over loud and clear as he said his name, and she felt a shiver of something primeval down her spine. Or maybe it was just the cold. She smiled at her self-appointed knight in shining armour and held out her hand.

"I'm Lydia Fletcher—and if you can get us there before the others I'll love you for ever."

His warm, strong and surprisingly slightly calloused fingers closed firmly round hers, and she felt the world shift a little under her feet. And not just hers, apparently. She saw the shockwave hit his eyes, felt the recognition of something momentous passing between them, and in that crazy and insane instant she wondered if anything would ever be the same again…

VALTIERI'S BRIDE

BY
CAROLINE ANDERSON

First published in Great Britain 2012
by Mills & Boon, an imprint of Harlequin (UK) Limited,
Eton House, 18-24 Paradise Road, Richmond, Surrey TW9 1SR

© Caroline Anderson 2012

ISBN: 978 0 263 89445 5
ebook ISBN: 978 1 408 97118 5

23-0712

Harlequin (UK) policy is to use papers that are natural, renewable and recyclable products and made from wood grown in sustainable forests. The logging and manufacturing processes conform to the legal environmental regulations of the country of origin.

Printed and bound in Spain
by Blackprint CPI, Barcelona

Caroline Anderson has the mind of a butterfly. She's been a nurse, a secretary, a teacher, run her own soft furnishing business, and now she's settled on writing. She says, 'I was looking for that elusive something. I finally realised it was variety, and now I have it in abundance. Every book brings new horizons and new friends, and in between books I have learned to be a juggler. My teacher husband John and I have two beautiful and talented daughters, Sarah and Hannah, umpteen pets, and several acres of Suffolk that nature tries to reclaim every time we turn our backs!' Caroline also writes for the Mills & Boon® Medical Romance™ series.

CHAPTER ONE

WHAT *on earth* was she doing?

As the taxi pulled up in front of the Jet Centre at London City Airport, he paused, wallet in hand, and stared spellbound across the drop-off point.

Wow. She was *gorgeous*.

Even in the crazy fancy-dress outfit, her beauty shone out like a beacon. Her curves—soft, feminine curves—were in all the right places, and her face was alight with laughter, the skin pale and clear, her cheeks tinged pink by the long blonde curls whipping round her face in the cutting wind. She looked bright and alive and impossibly lovely, and he felt something squeeze in his chest.

Something that had been dormant for a very long time.

As he watched she anchored the curls absently with one hand, the other gesturing expressively as she smiled and talked to the man she'd stopped at the entrance. She was obviously selling something. Goodness knows what, he couldn't read the piece of card she was brandishing from this distance, but the man laughed and raised a hand in refusal and backed away, entering the building with a chuckle.

Her smile fading, she turned to her companion, more sensibly dressed in jeans and a little jacket. Massimo flicked his eyes over her, but she didn't hold his attention. Not like the blonde, and he found his eyes drawn back to her against his will.

Dio, she was exquisite. By rights she should have looked an utter tramp but somehow, even in the tacky low-cut dress and a gaudy plastic tiara, she was, quite simply, riveting. There was something about her that transcended all of that, and he felt himself inexplicably drawn to her.

He paid the taxi driver, hoisted his flight bag over his shoulder and headed for the entrance. She was busy again, talking to another man, and as the doors opened he caught her eye and she flashed a hopeful smile at him.

He didn't have time to pause, whatever she was selling, he thought regretfully, but the smile hit him in the solar plexus, and he set his bag down on the floor by the desk once he was inside, momentarily winded.

'Morning, Mr Valtieri. Welcome back to the Jet Centre. The rest of your party have arrived.'

'Thank you.' He cleared his throat and glanced over his shoulder at the woman. 'Is that some kind of publicity stunt?'

The official gave a quiet, mildly exasperated sigh and smiled wryly.

'No, sir. I understand she's trying to get a flight to Italy.'

Massimo felt his right eyebrow hike. 'In a *wedding dress*?'

He gave a slight chuckle. 'Apparently so. Some competition to win a wedding.'

He felt a curious sense of disappointment. Not that it made the slightest bit of difference that she was getting married; she was nothing to him and never would be, but nevertheless…

'We asked her to leave the building, but short of escorting her right back to the main road, there's little more we can do to get rid of her and she seems harmless enough. Our clients seem to be finding her quite entertaining, anyway.'

He could understand that. He was entertained himself—mesmerised, if he was honest. And intrigued—

'Whereabouts in Italy?' he asked casually, although the tightness in his gut was far from casual.

'I think I heard her mention Siena—but, Mr Valtieri, you really don't want to get involved,' he warned, looking troubled. 'I think she's a little…'

'Crazy?' he said drily, and the man's mouth twitched.

'Your word, sir, not mine.'

As they watched, the other man walked away and she gave her companion a wry little smile. She said something, shrugged her slender shoulders in that ridiculous meringue of a dress, then rubbed her arms briskly. She must be freezing! September was a strange month, and today there wasn't a trace of sunshine and a biting wind was whipping up the Thames estuary.

No! It was none of his business if she hadn't had the sense to dress for the weather, he told himself firmly, but then he saw another man approach the doors, saw the woman straighten her spine and go up to him, her face wreathed in smiles as she launched into a fresh charm offensive, and he felt his gut clench.

He knew the man slightly, more by reputation than anything else, and he was absolutely the last person this enchanting and slightly eccentric young woman needed to get involved with. And he would be flying to his private airfield, about an hour's drive from Siena. Close enough, if you were desperate…

He couldn't let it happen. He had more than enough on his conscience.

The doors parted with a hiss as he strode up to them, and he gave the other man a look he had no trouble reading. He told him—in Italian, and succinctly—to back off, and Nico shrugged and took his advice, smiling regretfully at the woman before moving away from her, and Massimo gave him a curt nod and turned to the woman, meeting her eyes again—vivid, startling blue eyes that didn't look at all happy with what he'd just done. There was no smile this time, just those eyes like blue ice-chips skewering him as he stood there.

Stunning eyes, framed by long, dark lashes. Her mouth, even without the smile, was soft and full and kissable— No! He sucked in a breath, and found himself drawing a delicate and haunting fragrance into his lungs.

It rocked him for a second, took away his senses, and when they came back they *all* came back, slamming into him with the force of an express train and leaving him wanting in a way he hadn't wanted for years. Maybe ever—

'What did you *say* to him?' Lydia asked furiously, hardly able to believe the way he'd dismissed that man with a few choice words—not that she'd understood one of them, of course, but there was more to language than vocabulary and he'd been pretty explicit, she was sure. But she'd been so close to success and she was really, really cross and frustrated now. 'He'd just offered me a seat in his plane!'

'Believe me, you don't want to go on his plane.'

'Believe me, I do!' she retorted, but he shook his head.

'No. I'm sorry, I can't let you do it, it just isn't safe,' he said, a little crisply, and she dropped her head back and gave a sharp sigh.

Damn. He must be airport security, and a higher authority than the nice young man who'd shifted them outside. She sensed there'd be no arguing with him. There was a quiet implacability about him that reminded her of her father, and she knew when she was beaten. She met his eyes again, and tried not to notice that they were the colour of dark, bitter chocolate, warm and rich and really rather gorgeous.

And unyielding.

She gave up.

'I would have been perfectly safe, I've got a minder and I'm no threat to anyone and nobody's complained, as far as I know, but you can call the dogs off, I'm going.'

To her surprise he smiled, those amazing eyes softening and turning her bones to mush.

'Relax, I'm nothing to do with Security, I just have a social conscience. I believe you need to go to Siena?'

Siena? Nobody, she'd discovered, was flying to Siena but it seemed, incredibly, that he might be, or else why would he be asking? She stifled the little flicker of hope. 'I thought you said it wasn't safe?'

'It wasn't safe with *Nico*.'

'And it's safe with you?'

'Safer. My pilot won't have been drinking, and I—' He broke off, and watched her eyes widen as her mind filled in the blanks.

'And you?' she prompted a little warily, when he left it hanging there.

He sighed sharply and raked a hand through his hair, rumpling the dark strands threaded with silver at the temples. He seemed impatient, as if he was helping her against his better judgement.

'He has a—reputation,' he said finally.

She dragged her eyes off his hair. It had flopped forwards, and her fingers itched to smooth it back, to feel the texture…

'And you don't?'

'Let's just say that I respect women.' His mouth flickered in a wry smile. 'If you want a reference, my lawyer and doctor brothers would probably vouch for me, as would my three sisters—failing that, you could phone Carlotta. She's worked for the family for hundreds of years, and she delivered me and looks after my children.'

He had children? She glanced down and clocked the wedding ring on his finger, and with a sigh of relief, she thrust a laminated sheet at him and dug out her smile again. This time, it was far easier, and she felt a flicker of excitement burst into life.

'It's a competition to win a wedding at a hotel near Siena. There are two of us in the final leg, and I have to get to the hotel first to win the prize. This is Claire, she's from the radio station doing the publicity.'

Massimo gave Claire a cursory smile. He wasn't in the least interested in Claire. She was obviously the minder, and pretty enough, but this woman with the crazy outfit and sassy mouth…

He scanned the sheet, scanned it again, shook his head in disbelief and handed it back, frankly appalled. 'You must be mad. You have only a hundred pounds, a wedding dress and a passport, and you have to race to Siena to win this wedding? What on *earth* is your fiancé thinking of to let you do it?'

'Not my fiancé. I don't have a fiancé, and if I did, I wouldn't need his permission,' she said crisply, those eyes turning to ice again. 'It's for my sister. She had an accident, and they'd planned—oh, it doesn't matter. Either you can help me or you can't, and if you can't, the clock's ticking and I really have to get on.'

She didn't have a fiancé? 'I can help you,' he said before he could let himself think about it, and he thrust out his hand. 'Massimo Valtieri. If you're ready to go, I can give you a lift to Siena now.'

He pronounced it Mah-*see*-mo, long and slow and drawn out, his Italian accent coming over loud and clear as he said his name, and she felt a shiver of something primeval down her spine. Or maybe it was just the cold. She smiled at her self-appointed knight in shining armour and held out her hand.

'I'm Lydia Fletcher—and if you can get us there before the others, I'll love you forever.'

His warm, strong and surprisingly slightly calloused fingers closed firmly round hers, and she felt the world shift a little under her feet. And not just hers, apparently. She saw the shockwave hit his eyes, felt the recognition of something momentous passing between them, and in that crazy and insane instant she wondered if anything would ever be the same again.

The plane was small but, as the saying goes, perfectly formed.

Very perfectly, as far as she was concerned. It had comfortable seats, lots of legroom, a sober pilot and a flight plan that without doubt would win her sister the wedding of her dreams.

Lydia could hardly believe her luck.

She buckled herself in, grabbed Claire's hand and hung on tight as the plane taxied to the end of the runway. 'We did it. We got a flight straight there!' she whispered, and Claire's face lit up with her smile, her eyes sparkling.

'I know. Amazing! We're going to do it. We can't fail. I just know you're going to win!'

The engines roared, the small plane shuddering, and then it was off like a slingshot, the force of their acceleration pushing her back hard into the leather seat as the jet tipped and climbed. The Thames was flying past, dropping rapidly below them as they rose into the air over London, and then they were heading out over the Thames estuary towards France, levelling off, and the seat belt light went out.

'Oh, this is so exciting! I'm going to update the diary,' Claire said, pulling out her little notebook computer, and Lydia turned her head and met Massimo's eyes across the narrow aisle.

He unclipped his seat belt and shifted his body so he was

facing her, his eyes scanning her face. His mouth tipped into a smile, and her stomach turned over—from the steep ascent, or from the warmth of that liquid-chocolate gaze?

'All right?'

'Amazing.' She smiled back, her mouth curving involuntarily in response to his, then turning down as she pulled a face. 'I don't know how to thank you. I'm so sorry I was rude.'

His mouth twitched. 'Don't worry. You weren't nearly as rude to me as I was to Nico.'

'What *did* you say to him?' she asked curiously, and he gave a soft laugh.

'I'm not sure it would translate. Certainly not in mixed company.'

'I think I got the gist—'

'I hope not!'

She gave a little laugh. 'Probably not. I don't know any street Italian—well, no Italian at all, really. And I feel awful now for biting your head off, but…well, it means a lot to me, to win this wedding.'

'Yes, I gather. You were telling me about your sister?' he said.

'Jennifer. She had an accident a few months ago and she was in a wheelchair, but she's getting better, she's on crutches now, but her fiancé had to give up his job to help look after her. They're living with my parents and Andy's working with Dad at the moment for their keep. My parents have got a farm—well, not really a farm, more of a smallholding, really, but they get by, and they could always have the wedding there. There's a vegetable packing barn they could dress up for the wedding reception, but—well, my grandmother lived in Italy for a while and Jen's always dreamed of getting married there, and now they haven't got enough money even for a glass of cheap bubbly and a few sandwiches. So when I heard about this competition I just jumped at it, but I never in my wildest dreams imagined we'd get this far, never mind get a flight to exactly the right place. I'm just so grateful I don't know where to start.'

She was gabbling. She stopped, snapped her mouth shut and gave him a rueful grin. 'Sorry. I always talk a lot when the adrenaline's running.'

He smiled and leant back, utterly charmed by her. More than charmed…

'Relax. I have three sisters and two daughters, so I'm quite used to it, I've had a lot of practice.'

'Gosh, it sounds like it. And you've got two brothers as well?'

'*Si*. Luca's the doctor and he's married to an English girl called Isabelle, and Gio's the lawyer. I also have a son, and two parents, and a million aunts and uncles and cousins.'

'So what do you do?' she asked, irresistibly curious, and he gave her a slightly lopsided grin.

'You could say I'm a farmer, too. We grow grapes and olives and we make cheese.'

She glanced around at the plane. 'You must make a heck of a lot of cheese,' she said drily, and he chuckled, soft and low under his breath, just loud enough for her to hear.

The slight huff of his breath made an errant curl drift against her cheek, and it was almost as if his fingertips had brushed lightly against her skin.

'Not that much,' he said, his eyes still smiling. 'Mostly we concentrate on our wine and olive oil—Tuscan olive oil is sharper, tangier than the oil from southern Italy because we harvest the olives younger to avoid the frosts, and it gives it a distinctive and rich peppery flavour. But again, we don't make a huge amount, we concentrate on quality and aim for the boutique market with limited editions of certified, artisan products. That's what I was doing in England—I've been at a trade fair pushing our oil and wine to restaurateurs and gourmet delicatessens.'

She sat up straighter. 'Really? Did you take samples with you?'

He laughed. 'Of course. How else can I convince people that our products are the best? But the timing was bad, because we're about to harvest the grapes and I'm needed at home. That's why we chartered the plane, to save time.'

Chartered. So it wasn't his. That made him more approachable, somehow and, if it was possible, even more attractive. As did the fact that he was a farmer. She knew about farming, about aiming for a niche market and going for quality rather than quantity. It was how she'd been brought up. She relaxed, hitched one foot up under her and hugged her knee under the voluminous skirt.

'So, these samples—do you have any on the plane that I could try?'

'Sorry, we're out of wine,' he said, but then she laughed and shook her head.

'That's not what I meant, although I'm sure it's very good. I was talking about the olive oil. Professional interest.'

'You grow olives on your farm in England?' he asked incredulously, and she laughed again, tightening his gut and sending need arrowing south. It shocked him slightly, and he forced himself to concentrate.

'No. Of course not. I've been living in a flat with a pot of basil on the window sill until recently! But I love food.'

'You mentioned a professional interest.'

She nodded. 'I'm a—' She was going to say chef, but could you be a chef if you didn't have a restaurant? If your kitchen had been taken away from you and you had nothing left of your promising career? 'I cook,' she said, and he got up and went to the rear of the plane and returned with a bottle of oil.

'Here.'

He opened it and held it out to her, and she sniffed it slowly, drawing the sharp, fruity scent down into her lungs. 'Oh, that's gorgeous. May I?'

And taking it from him, she tipped a tiny pool into her hand and dipped her finger into it, sucking the tip and making an appreciative noise. Heat slammed through him, and he recorked the bottle and put it away to give him something to do while he reassembled his brain.

He never, *never* reacted to a woman like this! What on earth was he thinking of? Apart from the obvious, but he didn't want to think about that. He hadn't looked at a woman in that way for years, hadn't thought about sex in he didn't know how long. So why now, why this woman?

She wiped up the last drop, sucking her finger again and then licking her palm, leaving a fine sheen of oil on her lips that he really, really badly want to kiss away.

'Oh, that is so good,' she said, rubbing her hands together to remove the last trace. 'It's a shame we don't have any bread or balsamic vinegar for dunking.'

He pulled a business card out of his top pocket and handed it to her, pulling his mind back into order and his eyes out of her cleavage. 'Email me your address when you get home, I'll send you some of our wine and oil, and also a traditional *aceto balsamico* made by my cousin in Modena. They only make a little, but it's the best I've ever tasted. We took some with us, but I haven't got any of that left, either.'

'Wow. Well, if it's as good as the olive oil, it must be fabulous!'

'It is. We're really proud of it in the family. It's nearly as good as our olive oil and wine.'

She laughed, as she was meant to, tucking the card into her bag, then she tipped her head on one side. 'Is it a family business?'

He nodded. 'Yes, most definitely. We've been there for

more than three hundred years. We're very lucky. The soil is perfect, the slopes are all in the right direction, and if we can't grow one thing on any particular slope, we grow another, or use it for pasture. And then there are the chestnut woods. We export a lot of canned chestnuts, both whole and puréed.'

'And your wife?' she asked, her curiosity getting the better of her. 'Does she help with the business, or do you keep her too busy producing children for you?'

There was a heartbeat of silence before his eyes clouded, and his smile twisted a little as he looked away. 'Angelina died five years ago,' he said softly, and she felt a wave of regret that she'd blundered in and brought his grief to life when they'd been having a sensible and intelligent conversation about something she was genuinely interested in.

She reached across the aisle and touched his arm gently. 'I'm so sorry. I wouldn't have brought it up if...'

'Don't apologise. It's not your fault. Anyway, five years is a long time.'

Long enough that, when confronted by a vivacious, dynamic and delightful woman with beautiful, generous curves and a low-cut dress that gave him a more than adequate view of those curves, he'd almost forgotten his wife...

Guilt lanced through him, and he pulled out his wallet and showed her the photos—him and Angelina on their wedding day, and one with the girls clustered around her and the baby in her arms, all of them laughing. He loved that one. It was the last photograph he had of her, and one of the best. He carried it everywhere.

She looked at them, her lips slightly parted, and he could see the sheen of tears in her eyes.

'You must miss her so much. Your poor children.'

'It's not so bad now, but they missed her at first,' he said gruffly. And he'd missed her. He'd missed her every single day, but missing her didn't bring her back, and he'd buried himself in work.

He was still burying himself in work.

Wasn't he?

Not effectively. Not any more, apparently, because suddenly he was beginning to think about things he hadn't thought about for years, and he wasn't ready for that. He couldn't deal with it, couldn't think about it. Not now. He had work to do, work that couldn't wait. Work he should be doing now.

He put the wallet away and excused himself, moving to sit with the others and discuss how to follow up the contacts they'd made and where they went from here with their marketing strategy, with his back firmly to Lydia and that ridiculous wedding dress that was threatening to tip him over the brink.

Lydia stared at his back, regret forming a lump in her throat.

She'd done it again. Opened her mouth and jumped in with both feet. She was good at that, gifted almost. And now he'd pulled away from her, and must be regretting the impulse that had made him offer her and Claire a lift to Italy.

She wanted to apologise, to take back her stupid and trite and intrusive question about his wife—Angelina, she thought, remembering the way he'd said her name, the way he'd almost tasted it as he said it, no doubt savouring the precious memories. But life didn't work like that.

Like feathers from a burst cushion, it simply wasn't possible to gather the words up and stuff them back in without trace. She just needed to move on from the embarrassing lapse, to keep out of his personal life and take his offer of a lift at face value.

And stop thinking about those incredible, warm chocolate eyes…

'I can't believe he's taking us right to Siena!' Claire said quietly, her eyes sparkling with delight. 'Jo will be so miffed when we get there first, she was so confident!'

Lydia dredged up her smile again, not hard when she thought about Jen and how deliriously happy she'd be to have her Tuscan wedding. 'I can't believe it, either. Amazing.'

Claire tilted her head on one side. 'What was he showing you? He looked sort of sad.'

She felt her smile slip. 'Photos of his wife. She died five years ago. They've got three little children—ten, seven and five, I think he said. Something like that.'

'Gosh. So the little one must have been tiny—did she die giving birth?'

'No. No, she can't have done. There was a photo of her with two little girls and a baby in her arms, so no. But it must have been soon after.'

'How awful. Fancy never knowing your mother. I'd die if I didn't have my mum to ring up and tell about stuff.'

Lydia nodded. She adored her mother, phoned her all the time, shared everything with her and Jen. What would it have been like never to have known her?

Tears welled in her eyes again, and she brushed them away crossly, but then she felt a light touch on her arm and looked up, and he was staring down at her, his face concerned.

He frowned and reached out a hand, touching the moisture on her cheek with a gentle fingertip.

'Lydia?'

She shook her head. 'I'm fine. Ignore me, I'm a sentimental idiot.'

He dropped to his haunches and took her hand, and she had a sudden and overwhelming urge to cry in earnest. 'I'm sorry. I didn't mean to distress you. You don't need to cry for us.'

She shook her head and sniffed again. 'I'm not. Not really.

I was thinking about my mother—about how I'd miss her—and I'm twenty-eight, not five.'

He nodded. 'Yes. It's very hard.' His mouth quirked in a fleeting smile. 'I'm sorry, I've neglected you. Can I get you a drink? Tea? Coffee? Water? Something stronger?'

'It's a bit early for stronger,' she said, trying for a light note, and he smiled again, more warmly this time, and straightened up.

'Nico would have been on the second bottle of champagne by now,' he said, and she felt a wave of relief that he'd saved her from what sounded more and more like a dangerous mistake.

'Fizzy water would be nice, if you have any?' she said, and he nodded.

'Claire?'

'That would be lovely. Thank you.'

He moved away, and she let her breath out slowly. She hadn't really registered, until he'd crouched beside her, just how big he was. Not bulky, not in any way, but he'd shed his jacket and rolled up his shirtsleeves, and she'd been treated to the broad shoulders and solid chest at close range, and then his narrow hips and lean waist and those long, strong legs as he'd straightened up.

His hands, appearing in her line of sight again, were clamped round two tall glasses beaded with moisture and fizzing gently. Large hands, strong and capable, no-nonsense.

Safe, sure hands that had held hers and warmed her to the core.

Her breasts tingled unexpectedly, and she took the glass from him and tried not to drop it. 'Thank you.'

'*Prego*, you're welcome. Are you hungry? We have fruit and pastries, too.'

'No. No, I'm much too excited to eat now,' she confessed,

sipping the water and hoping the cool liquid would slake the heat rising up inside her.

Crazy! He was totally uninterested in her, and even if he wasn't, she wasn't in the market for any more complications in her life. Her relationship with Russell had been fraught with complications, and the end of it had been a revelation. There was no way she was jumping back into that pond any time soon. The last frog she'd kissed had turned into a king-sized toad.

'How long before we land?' she asked, and he checked his watch, treating her to a bronzed, muscular forearm and strong-boned wrist lightly scattered with dark hair. She stared at it and swallowed. How ridiculous that an arm could be so sexy.

'Just over an hour. Excuse me, we have work to do, but please, if you need anything, just ask.'

He turned back to his colleagues, sitting down and flexing his broad shoulders, and Lydia felt her gut clench. She'd never, *never* felt like that about anyone before, and she couldn't believe she was reacting to him that way. It must just be the adrenaline.

One more hour to get through before they were there and they could thank him and get away—hopefully before she disgraced herself. The poor man was still grieving for his wife. What was she thinking about?

Ridiculous! She'd known him, what, less than two hours altogether? Scarcely more than one. And she'd already put her foot firmly in it.

Vowing not to say another thing, she settled back in her seat and looked out of the window at the mountains.

They must be the Alps, she realised, fascinated by the jagged peaks and plunging valleys, and then the mountains fell away behind them and they were moving over a chequered landscape of forests and small, neat fields. They were curiously ordered and disciplined, serried ranks of what must be olive trees and grape vines, she guessed, planted with geometric precision, the pattern of the fields interlaced with narrow winding roads lined with avenues of tall, slender cypress trees.

Tuscany, she thought with a shiver of excitement.

The seat belt light came on, and Massimo returned to his seat across the aisle from her as the plane started its descent.

'Not long now,' he said, flashing her a smile. And then they were there, a perfect touchdown on Tuscan soil with the prize almost in reach.

Jen was going to get her wedding. Just a few more minutes…

They taxied to a stop outside the airport building, and after a moment the steps were wheeled out to them and the door was opened.

'We're really here!' she said to Claire, and Claire's eyes were sparkling as she got to her feet.

'I know. I can't believe it!'

They were standing at the top of the steps now, and Massimo smiled and gestured to them. 'After you. Do you have the address of the hotel? I'll drive you there.'

'Are you sure?'

'I'd hate you not to win after all this,' he said with a grin.

'Wow, thank you, that's really kind of you!' Lydia said, reaching for her skirts as she took another step.

It happened in slow motion.

One moment she was there beside him, the next the steps had disappeared from under her feet and she was falling, tumbling end over end, hitting what seemed like every step until finally her head reached the tarmac and she crumpled on the ground in a heap.

Her scream was cut off abruptly, and Massimo hurled himself down the steps to her side, his heart racing. No! Please, she couldn't be dead…

She wasn't. He could feel a pulse in her neck, and he let his breath out on a long, ragged sigh and sat back on his heels to assess her.

Stay calm, he told himself. She's alive. She'll be all right.

But he wouldn't really believe it until she stirred, and even then…

'Is she all right?'

He glanced up at Claire, kneeling on the other side of her, her face chalk white with fear.

'I think so,' he said, but he didn't think any such thing. Fear was coursing through him, bringing bile rising to his throat. Why wasn't she moving? This couldn't be happening again.

Lydia moaned. Warm, hard fingers had searched for a pulse in her neck, and as she slowly came to, she heard him snap out something in Italian while she lay there, shocked and a little stunned, wondering if it was a good idea to open her eyes. Maybe not yet.

'Lydia? Lydia, talk to me! Open your eyes.'

Her eyes opened slowly and she tried to sit up, but he pressed a hand to her shoulder.

'Stay still. You might have a neck injury. Where do you hurt?'

Where didn't she? She turned her head and winced. 'Ow… my head, for a start. What happened? Did I trip? Oh, I can't believe I was so stupid!'

'You fell down the steps.'

'I know that—ouch.' She felt her head, and her hand came away bloodied and sticky. She stared at it. 'I've cut myself,' she said, and everything began to swim.

'It's OK, Lydia. You'll be OK,' Claire said, but her face

was worried and suddenly everything began to hurt a whole lot more.

Massimo tucked his jacket gently beside her head to support it, just in case she had a neck injury. He wasn't taking any chances on that, but it was the head injury that was worrying him the most, the graze on her forehead, just under her hair. How hard had she hit it? Hard enough to…

It was bleeding faster now, he realised with a wave of dread, a red streak appearing as she shifted slightly, and he stayed beside her on his knees, holding her hand and talking to her comfortingly in between snapping out instructions.

She heard the words '*ambulanza*' and '*ospedale*', and tried to move, wincing and whimpering with pain, but he held her still.

'Don't move. The ambulance is coming to take you to hospital.'

'I don't need to go to hospital, I'm fine, we need to get to the hotel!'

'No,' Massimo and Claire said in unison.

'But the competition.'

'It doesn't matter,' he said flatly. 'You're hurt. You have to be checked out.'

'I'll go later.'

'No.' His voice was implacable, hard and cold and somehow strange, and Lydia looked at him and saw his skin was colourless and grey, his mouth pinched, his eyes veiled.

He obviously couldn't stand the sight of blood, Lydia realised, and reached out her other hand to Claire.

She took it, then looked at Massimo. 'I'll look after her,' she said. 'You go, you've got lots to do. We'll be all right.'

His eyes never left Lydia's.

'No. I'll stay with you,' he insisted, but he moved out of the way to give her space.

She looked so frail suddenly, lying there streaked with

blood, the puffy layers of the dress rising up around her legs and making her look like a broken china doll.

Dio, he felt sick just looking at her, and her face swam, another face drifting over it. He shut his eyes tight, squeezing out the images of his wife, but they refused to fade.

Lydia tried to struggle up again. 'I want to go to the hotel,' she said to Claire, and his eyes snapped open again.

'No way.'

'He's right. Don't be silly. You just lie there and we'll get you checked out, then we'll go. There's still plenty of time.'

But there might not be, she realised, as she lay there on the tarmac in her ridiculous charity shop wedding dress with blood seeping from her head wound, and as the minutes ticked by her joy slid slowly away…

CHAPTER TWO

THE ambulance came, and Claire went with Lydia.

He wanted to go with her himself, he felt he ought to, felt the weight of guilt and worry like an elephant on his chest, but it wasn't his place to accompany her, so Claire went, and he followed in his car, having sent the rest of the team on with a message to his family that he'd been held up but would be with them as soon as he could.

He rang Luca on the way, in case he was there at the hospital in Siena that day as he sometimes was, and his phone was answered instantly.

'Massimo, welcome home. Good flight?'

He nearly laughed. 'No. Where are you? Which hospital?'

'Siena. Why?'

He did laugh then. Or was it a sob of relief? 'I'm on my way there. I gave two girls a lift in the plane, and one of them fell down the steps as we were disembarking. I'm following the ambulance. Luca, she's got a head injury,' he added, his heart pounding with dread, and he heard his brother suck in his breath.

'I'll meet you in the emergency department. She'll be all right, Massimo. We'll take care of her.'

He grunted agreement, switched off the phone and followed the ambulance, focusing on facts and crushing his fear and guilt down. It couldn't happen again. Lightning didn't strike twice, he told himself, and forced himself to follow the ambulance at a sensible distance while trying desperately to put Angelina firmly out of his mind...

Luca was waiting for him at the entrance.

He took the car away to park it and Massimo hovered by the ambulance as they unloaded Lydia and whisked her inside, Claire holding her hand and reassuring her. It didn't sound as if it was working, because she kept fretting about the competition and insisting she was all right when anyone could see she was far from all right.

She was taken away, Claire with her, and he stayed in the waiting area, pacing restlessly and driving himself mad with his imagination of what was happening beyond the doors. His brother reappeared moments later and handed him the keys, giving him a keen look.

'You all right?'

Hardly. 'I'm fine,' he said, his voice tight.

'So how do you know this woman?' Luca asked, and he filled him in quickly with the bare bones of the accident.

'Oh—she's wearing a wedding dress,' he warned. 'It's a competition, a race to win a wedding.'

A race she'd lost. If only he'd taken her arm, or gone in front, she would have fallen against him, he could have saved her...

'Luca, don't let her die,' he said urgently, fear clawing at him.

'She won't die,' Luca promised, although how he could say that without knowing—well, he couldn't. It was just a platitude, Massimo knew that.

'Let me know how she is.'

Luca nodded and went off to investigate, leaving him there to wait, but he felt bile rise in his throat and got abruptly to his feet, pacing restlessly again. How long could it take?

Hours, apparently, or at least it felt like it.

Luca reappeared with Claire.

'They're taking X-rays of her leg now but it looks like a sprained ankle. She's just a little concussed and bruised from her fall, but the head injury doesn't look serious,' he said.

'Nor did Angelina's,' he said, switching to Italian.

'She's not Angelina, Massimo. She's not going to die of this.'

'Are you sure?'

'Yes. Yes, I'm sure. She's had a scan. She's fine.'

It should have reassured him, but Massimo felt his heart still slamming against his ribs, the memories crowding him again.

'She's all right,' Luca said quietly. 'This isn't the same.'

He nodded, but he just wanted to get out, to be away from the hospital in the fresh air. Not going to happen. He couldn't leave Lydia, no matter how much he wanted to get away. And he could never get away from Angelina…

Luca took him to her.

She was lying on a trolley, and there was blood streaked all over the front of the hideous dress, but at least they'd taken her off the spinal board. 'How are you?' he asked, knowing the answer but having to ask anyway, and she turned her head and met his eyes, her own clouded with worry and pain.

'I'm fine, they just want to watch me for a while. I've got some bumps and bruises, but nothing's broken, I'm just sore and cross with myself and I want to go to the hotel and they won't let me leave yet. I'm so sorry, Massimo, I've got Claire, you don't need to wait here with me. It could be ages.'

'I do.' He didn't explain, didn't tell her what she didn't need to know, what could only worry her. But he hadn't taken Angelina's head injury seriously. He'd assumed it was nothing. He hadn't watched her, sat with her, checked her every few minutes. If he had—well, he hadn't, but he was damned if he was leaving Lydia alone for a moment until he was sure she was all right.

Luca went back to work, and while the doctors checked her over again and strapped her ankle, Massimo found some coffee for him and Claire and they sat and drank it. Not a good idea. The caffeine shot was the last thing his racing pulse needed.

'I need to make a call,' Claire told him. 'If I go just outside, can you come and get me if there's any news?'

He nodded, watching her leave. She was probably phoning the radio station to tell them about Lydia's accident. And she'd been so close to winning…

She came back, a wan smile on her face. 'Jo's there.'

'Jo?'

'The other contestant. Lydia's lost the race. She's going to be so upset. I can't tell her yet.'

'I think you should. She might stop fretting if it's too late, let herself relax and get better.'

Claire gave a tiny, slightly hysterical laugh. 'You don't know her very well, do you?'

He smiled ruefully. 'No. No, I don't.' And it was ridiculous that he minded the fact.

Lydia looked up as they went back in, and she scanned Claire's face.

'Did you ring the radio station?'

'Yes.'

'Has…' She could hardly bring herself to ask the question, but she took another breath and tried again. 'Has Jo got there yet?' she asked, and then held her breath. It was possible she'd been unlucky, that she hadn't managed to get a flight, that any one of a hundred things could have happened.

They hadn't. She could see it in Claire's eyes, she didn't

need to be told that Jo and Kate, her minder, were already there, and she felt the bitter sting of tears scald her eyes.

'She's there, isn't she?' she asked, just because she needed confirmation.

Claire nodded, and Lydia turned her head away, shutting her eyes against the tears. She was so, *so* cross with herself. They'd been so close to winning, and if she'd only been more careful, gathered up the stupid dress so she could see the steps.

She swallowed hard and looked back up at Claire's worried face. 'Tell her well done for me when you see her.'

'I will, but you'll see her, too. We've got rooms in the hotel for the night. I'll ring them now, let them know what's happening. We can go there when they discharge you.'

'No, I could be ages. Why don't you go, have a shower and something to eat, see the others and I'll get them to ring you if there's any change. Or better still, if you give me back my phone and my purse, I can call you and let you know when I'm leaving, and I'll just get a taxi.'

'I can't leave you alone!'

'She won't be alone, I'll stay with her. I'm staying anyway, whether you're here or not,' Massimo said firmly, and Lydia felt a curious sense of relief. Relief, and guilt.

And she could see the same emotions in Claire's face. She was dithering, chewing her lip in hesitation, and Lydia took her hand and squeezed it.

'There, you see? And his brother works here, so he'll be able to pull strings. It's fine, Claire. Just go. I'll see you later.' And she could get rid of Massimo once Claire had gone...

Claire gave in, reluctantly. 'OK, if you insist. Here, your things. I'll put them in your bag. Where is it?'

'I have no idea. Is it under the bed?'

'No. I haven't seen it.'

'It must have been left on the ground at the airport,' Massimo said. 'My men will have picked it up.'

'Can you check? My passport's in it.'

'*Si.*' He left them briefly, and when he came back he confirmed it had been taken by the others. 'I'll make sure you get it tonight,' he promised.

'Thanks. Right, Claire, you go. I'm fine.'

'You will call me and let me know what's going on as soon as you have any news?'

'Yes, I promise.'

Claire gave in, hugging Lydia a little tearfully before she left them.

Lydia swallowed. Damn. She was going to join in.

'Hey, it's all right. You'll be OK.'

His voice was gentle, reassuring, and his touch on her cheek was oddly comforting. Her eyes filled again.

'I'm causing everyone so much trouble.'

'That's life. Don't worry about it. Are you going to tell your family?'

Oh, cripes. She ought to phone Jen, but she couldn't. Not now. She didn't think she could talk to her just yet.

'Maybe later. I just feel so sleepy.'

'So rest. I'll sit with you.'

Sit with her and watch her. Do what he should have done years ago.

She shut her eyes, just for a moment, but when she opened them again he'd moved from her side. She felt a moment of panic, but then she saw him. He was standing a few feet away reading a poster about head injuries, his hands rammed in his pockets, tension radiating off him.

Funny, she'd thought it was because of the blood, but there was no sign of blood now apart from a dried streak on her dress. Maybe it was hospitals generally. Had Angelina been ill for a long time?

Or maybe hospitals just brought him out in hives. She could understand that. After Jen's accident, she felt the same herself, and yet he was still here, still apparently labouring under some misguided sense of obligation.

He turned his head, saw she was awake and came back to her side, his dark eyes searching hers.

'Are you all right?'

She nodded. 'My head's feeling clearer now. I need to ring Jen,' she said quietly, and he sighed and cupped her cheek, his thumb smoothing away a tear she hadn't realised she'd shed.

'I'm sorry, *cara*. I know how much it meant to you to win this for your sister.'

'It doesn't matter,' she said dismissively, although of course it would to Jen. 'It was just a crazy idea. They can get married at home, it's really not an issue. I really didn't think I'd win anyway, so we haven't lost anything.'

'Claire said Jo's been there for ages. She would probably have beaten you to it anyway,' he said. 'She must have got away very fast.'

She didn't believe it. He was only trying to make it better, to take the sting out of it, but before she had time to argue the doctor came back in, checked her over and delivered her verdict.

Massimo translated.

'You're fine, you need to rest for a few days before you fly home, and you need watching overnight, but you're free to go.'

She thanked the doctor, struggled up and swung her legs over the edge of the trolley, and paused for a moment, her head swimming.

'All right?'

'I'm fine. I need to call a taxi to take me to the hotel.'

'I'll give you a lift.'

'I can't take you out of your way! I've put you to enough trouble as it is. I can get a taxi. I'll be fine.'

But as she slid off the edge of the trolley and straightened up, Massimo caught the sheen of tears in her eyes.

Whatever she'd said, the loss of this prize was tearing her apart for her sister, and he felt guilt wash over him yet again. Logically, he knew he had no obligation to her, no duty that extended any further than simply flying her to Siena as he'd promised. But somehow, somewhere along the way, things had changed and he could no more have left her there at the door of the hospital than he could have left one of his children. And they were waiting for him, had been waiting for him far too long, and guilt tugged at him again.

'Ouch!'

'You can't walk on that ankle. Stay here.'

She stayed, wishing her flight bag was still with her instead of having been whisked away by his team. She could have done with changing out of the dress, but her comfy jeans and soft cotton top were in her bag, and she wanted to cry with frustration and disappointment and pain.

'Here.'

He'd brought a wheelchair, and she eyed it doubtfully.

'I don't know if the dress will fit in it. Horrible thing! I'm going to burn it just as soon as I get it off.'

'Good idea,' he said drily, and they exchanged a smile.

He squashed it in around her, and wheeled her towards the exit. Then he stopped the chair by the door and looked down at her.

'Do you really want to go to the hotel?' he asked.

She tipped her head back to look at him, but it hurt, and she let her breath out in a gusty sigh. 'I don't have a choice. I need a bed for the night, and I can't afford anywhere else.'

He moved so she could see him, crouching down beside her. 'You do have a choice. You can't fly for a few days, and you don't want to stay in a strange hotel on your own for all that time. And anyway, you don't have your bag, so why don't you come back with me?' he said, the guilt about his children growing now and the solution to both problems suddenly blindingly obvious.

'I need to get home to see my children, they've been patient long enough, and you can clean up there and change into your own comfortable clothes and have something to eat and a good night's sleep. Carlotta will look after you.'

Carlotta? Lydia scanned their earlier conversations and came up with the name. She was the woman who looked after his children, who'd worked for them for a hundred years, as he'd put it, and had delivered him.

Carlotta sounded good.

'That's such an imposition. Are you sure you don't mind?'

'I'm sure. It's by far the easiest thing for me. The hotel's the other way, and it would save me a lot of time I don't really have, especially by the time I've dropped your bag over there. And you don't honestly want to be there on your own for days, do you?'

Guilt swamped her, heaped on the disappointment and the worry about Jen, and she felt crushed under the weight of it all. She felt her spine sag, and shook her head. 'I'm so sorry. I've wasted your entire day. If you hadn't given me a lift…'

'Don't go there. What ifs are a waste of time. Yes or no?'

'Yes, please,' she said fervently. 'That would be really kind.'

'Don't mention it. I feel it's all my fault anyway.'

'Rubbish. Of course it's not your fault. You've done so much already, and I don't think I've even thanked you.'

'You have. You were doing that when you fell down the steps.'

'Was I?' She gave him a wry grin, and turned to look up

at him as they arrived at the car, resting her hand on his arm lightly to reassure him. 'It's really not your fault, you know.'

'I know. You missed your step. I know this. I still…'

He was still haunted, because of the head injury, images of Angelina crowding in on him. Angelina falling, Angelina with a headache, Angelina slumped over the kitchen table with one side of her face collapsed. Angelina linked up to a life support machine…

'Massimo?'

'I'm all right,' he said gruffly, and pressing the remote, he opened the door for her and settled her in, then returned the wheelchair and slid into the driver's seat beside her. 'Are you OK?'

'I'm fine.'

'Good. Let's go.'

She phoned Claire and told her what was happening, assured her she would be all right and promised to phone her the next day, then put the phone down in her lap and rested her head back.

Under normal circumstances, she thought numbly, she'd be wallowing in the luxury of his butter-soft leather, beautifully supportive car seats, or taking in the picture-postcard countryside of Tuscany as the car wove and swooped along the narrow winding roads.

As it was she gazed blankly at it all, knowing that she'd have to phone Jen, knowing she should have done it sooner, that her sister would be on tenterhooks, but she didn't have the strength to crush her hopes and dreams.

'Have you told your sister yet?' he asked, as if he'd read her mind.

She shook her head. 'No. I don't know what to say. If I hadn't fallen, we would have won. Easily. It was just so stupid, so clumsy.'

He sighed, his hand reaching out and closing over hers briefly, the warmth of it oddly comforting in a disturbing way. 'I'm sorry. Not because I feel it was my fault, because I know it wasn't, really, but because I know how it feels to let someone down, to have everyone's hopes and dreams resting on your shoulders, to have to carry the responsibility for someone else's happiness.'

She turned towards him, inhibited by the awful, scratchy dress that she couldn't wait to get out of, and studied his profile.

Strong. Clean cut, although no longer clean-shaven, the dark stubble that shadowed his jaw making her hand itch to feel the texture of it against her palm. In the dusk of early evening his olive skin was darker, somehow exotic, and with a little shiver she realised she didn't know him at all. He could be taking her anywhere.

She closed her eyes and told herself not to be ridiculous. He'd followed them to the hospital, got his brother in on the act, a brother she'd heard referred to as *il professore*, and now he was taking her to his family home, to his children, his parents, the woman who'd delivered him all those years ago. Forty years? Maybe. Maybe more, maybe less, but give or take.

Someone who'd stayed with the family for all that time, who surely wouldn't still be there if they were nasty people?

'What's wrong?'

She shrugged, too honest to lie. 'I was just thinking, I don't know you. You could be anyone. After all, I was going in the plane with Nico, and you've pointed out in no uncertain terms that that wouldn't have been a good idea, and I just don't think I'm a very good judge of character.'

'Are you saying you don't trust me?'

She found herself smiling. 'Curiously, I do, or I wouldn't be here with you.'

He flashed her a look, and his mouth tipped into a wry grin. 'Well, thanks.'

'Sorry. It wasn't meant to sound patronising. It's just been a bit of a whirlwind today, and I'm not really firing on all cylinders.'

'I'm sure you're not. Don't worry, you're safe with me, I promise, and we're nearly there. You can have a long lazy shower, or lie in the bath, or have a swim. Whatever you choose.'

'So long as I can get out of this horrible dress, I'll be happy.'

He laughed, the sound filling the car and making something deep inside her shift.

'Good. Stand by to be happy very soon.'

He turned off the road onto a curving gravelled track lined by cypress trees, winding away towards what looked like a huge stone fortress. She sat up straighter. 'What's that building?'

'The house.'

'House?' She felt her jaw drop, and shut her mouth quickly. That was their *house*?

'So…is this your land?'

'*Si.*'

She stared around her, but the light was fading and it was hard to tell what she was looking at. But the massive edifice ahead of them was outlined against the sunset, and as they drew closer she could see lights twinkling in the windows.

They climbed the hill, driving through a massive archway and pulling up in front of a set of sweeping steps. Security lights came on as they stopped, and she could see the steps were flanked by huge terracotta pots with what looked like olive trees in them. The steps rose majestically up to the biggest set of double doors she'd ever seen in her life. Strong doors, doors that would keep you safe against all invaders.

She had to catch her jaw again, and for once in her life she was lost for words. She'd thought, foolishly, it seemed, that it might shrink as they got closer, but it hadn't. If anything it had grown, and she realised it truly was a fortress.

An ancient, impressive and no doubt historically significant fortress. And it was his family home?

She thought of their modest farmhouse, the place she called home, and felt the sudden almost overwhelming urge to laugh. What on earth did he think of her, all tarted up in her ludicrous charity shop wedding dress and capering about outside the airport begging a lift from any old stranger?

'Lydia?'

He was standing by her, the door open, and she gathered up the dress and her purse and phone and squirmed off the seat and out of the car, balancing on her good leg and eyeing the steps dubiously.

How on earth—?

No problem, apparently. He shut the car door, and then to her surprise he scooped her up into his arms.

She gave a little shriek and wrapped her arms around his neck, so that her nose was pressed close to his throat in the open neck of his shirt. Oh, God. He smelt of lemons and musk and warm, virile male, and she could feel the beat of his heart against her side.

Or was it her own? She didn't know. It could have been either.

He glanced down at her, concerned that he might be hurting her. There was a little frown creasing the soft skin between her brows, and he had the crazy urge to kiss it away. He almost did, but stopped himself in time.

She was a stranger, nothing more, and he tried to ignore the feel of her against his chest, the fullness of her breasts pressing into his ribs and making his heart pound like a drum. She had her head tucked close to his shoulder, and he could feel the whisper of her breath against his skin. Under the antiseptic her hair smelled of fresh fruit and summer flowers, and he wanted to bury his face in it and breathe in.

He daren't look down again, though. She'd wrapped her arms around his neck and the front of the dress was gaping slightly, the soft swell of those beautiful breasts tempting him almost beyond endurance.

Crazy. Stupid. Whatever was the matter with him? He gritted his teeth, shifted her a little closer and turned towards the steps.

Lydia felt his body tense, saw his jaw tighten and she wondered why. She didn't have time to work it out, though, even if she could, because as he headed towards the house three children came tumbling down the steps and came to a sliding halt in front of them, their mouths open, their faces shocked.

'Pàpa?'

The eldest, a thin, gangly girl with a riot of dark curls and her father's beautiful eyes, stared from one of them to the other, and the look on her face was pure horror.

'I think you'd better explain to your children that I am *not* your new wife,' she said drily, and the girl glanced back at her and then up at her father again.

'Pàpa?'

He was miles away, caught up in a fairy-tale fantasy of carrying this beautiful woman over the threshold and then peeling away the layers of her bridal gown…

'Massimo? I think you need to explain to the children,' Lydia said softly, watching his face at close range. There was a tic in his jaw, the muscle jumping. Had he carried Angelina up these steps?

'It's all right, Francesca,' he said in English, struggling to find his voice. 'This is Miss Fletcher. I met her today at the airport, and she's had an accident and has to rest for a few days, so I've brought her here. Say hello.'

She frowned and asked something in Italian, and he smiled a little grimly and shook his head. 'No. We are *not* married. Say hello to Miss Fletcher, *cara*.'

'Hello, Miss Fletcher,' Francesca said in careful English, her smile wary but her shoulders relaxing a little, and Lydia smiled back at her. She felt a little awkward, gathered up in his arms against that hard, broad chest with the scent of his body doing extraordinary things to her heart, but there was nothing she could do about it except smile and hope his arms didn't break.

'Hello, Francesca. Thank you for speaking English so I can understand you.'

'That's OK. We have to speak English to Auntie Isabelle. This is Lavinia, and this is Antonino. Say hello,' she prompted.

Lydia looked at the other two, clustered round their sister. Lavinia was the next in line, with the same dark, glorious curls but mischief dancing in her eyes, and Antonino, leaning against Francesca and squiggling the toe of his shoe on the gravel, was the youngest. The baby in the photo, the little one who must have lost his mother before he ever really knew her.

Her heart ached for them all, and she felt a welling in her chest and crushed it as she smiled at them.

'Hello, Lavinia, hello, Antonino. It's nice to meet you,' she said, and they replied politely, Lavinia openly studying her, her eyes brimming over with questions.

'And this is Carlotta,' Massimo said, and she lifted her head and met searching, wise eyes in a wizened face. He spoke rapidly to her in Italian, explaining her ridiculous fancy-dress outfit no doubt, and she saw the moment he told her that they'd lost the competition, because Carlotta's face softened and she looked at Lydia and shook her head.

'Sorry,' she said, lifting her hands. 'So sorry for you. Come, I help you change and you will be happier, *si*?'

'*Si,*' she said with a wry chuckle, and Massimo shifted her more firmly against his chest and followed Carlotta puffing and wheezing up the steps.

The children were tugging at him and questioning him in Italian, and he was laughing and answering them as fast as he could. Bless their little hearts, she could see they were hanging on his every word.

He was the centre of their world, and they'd missed him, and she'd kept him away from them all these hours when they must have been desperate to have him back. She felt another shaft of guilt, but Carlotta was leading the way through the big double doors, and she looked away from the children and gasped softly.

They were in a cloistered courtyard, with a broad covered walkway surrounding the open central area that must cast a welcome shade in the heat of the day, but now in the evening it was softly lit and she could see more of the huge pots of olive trees set on the old stone paving in the centre, and on the low wall that divided the courtyard from the cloistered walkway geraniums tumbled over the edge, bringing colour and scent to the evening air.

But that wasn't what had caught her attention. It was the frescoed walls, the ancient faded murals under the shelter of the cloisters that took her breath away.

He didn't pause, though, or give her time to take in the beautiful paintings, but carried her through one of the several doors set in the walls, then along a short hallway and into a bedroom.

He set her gently on the bed, and she felt oddly bereft as he straightened up and moved away.

'I'll be in the kitchen with the children. Carlotta will tell me when you're ready and I'll come and get you.'

'Thank you.'

He smiled fleetingly and went out, the children's clamouring voices receding as he walked away, and Carlotta closed the door.

'Your bath,' she said, pushing open another door, and she saw a room lined with pale travertine marble, the white suite simple and yet luxurious. And the bath—she could stick her bandaged leg up on the side and just wallow. Pure luxury.

'Thank you.' She couldn't wait. All she wanted was to get out of the dress and into water. But the zip…

'I help you,' Carlotta said, and as the zip slid down, she was freed from the scratchy fabric at last. A bit too freed. She clutched at the top as it threatened to drift away and smiled at Carlotta.

'I can manage now,' she said, and Carlotta nodded.

'I get your bag.'

She went out, and Lydia closed the bedroom door behind her, leaning back against it and looking around again.

It was much simpler than the imposing and impressive entrance, she saw with relief. Against expectations it wasn't vast, but it was pristine, the bed made up with sparkling white linen, the rug on the floor soft underfoot, and the view from the French window would be amazing in daylight.

She limped gingerly over to the window and stared out, pressing her face against the glass. The doors opened onto what looked like a terrace, and beyond—gosh, the view must be utterly breathtaking, she imagined, because even at dusk it was extraordinary, the twinkling lights of villages and scattered houses sparkling in the twilight.

Moving away from the window, she glanced around her, taking in her surroundings in more detail. The floor was tiled, the ceiling beamed, with chestnut perhaps? Probably, with terracotta tiles between the beams. Sturdy, simple and homely—which was crazy, considering the scale of the place and the grandeur of the entrance! But it seemed more like a farm now, curiously, less of a fortress, and much less threatening.

And that established, she let go of the awful dress, kicked it away from her legs, bundled it up in a ball and hopped into the bathroom.

The water was calling her. Studying the architecture could wait.

CHAPTER THREE

WHAT was that noise?

Lydia lifted her head, water streaming off her hair as she surfaced to investigate.

'*Signorina? Signorina!*'

Carlotta's voice was desperate as she rattled the handle on the bathroom door, and Lydia felt a stab of alarm.

'What is it?' she asked, sitting up with a splash and sluicing the water from her hair with her hands.

'Oh, *signorina*! You are all right?'

She closed her eyes and twisted her hair into a rope, squeezing out the rest of the water and suppressing a sigh. 'I'm fine. I'm OK, really. I won't be long.'

'I wait, I help you.'

'No, really, there's no need. I'll be all right.'

'But Massimo say I no leave you!' she protested, clearly worried for some reason, but Lydia assured her again that she was fine.

'OK,' she said after a moment, sounding dubious. 'I leave your bag here. You call me for help?'

'I will. Thank you. *Grazie.*'

'*Prego.*'

She heard the bedroom door close, and rested her head back down on the bath with a sigh. The woman was kindness itself, but Lydia just wanted to be left alone. Her head ached, her ankle throbbed, she had a million bruises all over her body and she still had to phone her sister.

The phone rang, almost as if she'd triggered it with her thoughts, and she could tell by the ringtone it was Jen.

Oh, rats. She must have heard the news.

There was no getting round it, so she struggled awkwardly out of the bath and hobbled back to the bed, swathed in the biggest towel she'd ever seen, and dug out her phone and rang Jen back.

'What's going on? They said you'd had an accident! I've been trying to phone you for ages but you haven't been answering! Are you all right? We've been frantic!'

'Sorry, Jen, I was in the bath. I'm fine, really, it was just a little slip on the steps of a plane and I've twisted my ankle. Nothing serious.'

Well, she hoped it wasn't. She crossed her fingers, just to be on the safe side, and filled in a few more details. She didn't tell her the truth, just that Jo had got there first.

'I'm so sorry, we really tried, but we probably wouldn't have made it even without the accident.'

There was a heartbeat of hesitation, then Jen said, 'Don't worry, it really doesn't matter and it's not important. I just need you to be all right. And don't go blaming yourself, it's not your fault.'

Why did *everyone* say that? It *was* her fault. If she'd looked where she was going, taken a bit more care, Jen and Andy would have been having the wedding of their dreams in a few months' time. As it was, well, as it was they wouldn't, but she wasn't going to give Jen anything to beat herself up about, so she told her she was fine, just a little twinge—and nothing at all about the head injury.

'Actually, since I'm over here, I thought I'd stay on for a few days. I've found a farm where I can get bed and breakfast, and I'm going to have a little holiday.'

Well, it wasn't entirely a lie. It *was* a farm, she had a bed, and she was sure they wouldn't make her starve while she recovered.

'You do that. It sounds lovely,' Jen said wistfully, and Lydia screwed her face up and bit her lip.

Damn. She'd been so close, and the disappointment that Jen was trying so hard to disguise was ripping Lydia apart.

Ending the call with a promise to ring when she was coming home, she dug her clean clothes out of the flight bag and pulled her jeans on carefully over her swollen, throbbing ankle. The soft, worn fabric of the jeans and the T-shirt were comforting against her skin, chafed from her fall as well as the boning and beading in the dress, and she looked around for the offending article. It was gone. Taken away by Carlotta? She hoped she hadn't thrown it out. She wanted the pleasure of that for herself.

She put her trainers on, managing to squeeze her bandaged foot in with care, and hobbled out of her room in search of the others, but the corridor outside didn't seem to lead anywhere except her room, a little sitting room and a room that looked like an office, so she went back through the door to the beautiful cloistered courtyard and looked around for any clues.

There were none.

So now what? She couldn't just stand there and yell, nor could she go round the courtyard systematically opening all the doors. Not that there were that many, but even so.

She was sitting there on the low wall around the central courtyard, studying the beautiful frescoes and trying to work out what to do if nobody showed up, when the door nearest to her opened and Massimo appeared. He'd showered and changed out of the suit into jeans and a soft white linen shirt stark against his olive skin, the cuffs rolled back to reveal those tanned forearms which had nearly been her undoing on the plane, and her heart gave a tiny lurch.

Stupid.

He caught sight of her and smiled, and her heart did another little jiggle as he walked towards her.

'Lydia, I was just coming to see if you were all right. I'm sorry, I should have come back quicker. How are you? How's the head?'

'Fine,' she said with a rueful smile. 'I'm just a bit lost. I didn't want to go round opening all the doors, it seemed rude.'

'You should have shouted. I would have heard you.'

'I'm not in the habit of yelling for help,' she said drily, and he chuckled and came over to her side.

'Let me help you now,' he said, and offered her his arm. 'It's not far, hang on and hop, or would you rather I carried you?'

'I'll hop,' she said hastily, not sure she could cope with being snuggled up to that broad, solid chest again, with the feel of his arms strong and safe under her. 'I don't want to break you.'

He laughed at that. 'I don't think you'll break me. Did you find everything you needed? How's your room?'

She slipped her arm through his, conscious of the smell of him again, refreshed now by his shower and overlaid with soap and more of the citrusy cologne that had been haunting her nostrils all day. She wanted to press her nose to his chest, to breathe him in, to absorb the warmth and scent and maleness of him.

Not appropriate. She forced herself to concentrate.

'Lovely. The bath was utter bliss. I can't tell you how wonderful it was to get out of that awful dress. I hope Carlotta hasn't burned it, I want to do it myself.'

He laughed again, a warm, rich sound that echoed round the courtyard, and scanned her body with his eyes. 'It really didn't do you justice,' he said softly, and in the gentle light she thought she caught a glimpse of whatever it was she'd seen in his eyes at the airport.

But then it was gone, and he was opening the door and ushering her through to a big, brightly lit kitchen. Carlotta was busy at the stove, and the children were seated at a large table in the middle of the room, Antonino kneeling up and leaning over to interfere with what Lavinia was doing.

She pushed him aside crossly, and Massimo intervened before a fight could break out, diffusing it swiftly by splitting them up. While he was busy, Carlotta came and helped her to the table. She smiled at her gratefully.

'I'm sorry to put you to so much trouble.'

'Is no trouble,' she said. 'Sit, sit. Is ready.'

She sniffed, and smiled. 'It smells wonderful.'

'*Buono.* You eat, then you feel better. Sit!'

She flapped her apron at Lydia, and she sat obediently at the last place laid at the long table. It was opposite Francesca, and Massimo was at the end of the table on her right, bracketed by the two younger ones who'd been split up to stop them squabbling.

They were fractious—overtired, she thought guiltily, and missing their father. But Francesca was watching her warily. She smiled at the girl apologetically.

'I'm sorry I kept your father away from you for so long. He's been so kind and helpful.'

'He is. He helps everybody. Are you better now?'

'I'm all right. I've just got a bit of a headache but I don't think it's much more than that. I was so stupid. I tripped over the hem of my dress and fell down the steps of the plane and hit my head.'

Behind her, there was a clatter, and Francesca went chalk white, her eyes huge with horror and distress.

'*Scusami,*' she mumbled, and pushing back her chair, she

ran from the room, her father following, his chair crashing over as he leapt to his feet.

'Francesca!' He reached the door before it closed, and she could hear his voice calling as he ran after her. Horrified, uncertain what she'd done, she turned to Carlotta and found her with her apron pressed to her face, her eyes above it creased with distress.

'What did I say?' she whispered, conscious of the little ones, but Carlotta just shook her head and picked up the pan and thrust it in the sink.

'Is nothing. Here, eat. Antonino!'

He sat down, and Lavinia put away the book he'd been trying to tug away from her, and Carlotta picked up Massimo's overturned chair and ladled food out onto all their plates.

There was fresh bread drizzled with olive oil, and a thick, rich stew of beans and sausage and gloriously red tomatoes. It smelt wonderful, tasted amazing, but Lydia could scarcely eat it. The children were eating. Whatever it was she'd said or done had gone right over their heads, but something had driven Francesca from the room, and her father after her.

The same something that had made Massimo go pale at the airport, as he'd knelt on the tarmac at her side? The same something that had made him stand, rigid with tension, staring grimly at a poster when he thought she was asleep in the room at the hospital?

She pushed back her chair and hopped over to the sink, where Carlotta was scrubbing furiously at a pot. 'I'm sorry, I can't eat. Carlotta, what did I say?' she asked under her breath, and those old, wise eyes that had seen so much met hers, and she shook her head, twisting her hands in the dishcloth and biting her lips.

She put the pot on the draining board, and Lydia automatically picked up a tea towel and dried it, her hip propped against the edge of the sink unit as she balanced on her good leg. Another pot followed, and another, and finally Carlotta stopped scouring the pots as if they were lined with demons and her hands came to rest.

She hobbled over to the children, cleared up their plates, gave them pudding and then gathered them up like a mother hen.

'Wait here. Eat. He will come back.'

They left her there in the kitchen, their footsteps echoing along a corridor and up stairs, and Lydia sank down at the table and stared blankly at the far wall, going over and over her words in her head and getting nowhere.

Carlotta appeared again and put Francesca's supper in a microwave.

'Is she coming down again? I want to apologise for upsetting her.'

'No. Is all right, *signorina*. Her *pàpa* look after her.' And lifting the plate out of the microwave, she carried it out of the room on a tray, leaving Lydia alone again.

She poked at her food, but it was cold now, the beans congealing in the sauce, and she ripped up a bit of bread and dabbed it absently in the stew. What had she said, that had caused such distress?

She had no idea, but she couldn't leave the kitchen without finding out, and there was still a pile of washing up to do. She didn't know where anything lived, but the table was big enough to put it all on, and there was a dishwasher sitting there empty.

Well, if she could do nothing else while she waited, she could do that, she told herself, and pushing up her sleeves, she hopped over to the dishwasher and set about clearing up the kitchen.

He had to go down to her—to explain, or apologise properly, at the very least.

His stomach growled, but he ignored it. He couldn't eat,

not while his daughter was just settling into sleep at last, her sobs fading quietly away into the night.

He closed his eyes. Talking to Lydia, dredging it all up again, was the last thing he wanted to do, the very last, but he had no choice. Leaning over Francesca, he pressed a kiss lightly against her cheek, and straightened. She was sleeping peacefully now; he could leave her.

Leave her, and go and find Lydia, if she hadn't had the sense to pack up her things and leave. It seemed unlikely, but he couldn't blame her.

He found her in the kitchen, sitting with Carlotta over a cup of coffee, the kitchen sparkling. He stared at them, then at the kitchen. Carlotta had been upstairs until a short while ago, settling the others, and the kitchen had been in chaos, so how?

'She's OK now,' he said in Italian. 'Why don't you go to bed, Carlotta? You look exhausted and Roberto's worried about you.'

She nodded and got slowly to her feet, then rested her hand on Lydia's shoulder and patted it before leaving her side. 'I *am* tired,' she said to him in Italian, 'but you need to speak to Lydia. I couldn't leave her. She's a good girl, Massimo. Look at my kitchen! A good, kind girl, and she's unhappy. Worried.'

He sighed. 'I know. Did you explain?'

'No. It's not my place, but be gentle with her—and yourself.' And with that pointed remark, she left them alone together.

Lydia looked up at him and searched his eyes. 'What did she say to you?'

He gave her a fleeting smile. 'She told me you were a good, kind girl. And she told me to be gentle with you.'

Her eyes filled, and she looked away. 'I don't know what I said, but I'm so, so sorry.'

His conscience pricked him. He should have warned her. He sighed and scrubbed a hand through his hair.

'No. I should be apologising, not you. Forgive us, we aren't normally this rude to visitors. Francesca was upset.'

'I know that. Obviously I made it happen. What I don't know is why,' she said, looking up at him again with grief-stricken eyes.

He reached for a mug, changed his mind and poured himself a glass of wine. 'Can I tempt you?'

'Is it one of yours?'

'No. It's a neighbour's, but it's good. We could take it outside. I don't know if it's wise, though, with your head injury.'

'I'll take the risk,' she said. 'And then will you tell me what I said?'

'You know what you said. What you don't know is what it meant,' he said enigmatically, and picking up both glasses of wine, he headed for the door, glancing back over his shoulder at her. 'Can you manage, or should I carry you?'

Carry her? With her face pressed up against that taunting aftershave, and the feel of his strong, muscled arms around her legs? 'I can manage,' she said hastily, and pushing back her chair, she got to her feet and limped after him out into the still, quiet night.

She could hear the soft chirr of insects, the sound of a motorbike somewhere in the valley below, and then she saw a single headlight slicing through the night, weaving and turning as it followed the snaking road along the valley bottom and disappeared.

He led her to a bench at the edge of the terrace. The ground fell away below them so it felt as if they were perched on the edge of the world, and when she was seated he handed her the glass and sat beside her, his elbows propped on his knees, his own glass dangling from his fingers as he stared out over the velvet blackness.

For a while neither of them said anything, but then the tension got to her and she broke the silence.

'Please tell me.'

He sucked in his breath, looking down, staring into his glass as he slowly swirled the wine before lifting it to his lips.

'Massimo?' she prompted, and he turned his head and met her eyes. Even in the moonlight, she could see the pain etched into his face, and her heart began to thud slowly.

'Angelina died of a brain haemorrhage following a fall,' he began, his voice expressionless. 'Nothing serious, nothing much at all, just a bit of a bump. She'd fallen down the stairs and hit her head on the wall. We all thought she was all right, but she had a bit of a headache later in the day, and we went to bed early. I woke in the night and she was missing, and I found her in the kitchen, slumped over the table, and one side of her face had collapsed.'

Lydia closed her eyes and swallowed hard as the nausea threatened to choke her. What had she *done*? Not just by saying what she had at the table—the same table? But by bringing this on all of them, on Claire, on him, on the children—most especially little Francesca, her eyes wide with pain and shock, fleeing from the table. The image would stay with her forever.

'It wasn't your fault,' he said gently. 'You weren't to know. I probably should have told you—warned you not to talk about it in that way, and why. I let you walk right into it.'

She turned back to him, searching his face in the shadows. She'd known something was wrong when he was bending over her on the tarmac, and again later, staring at the poster. And yet he'd said nothing.

'Why didn't you *tell* me? I knew something was wrong, something else, something more. Luca seemed much more worried than my condition warranted, even I knew that, and he kept looking at you anxiously. I thought he was worried about me, but then I realised it was you he was worried about. I just didn't know why. You should have told me.'

'How could I? You had a head injury. How could I say to you, "I'm sorry, I'm finding this a bit hard to deal with, my wife died of the same thing and I'm a bit worried I might lose you, too." How could I say that?'

He'd been worried he could lose her?

No. Of course he hadn't meant that, he didn't know her. He meant he was worried she might be about to die, too. Nothing more than that.

'You should have left us there instead of staying and getting distressed. I had no business tangling you all up in this mess—oh, Massimo, I'm so sorry.'

She broke off, clamping her teeth hard to stop her eyes from welling over, but his warm hand on her shoulder was the last straw, and she felt the hot, wet slide of a tear down her cheek.

'*Cara*, no. Don't cry for us. It was a long time ago.'

'But it still hurts you, and it'll hurt you forever,' she said unevenly.

'No, it just brought the memories back. We're all right, really. We're getting there. Francesca's the oldest, she remembers Angelina the most clearly, and she's the one who bears the brunt of the loss, because when I'm not there the little ones turn to her. She has to be mother to them, and she's been so strong, but she's just a little girl herself.'

He broke off, his jaw working, and she laid her hand gently against it and sighed.

'I'm so sorry. It must have been dreadful for you all.'

'It was. They took her to hospital, and she died later that day—she was on life support and they tested her brain but there was nothing. No activity at all. They turned off the machine, and I came home and told the children that their mother was gone. That was the hardest thing I've ever had to do in my life.'

His voice broke off again, turning away this time, and Lydia closed her eyes and swallowed the anguished response. There was nothing she could say that wouldn't be trite or meaningless, and so she stayed silent, and after a moment he let out a long, slow breath and sat back against the bench.

'So, now you know,' he said, his voice low and oddly flat.

Wordlessly, she reached out and touched his hand, and he turned it, his fingers threading through hers and holding on tight.

They stayed like that for an age, their hands lying linked between them as they sipped their wine, and then he turned to her in the dim light and searched her face. He'd taken comfort from her touch, felt the warmth of her generous spirit seeping into him, easing the ache which had been a part of him for so long.

How could she do that with just a touch?

No words. Words were too hard, would have been trite. Did she know that?

Yes. He could see that she did, that this woman who talked too much actually knew the value of silence.

He lifted her hand and pressed it to his lips, then smiled at her sadly. 'Did you eat anything?'

She shook her head. 'No. Not really.'

'Nor did I. Shall we see what we can find? It's a very, very long time since breakfast.'

It wasn't exactly *haute cuisine*, but the simple fare of olive bread and ham and cheese with sweetly scented baby plum tomatoes and a bowl of olive oil and balsamic vinegar just hit the spot.

He poured them another glass of wine, but it didn't seem like a good idea and so she gave him the second half and he found some sparkling water for her. She realised she'd thought nothing of handing him her glass of wine for him to finish, and he'd taken it without hesitation and drunk from it without turning a hair.

How odd, when they'd only met a scant twelve hours ago. Thirteen hours and a few minutes, to be more exact.

It seemed more like a lifetime since she'd watched him getting out of the taxi, wondered if he'd be The One to make it happen. The guy she'd been talking to was funny and seemed nice enough, but he wasn't about to give her a lift and she knew that. But Massimo had looked at her as he'd gone into the Jet Centre foyer, his eyes meeting hers and locking…

She glanced up, and found him watching her with a frown.

'Why are you frowning?' she asked, and his mouth kicked up a fraction in one corner, the frown ironed out with a deliberate effort.

'No reason. How's your head now?'

She shrugged. 'OK. It just feels as if I fell over my feet and spent the day hanging about in a hospital.' It was rather worse than that, but he didn't need to know about every ache and pain. The list was endless.

She reached out and covered his hand. 'Massimo, I'm all right,' she said softly, and the little frown came back.

'Sorry. It's just a reflex. I look after people—it's part of my job description. Everyone comes to me with their problems.'

She smiled at him, remembering her conversation with Francesca.

'I'm sorry I kept your father away from you for so long. He's been so kind and helpful.'

'He is. He helps everybody.'

'You're just a fixer, aren't you? You fix everything for everybody all the time, and you hate it when things can't be fixed.'

His frown deepened for a moment, and then he gave a wry laugh and pulled his hand away, swirling the wine in her glass before draining it. 'Is it so obvious?'

She felt her lips twitch. 'Only if you're on the receiving end. Don't get me wrong, I'm massively grateful and just so sorry I've dragged you into this awful mess and upset everyone. I'm more than happy you're a fixer, because goodness only knows I seemed to need one today. I think I need a guardian angel, actually. I just have such a gift for getting into a mess and dragging everybody with me.'

She broke off, and he tipped his head on one side and that little crease between his eyebrows returned fleetingly. 'A gift?'

She sighed. 'Jen's accident was sort of my fault.'

He sat back, his eyes searching hers. 'Tell me,' he said softly, so she did.

She told him about Russell, about their trip to her parents' farm for the weekend, because Jen and Andy were going to be there as well and she hadn't seen them for a while. And she'd shown him the farm, and he'd seen the quad bike, and suggested they went out on it so she could show him all the fields.

'I didn't want to go with him. He was a crazy driver, and I knew he'd want to go too fast, so I said no, but then Jen offered to show him round. She wanted to get him alone, to threaten him with death if he hurt me, but he hurt her instead. He went far too fast, and she told him to stop but he thought she was just being chicken and she wasn't, she knew about the fallen tree hidden in the long grass, and then they hit it and the quad bike cartwheeled through the air and landed on her.'

He winced and closed his eyes briefly. 'And she ended up in a wheelchair?'

'Not for a few weeks. She had a fractured spine, and she

was in a special bed for a while. It wasn't displaced, the spinal cord wasn't severed but it was badly bruised and it took a long time to recover and for the bones to heal. She's getting better now, she's starting to walk again, but she lost her job and so did Andy, so he could look after her. He took away everything from them, and if I'd gone with him, if it had been me, then I might have been able to stop him.'

'You really think so? He sounds like an idiot.'

'He is an idiot,' she said tiredly. 'He's an idiot, and he was my boss, so I lost my job, too.'

'He sacked you?'

She gave him a withering look. 'I walked…and then his business folded without me, and he threatened to sue me if I didn't go back. I told him to take a flying hike.'

'What business was he in?'

'He had a restaurant. I was his chef.'

Hence the tidy kitchen, he realised. She was used to working in a kitchen, used to bringing order to chaos, used to the utensils and the work space and the arrangement of them that always to him defied logic. And his restaurant had folded without her?

'You told me you were a cook,' he rebuked her mildly. 'I didn't realise you were a chef.'

She quirked an eyebrow at him mockingly. 'You told me you were a farmer and you live in a flipping fortress! I think that trumps it,' she said drily, and he laughed and lifted his glass to her.

'Touché,' he said softly, and her heart turned over at the wry warmth in his eyes. 'I'm sorry,' he went on. 'Sorry about this man who clearly didn't deserve you, sorry about your sister, sorry about your job. What a mess. And all because he was a fool.'

'Absolutely.'

'Tell me more about him.'

'Like what?'

'Like why your sister felt she needed to warn him not to hurt you. Had you been hurt before?'

'No, but she didn't really like him. He wasn't always a nice man, and he took advantage of me—made me work ridiculous hours, treated me like a servant at times and yet he could be a charmer, too. He was happy enough to talk me into his bed once he realised I was a good chef—sorry, you really didn't need to know that.'

He smiled slightly. 'Maybe you needed to say it,' he suggested, and her laugh was a little brittle.

'There are so many things I could tell you about him. I said I was a lousy judge of character. I think he had a lot in common with Nico, perhaps.'

He frowned. 'Nico?'

'The guy at the airport?'

'Yes, I know who you mean. In what way? Was he a drinker?'

'Yes. Definitely. But not just a drinker. He was a nasty drunk, especially towards the end of our relationship. He seemed to change. Got arrogant. He used to be quite charming at first, but it was just a front. He—well, let's just say he didn't respect women either.'

His mouth tightened. 'I'm sorry. You shouldn't have had to tolerate that.'

'No, I shouldn't. So—tell me about your house,' she said, changing the subject to give them both a bit of a break. She reached out and tore off another strip of bread, dunking it in the oil that she couldn't get enough of, and looked up to see a strange look on his face. Almost—tender?

Nonsense. She was being silly. 'Well, come on, then,' she mumbled round the bread, and he smiled, the strange look disappearing as if she'd imagined it.

'It's very old. We're not sure of the origins. It seems it

might have been a Medici villa, but the history is a little cloudy. It was built at the time of the Florentine invasion.'

'So how come your family ended up with it?'

His mouth twitched. 'One of our ancestors took possession of it at the end of the seventeenth century.'

That made her laugh. 'Took possession?'

The twitch again, and a wicked twinkle in his eye. 'We're not quite sure how he acquired it, but it's been in the family ever since. He's the one who renamed the villa *Palazzo Valtieri*.'

Palazzo? She nearly laughed at that. Not just a fortress, then, but a proper, full-on palace. Oh, boy.

'I'll show you round it tomorrow. It's beautiful. Some of the frescoes are amazing, and the formal rooms in the part my parents live in are fantastic.'

'Your parents live here?' she asked, puzzled, because there'd been no mention of them. Not that they'd really had time, but—

'*Si*. It's a family business. They're away at the moment, snatching a few days with my sister Carla and her new baby before the harvest starts, but they'll be back the day after tomorrow.'

'So how many rooms are there?'

He laughed. 'I have no idea. I've never counted them, I'm too busy trying not to let it fall down. It's crumbling as fast as we can patch it up, but so long as we can cheat time, that's fine. It's quite interesting.'

'I'm sure it is. And now it's your turn to run it?'

His mouth tugged down at the corners, but there was a smile in his eyes. '*Si*. For my sins. My father keeps trying to interfere, but he's supposed to be retired. He doesn't understand that, though.'

'No. It must be hard to hand it over. My father wouldn't be able to do it. And the harvest is just starting?'

He nodded. 'The grape harvest is first, followed by the chestnuts and the olives. It's relentless now until the end of November, so you can see why I was in a hurry to get back.'

'And I held you up.'

'*Cara*, accidents happen. Don't think about it any more.' He pushed back his chair. 'I think it's time you went to bed. It's after midnight.'

Was it? When had that happened? When they were outside, sitting in the quiet of the night and watching the twinkling lights in the villages? Or now, sitting here eating bread and cheese and olive oil, drinking wine and staring into each other's eyes like lovers?

She nodded and pushed back her chair, and he tucked her arm in his so she could feel the solid muscle of his forearm under her hand, and she hung on him and hopped and hobbled her way to her room.

'Ring me if you need anything. You have my mobile number on my card. I gave it to you on the plane. Do you still have it?'

'Yes—but I won't need you.'

Well, not for anything she'd dream of asking him for…

His brows tugged together. 'Just humour me, OK? If you feel unwell in the night, or want anything, ring me and I'll come down. I'm not far away. And please, don't lock your door.'

'Massimo, I'm feeling all right. My headache's gone, and I feel OK now. You don't need to worry.'

'You can't be too careful,' he said, and she could see a tiny frown between his brows, as if he was still waiting for something awful to happen to her.

They reached her room and he paused at the door, staring down into her eyes and hesitating for the longest moment. And then, just when she thought he was going to kiss her, he stepped back.

'Call me if you need me. If you need anything at all.'

'I will.'

'Good. *Buonanotte*, Lydia,' he murmured softly, and turned and walked away.

CHAPTER FOUR

WHAT was she *thinking* about?

Of course he hadn't been about to kiss her! That bump on the head had obviously been more serious than she'd realised. Maybe a blast of fresh air would help her think clearly?

She opened the French doors onto the terrace and stood there for a moment, letting the night air cool her heated cheeks. She'd been so carried along on the moment, so lured by his natural and easy charm that she'd let herself think all sorts of stupid things.

Of course he wasn't interested in her. Why would he be? She'd been nothing but a thorn in his side since the moment he'd set eyes on her. And even if he hadn't, she wasn't interested! Well, that was a lie, of course she was interested, or she wouldn't even be thinking about it, but there was no way it was going anywhere.

Not after the debacle with Russell. She was sworn off men now for life, or at least for a good five years. And so far, it hadn't been much more than five months!

Leaving the doors open, she limped back to the bed and pulled her pyjamas out of her flight bag, eyeing them dubiously. The skimpy top and little shorts she'd brought for their weightlessness had seemed fine when she was going to be sharing a hotel room with Claire, but here, in this ancient historic house—*palazzo*, even, for heaven's sake! She wondered what on earth he'd make of them.

Nothing. Nothing at all, because he wasn't going to see her in her nightclothes! Cross with herself, her head aching and her ankle throbbing and her bruises giving her a fair amount of grief as well, she changed into the almost-pyjamas, cleaned her teeth and crawled into bed.

Oh, bliss. The pillows were cloud-soft, the down quilt light and yet snuggly, and the breeze from the doors was drifting across her face, bringing with it the scents of sage and lavender and night-scented stocks.

Exhausted, weary beyond belief, she closed her eyes with a little sigh and drifted off to sleep...

Her doors were open.

He hesitated, standing outside on the terrace, questioning his motives.

Did he *really* think she needed checking in the night? Or was he simply indulging his—what? Curiosity? Fantasy? Or, perhaps...need?

He groaned softly. There was no doubt that he *needed* her, needed the warmth of her touch, the laughter in her eyes, the endless chatter and the brilliance of her smile.

The silence, when she'd simply held his hand and offered comfort.

Thinking about that moment brought a lump to his throat, and he swallowed hard. He hadn't allowed himself to need a woman for years, but Lydia had got under his skin, penetrated his defences with her simple kindness, and he wanted her in a way that troubled him greatly, because it was more than just physical.

And he really wasn't sure he was ready for that—would ever be ready for that again. But the need...

He'd just check on her, just to be on the safe side. He couldn't let her lie there alone all night.

Not like Angelina.

Guilt crashed over him again, driving out the need and leaving sorrow in its wake. Focused now, he went into her room, his bare feet silent on the tiled floor, and gave his eyes a moment to adjust to the light.

Had she sensed him? Maybe, because she sighed and shifted, the soft, contented sound drifting to him on the night air. When had he last heard a woman sigh softly in her sleep?

Too long ago to remember, too soon to forget.

It would be so easy to reach out his hand, to touch her. To take her in his arms, warm and sleepy, and make love to her.

Easy, and yet impossibly wrong. What was it about her that made him feel like this, that made him think things he hadn't thought in years? Not since he'd lost Angelina.

He stood over her, staring at her in the moonlight, the thought of his wife reminding him of why he was here. Not to watch Lydia sleep, like some kind of voyeur, but to keep her safe. He focused on her face. It was peaceful, both sides the same, just as it had been when he'd left her for the night, and she was breathing slowly and evenly. As he watched she moved her arms, pushing the covers lower. Both arms, both working.

He swallowed. She was fine, just as she'd told him, he realised in relief. He could go to bed now, relax.

But it was too late. He'd seen her sleeping, heard that soft, feminine sigh and the damage was done. His body, so long denied, had come screaming back to life, and he wouldn't sleep now.

Moving carefully so as not to disturb her, he made his way back to the French doors and out onto the terrace. Propping his hands on his hips, he dropped his head back and sucked in a lungful of cool night air, then let it out slowly before dragging his hand over his face.

He'd swim. Maybe that would take the heat out of his blood. And if it was foolish to swim alone, if he'd told the children a thousand times that no one should ever do it—well, tonight was different.

Everything about tonight seemed different.

He crossed the upper terrace, padded silently down the worn stone steps to the level below and rolled back the thermal cover on the pool. The water was warm, steaming billowing from the surface in the cool night air, and stripping off his clothes, he dived smoothly in.

Something had woken her.

She opened her eyes a fraction, peeping through the slit between her eyelids, but she could see nothing.

She could hear something, though. Not loud, just a little, rhythmic splash—like someone swimming?

She threw off the covers and sat up, wincing a little as her head pounded and the bruises twinged with the movement. She fingered the egg on her head, and sighed. *Idiot*. First thing in the morning she was going to track down that dress and burn the blasted thing.

She inched to the edge of the bed, and stood up slowly, her ankle protesting as she put weight through it. Not as badly as yesterday, though, she thought, and limped out onto the terrace to listen for the noise.

Yes. Definitely someone swimming. And it seemed to be coming from straight ahead. As she felt her way cautiously across the stone slabs and then the grass, she realised that this was the terrace they'd sat on last night, or at least a part of it. They'd been further over, to her left, and straight ahead of her were railings, the top edge gleaming in the moonlight.

She made her way slowly to them and looked down, and

there he was. Well, there someone was, slicing through the water with strong, bold strokes, up and down, up and down, length after length through the swirling steam that rose from the surface of the pool.

Exorcising demons?

Then finally he slowed, rolled to his back and floated spread-eagled on the surface. She could barely make him out because the steam clouded the air in the moonlight, but she knew instinctively it was him.

And as if he'd sensed her, he turned his head and as the veil of mist was drawn back for an instant, their eyes met in the night. Slowly, with no sense of urgency, he swam to the side, folded his arms and rested on them, looking up at her.

'You're awake.'

'Something woke me, then I heard the splashing. Is it sensible to swim on your own in the dark?'

He laughed softly. 'You could always come in. Then I wouldn't be alone.'

'I haven't got any swimming things.'

'Ah. Well, that's probably not very wise then because neither have I.'

She sucked in her breath softly, and closed her eyes, suddenly embarrassed. Amongst other things. 'I'm sorry. I didn't realise. I'll go away.'

'Don't worry, I'm finished. Just close your eyes for a second so I don't offend you while I get out.'

She heard the laughter in his voice, then the sound of him vaulting out of the pool. Her eyes flew open, and she saw him straighten up, water sluicing off his back as he walked calmly to a sun lounger and picked up an abandoned towel. He dried himself briskly as she watched, unable to look away, mesmerised by those broad shoulders that tapered down to lean hips and powerful legs.

In the magical silver light of the moon, the taut, firm globes of his buttocks, paler than the rest of him, could have been carved from marble, like one of the statues that seemed to litter the whole of Italy. Except they'd be warm, of course, alive…

Her mouth dry, she snapped her eyes shut again and made herself breath. In, out, in, out, nice and slowly, slowing down, calmer.

'Would you like a drink?'

She jumped and gave a tiny shriek. 'Don't creep up on people like that!' she whispered fiercely, and rested her hand against the pounding heart beneath her chest.

Yikes. Her all but bare chest, in the crazily insubstantial pyjamas…

'I'm not really dressed for entertaining,' she mumbled, which was ridiculous because the scanty towel twisted round his hips left very little to the imagination.

His fingers, cool and damp, appeared under her chin, tilting her head up so she could see his face instead of just that tantalising towel. His eyes were laughing.

'That makes two of us. I tell you what, I'll go and put the kettle on and pull on my clothes, and you go and find something a little less…'

'Revealing?'

His smile grew crooked. 'I was going to say alluring.'

Alluring. Right.

'I'll get dressed,' she said hastily, and limped rather faster than was sensible back towards her room, shutting the doors firmly behind her.

He watched her hobble away, his eyes tracking her progress across the terrace in the skimpiest of pyjamas, the long slender legs that had been hidden until now revealed by those tiny shorts in a way that did nothing for his peace of mind.

Or the state of his body. He swallowed hard and tightened his grip on the towel.

So much for the swimming cooling him down, he thought wryly, and went into the kitchen through the side door, rubbed himself briskly down with the towel again and pulled on his clothes, then switched on the kettle. Would she be able to find him? Would she even know which way to go?

Yes. She was there, in the doorway, looking deliciously rumpled and sleepy and a little uncertain. She'd pulled on her jeans and the T-shirt she'd been wearing last night, and her unfettered breasts had been confined to a bra. Pity, he thought, and then chided himself. She was a guest in his house, she was injured, and all he could do was lust after her. He should be ashamed of himself.

'Tea, coffee or something else? I expect there are some herbal teabags or something like that.'

'Camomile?' she asked hopefully.

Something to calm her down, because her host, standing there in bare feet, a damp T-shirt clinging to the moisture on his chest and a pair of jeans that should have had a health warning on them hanging on his lean hips was doing nothing for her equilibrium.

Not now she knew what was underneath those clothes.

He poured boiling water into a cup for her, then stuck another cup under the coffee maker and pressed a button. The sound of the grinding beans was loud in the silence, but not loud enough to drown out the sound of her heartbeat.

She should have stayed in her room, kept out of his way.

'Here, I don't know how long you want to keep the teabag in.'

He put the mug down on the table and turned back to the coffee maker, and as she stirred the teabag round absently she watched him. His hands were deft, his movements precise as he spooned sugar and stirred in a splash of milk.

'Won't that keep you awake?' she asked, but he just laughed softly.

'It's not a problem, I'm up now for the day. After I've drunk this I'll go and tackle some work in my office, and then I'll have breakfast with the children before I go out and check the grapes in each field to see if they're ripe.'

'Has the harvest started?'

'La vendemmia?' He shook his head. 'No. If the grapes are ripe, it starts tomorrow. We'll spend the rest of the day making sure we're ready, because once it starts, we don't stop till it's finished. But today—today should be pretty routine.'

So he might have time to show her round...

'Want to come with me and see what we do? If you're interested, of course. Don't feel you have to.'

If she was interested? She nearly laughed. *The farm*, she told herself firmly. He was talking about the *farm*.

'That would be great, if I won't be in your way?'

'No, of course not. It might be dull, though, and once I leave the house I won't be back for hours. I don't know if you're feeling up to it.'

Was he trying to get out of it? Retracting his invitation, thinking better of having her hanging around him all day like a stray kitten that wouldn't leave him alone?

'I can't walk far,' she said, giving him a get-out clause, but he shook his head.

'No, you don't have to. We'll take the car, and if you don't feel well I can always bring you back, it's not a problem.'

That didn't sound as if he was trying to get out of it, and she was genuinely interested.

'It sounds great. What time do you want to leave?'

'Breakfast is at seven. We'll go straight afterwards.'

It was fascinating.

He knew every inch of his land, every nook and cranny,

every slope, every vine, almost, and as he stood on the edge of
a little escarpment pointing things out to her, his feet planted
firmly in the soil, she thought she'd never seen anyone who
belonged so utterly to their home.

He looked as if he'd grown from the very soil beneath his
feet, his roots stretching down into it for three hundred years.
It was a part of him, and he was a part of it, the latest guardian in its history, and it was clear that he took the privilege
incredibly seriously.

As they drove round the huge, sprawling estate to check
the ripeness of the grapes on all the slopes, he told her about
each of the grape varieties which grew on the different soils
and orientations, lifting handfuls of the soil so she could see
the texture, sifting it through his fingers as he talked about
moisture content and pH levels and how it varied from field
to field, and all the time his fingers were caressing the soil
like a lover.

He mesmerised her.

Then he dropped the soil, brushed off his hands and gave
her a wry smile.

'I'm boring you to death. Come on, it's time for lunch.'

He helped her back to the car, frowning as she trod on some
uneven ground and gave a little cry as her ankle twisted.

'I'm sorry, it's too rough for you. Here.' And without hesitating he scooped her off her feet and set her back on the pas-
senger seat, shut the door and went round and slid in behind
the wheel.

He must have been mad to bring her out here on the
rough ground in the heat of the day, with a head injury and
a sprained ankle. He hadn't been thinking clearly, what with
the upset of yesterday and Francesca's scene at the table and
then the utter distraction of her pyjamas—even if he'd been
intending to go back to bed, there was no way he would have
slept. In fact, he doubted if he'd ever sleep again!

He put her in the car, drove back to the villa and left her there with Carlotta. He'd been meaning to show her round the house, but frankly, even another moment in her company was too dangerous to contemplate at the moment.

He made a work-related excuse, and escaped.

He had a lot to do, he'd told her as he'd hurried off, because *la vendemmia* would start the following day.

So much for her tour of the house, she thought, but maybe it was as well to keep a bit of distance, because her feelings for him were beginning to confuse her.

Roberto brought the children home from school at the end of the afternoon, and she heard them splashing in the pool. She'd been contemplating the water herself, but without a suit it wasn't a goer, so she'd contented herself with sitting in the sun for a while and relaxing.

She went over to the railings and looked down, and saw all three of them in the water, with Carlotta and Roberto sitting in the shade watching them and keeping order. Carlotta glanced up at her and waved her down, and she limped down the steps and joined them.

It looked so inviting. Was her face a giveaway? Maybe, because Carlotta got to her feet and went to a door set in the wall of the terrace, under the steps. She emerged with a sleek black one-piece and offered it to her. 'Swim?' she said, encouragingly.

It was so, so tempting, and the children didn't seem to mind. Lavinia swam to the edge and grinned at her, and Antonino threw a ball at her and missed, and then giggled because she threw it back and bounced it lightly off his head. Only Francesca kept her distance, and she could understand why. It was the first time she'd seen her since supper last night, and maybe now she'd find a chance to apologise.

She changed in the cubicle Carlotta had taken the costume

from, and sat on the edge of the pool to take off her elastic ankle support.

'Ow. It looks sore.'

She glanced up, and saw Francesca watching her warily, her face troubled.

'I'm all right,' she assured her with a smile. 'I was really stupid to fall like that. I'm so sorry I upset you last night.'

She shrugged, and returned the smile with a tentative one of her own. 'Is OK. I was just tired, and *Pàpa* had been away for days, and—I'm OK. Sometimes, I just remember…'

She nodded, trying to understand what it must be like to be ten and motherless, and coming up with nothing even close, she was sure.

'I'm sorry.' She slipped into the water next to Francesca, and reached out and touched her shoulder gently. Then she smiled at her. 'I wonder, would you teach me some words of Italian?'

'Sure. What?'

'Just basic things. Sorry. Thank you. Hello, goodbye—just things like that.'

'Of course. Swim first, then I teach you.'

And she smiled, a dazzling, pretty smile like the smile of her mother in the photograph, and it nearly broke Lydia's heart.

He came into the kitchen as she was sitting there with the children, Francesca patiently coaching her.

'No! *Mee dees-pya-che*,' said Francesca, and Lydia repeated it, stretching the vowels.

'That's good. *Ciao, bambini!*'

'*Ciao, Pàpa!*' the children chorused, and he came over and sat down with them.

'I'm teaching Lydia *Italiano*,' Francesca told him, grinning at him.

He smiled back, his eyes indulgent. *'Mia bella ragazza,'* he said softly, and her smile widened, a soft blush colouring her cheeks.

'So what do you know?' he asked Lydia, and she laughed ruefully.

'Mi dispiace—I thought sorry was a word I ought to master pretty early on, with my track record,' she said drily, and he chuckled.

'Anything else?'

'Grazie mille—I seem to need that a lot, too! And *per favore*, because it's rude not to say please. And *prego*, just in case I ever get the chance to do something that someone thanks me for. And that's it, so far, but I think it's the most critical ones.'

He laughed. 'It's a good start. Right, children, bedtime. Say goodnight.'

'Buonanotte, Lydia,' they chorused, and she smiled at them and said, *'Buonanotte,'* back.

And then she looked at Francesca, and added, *'Grazie mille*, Francesca,' her eyes soft, and Francesca smiled back.

'Prego. We do more tomorrow?'

'Si.'

She grinned, and then out of the blue she came over to Lydia and kissed her on both cheeks. 'Goodnight.'

'Goodnight, Francesca.'

He ushered them away, although Francesca didn't really need to go to bed this early, but she'd lost sleep the night before and she was always happy to lie in bed and read.

He chivvied them through the bathroom, checked their teeth, redid Antonino's and then tucked them up. As he bent to kiss Francesca goodnight, she slid her arms round his neck and hugged him. 'I like Lydia,' she said. 'She's nice.'

'She is nice,' he said. 'Thank you for helping her.'

'It's OK. How long is she staying?'

'I don't know. A few days, just until she's better. You go to sleep, now.'

He turned off her top light, leaving the bedside light on so she could read for a while, and went back down to the kitchen.

Lydia was sitting there studying an English-Italian dictionary that Francesca must have lent her, and he poured two glasses of wine and sat down opposite her.

'She's a lovely girl.'

'She is. She's very like her mother. Kind. Generous.'

Lydia nodded. 'I'm really sorry you lost her.'

He smiled, but said nothing. What was there to say? Nothing he hadn't said before.

'So, the harvest starts tomorrow,' Lydia said after a moment.

'*Si*. You should come down. Carlotta brings lunch for everyone at around twelve-thirty. Come with her, I'll show you what we do.'

Massimo left before dawn the following morning, and she found Carlotta up to her eyes in the kitchen.

'How many people are you feeding?' she asked.

Carlotta's face crunched up thoughtfully, and she said something in Italian which was meaningless, then held up her outspread hands and flashed them six times. Sixty. *Sixty?*

'Wow! That's a lot of work.'

'*Si*. Is lot of work.'

She looked tired at the very thought, and Lydia frowned slightly and began to help without waiting to be asked. They loaded the food into a truck at twelve, and Roberto, Carlotta's husband, drove them down to the centre of operations.

They followed the route she'd travelled with Massimo the day before, bumping along the gravelled road to a group of buildings. It was a hive of activity, small tractors and pickup trucks in convoy bringing in the grapes, a tractor and trailer with men and women crowded on the back laughing and joking, their spirits high.

Massimo met them there, and helped her down out of the truck with a smile. 'Come, I'll show you round,' he said, and led her to the production line.

Around the tractors laden with baskets of grapes, the air was alive with the hum of bees. Everyone was covered in sticky purple grape juice, the air heavy with sweat and the sweet scent of freshly pressed grapes, and over the sound of excited voices she could hear the noise of the motors powering the pumps and the pressing machines.

'It's fascinating,' she yelled, and he nodded.

'It is. You can stay, if you like, see what we do with the grapes.'

'Do you need me underfoot?' she asked, and his mouth quirked.

'I'm sure I'll manage. You ask intelligent questions. I can live with that.'

His words made her oddly happy, and she smiled. 'Thank you. They seem to be enjoying themselves,' she added, gesturing to the laughing workers, and he grinned.

'Why wouldn't they be? We all love the harvest. And anyway, it's lunchtime,' he said pragmatically as the machines fell silent, and she laughed.

'So it is. I'm starving.'

The lunch was just a cold spread of bread and cheese and ham and tomatoes, much like their impromptu supper in the middle of the first night, and the exhausted and hungry workers fell on it like locusts.

'Carlotta told me there are about sixty people to feed. Does she do this every day?'

'Yes—and an evening meal for everyone. It's too much for her, but she won't let anyone else take over, she insists on being in charge and she's so fussy about who she'll allow in her kitchen it's not easy to get help that she'll accept.'

She nodded. She could understand that. She'd learned the art of delegation, but you still had to have a handle on everything that was happening in the kitchen and that took energy and physical resources that Carlotta probably didn't have any more.

'How old is she?'

Massimo laughed. 'It's a state secret and more than my life's worth to reveal it. Roberto's eighty-two. She tells me it's none of my business, which makes it difficult as she's on the payroll, so I had to prise it out of Roberto. Let's just say there's not much between them.'

That made her chuckle, but it also made her think. Carlotta hadn't minded her helping out in the kitchen this morning, or the other night—in fact, she'd almost seemed grateful. Maybe she'd see if she could help that afternoon. 'I think I'll head back with them,' she told him. 'It's a bit hot out here for me now anyway, and I could do with putting my foot up for a while.'

It wasn't a lie, none of it, but she had no intention of putting her foot up if Carlotta would let her help. And it would be a way to repay them for all the trouble she'd caused.

It was an amazing amount of work.

It would have been a lot for a team. For Carlotta, whose age was unknown but somewhere in the ballpark of eighty-plus, it was ridiculous. She had just the one helper, Maria, who sighed with relief when Lydia offered her assistance.

So did Carlotta.

Oh, she made a fuss, protested a little, but more on the lines of 'Oh, you don't really want to,' rather than, 'No, thank you, I don't need your help.'

So she rolled up her sleeves and pitched in, peeling and

chopping a huge pile of vegetables. Carlotta was in charge of browning the diced chicken, seasoning the tomato-based sauce, tasting.

That was fine. This was her show. Lydia was just going along for the ride, and making up for the disaster of her first evening here, but by the time they were finished and ready to serve it on trestle tables under the cherry trees, her ankle was paying for it.

She stood on one leg like a stork, her sore foot hooked round her other calf, wishing she could sit down and yet knowing she was needed as they dished up to the hungry hordes.

They still looked happy, she thought. Happy and dirty and smelly and as if they'd had a good day, and there was a good deal of teasing and flirting going on, some of it in her direction.

She smiled back, dished up and wondered where Massimo was. She found herself scanning the crowd for him, and told herself not to be silly. He'd be with the children, not here, not eating with the workers.

She was wrong. A few minutes later, when the queue was thinning out and she was at the end of her tether, she felt a light touch on her waist.

'You should be resting. I'll take over.'

And his firm hands eased her aside, took the ladle from her hand and carried on.

'You don't need to do that. You've been working all day.'

'So have you, I gather, and you're hurt. Have you eaten?'

'No. I was waiting till we'd finished.'

He ladled sauce onto the last plate and turned to her. 'We're finished. Grab two plates, we'll go and eat. And you can put your foot up. You told me you were going to do that and I hear you've been standing all day.'

They sat at the end of a trestle, so she was squashed be-

tween a young girl from one of the villages and her host, and
the air was heady with the scent of sweat and grape juice and
the rich tomato and basil sauce.

He shaved cheese over her pasta, his arm brushing hers
as he held it over her plate, and the soft chafe of hair against
her skin made her nerve-endings dance.

'So, is it a good harvest?' she asked, and he grinned.

'Very good. Maybe the best I can remember. It'll be a vintage year for our Brunello.'

'Brunello? I thought that was only from Montalcino?'

'It is. Part of the estate is in the Montalcino territory. It's
very strictly regulated, but it's a very important part of our
revenue.'

'I'm sure.' She was. During the course of her training
and apprenticeships she'd learned a lot about wines, and she
knew that Brunellos were always expensive, some of them
extremely so. Expensive, and exclusive. Definitely niche market.

Her father would be interested. He'd like Massimo, she
realised. They had a lot in common, in so many ways, for all
the gulf between them.

Deep in thought, she ate the hearty meal, swiped the last
off the sauce from her plate with a chunk of bread and licked
her lips, glancing up to see him watching her with a smile on
his face.

'What?'

'You. You really appreciate food.'

'I do. Carlotta's a good cook. That was delicious.'

'Are you making notes?'

She laughed. 'Only mental ones.'

He glanced over her head, and a smile touched his face.
'My parents are back. They're looking forward to meeting
you.'

Really? Like this, covered in tomato sauce and reeking of

chopped onions? She probably had an orange tide-line round her mouth, and her hair was dragged back into an elastic band, and—

'Mamma, *Pàpa*, this is Lydia.'

She scrambled to her feet, wincing as her sore ankle took her weight, and looked up into the eyes of an elegant, beautiful, immaculately groomed woman with clear, searching eyes.

'Lydia. How nice to meet you. Welcome to our home. I'm Elisa Valtieri, and this is my husband, Vittorio.'

'Hello. It's lovely to meet you, too.' Even if she did look a fright.

She shook their hands, Elisa's warm and gentle, Vittorio's rougher, his fingers strong and hard, a hand that wasn't afraid of work. He was an older version of his son, and his eyes were kind. He reminded her of her father.

'My son tells me you've had an accident?' Elisa said, her eyes concerned.

'Yes, I was really stupid, and he's been unbelievably kind.'

'And so, I think, have you. Carlotta is singing your praises.'

'Oh.' She felt herself colour, and laughed a little awkwardly. 'I didn't have anything else to do.'

'Except rest,' Massimo said drily, but his smile was gentle and warmed her right down to her toes.

And then she glanced back and found his mother looking at her, curiosity and interest in those lively brown eyes, and she excused herself, mumbling some comment about them having a lot to catch up on, and hobbled quickly back to Carlotta to see if there was anything she could do to help.

Anything, other than stand there while his mother eyed her speculatively, her eyes asking questions Lydia had no intention of answering.

If she even knew the answers…

CHAPTER FIVE

'YOU ran away.'

She was sitting outside her room on a bench with her foot up, flicking through a magazine she'd found, and she looked up guiltily into his thoughtful eyes.

'I had to help Carlotta.'

'And it was easier than dealing with my mother,' he said softly, a fleeting smile in his eyes. 'I'm sorry, she can be a little…'

'A little…?'

He grinned slightly crookedly. 'She doesn't like me being on my own. Every time I speak to a woman under fifty, her radar picks it up. She's been interrogating me for the last three hours.'

Lydia laughed, and she put the magazine down, swung her foot to the ground and patted the bench. 'Want to hide here for a while?'

His mouth twitched. 'How did you guess? Give me a moment.'

He vanished, then reappeared with a bottle of wine and two glasses. 'Prosecco?'

'Lovely. Thanks.' She took a glass from him, sniffing the bubbles and wrinkling her nose as she sipped. 'Mmm, that's really nice. So, how was the baby?'

'Beautiful, perfect, amazing, the best baby in the world—

oh, apart from all their other grandchildren. This is the sixth, and Luca and Isabelle are about to make it seven. Their second is due any time now.'

'Wow. Lots of babies.'

'Yes, and she loves it. Nothing makes her happier. Luca and Isabelle and my brother Gio are coming over tomorrow for dinner with some neighbours, by the way. I'd like you to join us, if you can tolerate it.'

She stared at him. 'Really? I'm only here by default, and I feel such a fraud. I really ought to go home.'

'How's your head now?'

She pulled a face. 'Better. I'm still getting the odd headache, but nothing to worry about. It's my ankle and the other bruises and scrapes that are sorest. I think I hit every step.'

He frowned. 'I'm sorry. I didn't really think about the things I can't see.'

Well, that was a lie. He thought about them all the time, but there was no way he was confessing that to Lydia. 'So—will you join us?'

She bit her lip, worrying it for a moment with her teeth, which made him want to kiss her just to stop her hurting that soft, full mouth that had been taunting him for days. *Dio*, the whole damn woman had been taunting him for days—

'Can I think about it?'

A kiss? No. No! Not a kiss!

'Of course,' he said, finally managing to unravel his tongue long enough to speak. 'Of course you may. It won't be anything impressive, Carlotta's got enough to do as it is, but my mother wanted to see Isabelle and Luca before the baby comes, and Gio's coming, and so my mother's invited Anita and her parents, and so it gets bigger—you know how it is.'

She laughed softly. 'I can imagine. Who's Anita?'

'The daughter of our neighbours. She and Gio had a thing a

while back, and my mother keeps trying to get them together again. Can't see it working, really, but she likes to try.'

'And how do they feel?'

He laughed abruptly. 'I wouldn't dare ask Gio. He has a fairly bitter and twisted attitude to love. Comes from being a lawyer, I suppose. His first line of defence is always a pre-nuptial agreement.'

She raised an eyebrow. 'Trust issues, then. I can under-stand that. I have a few of my own after Russell.'

'I'm sure. People like that can take away something pre-cious, a sort of innocence, a naivety, and once it's gone you can never get it back. Although I have no idea what happened to Gio. He won't talk about it.'

'What about Anita? What's she like?'

His low chuckle made her smile. 'Anita's a wedding plan-ner. What do you think?'

'I think she might like to plan her own?'

'Indeed. But Gio can't see what's under his nose, even if Mamma keeps putting her there.' He tipped his head on one side. 'It could be an interesting evening. And if you're there, it might take the heat off Gio, so he'll probably be so busy being grateful he'll forget to quiz me about you, so it could be better all round!'

She started to laugh at that, and he joined in with another chuckle and topped up her glass.

'Here's to families and their politics and complications,' he said drily, and touched his glass to hers.

'Amen to that,' she said, remembering guiltily that she'd meant to phone Jen again. 'I heard from Claire, by the way—she's back home safely, and she said Jo's ecstatic about win-ning.'

'How's your sister about it?'

She pulled a face. 'I'm not sure. She was putting on a brave face, but I think she's gutted. I know none of us expected me to win but, you know, it would have been so nice.'

He nodded. 'I'm sorry.'

'Don't be. You've done more than enough.' She drained her glass and handed it to him. 'I'm going to turn in. I need to rest my leg properly, and tomorrow I need to think about arranging a flight back home.'

'For tomorrow?' He sounded startled, and she shook her head.

'No. I thought maybe the next day? I probably ought to phone the hospital and get the go-ahead to fly.'

'I can take you there if you want a check-up.'

'You've got so much to do.'

'Nothing that's more important,' he said, and although it wasn't true, she knew that for him there was nothing more important than making sure there wasn't another Angelina.

'I'll see what they say,' she compromised. There was always the bus, surely? She'd ask Carlotta in the morning.

She got to her feet, and he stood up and took her hand, tucking it in the crook of his arm and helping her to the French doors. Quite unnecessarily, since she'd been hobbling around without help since the second day, really, but it was still nice to feel the strength of his arm beneath her hand, the muscles warm and hard beneath the fine fabric of his shirt.

Silk and linen, she thought, sampling the texture with her fingertips, savouring it.

He hesitated at the door, and then just when she thought he was going to walk away, he lowered his head and touched his lips to hers, sending rivers of ice and fire dancing over her skin.

It was a slow kiss, lingering, thoughtful, their mouths the only point of contact, but then the velvet stroke of his tongue against her lips made her gasp softly and part them for him, and everything changed.

He gave a muffled groan and deepened the kiss, searching the secret recesses of her mouth, his tongue finding hers and dancing with it, retreating, tangling, coaxing until she thought her legs would collapse.

Then he eased away, breaking the contact so slowly so that for a tiny second their lips still clung.

'*Buonanotte*, Lydia,' he murmured unevenly, his breath warm against her mouth, and then straightening slowly, he took a step back and turned briskly away, gathering up the glasses and the bottle as he went without a backwards glance.

She watched him go, then closed the curtains and undressed, leaving the doors open. The night was warm still, the light breeze welcome, and she lay there in the darkness, her fingertips tracing her lips, and thought about his kiss...

He must have been mad to kiss her!

Crazy. Insane. If he hadn't walked away, he would have taken her right there, standing on the terrace in full view of anyone who walked past.

He headed for the stairs, but then hesitated. He wouldn't sleep—but what else could he do? His office was next to her room, and he didn't trust himself that close to her. The pool, his first choice of distraction for the sheer physical exertion it offered, was too close to her room, and she slept with her doors open. She'd hear him, come and investigate, and...

So not the pool, then.

Letting out a long, weary sigh, he headed slowly up the stairs to his room, and sat on the bed, staring at the photograph of Angelina on his bedside table.

He'd loved her—really, deeply and enduringly loved her. But she was gone, and now, as he looked at her face, another face seemed superimposed on it, a face with laughing eyes and a soft, full bottom lip that he could still taste.

He groaned and fell back against the pillows, staring up

at the ceiling. The day after tomorrow, she'd be gone, he told himself, and then had to deal with the strange and unsettling sense of loss he felt at the thought that he was about to lose her.

She didn't sleep well.

Her dreams had been vivid and unsettling, and as soon as she heard signs of life, she got up, showered and put on her rinsed-out underwear, and then sat down on the edge of the bed and sighed thoughtfully as she studied her clothes.

She couldn't join them for dinner—not if their neighbours were coming. She'd seen Elisa, seen the expensive and elegant clothes she'd worn for travelling back home from her daughter's house, and the only things she had with her were the jeans and top she'd been wearing now for two days, including all the cooking she'd done yesterday.

No way could she wear them to dinner, even if she'd earn Gio's undying gratitude and give Elisa something else to think about! She put the clothes on, simply because she had absolutely no choice apart from the wedding dress Carlotta had stuffed in a bag for her and which she yet had to burn, and went outside and round the corner to the kitchen.

Carlotta was there, already making headway on the lunch preparations, and the children were sitting at the table eating breakfast. For a slightly crazy moment, she wondered if they could tell what she'd been dreaming about, if the fact that she'd kissed their father was written all over her face.

She said good morning to them, in her best Italian learned yesterday from Francesca, asked them how they were and then went over to Carlotta. '*Buongiorno*, Carlotta,' she said softly, and Carlotta blushed and smiled at her and patted her cheek.

'*Buongiorno, signorina,*' she said. 'Did you have good sleep?'

'Very good,' she said, trying not to think of the dreams and blushing slightly anyway. 'What can I do to help you?'

'No, no, you sit. I can do it.'

'You know I can't do that,' she chided softly. She stuck a mug under the coffee machine, pressed the button and waited, then added milk and went back to Carlotta, sipping the hot, fragrant brew gratefully. 'Oh, that's lovely. Right. What shall I do first?'

Carlotta gave in. 'We need to cut the meat, and the bread, and—'

'Just like yesterday?'

'*Si.*'

'So I'll do that, and you can make preparations for tonight. I know you have dinner to cook for the family as well as for the workers.'

Her brow creased, looking troubled, and Lydia could tell she was worried. Exhausted, more like. 'Look, let me do this, and maybe I can give you a hand with that, too?' she offered, but that was a step too far. Carlotta straightened her gnarled old spine and plodded to the fridge.

'I do it,' she said firmly, and so Lydia gave in and concentrated on preparing lunch for sixty people in the shortest possible time, so she could move on to cooking the pasta sauce for the evening shift with Maria. At least that way Carlotta would be free to concentrate on dinner.

Massimo found her in the kitchen at six, in the throes of draining gnocci for the workers, and she nearly dropped the pan. Crazy. Ridiculous, but the sight of him made her heart pound and she felt like a gangly teenager, awkward and confused because of the kiss.

'Are you in here again?' he asked, taking the other side of the huge pan and helping her tip it into the enormous strainer.

'Looks like me,' she said with a forced grin, but he just

frowned and avoided her eyes, as if he, too, was feeling awkward and uncomfortable about the kiss.

'Did you speak to the hospital?' he asked, and she realised he would be glad to get rid of her. She'd been nothing but trouble for him, and she was unsettling the carefully constructed and safe status quo he'd created around them all.

'Yes. I'm fine to travel,' she said, although it wasn't quite true. They'd said they needed to examine her, and when she'd said she was too busy, they'd fussed a bit but what could they do? So she'd booked a flight. 'I've got a seat on a plane at three tomorrow afternoon from Pisa,' she told him, and he frowned again.

'Really? You didn't have to go so soon,' he said, confusing her even more.

'It's not soon. It'll be five days—that's what they said, and I've been under your feet long enough.'

And any longer, she realised, and things were going to happen between them. There was such a pull every time she was with him, and that kiss last night—

She thrust the big pot at him. 'Here, carry the *gnocci* outside for me. I'll bring the sauce.'

He followed her, set the food down for the workers and stood at her side, dishing up.

'So can I persuade you to join us for dinner?' he asked, but she shook her head.

'I've got nothing to wear,' she said, feeling safe because he couldn't argue with that, but she was wrong.

'You're about the same size as Serena. I'm sure she wouldn't mind if you borrowed something from her wardrobe. She always leaves something here. Carlotta will show you.'

'Carlotta's trying to prepare a meal for ten people this evening, Massimo. She doesn't have time to worry about clothes for me.'

'Then I'll take you,' he said, and the moment the serving was finishing, he hustled her back into the house before she could argue.

He was right. She and Serena were about the same size, something she already knew because she'd borrowed her costume to swim in, and she found a pair of black trousers that were the right length with her flat black pumps, and a pretty top that wasn't in the first flush of youth but was nice enough.

She didn't want to take anything too special, but she didn't think Serena would mind if she borrowed that one, and it was good enough, surely, for an interloper?

She went back to the kitchen, still in her jeans and T-shirt, and found Carlotta sitting at the table with her head on her arms, and Roberto beside her wringing his hands.

'Carlotta?'

'She is tired, *signorina*,' he explained worriedly. 'Signora Valtieri has many people for dinner, and my Carlotta…'

'I'll do it,' she said quickly, sitting down and taking Carlotta's hands in hers. 'Carlotta, tell me what you were going to cook them, and I'll do it.'

'But Massimo said…'

'Never mind what he said. I can cook and be there at the same time. Don't worry about me. We can make it easy. Just tell me what you're cooking, and Roberto can help me find things. We'll manage, and nobody need ever know.'

Her eyes filled with tears, and Lydia pulled a tissue out of a box and shoved it in her hand. 'Come on, stop that, it's all right. We've got cooking to do.'

Well, it wasn't her greatest meal ever, she thought as she sat with the others and Roberto waited on them, but it certainly didn't let Carlotta down, and from the compliments going back to the kitchen via Roberto, she knew Carlotta would be feeling much less worried.

As for her, in her borrowed top and trousers, she felt underdressed and overawed—not so much by the company as by the amazing dining room itself. Like her room and the kitchen, it opened to the terrace, but in the centre, with two pairs of double doors flung wide so they could hear the tweeting and twittering of the swallows swooping past the windows.

But it was the walls which stunned her. Murals again, like the ones in the cloistered walkway around the courtyard, but this time all over the ornate vaulted ceiling as well.

'Beautiful, isn't it?' Gio said quietly. 'I never get tired of looking at this ceiling. And it's a good way to avoid my mother's attention.'

She nearly laughed at that. He was funny—very funny, very quick, very witty, very dry. A typical lawyer, she thought, used to brandishing his tongue in court like a rapier, slashing through the opposition. He would be formidable, she realised, and she didn't envy the woman who was so clearly still in love with him.

Anita was lovely, though. Strikingly beautiful, but warm and funny and kind, and Lydia wondered if she realised just how often Gio glanced at her when she'd looked away.

Elisa did, she was sure of it.

And then she met Massimo's eyes, and realised he was studying her thoughtfully.

'Excuse me, I have to go and do something in the kitchen,' she murmured. 'Carlotta very kindly let me experiment with the dessert, and I need to put the finishing touches to it.'

She bolted, running along the corridor and arriving in the kitchen just as Carlotta had put out the bowls.

'Roberto say you tell them I cook everything!' she said, wringing her hands and hugging her.

Lydia hugged her back. 'You did, really. I just helped you. You told me exactly what to do.'

'You *know* what to do. You such good *cuoca*—good cook. Look at this! So easy—so beautiful. *Bellisima!*'

She spread her hands wide, and Lydia looked. Five to a tray, there were ten individual gleaming white bowls, each containing glorious red and black frozen berries fogged with icy dew, and in the pan on the stove Roberto was gently heating the white chocolate sauce. Sickly sweet, immensely sticky and a perfect complement to the sharp berries, it was her favourite no-frills emergency pud, and she took the pan from Roberto, poured a swirl around the edge of each plate and then they grabbed a tray each and went back to the dining room.

'I hope you like it,' she said brightly. 'If not, please don't blame Carlotta, I made her let me try it!'

Elisa frowned slightly, but Massimo just gave her a level look, and as she set the plate down in front of him, he murmured, 'Liar,' softly, so only she could hear.

She flashed him a smile and went back to her place, between Gio and Anita's father, and opposite Isabelle. 'So, tell me, what's it like living in Tuscany full-time?' she asked Isabelle, although she could see that she was blissfully contented and the answer was going to be biased.

'Wonderful,' Isabelle said, leaning her head against Luca's shoulder and smiling up at him. 'The family couldn't have been kinder.'

'That's not true. I tried to warn you off,' Gio said, and Luca laughed.

'You try and warn everybody off,' he said frankly, 'but luckily for me she didn't listen to you. Lydia, this dessert is amazing. Try it, *cara.*'

He held a spoonful up to Isabelle's lips, and Lydia felt a lump rise in her throat. Their love was so open and uncomplicated and genuine, so unlike the relationship she'd had with Russell. Isabelle and Luca were like Jen and Andy, unashamedly devoted to each other, and she wondered with a little ache what it must feel like to be the centre of someone's world, to be so clearly and deeply loved. *That* would be amazing.

She glanced across the table, and found Massimo watching her, his eyes thoughtful. He lifted his spoon to her in salute.

'Amazing, indeed.'

She blinked. He was talking about the dessert, not about love. Nothing to do with love, or with her, or him, or the two of them, or that kiss last night.

'Thank you,' she said, a little breathlessly, and turned her attention to the sickly, sticky white chocolate sauce. If she glued her tongue up enough with that, maybe it would keep it out of trouble.

'So how much of that was you, and how much was Carlotta?'

It was midnight, and everyone else had left or gone to bed. They were alone in the kitchen, putting away the last of the serving dishes that she'd just washed by hand, and Massimo was making her a cup of camomile tea.

'Honestly? I gave her a hand.'

'And the dessert?'

'Massimo, she was tired. She had all the ingredients for my quick fix, so I just improvised.'

'Hmm,' he said, but he left it at that, to her relief. She sensed he didn't believe her, but he had no proof, and Carlotta had been so distraught.

'Right, we're done here,' he said briskly. 'Let's go outside and sit and drink this.'

They went on her bench, outside her room, and sat in companionable silence drinking their tea. At least, it started out companionable, and then last night's kiss intruded, and she felt the tension creep in, making the air seem to fizz with the sparks that passed between them.

'You don't have to go tomorrow, you know,' he said, breaking the silence after it had stretched out into the hereafter.

'I do. I've bought a ticket.'

'I'll buy you another one. Wait a few more days.'

'Why? So I can finish falling for you? That's not a good idea, Massimo.'

He laughed softly, and she thought it was the saddest sound she'd ever heard. 'No. Probably not. I have nothing to offer you, Lydia. I wish I did.'

'I don't want anything.'

'That's not quite true. We both want something. It's just not wise.'

'Is it ever?'

'I don't know. Not for us, I don't think. We've both been hurt enough by the things that have happened, and I don't know about you but I'm not ready to try again. I have so many demands on me, so many calls on my time, so much *duty*.'

She put her cup down very carefully and turned to face him. 'We could just take tonight as it comes,' she said quietly, her heart in her mouth. 'No strings, just one night. No duty, no demands. Just a little time out from reality, for both of us.'

The silence was broken only by the beating of her heart, the roaring in her ears so loud that she could scarcely hear herself think. For an age he sat motionless, then he lifted a hand and touched her cheek.

'Why, *cara*? Why tonight?'

'Because it's our last chance?'

'Why me?'

'I don't know. It just seems right.'

Again he hesitated, then he took her hand and pressed it to his lips. 'Give me ten minutes. I need to check the children.'

She nodded, her mouth dry, and he brushed her lips with his and left her there, her fingers resting on the damp, tingling skin as if to hold the kiss in place.

Ten minutes, she thought. Ten minutes, and my life will change forever.

He didn't come back.

She gave up after half an hour, and went to bed alone, humiliated and disappointed. How stupid, to proposition a man so far out of her league. He was probably still laughing at her in his room.

He wasn't. There was a soft knock on the door, and he walked in off the terrace. 'Lydia? I'm sorry I was so long. Are you still awake?'

She propped herself up on one elbow, trying to read his face, but his back was to the moonlight. 'Yes. What happened? I'd given up on you.'

'Antonino woke. He had a nightmare. He's all right now, but I didn't want to leave him till he was settled.'

He sat on the edge of the bed, his eyes shadowed in the darkness, and she reached for the bedside light. He caught her hand. 'No. Leave it off. Let's just have the moonlight.'

He opened the curtains wide, but closed the doors—for privacy? She didn't know, but she was grateful that he had because she felt suddenly vulnerable as he stripped off his clothes and turned back the covers, lying down beside her and taking her into his arms.

The shock of that first contact took their breath away, and he rested his head against hers and gave a shuddering sigh. 'Oh, Lydia, *cara*, you feel so good,' he murmured, and then after that she couldn't understand anything he said, because his voice deepened, the words slurred and incoherent. He was speaking Italian, she realised at last, his breath trembling over her body with every groaning sigh as his hands cupped and moulded her.

She arched against him, her body aching for him, a need like no need she'd ever felt swamping her common sense and turning her to jelly. She ran her hands over him, learning his contours, the feel of his skin like hot silk over the taut, corded muscles beneath, and then she tasted him, her tongue testing the salt of his skin, breathing in the warm musk and the lingering trace of cologne.

He seemed to be everywhere, his hands and mouth caressing every part of her, their legs tangling as his mouth returned to hers and he kissed her as if he'd die without her.

'Please,' she whispered, her voice shaking with need, and he paused, fumbling for something on the bedside table.

Taking care of her, she realised, something she'd utterly forgotten, but not him. He'd remembered, and made sure that she was safe with him.

No strings. No repercussions.

Then he reached for her, taking her into his arms, and as he moved over her she stopped thinking altogether and just *felt*.

He woke to the touch of her hand on his chest, lying lightly over his heart.

She was asleep, her head lying on his shoulder, her body silvered by the moonlight. He shifted carefully, and she sighed and let him go, so he could lever himself up and look down at her.

There was a dark stain over one hipbone. He hadn't noticed it last night, but now he did. A bruise, from her fall. And there was another, on her shoulder, and one on her thigh, high up on the side. He kissed them all, tracing the outline with his lips, kissing them better like the bruises of a child.

It worked, his brother Luca told him, because the caress

released endorphins, feel-good hormones, and so you really could kiss someone better, but only surely if they were awake—

'Massimo?'

He turned his head and met her eyes. 'You're hurt all over.'

'I'm all right now.'

She smiled, reaching up and cradling his jaw in her hand, and he turned his face into her hand and kissed her palm, his tongue stroking softly over the sensitive skin.

'What time is it?'

He glanced at his watch and sighed. 'Two. Just after.'

Two. Her flight was in thirteen hours.

She swallowed hard and drew his face down to hers. 'Make love to me again,' she whispered.

How could he refuse? How could he walk away from her, even though it was madness?

Time out, she'd said, from reality. He needed that so badly, and he wasn't strong enough to resist.

Thirteen hours, he thought, and as he took her in his arms again, his heart squeezed in his chest.

Saying goodbye to the children and Carlotta and Roberto was hard. Saying goodbye to Massimo was agony.

He'd parked at the airport, in the short stay carpark, and they'd had lunch in the café, sitting outside under the trailing pergola. She positioned herself in the sun, but it didn't seem to be able to warm her, because she was cold inside, her heart aching.

'Thank you for everything you've done for me,' she said, trying hard not to cry, but it was difficult and she felt a tear escape and slither down her cheek.

'Oh, *bella*.' He sighed, and reaching out his hand, he brushed it gently away. 'No tears. Please, no tears.'

'Happy tears,' she lied. 'I've had a wonderful time.'

He nodded, but his eyes didn't look happy, and she was sure hers didn't. She tried to smile.

'Give my love to the children, and thank Francesca again for my Italian lessons.'

He smiled, his mouth turning down at the corners ruefully. 'They'll miss you. They had fun with you.'

'They'll forget me,' she reassured him. 'Children move on very quickly.'

But maybe not if they'd been hurt in the past, he thought, and wondered if this had been so safe after all, so without consequences, without repercussions.

Maybe not.

He left her at the departures gate, standing there with his arms round her while she hugged him tight. She let him go, looked up, her eyes sparkling with tears.

'Take care,' she said, and he nodded.

'You, too. Safe journey.'

And without waiting to see her go through the gate, he walked away, emotions raging through him.

Madness. He'd thought he could handle it, but—

He'd got her address from her, so he could send her a crate of wine and oil.

That was all, he told himself. Nothing more. He certainly wasn't going to contact her, or see her again—

He sucked in a breath, surprised by the sharp stab of loss. Ships in the night, he told himself more firmly. They'd had a good time but now it was over, she was gone and he could get on with his life.

How hard could it be?

CHAPTER SIX

'WHY don't you just go and see her?'

Massimo looked up from the baby in his arms and forced himself to meet his brother's eyes.

'I don't know what you mean.'

'Of course you do. You've been like a grizzly bear for the last two weeks, and even your own children are avoiding you.'

He frowned. Were they? He hadn't noticed, he realised in horror, and winced at the wave of guilt. But…

'It's not a crime to want her, you know,' Luca said softly.

'It's not that simple.'

'Of course not. Love never is.'

His head jerked up again. 'Who's talking about love?' he snapped, and Luca just raised an eyebrow silently.

'I'm *not* in love with her.'

'If you say so.'

He opened his mouth to say, 'I do say so,' and shut it smartly. 'I've just been busy,' he said instead, making excuses. 'Carlotta's been ill, and I've been trying to juggle looking after the children in the evenings and getting them ready for school without neglecting all the work of the grape harvest.'

'But that's over now—at least the critical bit. And you're wrong, you know, Carlotta isn't ill, she's old and tired and she needs to stop working before she becomes ill.'

Massimo laughed out loud at that, startling his new nephew

and making him cry. He shushed him automatically, soothing the fractious baby, and then looked up at Luca again. 'I'll let you tell her that.'

'I have done. She won't listen because she thinks she's indispensable and she doesn't want to let anybody down. And she's going to kill herself unless someone does something to stop her.'

And then it dawned on him. Just the germ of an idea, but if it worked...

He got to his feet, wanting to get started, now that the thought had germinated. He didn't know why he hadn't thought of it before, except he'd been deliberately putting it—her—out of his mind.

'I think I'll take a few days off,' he said casually. 'I could do with a break. I'll take the car and leave the children here. Mamma can look after them. It'll keep her off Gio's back for a while and they can play with little Annamaria while Isabelle rests.'

Luca took the baby from him and smiled knowingly.

'Give her my love.'

He frowned. 'Who? I don't know what you're talking about. This is a business trip. I have some trade samples to deliver.'

His brother laughed and shut the door behind him.

'Do you know anyone with a posh left-hand-drive Mercedes with a foreign number plate?'

Lydia's head jerked up. She did—but he wouldn't be here. There was no way he'd be here, and certainly not without warning—

'Tall, dark-haired, uber-sexy. Wow, in fact. Very, *very* wow!'

Her mouth dried, her heart thundering. No. Surely not—not when she was just getting over him—

'Let me see.'

She leant over Jen's shoulder and peeped through the doorway, and her heart, already racing, somersaulted in her chest. Over him? Not a chance. She'd been fooling herself for over two weeks, convincing herself she didn't care about him, it had just been a holiday romance, and one sight of him and all of it had come slamming back. She backed away, one hand on her heart, trying to stop it vaulting out through her ribs, the other over her mouth holding back the chaotic emotions that were threatening to erupt.

'It's him, isn't it? Your farmer guy. You never said he was that hot!'

No, she hadn't. She'd said very little about him because she'd been desperately trying to forget him and avoid the inevitable interrogation if she so much as hinted at a relationship. But—farmer? Try millionaire. More than that. Try serious landowner, old-money, from one of Italy's most well-known and respected families. Not a huge brand name, but big enough, she'd discovered when she'd checked on the internet in a moment of weakness and aching, pathetic need.

And try lover—just for one night, but the most magical, memorable and relived night of her life.

She looked down at herself and gave a tiny, desperate scream. She was cleaning tack—old, tatty tack from an even older, tattier pony who'd finally met his maker, and they were going to sell it. Not for much, but the saddle was good enough to raise a couple of hundred pounds towards Jen's wedding.

'He's looking around.'

So was she—for a way to escape from the tack room and back to the house without being seen, so she could clean up and at least look slightly less disreputable, but there was no other way out, and...

'He's seen me. He's coming over. Hi, there. Can I help?'

'I hope so. I'm looking for Lydia Fletcher.'

His voice made her heart thud even harder, and she backed into the shadows, clutching the filthy, soapy rag in a desperate fist.

'She's here,' Jen said, dumping her in it and flashing him her most charming smile. 'I'm her sister, Jen—and she's rather grubby, so she probably doesn't want you to see her like that, so why don't I take you over to the house and make you a cup of tea—'

'I don't mind if she's grubby. She's seen me looking worse, I'm sure.'

And before Jen could usher him away, he stepped past her into the tack room, sucking all the air out of it in that simple movement.

'*Ciao, bella,*' he said softly, a smile lurking in his eyes, and she felt all her resolve melt away to nothing.

'*Ciao,*' she echoed, and then toughened up. 'I didn't expect to see you again.'

She peered past him at Jen, hovering in the doorway. 'Why don't you go and put the kettle on?' she said firmly.

With a tiny, knowing smile, Jen took a step away, then mouthed, '*Be nice!*'

Nice? She had no intention of being anything *but* nice, but she also had absolutely no intention of being anything more accommodating. He'd been so clear about not wanting a relationship, and she'd thought she could handle their night together, thought she could walk away. Well, she wasn't letting him in again, because she'd never get over it a second time.

'You could have warned me you were coming,' she said when Jen had gone, her crutches scrunching in the gravel. 'And don't tell me you lost my phone number, because it was on the same piece of paper as my address, which you clearly have or you wouldn't be here.'

'I haven't lost it. I didn't want to give you the chance to avoid me.'

'You thought I would?'

'I thought you might want to, and I didn't want you to run away without hearing me out.' He looked around, studying the dusty room with the saddle racks screwed to the old beams, the saddle horse in the middle of the room with Bruno's saddle on it, half-cleaned, the hook dangling from the ceiling with his bridle and stirrup leathers hanging from it, still covered in mould and dust and old grease.

Just like her, really, smeared in soapy filth and not in any way dressed to impress.

'Evocative smell.' He fingered the saddle flap, rubbing his fingertips together and sniffing them. 'It takes me back. I had a friend with horses when I was at boarding school over here, and I stayed with him sometimes. We used to have to clean the tack after we rode.'

He smiled, as if it was a good memory, and then he lifted his hand and touched a finger to her cheek. 'You've got dirt on your face.'

'I'm sure. And don't you dare spit on a tissue and rub it off.'

He chuckled, and shifting an old riding hat, he sat down on a rickety chair and crossed one foot over the other knee, his hands resting casually on his ankle as if he really didn't care how dirty the chair was.

'Well, don't let me stop you. You need to finish what you're doing—at least the saddle.'

She did. It was half-done, and she couldn't leave it like that or it would mark. She scrunched the rag in her fingers and nodded. 'If you don't mind.'

'Of course not. I didn't know you had a horse,' he added, after a slight pause.

'We don't—not any more.'

His eyes narrowed, and he leant forwards. 'Lydia?' he said

softly, and she sniffed and turned away, reaching for the saddle soap.

'He died,' she said flatly. 'We don't need the tack, so I'm going to sell it. It's a crime to let it rot out here when someone could be using it.'

'I'm sorry.'

'Don't be. He was ancient.'

'But you loved him.'

'Of course. That's what life's all about, isn't it? Loving things and losing them?' She put the rag down and turned back to him, her heart aching so badly that she was ready to howl her eyes out. 'Massimo, why are you here?'

'I promised you some olive oil and wine and balsamic vinegar.'

She blinked, and stared at him, dumbfounded. 'You drove all this way to deliver me *olive oil*? That's ridiculous. Why are you really here, in the middle of harvest? And what was that about not wanting me to run away before hearing you out?'

He smiled slowly—reluctantly. 'OK. I have a proposition for you. Finish the saddle, and I'll tell you.'

'Tell me now.'

'I'll tell you while you finish,' he compromised, so she picked up the rag again and reapplied it to the saddle, putting on rather more saddle soap than was necessary. He watched her, watched the fierce way she rubbed the leather, the pucker in her brow as she waited for him to speak.

'So?' she prompted, her patience running out.

'So—I think Carlotta is unwell. Luca says not, and he's the doctor. He says she's just old, and tired, and needs to stop before she kills herself.'

'I agree. She's been too old for years, probably, but I don't suppose she'll listen if you tell her that.'

'No. She won't. And the trouble is she won't allow anyone else in her kitchen.' He paused for a heartbeat. 'Anyone except *you*.'

She dropped the rag and spun round. 'Me!' she squeaked, and then swallowed hard. 'I—I don't understand! What have I got to do with anything?'

'We need someone to feed everybody for the harvest. After that, we'll need someone as a housekeeper. Carlotta won't give that up until she's dead, but we can get her local help, and draft in caterers for events like big dinner parties and so on. But for the harvest, we need someone she trusts who can cater for sixty people twice a day without getting in a flap—someone who knows what they're doing, who understands what's required and who's available.'

'I'm not available,' she said instantly, and he felt a sharp stab of disappointment.

'You have another job?'

She shook her head. 'No, not really, but I'm helping with the farm, and doing the odd bit of outside catering, a bit of relief work in the pub. Nothing much, but I'm trying to get my career back on track and I can't do that if I'm gallivanting about all over Tuscany, however much I want to help you out. I have to earn a living—'

'You haven't heard my proposition yet.'

She stared at him, trying to work out what he was getting at. What he was offering. She wasn't sure she wanted to know, because she had a feeling it would involve a lot of heartache, but—

'What proposition? I thought that was your proposition?'

'You come back with me, work for the harvest and I'll give your sister her wedding.'

She stared at him, confused. She couldn't have heard him right. 'I don't understand,' she said, finding her voice at last.

'It's not hard. The hotel was offering the ceremony, a reception for—what, fifty people?—a room for their wedding night, accommodation for the night before for the bridal party, a food and drink package—anything I've missed?'

She shook her head. 'Flowers, maybe?'

'OK. Well, we can offer all that. There's a chapel where they can marry, if they're Catholic, or they could have a blessing there and marry in the Town Hall, or whatever they wanted, and we'll give them a marquee with tables and chairs and a dance floor, and food and wine for the guests. And flowers. And if they don't want to stay in the guest wing of the villa, there's a lodge in the woods they can have the use of for their honeymoon.'

Her jaw dropped, and her eyes suddenly filled with tears. 'That's ridiculously generous! Why would you do this for them?'

'Because if I hadn't distracted you on the steps, you wouldn't have fallen, and your sister would have had her wedding.'

'No! Massimo, it wasn't your fault! I don't need your guilt as well as my own! This is not your problem.'

'Nevertheless, you would have won if you hadn't fallen, and yet when I took you back to my home that night you just waded in and helped Carlotta, even though you were hurt and disappointed. You didn't need to do that, but you saw she was struggling, and you put your own worries and injuries out of your mind and just quietly got on with it, even though you were much more sore than you let on.'

'What makes you say that?'

He smiled tenderly. 'I saw the bruises, cara. All over your body.'

She blushed furiously, stooping to pick the rag up off the floor, but it was covered in dust and she put it down again. The saddle was already soaped to death.

'And that dinner party—I know quite well that all of those dishes were yours. Carlotta doesn't cook like that, and yet you left an old woman her pride, and for that alone, I would give you this wedding for your sister.'

The tears spilled down her cheeks, and she scrubbed them away with the backs of her hands. Not a good idea, she realised instantly, when they were covered in soapy filth, but he was there in front of her, a tissue in his hand, wiping the tears away and the smears of dirt with them.

'Silly girl, there's no need to cry,' he tutted softly, and she pushed his hand away.

'Well, of course I'm crying, you idiot!' she sniffed, swallowing the tears. 'You're being ridiculously generous. But I can't possibly accept.'

'Why not? We need you—and that is real and genuine. I knew you'd refuse the wedding if I just offered it, but we really need help with the harvest, and it's the only way Carlotta will allow us to help her. If we do nothing, she'll work herself to death, but she'll be devastated if we bring in a total stranger to help out.'

'I was a total stranger,' she reminded him.

He gave that tender smile again, the one that had unravelled her before. 'Yes—but now you're a friend, and I'm asking you, as a friend, to help her.'

She swallowed. 'And in return you'll give Jen this amazing wedding?'

'*Si.*'

'And what about us?'

Something troubled flickered in his eyes for a second until the shutters came down. 'What about us?'

'We agreed it was just for one night.'

'Yes, we did. No strings. A little time out from reality.'

'And it stays that way?'

He inclined his head. '*Si.* It stays that way. It has to.'

Did it? She felt—what? Regret? Relief? A curious mix-

ture of both, probably, although if she was honest she might
have been hoping…

'Can I think about it?'

'Not for long. I have to return first thing tomorrow morning. I would like to take you with me.'

She nodded. 'Right. Um. I need to finish this—what are
you *doing*?'

He'd taken off his jacket, slung it over the back of the chair
and was rolling up his sleeves. 'Helping,' he said, and taking
a clean rag from the pile, he buffed the saddle to a lovely, soft
sheen. 'There. What else?'

It took them half an hour to clean the rest of Bruno's tack, and
then she led him back to the house and showed him where he
could wash his hands in the scullery sink.

'Don't mention any of this to Jen, not until I've made up
my mind,' she warned softly, and he nodded.

Her sister was in the kitchen, and she pointed her in the
direction of the kettle and ran upstairs to shower. Ten minutes later, she was back down in the kitchen with her hair in
soggy rats' tails and her face pink and shiny from the steam,
but at least she was clean.

He glanced up at her and got to his feet with a smile.
'Better now?'

'Cleaner,' she said wryly. 'Is Jen looking after you?'

Jen was, she could see that. The teapot was on the table,
and the packet of biscuits they'd been saving for visitors was
largely demolished.

'She's been telling me all about you,' he said, making her
panic, but Jen just grinned and helped herself to another bis-
cuit.

'I've invited him to stay the night,' she said airily, dunking it in her tea while Lydia tried not to panic yet again.

'I haven't said yes,' he told her, his eyes laughing as he

registered her reaction. 'There's a pub in the village with a sign saying they do rooms. I thought I might stay there.'

'You can't stay there. The pub's awful!' she said without thinking, and then could have kicked herself, because realistically there was nowhere else for miles.

She heard the door open, and the dogs came running in, tails wagging, straight up to him to check him out, and her mother was hard on their heels.

'Darling? Oh!'

She stopped in the doorway, searched his face as he straightened up from patting the dogs, and started to smile. 'Hello. I'm Maggie Fletcher, Lydia's mother, and I'm guessing from the number plate on your car you must be her Italian knight in shining armour.'

He laughed and held out his hand. 'Massimo Valtieri—but I'm not sure I'm any kind of a knight.'

'Well, you rescued my daughter, so I'm very grateful to you.'

'She hurt herself leaving my plane,' he pointed out, 'so really you should be throwing me out, not thanking me!'

'Well, I'll thank you anyway, for trying to get her there in time to win the competition. I always said it was a crazy idea.'

'Me, too.' He smiled, and Lydia ground her teeth. The last thing she needed was him cosying up to her mother, but it got worse.

'I promised her some produce from the estate, and I thought, as I had a few days when I could get away, I'd deliver it in person. I'll bring it in, if I may?'

'Of course! How very kind of you.'

It wasn't kind. It was an excuse to bribe her into going back there to feed the troops by dangling a carrot in front of her that he knew perfectly well she'd be unable to resist. Two carrots, really, because as well as Jen's wedding, which was giving her the world's biggest guilt trip, there was the problem of the aging and devoted Carlotta, who'd become her friend.

'I'll help you,' she said hastily, following him out to the car so she could get him alone for a moment.

He was one step ahead of her, though, she realised, because as he popped the boot open, he turned to her, his face serious. 'Before you say anything, I'm not going to mention it to your family. This is entirely your decision, and if you decline, I won't say any more about it.'

Well, damn. He wasn't even going to *try* to talk her into it! Which, she thought with a surge of disappointment, could only mean that he really wasn't interested in picking up their relationship, and was going to leave it as it stood, as he'd said, with just that one night between them.

Not that she wanted him to do anything else. She really didn't want to get involved with another man, not after the hatchet job Russell had done on her self-esteem, and not when she was trying to resurrect her devastated career, but...

'Here. This is a case of our olive oils. There are three types, different varietals, and they're quite distinctive. Then this is a case of our wines—including a couple of bottles of vintage Brunello. You really need to save them for an important occasion, they're quite special. There's a nice *vinsanto* dessert wine in there, as well. And this is the *aceto balsamico* I promised you, from my cousin in Modena.'

While she was still standing there open-mouthed, he reached into a cool box and pulled out a leg of lamb and a whole Pecorino cheese.

'Something for your mother's larder,' he said with a smile, and without any warning she burst into tears.

'Hey,' he said softly, and wrapping his arms around her, he drew her up against his chest. He could feel the shudders running through her, and he cradled her against his heart and rocked her, shushing her gently. 'Lydia, please, *cara*, don't cry.'

'I'm not,' she lied, bunching her fists in his shirt and burrowing into his chest, and he chuckled and hugged her.

'I don't think that's quite true,' he murmured. 'Come on, it's just a few things.'

'It's nothing to do with the things,' she choked out. Her fist hit him squarely in the chest. 'I didn't think I'd ever see you again, and I was trying to move on, and then you just come back into my life and drop this bombshell on me about the wedding, and of all the times to choose, when I'm already…'

Realisation dawned, and he stroked her hair, gentling her. 'Oh, *cara*, I'm sorry. When did he die, the pony?'

She sniffed hard and tried to pull away, but he wouldn't let her, he just held her tight, and after a moment she went still, unyielding but resigned. 'Last week,' she said, her voice clogged with tears. 'We found him dead in the field.'

'And you haven't cried,' he said.

She gave up fighting and let her head rest against his chest. 'No. But he was old.'

'We lost our dog last year. She was very, very old, and she'd been getting steadily worse. After she died, I didn't cry for weeks, and then one day it suddenly hit me and I disintegrated. Luca said he thought it was to do with Angelina. Sometimes grief is like that. We can't acknowledge it for the things that really hurt, and then something else comes along, and it's safe then to let go, to let out the hurt that you can't face.'

She lifted her head and looked up at him through her tears. 'But I don't hurt.'

'Don't you? Even after Russell treated you the way he did? For God's sake, Lydia, he was supposed to be your lover, and yet when he'd crippled your sister, his only reaction was anger that you'd left him and his business was suffering! What kind of a man is that? Of course you're hurting.'

She stared at him, hearing her feelings put into words somehow making sense of them all at last. She eased away from him, needing a little space, her emotions settling now.

'You know I can't say no, don't you? To your proposition?'

His mouth quirked slightly and he nodded slowly and let her go. 'Yes. I do know, and I realise it's unfair to ask this of you, but—I need help for Carlotta, and you need the wedding. This way, we both win.'

Or lose, depending on whether or not he could keep his heart intact, seeing her every day, working alongside her, knowing she'd be just there in the room beside his office, taunting him even in her sleep.

She met his eyes, her own troubled. 'I don't want an affair. I can't do it. One night was dangerous enough. I'm not ready, and I don't want to hurt your children.'

He nodded. 'I know. And I agree. If I wanted an affair, it would be with a woman my children would never meet, someone they wouldn't lose their hearts to. But I would like to be your friend, Lydia. I don't know if that could work but I would like to try.'

No. It couldn't work. It was impossible, because she was already more than half in love with him, but—Jen needed her wedding, and she'd already had it snatched away from her once. This was another chance, equally as crazy, equally as dangerous, if not more so.

It was a chance she had to take.

'OK, I'll do it,' she said, without giving herself any further time to think, and his shoulders dropped slightly and he smiled.

'*Grazie, cara. Grazie mille.* And I know you aren't doing it for me, but for your sister and also for Carlotta, and for that, I thank you even more.'

He hugged her—just a gentle, affectionate hug between friends, or so he told himself as she slid her arms round him and hugged him back, but the feel of her in his arms, the soft pressure of her breasts, the smell of her shampoo and the warmth of her body against his all told him he was lying.

He was in this right up to his neck, and if he couldn't hold it together for the next two months—but he had to. There was no choice. Neither of them was ready for this.

He let her go, stepped back and dumped the lamb and the cheese in her arms. 'Let's go back in.'

'Talk to me about your dream wedding,' he said to Jen, after they'd taken all the things in from the car.

Her smile tugged his heartstrings. 'I don't dream about my wedding. The last time I did that, it turned into a nightmare for Lydia, so I'm keeping my feet firmly on the ground from now on, and we're going to do something very simple and quiet from here, and it'll be fine.'

'What if I was to offer you the *palazzo* as a venue?' he suggested, and Jen's jaw dropped.

'What?' she said, and then shook her head. 'I'm sorry, I don't understand.'

'The same deal as the hotel.'

She stared, looking from Lydia to Massimo and back again, and shook her head once more. 'I don't...'

'They need me,' Lydia explained. 'Carlotta's not well, and if I cook for the harvest season, you can have your wedding. I don't have another job yet, and it's good experience and an interesting place to work, so I thought it might be a good idea.'

'I've brought a DVD of my brother's wedding so you can see the setting. It might help you to decide.'

He handed it to her, and she handed it straight back.

'There's a catch,' she said, her voice strained. 'Lydia?'

'No catch. I work, you get the wedding.'

'But—that's so generous!'

'Nonsense. We'd have to pay a caterer to do the job, and it would cost easily as much.'

'But—Lydia, what about you? You were looking for another job, and you were talking about setting up an outside catering business. How can you do that if you're out of the country? No, I can't let you do it!'

'Tough, kid,' she said firmly, squashing her tears again. Heavens, she never cried, and this man was turning her into a fountain! 'I'm not doing it just for you, anyway. This is a job—a real job, believe me. And you know what I'm like. I'd love to know more about Italian food—real, proper country food—and this is my chance, so don't go getting all soppy on me, all right? My catering business will keep. Just say thank you and shut up.'

'Thank you and shut up,' she said meekly, and then burst into tears.

Lydia cooked the leg of lamb for supper and served it with rosemary roast potatoes and a redcurrant *jus*, and carrots and runner beans from the garden, and they all sat round at the battered old kitchen table with the dogs at their feet and opened one of the bottles of Brunello.

'It seems wrong, drinking it in here,' she said apologetically, 'but Andy's doing the accounts on the dining table at the moment and it's swamped.'

'It's not about the room, it's about the flavour. Just try it,' he said, watching her closely.

So she swirled it, sniffed it, rolled it round on her tongue and gave a glorious sigh. 'That is *the* most gorgeous wine I have ever tasted,' she told him, and he inclined his head and smiled.

'Thank you. We're very proud of it, and it's a perfect complement to the lamb. It's beautifully cooked. Well done.'

'Thank you. Thank you for trusting me with it.' She smiled back, suddenly ridiculously happy, and then the men started to talk about farming, and Jen quizzed her about the *palazzo*, because she'd hardly said anything about it since she'd come home.

'It sounds amazing,' Jen said, wide-eyed. 'We'll have to look at that video.'

'You will. It's great. The frescoes are incredible, and the view is to die for, especially at night, when all you can see is the twinkling lights in the distance. It's just gorgeous, and really peaceful. I know it'll sound ridiculous, but it reminded me of home, in a way.'

'I don't think that's ridiculous,' Massimo said, cutting in with a smile. 'It's a home, that's all, just in a beautiful setting, and that's what you have here—a warm and loving family home in a peaceful setting. I'm flattered that you felt like that about mine.'

The conversation drifted on, with him telling them more about the farm, about the harvest and the soil and the weather patterns, and she could have sat there for hours just listening to his voice, but she had so much to do before they left in the morning, not least gathering together her clothes, so she left them all talking and went up to her room.

Bearing in mind she'd be flying back after the harvest was over, she tried to be sensible about the amount she took, but she'd need winter clothes as well as lighter garments, and walking boots so she could explore the countryside, and something respectable in case he sprang another dinner on her—

'You look lost.'

She looked up from her suitcase and sighed. 'I don't know what to take.'

'Your passport?'

'Got that,' she said, waggling it at him with a smile. 'It's clothes. I want enough, but not too much. I don't know what the weather will be like.'

'It can get cold. Bring warm things for later, but don't worry. You can buy anything you don't have.'

'I'm trying to stick to a sensible baggage allowance for when I come back.'

'Don't bother. I'll pay the excess. Just bring what you need.'

'What time are we leaving?'

'Seven.'

'Seven?' she squeaked, and he laughed.

'That's a concession. I would have left at five, or maybe six.'

'I'll be ready whenever you tell me. Have you been shown to your room?'

'*Si.* And the bathroom is opposite?'

'Yes. I'm sorry it doesn't have an *en suite* bathroom—'

'Lydia, stop apologising for your home,' he said gently. 'I'm perfectly capable of crossing a corridor. I'll see you at six for breakfast, OK?'

'OK,' she said, and for a heartbeat she wondered if he'd kiss her goodnight.

He didn't, and she spent a good half-hour trying to convince herself she was glad.

They set off in the morning shortly before seven, leaving Jen and Andy still slightly stunned and busy planning their wedding, and she settled back in the soft leather seat and wondered if she'd completely lost her mind.

'Which way are we going?' she asked as they headed down to Kent.

'The quickest route—northern France, across the Alps in Switzerland, past Lake Como and onto the A1 to Siena. We'll stay somewhere on the way. I don't want to drive through the Alps when I'm tired, the mountain roads can be a little tricky.'

Her heart thudded. They were staying somewhere overnight?

Well, of course they were, he couldn't possibly drive whatever distance it was from Suffolk to Tuscany in one day, but somehow she hadn't factored an overnight stop into her calculations, and the journey, which until now had seemed simple and straightforward, suddenly seemed fraught with the danger of derailing their best intentions.

CHAPTER SEVEN

'LYDIA?'

She stirred, opened her eyes and blinked.

He'd pulled up in what looked like a motorway service area, and it was dark beyond the floodlit car park. She yawned hugely and wrapped her hand around the back of her neck, rolling her head to straighten out the kinks.

'Oh, ow. What time is it? I feel as if I've been asleep for hours!'

He gave her a wry, weary smile. 'You have. It's after nine, and I need to stop for the night before I join you and we have an accident.'

'Where are we?'

'A few miles into Switzerland? We're getting into the mountains and this place has rooms. It's a bit like factory farming, but it's clean and the beds are decent. I'd like to stop here if they have any vacancies.'

'And if they don't?'

He shrugged. 'We go on.'

But he must be exhausted. They'd only stopped twice, the last time at two for a late lunch. What if they only have one room? she thought, and her heart started to pound. How strong was her resolve? How strong was his?

She never found out. They had plenty of space, so he booked two rooms and carried her suitcase for her and put it down at the door. 'We should eat fairly soon, but I thought you might want to freshen up. Ten minutes?'

'Ten minutes is fine,' she said, and let herself into her lonely, barren motel room. It was clean and functional as he'd promised, just another generic hotel room like all the rest, and she wished that for once in her life she had the courage to go after the thing she really wanted.

Assuming the thing—the person—really wanted her, of course, and he'd made it clear he didn't.

She stared at herself in the bathroom mirror. What was she *thinking* about? She didn't want him! She wasn't ready for another relationship. Not really, not if she was being sensible. She wanted to get her career back on track, to refocus her life and remember where she was going and what she was doing. She certainly didn't need to get her heart broken by a sad and lonely workaholic ten years her senior, with three motherless children and a massively demanding business empire devouring all his time.

Even if he was the most fascinating and attractive man she'd ever met in her life, and one of the kindest and most thoughtful. He was hurting, too, still grieving for his wife, and in no way ready to commit to another relationship, no matter how deeply she might fall in love with him. He wouldn't hurt her intentionally, but letting herself get close to him—that was a recipe for disaster if nothing else was.

'Lydia?'

There was a knock at the bedroom door, and she turned off the bathroom light and opened it. Massimo was standing there in the corridor, in a fresh shirt and trousers, his hair still damp from the shower. He looked incredible.

'Are you ready for dinner?'

She conjured up a smile. 'Give me ten seconds.'

She picked up her bag, gave her lips a quick swipe of translucent colour as a concession to vanity and dragged a comb through her hair. And then, just out of defiance, she added a spritz of scent.

She might be travel weary, and she might not be about to get involved with him, but she still had her pride.

The dinner was adequate. Nothing more, nothing less.

He was tired, she was tired—and yet still they lingered, talking for an hour over their coffee. She asked about Isabelle and Luca's baby, and how the children were, and he asked her about Jen's progress and if she'd be off the crutches by the time of the wedding, whenever it would be.

They talked about his time at boarding school, and she told him about her own schooling, in a village just four miles from where she lived.

And then finally they both fell silent, and he looked at his watch in disbelief.

'It's late and tomorrow will be a hard drive,' he said. 'We should go to bed.'

The word *bed* reverberated in the air between them, and then she placed her napkin on the table and stood up a little abruptly. 'You're right. I'm sorry, you should have told me to shut up.'

He should. He should have cut it short and gone to bed, instead of sitting up with her and hanging on her every word. He paid the bill and escorted her back to her room, leaving a clear gap between them as he paused at her door.

Not because he wanted to, but because he didn't, and if he got any closer, he didn't trust himself to end it there.

'*Buonanotte, bella,*' he said softly. 'I'll wake you at five thirty.'

She nodded, and without looking back at him, she opened the door of her room, went in and closed it behind her. He stared at it for a second, gave a quiet, resigned laugh and let himself into his own room.

This was what he'd wanted, wasn't it? For her to keep her distance, to enable him to do the same?

So why did he suddenly feel so lonely?

It was like coming home.

This time, when she saw the fortress-like building standing proudly on the hilltop, she felt excitement and not trepidation, and when the children came tumbling down the steps to greet them, there was no look of horror, but shrieks of delight and hugs all round.

Antonino just wanted his father, but Francesca hugged her, and Lavinia hung on her arm and grinned wildly. 'Lydia!' she said, again and again, and then Carlotta appeared at the top of the steps and welcomed her—literally—with open arms.

'*Signorina*! You come back! Oh!'

She found herself engulfed in a warm and emotional hug, and when Carlotta let her go, her eyes were brimming. She blotted them, laughing at herself, and then taking Lydia by the hand, she led her through the courtyard to her old room.

This time there were flowers on the chest of drawers, and Roberto brought in her luggage and put it down and hugged her, too.

'*Grazie mille, signorina,*' he said, his voice choked. 'Thank you for coming back to help us.'

'Oh, Roberto, it's my pleasure. There's so much Carlotta can teach me, and I'm really looking forward to learning.'

'I teach,' she said, patting her hand. 'I teach you everything!'

She doubted it. Carlotta's knowledge of traditional dishes was a rich broth of inheritance, and it would take more than a few experiments to capture it, but it would still be fascinating.

They left her to settle in, and a moment later there was a tap at the French doors.

'The children and I are going for a swim. Want to join us?'

She was so tempted. It was still warm here, much warmer than in England, although she knew the temperature would drop once it was dark. The water in the pool would be warm and inviting, though, and it would be fun playing with the children, but she felt a shiver of danger, and not just from him.

'I don't think so. I'm a bit tired. I might rest for a little while.'

He nodded, smiled briefly and walked away, and she closed the door and shut the curtains, just to make the point.

The children were delightful, but they weren't why she was here, and neither was he. And the more often she reminded herself of that, the better, because she was in serious danger of forgetting.

She didn't have time to think about it.

The harvest season was in full swing, and from first thing the following morning, she was busy. Carlotta still tried to do too much, but she just smiled and told her she was allowed to give orders and that was all, and after the first two days she seemed happy to do that.

She even started taking a siesta in the middle of the day, which gave Lydia time to make a lot of the preparations for the evening without prodding Carlotta's conscience.

And every evening, she dished up the food to the workers and joined them for their meal.

They seemed pleased to see her, and there was a bit of flirting and whistling and nudging, but she could deal with that. And then Massimo appeared at her side, and she heard a ripple of laughter and someone said something she'd heard a few times before when he was about. She'd also heard him say it to Francesca on occasions.

'What does *bella ragazza* mean?' she asked in a quiet moment as they were finishing their food, and he gave a slightly embarrassed laugh.

'Beautiful girl.'

She studied his face closely, unconvinced. 'Are you sure? Because they only say it when you're near me.'

He pulled a face. 'OK. It's usually used for a girlfriend.'

'They think I'm your *girlfriend*?' she squeaked, and he cleared his throat and pushed the food around his plate.

'Ignore them. They're just teasing us.'

Were they? Or could they see the pull between them? Because ignore it as hard as she liked, it wasn't going away, and it was getting stronger with every day that passed.

A few days later, while she was taking a breather out on the terrace before lunch, Isabelle appeared. She was pushing a pram, and she had a little girl in tow.

'Lydia, hi. I was hoping to find you. Mind if we join you?'

She stood up, pleased to see her again, and hugged her. 'Of course I don't mind. Congratulations! May I see?'

'Sure.'

She peered into the pram, and sighed. 'Oh, he's gorgeous. So, so gorgeous! All that dark hair!'

'Oh, yes, he's his daddy's boy. Sometimes I wonder where my genes went in all of this.' She laughed, and Lydia smiled and reached out to touch the sleeping baby's outstretched hand.

It clenched reflexively, closing on her fingertip, and she gave a soft sigh and swallowed hard.

He looked just like the picture of Antonino with his mother in the photo frame in the kitchen. Strong genes, indeed, she thought, and felt a sudden, shocking pang low down in her abdomen, a need so strong it was almost visceral.

She eased her finger away and straightened up. 'Can I get you a drink? And what about your little girl?'

'Annamaria, do you want a drink, darling?'

'Juice!'

'Please.'

'P'ees.'

'Good girl. I'd love a coffee, if you've got time? And anything juice-related with a big slosh of water would be great. We've got a feeder cup.'

They went into the kitchen, and she found some biscuits and took them out into the sun again with the drinks, and sat on the terrace under the pergola, shaded by the jasmine.

'Are you completely better now, after your fall?' Isabelle asked her, and she laughed and brushed it aside.

'I'm fine. My ankle was the worst thing, really, but it's much better now. It still twinges if I'm careless, but it's OK. How about you? Heavens, you've had a baby, that's much worse!'

Isabelle laughed and shook her head. 'No. It was harder than when Annamaria was born, but really very straightforward, and you know Luca's an obstetrician?'

'Yes, I think so. I believe Massimo mentioned it. I know he's a doctor, he met us at the hospital when I had the fall and translated everything for me. So did he deliver him? What's he called, by the way?'

'Maximus—Max for short, after his uncle. Maximus and Massimo both mean the greatest, and my little Max was huge, so he really earned it. And yes, Luca did help deliver him, but at home with a midwife. Not like last time. He nearly missed Annamaria's birth, and I was at home on my own, so this time he kept a very close eye on me!'

'I'll bet. Wow. You're very brave having them at home.'

'No, I just have confidence in the process. I'm a midwife.'

'Is that how you met?'

She laughed. 'No. We met in Florence, in a café. We ended

up together by a fluke, really.' She tipped her head on one side. 'So what's the story with you and Massimo?'

She felt herself colour and pretended to rearrange the biscuits. 'Oh, nothing, really. There is no story. He gave me a lift, I had an accident, he rescued me, and now I'm doing Carlotta's job so she doesn't kill herself.'

Isabelle didn't look convinced, but there was no way Lydia was going into details about her ridiculous crush or their one-night stand! But Luca's wife wasn't so easily put off. She let the subject drop for a moment, but only long enough to lift the now-crying baby from the pram and cradle him in her arms as she fed him.

Spellbound, Lydia watched the baby's tiny rosebud mouth fasten on his mother's nipple, saw the look of utter contentment on Isabelle's face, and felt a well of longing fill her chest.

'He's a good man, you know. A really decent guy. He'd be worth the emotional investment, but only if you're serious. I'd hate to see him hurt.'

'He won't get hurt. We're not getting involved,' she said firmly. 'Yes, there's something there, but neither of us want it.'

Isabelle's eyes were searching, and Lydia felt as if she could see straight through her lies.

Lies? Were they?

Oh, yes. Because she did want it, even though it was crazy, even though she'd get horribly badly hurt. And she'd thought Russell had hurt her? He didn't even come close to what Massimo could do if she let him into her heart.

'He's not interested in an emotional investment,' she said, just in case there was any misunderstanding, but Isabelle just raised a brow slightly and smiled.

'No. He doesn't *think* he is, but actually he's ready to love again. He just hasn't realised it.'

'No, he isn't. We've talked about it—'

'Men don't talk. Not really. It's like pulling teeth. He's telling you what he thinks he ought to feel, not what he feels.'

She glanced up, at the same time as Lydia heard crunching on the gravel.

'Talk of the devil, here they are,' Isabelle said, smiling at her husband and his brother, and not wanting to get involved any deeper in this conversation, Lydia excused herself and went back to the kitchen.

Seconds later Massimo was in there behind her. 'I've come to tell you we've almost finished. The last of the vines are being stripped now and everyone's having the afternoon off.'

'So no lunch?'

He raised an eyebrow. 'I don't think you'll get away with that, but no evening meal, certainly. Not today. And tomorrow we're moving on to the chestnut woods. So tonight I'm taking you out for dinner, to thank you.'

'You don't need to do that. You're paying for my sister's wedding. That's thanks enough.'

He brushed it aside with a flick of his hand, and smiled. 'Humour me. I want to take you out to dinner. There's a place we eat from time to time—fantastic food, Toscana on a fork. The chef is Carlotta's great-nephew. I think you'll find it interesting. Our table's booked for eight.'

'What if I want an early night?'

'Do you?'

She gave in and smiled. 'No, not really. It sounds amazing. What's the dress code?'

'Clean. Nothing more. It's where the locals eat.'

'Your mother's a local,' she said drily, and he chuckled.

'My mother always dresses for the occasion. I'll wear jeans and a jacket, no tie. Does that help?'

She smiled. 'It does. Thank you. Help yourselves to coffee, I need to get on with lunch.'

* * *

Jeans and a jacket, no tie.

So what did that mean for her? Jeans? Best jeans with beaded embroidery on the back pockets and a pretty top?

Black trousers and a slinky top with a cardi over it?

A dress? How about a long skirt?

Clean. That was his first stipulation, so she decided to go with what was comfortable. And by eight, it would be cool, and they'd be coming back at about eleven, so definitely cooler.

Or maybe…

She'd just put the finishing touches to her makeup, not too much, just enough to make her feel she'd made the effort, when there was a tap on her door.

'Lydia? I'm ready to go when you are.'

She opened the door and scanned him. Jeans—good jeans, expensive jeans, with expensive Italian leather loafers and a handmade shirt, the leather jacket flung casually over his shoulder hanging from one finger.

He looked good enough to eat, and way up the scale of clean, so she was glad she'd changed her mind at the last minute and gone for her one decent dress. It wasn't expensive, but it hung like a dream to the asymmetric hem and made her feel amazing, and from the way he was scanning her, he wasn't disappointed.

'Will I do?' she asked, twirling slowly, and he said nothing for a second and then gave a soft huff of laughter.

'Oh, yes. I think so.'

His eyes were still trailing over her, lingering on the soft swell of her breasts, the curve of her hip, the hint of a thigh—

He pulled himself together and jerked his eyes back up to meet hers. 'You look lovely,' he said, trying not to embarrass himself or her. 'Are you ready to go?'

'I just need a wrap for later.' She picked up a pretty pashmina the same colour as her eyes, and her bag, and shut the door behind her. 'Right, then. Let's go get Toscana on a fork!'

It was a simple little building on one side of a square in the nearby town.

From the outside it looked utterly unpretentious, and it was no different inside. Scrubbed tables, plain wooden chairs, simple décor. But the smell was amazing, and the place was packed.

'Massimo, *ciao!*'

He shook hands with a couple on the way in, introduced her as a friend from England, and ushered her past them to the table he'd reserved by the window.

'Is it always this busy?'

His lips twitched in a smile. 'No. Sometimes it's full.'

She looked around and laughed. 'And these are all locals?'

'Mostly. Some will be tourists, people who've bothered to ask where they should eat.'

She looked around again. 'Is there a menu?'

'No. He writes it on a board—it's up there. Tonight it's a casserole of wild boar with plums in a red wine reduction.'

'And that's it?'

'No. He cooks a few things every night—you can choose from the board, but the first thing up is always his dish of the day, and it's always worth having.'

She nodded. 'Sounds great.'

He ordered a half-carafe of house wine to go with it— again, the wine was always chosen to go with the meal and so was the one to go for, he explained—and then they settled back to wait.

'So—are you pleased with the harvest?' she asked to fill the silence, and he nodded.

'*Si.* The grapes have been exceptional this year, it should be an excellent vintage. We need that. Last year was not so good, but the olives were better, so we made up for it.'

'And how are the olives this year?'

'Good so far. It depends on the weather. We need a long, mild autumn to let them swell and ripen before the first frosts. We need to harvest early enough to get the sharp tang from the olives, but not so early that it's bitter, or so late that it's sweet and just like any other olive oil.'

She smiled. 'That's farming for you. Juggling the weather all the time.'

'*Si*. It can be a disaster or a triumph, and you never know. We're big enough to weather it, so we're fortunate.'

'We're not. We had a dreadful year about three years ago, and I thought we'd go under, but then the next year we had bumper crops. It's living on a knife edge that's so hard.'

'Always. Always the knife edge.'

Her eyes met his, and the smile that was hovering there was driven out by an intensity that stole her breath away. 'You look beautiful tonight, *cara*,' he said softly, reaching out to touch her hand where it lay on the table top beside her glass.

She withdrew it, met his eyes again warily. 'I thought we weren't going to do this?'

'We're not doing anything. It was a simple compliment. I would say the same to my sister.'

'No, you wouldn't. Not like that.' She picked up her glass of water and drained the last inch, her mouth suddenly dry. 'At least, I hope not.'

His mouth flicked up briefly at the corners. 'Perhaps not quite like that.'

He leant back as the waiter appeared, setting down bread and olive oil and balsamic vinegar, and she tore off a piece of bread and dunked it, then frowned thoughtfully as the taste exploded on her tongue. 'Is this yours?'

He smiled. 'Yes. And the *balsamico* is from my cousin.'

'And the wild boar?'

'I have no idea. If it's from our estate, I don't know about it. The hunting season doesn't start until November.'

She smiled, and the tension eased a little, but it was still there, simmering under the surface, the compliment hovering at the fringes of her consciousness the whole evening. It didn't spoil the meal. Rather, it heightened the sensations of taste and smell and texture, as if somehow his words had brought her alive again and set her free.

'This casserole is amazing,' she said after the first mouthful. 'I want the recipe.'

He laughed at that. 'He won't give it to you. Women offer to sleep with him, but he never reveals his secrets.'

'Does he sleep with them anyway?'

He chuckled again. 'I doubt it. His wife would skin him alive.'

'Good for her. She needs to keep him. He's a treasure. And I've never been that desperate for a recipe.'

'I'm glad to hear it.' He was. He didn't even want to think about her sleeping with anybody else, even if she wasn't sleeping with him. And she wasn't.

She really, really wasn't. He wasn't going to do that again, it was emotional suicide. It had taken him over a week before he could sleep without waking aroused and frustrated in a tangle of sheets, aching for her.

He returned his attention to the casserole, mopping up the last of the sauce with a piece of bread until finally the plate was clean and he had no choice but to sit back and look up and meet her eyes.

'That was amazing,' she said. 'Thank you so much.'

'Dessert?'

She laughed a little weakly. 'I couldn't fit it in. Coffee, though—I could manage coffee.'

He ordered coffee, and they lingered over it, almost as if

they daren't leave the safety of the little *trattoria* for fear of what they might do. But then they ran out of words, out of stalling tactics, and their eyes met and held.

'Shall we go?'

She nodded, getting to her feet even though she knew what was going to happen, knew how dangerous it was to her to leave with him and go back to her room—because they would end up there, she was sure of it, just as they had before, and all their good intentions would fall at the first hurdle…

CHAPTER EIGHT

THEY didn't speak on the way back to the *palazzo*.

She sat beside him, her heart in her mouth, the air between them so thick with tension she could scarcely breathe. They didn't touch. All the way to her bedroom door, there was a space between them, as if they realised that the slightest contact would be all it took to send them up in flames.

Even when he shut the door behind them, they still hesitated, their eyes locked. And then he closed his eyes and murmured something in Italian. It could have been a prayer, or a curse, or just a 'what the hell am I doing?'

She could understand that. She was doing it herself, but she was beyond altering the course of events. She'd been beyond it, she realised, the moment he'd walked into the tack room at home and smiled at her.

He opened his eyes again, and there was resignation in them, and a longing that made her want to weep. He lifted his hand and touched her cheek, just lightly, but it was enough.

She turned her face into his hand, pressing her lips to his palm, and with a ragged groan he reeled her in, his mouth finding hers in a kiss that should have felt savage but was oddly tender for all its desperation.

His jacket hit the floor, then his shirt, stripped off over his head, and he spun her round, searching for the zip on her dress and following its progress with his lips, scorching a trail of fire down her spine. It fell away, and he unclipped her bra and turned her back to face him, easing it away and sighing softly as he lowered his head to her breasts.

She felt the rasp of his stubble against the sensitised skin, the heat of his mouth closing over one nipple, then the cold as he blew lightly against the dampened flesh.

She clung to his shoulders, her legs buckling, and he scooped her up and dropped her in the middle of the bed, stripping off the rest of his clothes before coming down beside her, skin to skin, heart to heart.

There was no foreplay. She would have died if he'd made her wait another second for him. Incoherent with need, she reached for him, and he was there, his eyes locking with hers as he claimed her with one long, slow thrust.

His head fell against hers, his eyes fluttering closed, a deep groan echoing in her ear. Her hands were on him, sliding down his back, feeling the powerful muscles bunching with restraint, the taut buttocks, the solid thighs bracing him as he thrust into her, his restraint gone now, the desperation overwhelming them, driving them both over the edge into frenzy.

She heard a muffled groan, felt his lips against her throat, his skin like hot, wet silk under her hands as his hard body shuddered against hers. For a long time he didn't move, but then, his chest heaving, he lifted his head to stare down into her eyes.

'Oh, *cara*,' he murmured roughly, and then gathering her against his heart he rolled to his side and collapsed against the pillows, and they lay there, limbs entangled, her head on his chest, and waited for the shockwaves to die away.

'I thought we weren't going to do that.'

He glanced down at her, and his eyes were filled with regret and despair. 'It looks like we were both wrong.'

His eyes closed, as if he couldn't bear to look at her, and easing away from her embrace he rolled away and sat up on the edge of the bed, elbows braced on his knees, dropping his head into his hands for a moment. Then he raked his fingers through his hair and stood up, pulling on his clothes.

'I have to check the children,' he said gruffly.

'We need to talk.'

'Yes, but not now. Please, *cara*. Not now.'

He couldn't talk to her now. He had to get out of there, before he did something stupid like make love to her again.

Make love? Who was he kidding? He'd slaked himself on her, with no finesse, no delicacy, no patience. And he'd promised her—promised himself, but promised *her*—that this wouldn't happen again.

Shaking his head in disgust, he pushed his feet into his shoes, slung his jacket over his shoulder and then steeled himself to look at her.

She was still lying there, curled on her side on top of the tangled bedding, her eyes wide with hurt and confusion.

'Massimo?'

'Later. Tomorrow, perhaps. I have to go. If Antonino wakes—'

She nodded, her eyes closing softly as she bit her lip. Holding back the tears?

He was despicable. All he ever did was make this woman cry.

He let himself out without another word, and went through to his part of the house, up the stairs to the children to check that they were all in bed and sleeping peacefully.

They were. Antonino had kicked off the covers, and he eased them back over his son and dropped a kiss lightly on his forehead. He mumbled in his sleep and rolled over, and he went out, leaving the door open, and checked the girls.

They were both asleep, Francesca's door closed, Lavinia's open and her nightlight on.

He closed the landing door that led to his parents' quarters, as he always did when he was in the house, and then he made his way back down to the kitchen and poured himself a glass of wine.

Why? Why on earth had he been so stupid? After all his lectures to himself, how could he have been so foolish, so weak, so self-centred?

He'd have to talk to her, he realised, but he had no idea what he would say. He'd promised her—promised! And yet again he'd failed.

He propped his elbows on the table and rested his face in his hands. Of all the idiotic things—

'Massimo?'

Her voice stroked him like a lover's touch, and he lifted his head and met her eyes.

'What are you doing here?' he asked, his voice rough.

'I came to get a drink,' she said uncertainly.

He shrugged. 'Go ahead, get it.'

She stayed there, her eyes searching his face. 'Oh, Massimo, don't beat yourself up. We were deluded if we thought this wouldn't happen. It was so obvious it was going to and I can't believe we didn't realise. What we need to work out is what happens now.'

He gave a short, despairing laugh and pushed back his chair. 'Nothing, but I have no idea how to achieve that. All I know that whenever I'm with you, I want you, and I can't just have what I want. I'm not a tiny child, I understand the word no, I just can't seem to use it to myself. Wine?'

She shook her head. 'Tea. I'll make it.'

He watched her as she took out a mug from the cupboard, put a teabag in it, poured on boiling water, her movements automatic. She was wearing a silky, figure-hugging dressing gown belted round her waist, and he'd bet his life she had those tiny little pyjamas on underneath.

'Just tell me this,' she said at last, turning to face him. 'Is there any reason why we can't have an affair? Just—discreetly?'

'Here? In this house? Are you crazy? I have children here and they have enough to contend with without waking in the night from a bad dream and finding I'm not here because I'm doing something stupid and irresponsible for my own gratification.'

She sat down opposite him, cradling the tea in her hands and ignoring his stream of self-hatred. 'So what do you normally do?'

Normally? *Normally?* he thought.

'Normally, I don't have affairs,' he said flatly. 'I suppose, if I did, it would be elsewhere.' He shrugged. 'Arranged meetings—afternoon liaisons when the children are at school, lunchtimes, coffee.'

'And does it work?'

He laughed a little desperately. 'I have no idea. I've never tried.'

She stared at him in astonishment. 'What? In five years, you've never had an affair?'

'Not what you could call an affair, no. I've had the odd liaison, but nothing you could in any way call a relationship.' He sighed shortly, swirled his wine, put it down again.

'You have to see it from my point of view. I have obligations, responsibilities. I would have to be very, very circumspect in any relationship with a woman.'

'Because of the children.'

'Mostly, but because of all sorts of things. Because of my duties and responsibilities, the position I hold within the family, the business—any woman I was to become involved with would have to meet a very stringent set of criteria.'

'Not money-grabbing, not lying, not cheating, not looking for a meal ticket or an easy family or status in the community.'

'Exactly. And it's more trouble than it's worth. I don't need it. I can live without the hassle. But it's more than that. If I make a mistake, many people could suffer. And besides, I don't have the time to invest in a relationship, not to do it justice. And nor do you, not if you're going to reinvent yourself and relaunch your career.'

He'd be worth the emotional investment, but only if you're serious.

Oh, Isabelle, you're so right, she thought. But was she serious? Serious enough? Could she afford to dedicate the emotional energy needed, to a man who was so clearly focused on his family life and business that women weren't considered necessary?

If she felt she stood the slightest chance, then yes, she realised, she could be very, very serious indeed about this man. But he wasn't ever going to be serious about her. Not serious enough to let her into all parts of his life, and there was no way she'd pass his stringent criteria test.

No job, for a start. No independent wealth—no wealth of any sort. And besides, he was right, she needed to get her career back on track. It had been going so well...

'So what happens now? We can't have an affair here, because of the children, and yet we can't seem to stick to that. So what do we do? Because doing nothing doesn't seem to work for us, Massimo. We need a plan.'

He gave a wry laugh and met her eyes again, his deadly serious. 'I have no idea, *cara.* I just know I can't be around you.'

'So we avoid each other?'

'We're both busy. It shouldn't be so hard.'

They were busy, he was right, but she felt a pang of loss even though she knew it made sense.

'OK. I'll keep out of your way if you keep out of mine.'

He inclined his head, then looked up as she got to her feet.

'You haven't finished your tea.'

'I'll take it with me,' she said, and left him sitting there wondering why he felt as if he'd just lost the most precious thing in the world, and yet didn't quite know what it was.

Nice theory, she thought later, when her emotions had returned to a more even keel. It just didn't have a hope of working in practice.

How could they possibly avoid each other in such an intimate setting?

Answer—they couldn't. He was in and out of the kitchen all the time with the children, and she was in and out of his workspace twice a day at least with food for the team of workers.

They were gathering chestnuts this week, in the *castagneti*, the chestnut woods on the higher slopes at the southern end of the estate. Carlotta told her all about it, showed her the book of chestnut recipes she'd gathered, many handed down from her mother or her grandmother, and she wanted to experiment.

So she asked Massimo one lunchtime if she could have some for cooking.

'Sure,' he said briskly. 'Help yourself. Someone will give you a basket.'

She shouldn't have been hurt. It was silly. She knew why he was doing it, why he hadn't met her eyes for more than a fleeting second, because in that fleeting second she'd seen something in his eyes that she recognised.

A curious mixture of pain and longing, held firmly in check.

She knew all about that.

She gathered her own chestnuts, joining the workforce and taking good-natured and teasing advice, most of which she didn't understand, because her Italian lessons with Francesca hadn't got that far yet—and in any case, she was very conscious of not getting too close to his children, for fear of them forming an attachment to her that would only hurt them when she went home again, so she hadn't encouraged it.

But she understood the gist. Sign language was pretty universal, and she learned how to split open the cases without hurting her fingers and remove the chestnuts—huge chestnuts, *marrone*, apparently—and that night after she'd given them all their evening meal, she went into the kitchen to experiment.

And he was there, sitting at the kitchen table with a laptop and a glass of wine.

'Oh,' she said, and stood there stupidly for a moment.

'Problem?'

'I was going to try cooking some of the chestnuts.'

His eyes met hers, and he shut the laptop and stood up. 'It's fine. I'll get out of your way.'

She looked guarded, he thought, her sunny smile and open friendliness wiped away by his lack of control and this overwhelming need that stalked him hour by hour. It saddened him. Greatly.

'You don't have to go.'

'I do,' he said wearily. 'I can't be around you, *cara*. It's too difficult. I thought I could do this, but I can't. The only way is to keep my distance.'

'But you can't. We're falling over each other all the time.'

'There's no choice.'

There was, she thought. They could just go with the flow, make sure they were discreet, keep it under control, but he didn't seem to think they could do that successfully, and he'd left the kitchen anyway.

She sat down at the table, in the same chair, feeling the warmth from his body lingering in the wood, and opened Carlotta's recipe book. Pointless. It was in Italian, and she didn't understand a word.

Frustration getting the better of her, she dropped her head into her hands and growled softly.

'Lydia, don't.'

'Don't what? I thought you'd gone,' she said, lifting her head.

'I had.' He sat down opposite her and took her hand in his, the contact curiously disturbing and yet soothing all at once.

'This is driving me crazy,' he admitted softly.

'Me, too. There must be another way. We can't avoid each other successfully, so why don't we just work alongside each other and take what comes? We know it's not long-term, we know you're not looking for commitment and I'm not ready to risk it again, and I have to go back and try and relaunch my career in some direction.'

He let go of her hand and sat back. 'Any ideas for that?' he said, not running away again as she'd expected, but staying to have a sensible conversation, and she let herself relax and began to talk, outlining her plans, such as they were.

'I've been thinking more and more about outside catering, using produce from my parents' farm. There are plenty of people with money living in the nearby villages, lots of second homes with people coming up for the weekend and bringing friends. I'm sure there would be openings, I just have to be there to find them.'

'It could be a bit seasonal.'

'Probably. Easter, summer and winter—well, Christmas and New Year, mostly. There's always lots of demand around

Christmas, and I need to be back by then. Will the olive harvest be over?'

'Almost certainly. If it's not, we can manage if you need to return.' He stood up and put the kettle on. 'I was thinking we should invite your sister and her fiancé over to meet Anita so she can start the ball rolling.'

'Anita?'

'*Si*. They'll need a wedding planner.'

'They can't afford a wedding planner!'

'It's part of the package. I'm not planning it, I simply don't have the time or the expertise, and Jen can't plan a wedding in a strange place from a distance of two thousand kilometres, so we need Anita.'

'I could do it. I'm here.'

'But do you have the necessary local contacts? No. And besides, you're already busy.'

'Can I do the catering?'

He smiled tolerantly. 'Really? Wouldn't you rather enjoy your sister's wedding?'

'No. I'd rather cut down the cost of it to you. I feel guilty enough—'

'Don't feel guilty.'

'But I do. I know quite well what cooks get paid, and it doesn't stack up to the cost of a wedding in just three months!'

He smiled again. 'We pay our staff well.'

She snorted rudely, and found a mug of tea put down in front of her.

'Don't argue with me, *cara*,' he said quietly. 'Just ask your sister when she could come over, and arrange the flights and check that Anita is free to see them.'

'Only if you'll let me do the catering.'

He rolled his eyes and laughed softly. 'OK, you can do the catering, but Anita will give you menu options.'

'No. I want to do the menus.'

'Why are you so stubborn?'

'Because it's my job!'

'To be stubborn?'

'To plan menus. And don't be obtuse.'

His mouth twitched and he sat down opposite her again, swirling his wine in the glass. 'I thought you were going to cook chestnuts?'

'I can't read the recipe book. My Italian is extremely limited so it's a non-starter.'

He took it from her, opened it and frowned. 'Ah. Well, some of it is in a local dialect anyway.'

'Can you translate?'

'Of course. But you'd need to know more than just classic Italian to understand it. Which recipe did you want to try?'

She raised an eyebrow. 'Well, how do I know? I don't know what they are.'

'I'll read them to you.'

'You know what? I'll do it in the morning, with Carlotta. She'll be able to tell me which are her favourites.'

'I can tell you that. She feeds them to us regularly. She does an amazing mousse for dessert, and stuffing for roast boar which is incredible. You should get her to teach you those if nothing else. Anyway, tomorrow won't work. There's a fair in the town.'

'Carlotta said there was a day off, but nobody told me why.'

'To celebrate the end of *La Vendemmia*. They hold one every year. Then in a few weeks there's the chestnut fair, and then after *La Raccolta*, the olive harvest, there's another one. It's a sort of harvest festival gone mad. You ought to go tomorrow, it's a good day out.'

'Will you be there?'

He nodded. 'All of us will be there.'

'I thought we were avoiding each other?'

He didn't smile, as she'd expected. Instead he frowned,

his eyes troubled. 'We are. I'll be with my children. Roberto and Carlotta will be going. I'm sure they'll give you a lift.'

And then, as if she'd reminded him of their unsatisfactory arrangement, he stood up. 'I'm going to do some work. I'll see you tomorrow.'

She did see him, but only because she kept falling over him.

Why was it, she thought, that if you lost someone in a crowd of that size you'd never be able to find them again, and yet every time she turned round, he was there?

Sometimes he didn't see her. Equally, probably, there were times when she didn't see him. But there were times when their eyes met, and held. And then he'd turn away.

Well, this time she turned away first, and made her way through the crowd in the opposite direction.

And bumped into Anita.

'Lydia! I was hoping I'd see you. Come, let's find a quiet corner for a coffee and a chat. We have a wedding to plan!'

She looked around at the jostling crowd and laughed. 'A quiet corner?'

'There must be one. Come, I know a café bar on a side street. We'll go there.'

They had to sit outside, but the sunshine was lovely and it was relatively quiet away from the hubbub and festival atmosphere of the colourful event.

'So—this wedding. Massimo tells me your sister's coming over soon to talk about it. Do you know what she wants?'

Lydia shrugged, still uncomfortable about him spending money on Anita's services. 'The hotel was offering a fairly basic package,' she began, and Anita gave a soft laugh.

'I know the hotel. It would have been basic, and they would have talked it up to add in all sorts of things you don't really need.'

'Well, they wouldn't, because she hasn't got any money, which is why I'm working here now.'

Anita raised an eyebrow slightly. 'Is that the only reason?' she asked softly. 'Because I know these Valtieri men. They're notoriously addictive.'

Poor Anita. Lydia could see the ache in her eyes, knew that she could understand. Maybe, for that reason, she let down her guard.

'No. It's not the only reason,' she admitted quietly. 'Maybe, subconsciously, it gave me an excuse to spend time with him, but trust me, it's not going to come to anything.'

'Don't be too sure. He's lonely, and he's a good man. He can be a bit of a recluse—he shuts himself away and works rather than deal with his emotions, but he's not alone in that. It's a family habit, I'm afraid.'

She shook her head. 'I *am* sure nothing will come of it. We've talked about it,' she said, echoing her conversation with Isabelle and wondering if both women could be wrong or if it was just that they were fond of him and wanted him to be happy.

'He needs someone like you,' Anita said, 'someone honest and straightforward who isn't afraid of hard work and under-stands the pressures and demands of an agricultural lifestyle. He said your family are lovely, and he felt at home there with them. He said they were refreshingly unpretentious.'

She laughed at that. 'We've got nothing to be pretentious about,' she pointed out, but Anita just smiled.

'You have to understand where he's coming from. He has women after him all the time. He's a very, very good catch, and Gio is worried that some money-seeking little tart will get her claws into him.'

'Not a chance. He's much too wary for that, believe me. He has strict criteria. Anyway, I thought we were talking about the wedding?'

Anita smiled wryly and let it go, but Lydia had a feeling that the subject was by no means closed…

'What are you doing?'

A pair of feet appeared in her line of sight, slender feet clad in beautiful, soft leather pumps. She straightened up on her knees and looked up at his mother, standing above her on the beautiful frescoed staircase.

'I'm helping Carlotta.'

'It's not your job to clean. She has a maid for that.'

'But the maid's sick, so I thought I'd help her.'

Elisa frowned. 'I didn't know that. Why didn't Carlotta tell me?'

'Because she doesn't?' she suggested gently. 'She just gets on with it.'

'And so do you,' his mother said softly, coming down to her level. 'Dear girl, you shouldn't be doing this. It's not part of your job.'

'I don't have a job, Signora Valtieri. I have a bargain with your son. I help out, my sister gets her wedding, which is incredibly generous, so if there's some way I can help, I just do it.'

'You do, don't you, without any fuss? You are a quite remarkable girl. It's a shame you have to leave.'

'I don't think he thinks so.'

'My son doesn't know what's good for him.'

'And you do?'

'Yes, I do, and I believe you could be.'

She stared at Elisa, stunned. 'But—I'm just a chef. A nobody.'

'No, you are not a nobody, Lydia, and we're just farmers like your people.'

'No.' She laughed at that and swept an arm around her to underline her point. 'No, you're not just farmers, *signora*. My family are just farmers. You own half of Tuscany and a *palazzo*, with incredibly valuable frescoes on the walls painted by Old Masters. There is a monumental difference.'

'I think not—and please stop calling me *signora*. My name, as you well know, is Elisa. Come. Let's go and get some coffee and have a chat.'

She shook her head. 'I can't. I have work to do—lunch to prepare for everyone in a minute. I was just giving the stairs a quick sweep.'

'So stop now, and come, just for a minute. Please? I want to ask you something.'

It was a request, but from his mother it was something on the lines of an invitation to Buckingham Palace. You didn't argue. You just went.

So she went, leaving the ornate and exquisitely painted staircase hall and following her into the smaller kitchen which served their wing of the house.

'How do you take your coffee? Would you like a cappuccino?'

'That would be lovely. Thank you.'

Bone china cups, she thought, and a plate with little Amaretti biscuits. Whatever this was about, it was not going to be a quick anything, she realised.

'So,' Elisa said, setting the tray down at a low table between two beautiful sofas in the formal *salon* overlooking the terrace. 'I have a favour to ask you. My son tells me you're contemplating starting a catering business. I would like to commission you.'

Lydia felt her jaw drop. 'Commission?' she echoed faintly. 'For what?'

'I'm having a meeting of my book group. We get together every month over dinner and discuss a book we've read, and this time it's my turn. I would like you to provide the meal for us. There will be twenty people, and we will need five courses.'

She felt her jaw sag again. 'When?'

'Wednesday next week. The chestnuts should be largely harvested by then, and the olive harvest won't have started yet. So—will you do it?'

'Is there a budget?'

Elisa shrugged. 'Whatever it takes to do the job.'

Was it a test? To see if she was good enough? Or a way to make her feel valued and important enough to be a contender for her son? Or was it simply that she needed a meal provided and Carlotta was too unwell?

It didn't matter. Whatever the reason, she couldn't refuse. She looked into Elisa's eyes.

'Yes. Yes, I'll do it,' she said. 'Just so long as you'll give me a reference.'

Elisa put her cup down with a satisfied smile. 'Of course.'

CHAPTER NINE

THE book club dinner seemed to be going well.

She was using her usual kitchen—the room which histori-cally had always been the main kitchen in the house, although it was now used by Massimo and his children, and for pre-paring the harvest meals.

She needed the space. Twenty people were quite hard to cater for if the menu was extravagant, and she'd drafted in help in the form of Maria, the girl who'd been helping her with the meals all along.

The *antipasti* to start had been a selection of tiny canapés, all bite-sized but labour intensive. Massimo had dropped in and tasted them, and she'd had to send him away before he'd eaten them all.

Then she'd served penne pasta with crayfish in a sauce of cream with a touch of fresh chilli, followed by a delicate lemon sorbet to cleanse the palette.

For the main, she'd sourced some wild boar with Carlotta's help, and she'd casseroled it with fruit and lots of wine and garlic, reducing it to a rich, dark consistency. Massimo, yet again, had insisted on tasting it, dipping his finger in the sauce and sucking it, and said it was at least as good as Carlotta's great-nephew's. Carlotta agreed, and asked her for the recipe, which amazed her.

She'd served it on a chestnut, apple and sweet potato mash,

with fresh green beans and fanned Chantenay carrots. And now it was time for the dessert, individual portions of perfectly set and delicate pannacotta under a spun sugar cage, with fresh autumn raspberries dusted with vanilla sugar and drizzled with dark chocolate. If that didn't impress them, nothing would, she thought with satisfaction.

She carried them through with Maria's help, set them down in front of all the guests and then left them to it. She put the coffee on to brew in Elisa's smaller kitchen, with homemade *petit fours* sitting ready on the side, and then headed back to her kitchen to start the massive clean-up operation.

But Massimo was in there, up to his wrists in suds, scrubbing pans. The dishwasher was sloshing quietly in the background, and there was no sign of Maria.

'I sent her home,' he said in answer to her question. 'It's getting late, and she's got a child.'

'I was going to pay her.'

'I've done it. Roberto's taken her home. Why don't you make us both a coffee while I finish this?'

She wasn't going to argue. Her head was aching, her feet were coming out in sympathy and she hadn't sat down for six hours. More, probably.

'Are they happy?'

She shrugged. 'They didn't say not and they seemed to eat it all, mostly.'

'Well, that's a miracle. There are some fussy women amongst them. I don't know why my mother bothers with them.'

He dried his hands and sat down opposite her, picking up his coffee. 'Well done,' he said, and the approval in his voice warmed her.

'I'll reserve judgement until I get your mother's verdict,' she said, because after all he hadn't been her client.

'Don't bother. It was the best food this house has seen in decades. You did an amazing job.'

'I loved it,' she confessed with a smile. 'It was great to do something a bit more challenging, playing with flavours and presentation and just having a bit of fun. I love it. I've always loved it.'

He nodded slowly. 'Yes, I can see that. And you're very good at it. I don't suppose there's any left?'

She laughed and went to the fridge. 'There's some of the boar casserole, and a spare pannacotta. Haven't you eaten?'

He pulled a face. 'Kid's food,' he admitted. 'My father and I took them out for pizza. There didn't seem to be a lot of room in here.'

She plated him up some of the casserole with the vegetables, put it in the microwave and reheated it, then set it down in front of him and watched him eat. It was the best part of her job, to watch people enjoying the things she'd created, and he was savouring every mouthful.

She felt a wave of sadness and regret that there was no future for them, that she wouldn't spend the rest of her life creating wonderful, warming food and watching him eat it with relish.

She'd had the girls in with her earlier in the day, and she'd let them help her make the *petit fours* from homemade marzipan. That, too, had given her pangs of regret and a curious sense of loss. Silly, really. She'd never had them, so how could she feel that she'd lost them?

And after he'd eaten so much marzipan she was afraid he'd be sick, Antonino had stood up at the sink on an upturned box and washed up the plastic mixing bowls, soaking himself and the entire area in the process and having a great time with the bubbles. Such a sweet child, and the spitting image of his father. He was going to be a good-looking man one day, but she wouldn't be there to see it.

Or watch his father grow old.

She took away his plate, and replaced it with the pannacotta. He pressed the sugar cage with his fingertip, and frowned as it shattered gently onto the plate. 'How did you make it?' he asked, fascinated. 'I've never understood.'

'Boil sugar and water until it's caramelised, then trail it over an oiled mould. It's easy.'

He laughed. 'For you. I can't even boil an egg. Without Carlotta my kids would starve.'

'No. They'd eat pizza,' she said drily, and he gave a wry grin.

'Probably.' He dug the spoon into the pannacotta and scooped up a raspberry with it, then sighed as it melted on his tongue. 'Amazing,' he mumbled, and scraped the plate clean.

Then he put the spoon down and pushed the plate away, leaning back and staring at her. 'You really are an exceptional chef. If there's any justice, you'll do well in your catering business. That was superb.'

'Thank you.' She felt his praise warm her, and somehow that was more important than anyone else's approval. She washed his plate and their coffee cups, then turned back to him, her mind moving on to the real reason she was here.

'Massimo, I need to talk to you about Jen and the wedding. They'll be here in two days, and I need to pick them up from the airport somehow.'

'I'll do it,' he offered instantly. 'My mother's preparing the guest wing for them, but she wanted to know if they needed one room or two.'

'Oh, one. Definitely. She needs help in the night sometimes. Is there a shower?'

'A wet room. That was one of the reasons for the choice. And it's got French doors out to the terrace around the other side. Come. I'll show you. You can tell me which room would be the best for them.'

She went, and was blown away by their guest suite. Two bedrooms, both large, twin beds in one and a huge double in the other, with a wet room between and French doors out onto the terrace. And there was a small sitting room, as well, a private retreat, with a basic kitchen for making drinks and snacks.

'This will be just perfect. Give them the double room. She wakes in the night quite often, having flashbacks. They're worse if Andy's not beside her.'

'Poor girl.'

She nodded, still racked with guilt. She always would be, she imagined. It would never go away, just like his guilt over Angelina slumped over the kitchen table, unable to summon help.

She felt his finger under her chin, tilting her face up to his so he could look into her eyes.

'It was not your fault,' he said as if he could read her mind.

Her eyes were steady, but sad. 'Any more than Angelina's death was your fault. Bad things happen. Guilt is just a natural human reaction. Knowing it and believing it are two different things.'

He felt his mouth tilt into a smile, but what kind of a smile it was he couldn't imagine. It faded, as he stared into her eyes, seeing the ache in them, the longing, the emptiness.

He needed her. Wanted her like he had never wanted anyone, but there was too much at stake to risk upsetting the status quo, for any of them.

He dropped his hand. 'What time do they arrive?' he asked, and the tension holding them eased.

For now.

They collected Jen and Andy from Pisa airport at midday on Friday, and they were blown away by their first view of the *palazzo.* By the time they'd pulled up at the bottom of the steps, Jen's eyes were like saucers, but all Lydia could think about was how her sister would get up the steps.

She hadn't even thought about it, stupidly, and now—

'Come here, gorgeous,' Andy said, unfazed by the sight of them, and scooping Jen up, he grinned and carried her up the steps to where Roberto was waiting with the doors open.

Massimo and Lydia followed, carrying their luggage and the crutches, and as they reached the top their eyes met and held.

The memory was in her eyes, and it transfixed him. The last woman to be carried up those steps had been her in that awful wedding dress—the dress that was still hanging on the back of his office door, waiting for her to ask for it and burn it.

He should let her. Should burn it himself, instead of staring at it for hour after hour and thinking of her.

He dragged his eyes away and forced himself to concentrate on showing them to their rooms.

'I'll leave you with Lydia. If you need anything, I'll be in the office.'

And he walked away, crossing the courtyard with a firm, deliberate stride. She dragged her eyes off him and closed the door, her heart still pounding from that look they'd exchanged at the top of the steps.

Such a short time since he'd carried her up them, and yet so much had happened. Nothing obvious, nothing apparently momentous, and yet nothing would ever be quite the same as it had been before.

Starting with her sister's wedding.

'Wow—this is incredible!' Jen breathed, leaning back on Andy and staring out of the French doors at the glorious view. 'So beautiful! And the house—my God, Lydia, it's fantastic! Andy, did you see those paintings on the wall?'

Lydia gave a soft laugh. 'Those are the rough ones. There are some utterly stunning frescoes in the main part of the house, up the stairwell, for instance, and in the dining room. Absolutely beautiful. The whole place is just steeped in history.'

'And we're going to get married from here. I can't believe it.'

'Believe it.' She glanced at her watch. 'Are you hungry? There's some soup and cheese for lunch, and we'll eat properly tonight. Anita's coming over before dinner to talk to you and show you where the marquee will go and how it all works—they've had Carla's wedding and Luca's here, so they've done it all before.'

'Not Massimo's?'

She had no idea. It hadn't been mentioned. 'I don't know. Maybe not. So—lunch. Do you want a lie down for a while, or shall I bring you something over?'

'Oh, I don't want to make work for you,' Jen said, but Lydia could see she was flagging, and she shook her head.

'I don't mind. I'll bring you both something and you can take it easy for a few hours. Travelling's always exhausting.'

Anita arrived at five, and by six Gio had put in an appearance, rather as she'd expected.

He found Lydia in the kitchen, and helped himself to a glass of Prosecco from the fridge and a handful of canapés.

'Hey,' she said, slapping his wrist lightly when he went back for more. 'I didn't know you were involved in the wedding planning.'

'I'm not,' he said with a cocky grin. 'I'm just here for the food.'

And Anita, she thought, but she didn't say that. She knew he'd turn from the smiling playboy to the razor-tongued lawyer the instant she mentioned the woman's name. Instead she did a little digging on another subject.

'So, how many weddings have there been here recently?' she asked.

'Two—Carla and Luca.'

'Not Massimo?'

'No. He got married in the *duomo* and they went back to her parents' house. Why?'

She shrugged. 'I just didn't want to say anything that hit a nerve.'

'I think you hit a nerve,' he said, 'even without speaking. You unsettle him.'

Was it so obvious? Maybe only to someone who was looking for trouble.

'Relax, Gio,' she said drily. 'You don't need to panic and get out your pre-nup template. This is going nowhere.'

'Shame,' he said, pulling a face, 'you might actually be good for him,' and while she was distracted he grabbed another handful of canapés.

She took the plate away and put it on the side. 'Shame?' she asked, and he shrugged.

'He's lonely. Luca likes you, so does Isabelle. And so does our mother, which can't be bad. She's a hard one to please.'

'Not as hard as her son,' she retorted. 'And talking of Massimo, why don't you go and find him and leave me in peace to cook? You're distracting me.'

'Wouldn't want to do that. You might ruin the food, and I've come all the way from Florence for it.'

And he sauntered off, stealing another mouthful from the plate in passing.

The dinner went well, and Anita came back the following day to go through the plans in detail, after talking to Jen and Andy the night before.

'She's amazing,' Jen said later. 'She just seems to know what I want, and she's got the answers to all of my questions.'

'Good,' she said, glad they'd got on well, because hearing the questions she'd realised there was no way someone without in-depth local knowledge could have answered them.

They were getting married the first weekend in May, in the town hall, and coming back to the *palazzo* for the marquee reception. They talked food, and she asked Anita for the catering budget and drew a blank. 'Whatever you need,' she was told, and she shook her head.

'I need to know.'

'I allow between thirty and eighty euros a head for food. Do whatever you want, he won't mind. Just don't make it cheap. That would insult him.'

'What about wine?'

'Prosecco for reception drinks, estate red and white for the meal, estate vinsanto for the dessert, champagne for toasts—unless you'd rather have prosecco again?'

'Prosecco would be fine. I prefer it,' Jen said, looking slightly stunned. 'Lydia, this seems really lavish.'

'Don't worry, Jen, she's earned it,' Anita said. 'He's been working her to the bone over the harvest season, and it's not finished yet.'

It wasn't, and there was a change in the weather. Saturday night was cold and clear, and there was a hint of frost on the railings. Winter was coming, and first thing on Monday morning Roberto, not Massimo, took Jen and Andy to the airport because *la Raccolta*, the olive harvest, was about to begin.

Jen hugged her goodbye, her eyes welling. 'It's going to be amazing. I don't know how to thank you.'

'You don't need to thank me. Just go home and concentrate on getting better, and don't buy your wedding dress until I'm there. I don't want to miss that.'

'What, with your taste in wedding dresses?' Massimo said, coming up behind them with a teasing smile that threatened to double her blood pressure.

'It was five pounds!'

'You were cheated,' he said, laughing, and kissed Jen good-bye, slapping Andy on the back and wishing them a safe journey. 'I have to go—I'm needed at the plant. We have a problem with the olive press. I'll see you in May.'

She waved them off, feeling a pang of homesickness as they went, but she retreated to the kitchen where Carlotta was carving bread.

'Here we go again, then,' she said with a smile, and Carlotta smiled back and handed her the knife.

'I cut the *prosciutto*,' she said, and turned on the slicer.

He was late back that night—more problems with the *frantoio*, so Roberto told her, and Carlotta was exhausted.

Elisa and Vittorio were out for dinner, and so apart from Roberto and Carlotta, she was alone in the house with the children. And he was clearly worried for his wife.

'Go on, you go and look after her. Make her have an early night. I'll put the children to bed and look after them.'

'Are you sure?'

'Of course. They don't bite.'

He smiled gratefully and went, and she found the children in the sitting room. Antonino and Lavinia were squabbling again, and Francesca was on the point of tears.

'Who wants a story?' she asked, and they stopped fighting and looked up at her.

'Where's *Pàpa*?' Lavinia asked, looking doubtful.

'Working,' she said, because explaining what he was doing when she didn't really understand was beyond her. But they seemed to accept it, and apart from tugging his sister's hair again, even Antonino co-operated.

More or less. There was some argument about whether or not they needed a bath, but she was pretty sure no child had died from missing a single bath night, so she chivvied them into their pyjamas, supervised the teeth cleaning and ushered them into Antonino's bedroom.

It was a squeeze, but they all fitted on the bed somehow, and he handed her his favourite story book.

It was simple enough, just about, that she could fudge her way through it, but her pronunciation made them all laugh, and Francesca coached her. Then she read it again, much better this time, and gradually Antonino's eyelids began to wilt.

She sent the girls out, tucked him up and, on impulse, she kissed him goodnight.

He was already asleep by the time she reached the door, and Lavinia was in bed. Francesca, though, looked unhappy still, so after she'd settled her sister, she went into the older girl's room and gave her a hug.

She wasn't surprised when she burst into tears. She'd been on the brink of it before, and Lydia took her back downstairs and made her a hot drink and they curled up on the sofa in the sitting room next to the kitchen and talked.

'He's always working,' she said, her eyes welling again. 'He's never here, and Nino and Vinia always fight, and then Carlotta gets cross and upset because she's tired, and it's always me to stop them fighting, and—'

She broke off, her thin shoulders racked with sobs, and Lydia pulled her into her arms and rocked her, shushing her gently as she wept.

'—she's the one who bears the brunt of the loss, because when I'm not there the little ones turn to her. She has to be mother to them, and she's been so strong, but she's just a little girl herself—'

Poor, poor little thing. She was so stoic, trying to ease the burden on her beloved *pàpa*, and he was torn in half by his responsibilities. It was a no-win situation, and there was nothing she could do to change it, but maybe, just this one night, she'd made it a little easier.

She cradled Francesca in her arms until the storm of weeping had passed, and then they put on a DVD and snuggled up together to watch it.

Lydia couldn't understand it, but it didn't matter, and after a short while Francesca dropped off to sleep on Lydia's shoulder. She shifted her gently so she was lying with her head on her lap, and she stroked her hair as she settled again.

Dear, sweet child. Lydia was falling for her, she realised. Falling for them all. For the first time in her life she felt truly at home, truly needed, as if what she did really made a difference.

She sifted the soft, dark curls through her fingers and wondered what the future held for her and for her brother and sister.

She'd never know. Her time here was limited, they all knew that, and yet she'd grown to love them all so much that to leave them, never to know what became of them, how their lives panned out—it seemed unthinkable. She felt so much a part of their family, and it would be so easy to imagine living here with them, maybe adding to the family in time.

She squeezed her eyes shut and bit her lips.

No. It was never going to happen. She was going, and she had to remember that.

But not yet, she thought, a fine tendril of hair curled around her finger. Not now. For now, she'd just sit there with Francesca, and they'd wait for Massimo to return.

It was so late.

His mother would have put the children to bed, he thought, but yet again he'd missed their bedtime story, yet again he'd let them down.

The lights were on in the sitting room, and he could hear the television. Odd. He paused at the door, thinking the children must have left everything on, and he saw Lydia asleep on the sofa, Francesca sprawled across her lap.

Why Lydia? And why wasn't Francesca in bed?

He walked quietly over and looked down at them. They were both sound asleep, and Lydia was going to have a dreadful crick in her neck, but he was filthy, and if he was to carry Francesca up to bed, he needed a shower.

He backed out silently, went upstairs and showered, then threw on clean clothes and ran lightly downstairs.

'Lydia?' he murmured softly, touching her on the shoulder, and she stirred slightly and winced.

'Oh—you're home,' she whispered.

'*Si.* I'll take her.'

He eased her up into his arms, and Francesca snuggled close.

'She missed you,' Lydia said. 'The little ones were tired and naughty.'

'I'm sorry.'

'Don't be. It's not your fault.'

'Why are you here? My mother should be putting them to bed. I sent her a text.'

'They're out for dinner.'

He dropped his head back with a sigh. 'Of course. Oh, Lydia, I'm so sorry.'

'It's fine. Put her to bed.'

He did, settling her quickly, earning a sleepy smile as he kissed her goodnight. But by the time he got downstairs again, the television was off and the sitting room was in darkness.

It was over.

La Raccolta was finished, the olive oil safely in the huge lidded terracotta urns where it would mature for a while before being bottled.

The fresh olive oil, straight from the press, was the most amazing thing she'd ever tasted, and she'd used it liberally in the cooking and on *bruschetta* as an appetiser for the family's meals.

Of all the harvests, she'd found the olive harvest the most fascinating. The noise and smell in the pressing room was amazing, the huge stone wheels revolving on edge in the great stainless steel bowl of the *frantoio*, the olive press, crushing the olives to a purple paste. It was spread on circular felt discs and then stacked and pressed so that the oily juice dribbled out and ran into a vat, where it separated naturally, the bright green oil floating to the top.

Such a simple process, really, unchanged for centuries, and yet so very effective.

Everything in there had been covered in oil, the floor especially, and she knew that every time she smelt olive oil now, she'd see that room, hear the sound of the *frantoio* grinding the olives, see Massimo tossing olives in the palm of his hand, or checking the press, or laughing with one of the workers.

It would haunt her for the rest of her life, and the time had come so quickly.

She couldn't believe she was going, but she was. She'd grown to love it, not just because of him, but because of all his family, especially the children.

They were sad she was leaving, and on her last night she cooked them a special meal of their own, with a seafood risotto for their starter, and a pasta dish with chicken and pesto, followed by the dessert of frozen berries with hot white chocolate sauce that was always everyone's favourite.

'I don't want you to go,' Francesca said sadly as they finished clearing up.

Massimo, coming into the room as she said it, frowned. 'She has to go, *cara*. She has a business to run.'

'No, she doesn't. She has a job here, with us.'

Her heart squeezed. 'But I don't, sweetheart,' she said gently. 'I was only here to help Carlotta with the harvest. It's finished now. I can't just hang around and wait for next year. I have to go and cook for other people.'

'You could cook for us,' she reasoned, but Lydia shook her head.

'No. Carlotta would feel hurt. That's her job, to look after you. And your *pàpa* is right, I have to go back to my business.'

'Not go,' Lavinia said, her eyes welling. '*Pàpa, no!*' She ran to him, begging him in Italian, words she couldn't understand.

'What's she saying?' she asked, and Lavinia turned to look at her, tugging at her father and pleading, and he met her eyes reluctantly.

'She wants you to stay. She said—'

He broke off, but Francesca wouldn't let him stop.

'Tell her what Lavinia said, *Pàpa*,' she prompted, and he closed his eyes briefly and then went on.

'*Pàpa* is unhappy when aren't you're here,' he said grudgingly, translating directly as Lavinia spoke. 'Please don't go. We missed you when you went home before.' He hesitated, and she nudged him. 'It's lovely when you're here,' he went on, his bleak eyes locked with hers, 'because you make *Pàpa* laugh. He never laughs when you're not here.'

A tear slipped over and slid down her cheek, but she didn't seem to notice. Their eyes were locked, and he could see the anguish in them. He swallowed hard, his arm around Lavinia's skinny little shoulders holding her tight at his side.

Was it true? Was he unhappy when she wasn't there, unhappy enough that even the children could see it? Did he really not laugh when she wasn't there?

Maybe.

Lydia pressed her fingers to her lips, and shook her head. 'Oh, Lavinia. I'm sorry. I don't want to make your *pàpa* unhappy, or any of you, but I have to go home to my family.'

She felt little arms around her hips, and looked down to find Antonino hugging her, his face buried in her side. She laid a hand gently on his hair and stroked it, aching unbearably inside. She'd done this, spent so much time with them that she was hurting them now by leaving, and she never meant to hurt them. 'I'm sorry,' she said to him, *'mi dispiace.'* And his little arms tightened.

'Will you read us a story?' Francesca asked.

She'd be leaving for the airport before three in the morning, long before the children were up, so this was her last chance to read to them. Her last chance ever? 'Of course I will,' she said, feeling choked. She'd done it a few times since the night of the *frantoio* breakdown, and she loved it. Too much.

They were already in their pyjamas, and she ushered them up to bed, supervised the teeth cleaning as she'd done before, and then they settled down on Antonino's bed, all crowded round while she read haltingly to them in her awful, amateurish Italian.

She could get the expressions right, make it exciting—that was the easy bit. The pronunciation was harder, but it was a book they knew, so it didn't really matter.

What mattered was lying propped up against the wall, with Antonino under one arm and Lavinia under the other, and Francesca curled up by her knees leaning against the wall and watching her with wounded eyes.

She was the only one of them to remember her mother, and for a few short weeks, Lydia realised, she'd slipped into the role without thinking, unconsciously taking over some of the many little things a mother did. Things like making cupcakes, and birthday cards for Roberto. She'd stopped the two little ones fighting, and hugged them when they'd hurt themselves, and all the time she'd been playing happy families and ignoring the fact that she'd be going away soon, going back to her real life at home.

And now she had to go.

She closed the book, and the children snuggled closer, stretching out the moment.

Then Massimo's frame filled the doorway, his eyes shadowed in the dim light.

'Come on. Bedtime now. Lydia needs to pack.'

It was a tearful goodnight, for all of them, and as soon as she could she fled to her room, stifling the tears.

She didn't have to pack. She'd done it ages ago, been round all the places she might have left anything, and there was nothing to do now, nothing to distract her.

Only Lavinia's words echoing in her head.

He never laughs when you're not here.

The knock was so quiet she almost didn't hear it.

'Lydia?'

She opened the door, unable to speak, and met his tortured eyes.

And then his arms closed around her, and he held her hard against his chest while she felt the shudders run through him.

They stayed like that for an age, and then he eased back and looked down at her.

His eyes were raw with need, and she led him into the room and closed the door.

Just one last time…

CHAPTER TEN

'Is it true?'

He turned his head and met her eyes in the soft glow of the bedside light, and his face was shuttered and remote.

'Is what true?'

'That you don't laugh when I'm not here?'

He looked away again. 'You don't want to listen to what the children say.'

'Why not, if it's true? Is it?'

He didn't answer, so she took it as a yes. It made her heart ache. If only he'd believe in them, if only he'd let her into his heart, his life, but all he would say was no.

'Talk to me,' she pleaded.

He turned his head back, his eyes unreadable.

'What is there to say?'

'You could tell me how you really feel. That would be a good start.'

He laughed, a harsh, abrupt grunt full of pain. 'I can't,' he said, his accent stronger than she'd ever heard it. 'I can't find the words, I don't have the language to do this in English.'

'Then tell me in Italian. I won't understand, but you can say it then out loud. You can tell me whatever you like, and I can't hold you to it.'

He frowned, but then he reached out and stroked her face, his fingers trembling. His mouth flickered in a sad smile, and then he started to speak, as if she'd released something inside him that had been held back for a long, long time.

She didn't understand it, but she understood the tone—the gentleness, the anguish, the pain of separation.

And then, his eyes locked with hers, he said softly, *'Ciao, mia bella ragazza. Te amo...'*

She reached out and cradled his jaw, her heart breaking. *Ciao* meant hello, but it also meant goodbye.

'It doesn't have to be goodbye,' she said softly. 'I love you, too—so much.'

He shook his head. 'No. No, *cara*, please. I can't let you love me. I can't let you stay. You'll be hurt.'

'No!'

'Yes. I won't let you.'

'Would you stop that?' she demanded, angry now. 'The first time I met you, you said I couldn't go in the plane with Nico because it wasn't safe. Now you're telling me I can't love you because I'll get hurt! Maybe I want to take the risk, Massimo? Maybe I *need* to take the risk.'

'No. You have a life waiting for you, and one day there will be some lucky man...'

'I don't want another man, I want you.'

'No! I have nothing to give you. I'm already pulled in so many ways. How can I be fair to you, or the children, or my work, my family? How can I do another relationship justice?'

'Maybe I could help you. Maybe I could make it easier. Maybe we could work together?'

'No. You love your family, you have your career. If I let you give it all up for me, what then? What happens when we've all let you into our hearts and then you leave?'

'I won't leave!'

'You don't know that. You've been here less than three months. What happens in three years, when we have another child and you decide you're unhappy and want to go? I don't have time for you, I can't give you what you need. I don't even have enough time now to sleep! Please, *cara*. Don't make it harder. You'll forget me soon.'

'No. I'll never forget you. I'll never stop loving you.'

'You will. You'll move on. You'll meet someone and marry him and have children of your own in England, close to your family, and you'll look back and wonder what you saw in this sad and lonely old man.'

'Don't be ridiculous, you're not old, and you're only sad and lonely because you won't let anybody in!'

His eyes closed, as if he couldn't bear to look at her any longer. 'I can't. The last time I let anyone into my life, she lost her own, and it was because I was too busy, too tired, too overstretched to be there for her.'

'It wasn't your fault!'

'Yes, it was! I was *here*! I was supposed to be looking after her, but I was lying in my bed asleep while she was dying.'

'She should have woken you! She should have told you she was sick. It was not your fault!'

'No? Then why do I wake every night hearing her calling me?'

He threw off the covers and sat up, his legs over the edge of the bed, his head in his hands, his whole body vibrating with tension. 'I can't do this, Lydia! Please, don't ask me to. I can't do it.'

Why do I wake every night hearing her calling me?

His words echoing in her head, her heart pounding, she knelt up behind him, her arms around him, her body pressed to his in comfort.

'It wasn't your fault,' she said gently. 'You weren't responsible, but you're holding yourself responsible, and you have to forgive yourself. It wasn't my fault Jen had her accident, but I've blamed myself, and it has taken months to accept that it wasn't my fault and to forgive myself for not stopping him.

You have to do the same. You have to accept that you weren't
at fault—'

'But I was! I should have checked on her.'

'You were asleep! What time of year was it?'

'Harvest,' he admitted, his voice raw. 'The end of *La
Raccolta*.'

Right at the end of the season. Now, in fact. Any time now.
Her heart contracted, and she sank back down onto her feet,
her hands against his back.

'You were exhausted, weren't you? Just as you're exhausted
now. And she didn't want to disturb you, so she went down
to the kitchen for painkillers.'

He sucked in a breath, and she knew she was right.

'She probably wasn't thinking clearly. Did she suffer from
headaches?'

'Yes. All the time. They said she had a weakness in the
vessels.'

'So it could have happened at any time?'

'*Si*. But it happened when I was there, and it happened
slowly, and if I'd realised, if I hadn't thought she was with
the baby, if I'd known…'

'If you'd been God, in fact? If you'd been able to see inside her head?'

'They could have seen inside her head. She'd talked of
going to the doctor about her headaches, but we were too busy,
and she'd just had the baby, and it was the harvest, and…'

'And there was just no time. Oh, Massimo. I'm so sorry,
but you know it wasn't your fault. You can't blame yourself.'

'Yes, I can. I can, and I have to, because my guilt and my
grief is all I have left to give her! I can't even love her any
more because you've taken that from me!' he said harshly,
his voice cracking.

The pain ran through her like a shockwave.

How could he tell her that he loved her, and yet cling to his guilt and grief so that he could hold onto Angelina?

He couldn't. Not if he really loved her. Unless...

'Why are you doing this to me?' she asked quietly. 'To yourself? To your children? You wear your grief and your guilt like a hair shirt to torture yourself with, but it's not just you you're torturing, you're torturing me, as well, and your children. And they don't deserve to be tortured just because you're too much of a coward to let yourself love again!'

'I am not a coward!'

'Then prove it!' she begged. 'Let yourself love again!'

He didn't answer, his shoulders rigid, unmoving, and after what felt like forever, she gave up. She'd tried, and she could do no more.

Shaking, she eased away from him and glanced at her watch.

'We have to leave in half an hour. I'm going to shower,' she said, as steadily as she could.

And she walked into the bathroom, closed the door and let the tears fall...

He didn't come into the airport building this time.

He gave her a handful of notes to pay for her excess baggage, put her luggage on the pavement at the drop-off point and then hesitated.

'I'll see you in May,' he said, his voice clipped and harsh.

His eyes were raw with pain, and she wanted to weep for him, and for herself, and for the children, but now wasn't the time.

'Yes. I'll be in touch.'

'Anita will email you. She's in charge. I'll be too busy.'

Of course he would.

'Take care of yourself,' she said softly. And going up on tiptoe, she pressed her lips to his cheek.

His arms came round her, and for the briefest moment he rested his head against hers. *'Ciao, bella,'* he said softly, so softly that she scarcely heard him, and then he was straightening up, moving back, getting into the car.

He started the engine and drove away, and she watched his tail lights until they disappeared. Then she gathered up her luggage and headed for the doors.

It was the worst winter of her life.

The weather was glorious, bright winter sunshine that seemed to bounce right off her, leaving her cold inside. She found work in the pub down the road, and she created a website and tried to promote her catering business.

It did well, better than she'd expected, but without him her life was meaningless.

Jen found her one day in mid-January, staring into space.

'Hey,' she said softly, and came and perched beside her on the back of the sofa, staring out across the valley.

'Hey yourself. How are you doing?'

'OK. We've had another email from Anita. She wants to know about food.'

She could hardly bring herself to think about food. For a while she'd thought she was pregnant she'd felt so sick, but she wasn't. The test said no, her body said no and her heart grieved for a child that never was and never would be. And still she felt sick.

'What does she want to know? I've given her menu plans.'

'Something about the carpaccio of beef?'

She sighed. 'OK. I'll contact her.'

It was nothing to do with the beef. It was about Massimo.

'He's looking awful,' Anita said. 'He hasn't smiled since you left.'

Nor have I, she thought, *but there's nothing I can do, either for him or me.*

She didn't reply to the email. Two hours later her phone rang.

'I can't help you, Anita,' she said desperately. 'He won't listen to me.'

'He won't listen to anyone—Luca, Carlotta, his mother—even Gio's on your side, amazingly, but he just says he doesn't want to talk about it. And we're all worried. We're really worried.'

'I'm sorry, I can't do any more,' she said again, choked, and hung up.

Jen found her in her room, face down on the bed sobbing her heart out, and she lay down beside her and held her, and gradually it stopped hurting and she was numb again.

Better, in a strange kind of way.

January turned into February, and then March, and finally Jen was able to walk without the crutches.

'That's amazing,' Lydia said, hugging her, her eyes filling with tears. 'I'm so glad.'

'So am I.' Jen touched her cheek gently. 'I'm all right now, Lydia. I'm going to be OK. Please stop hurting yourself about it.'

'I'm not,' she said, and realised it was true, to an extent. Oh, it would always hurt to know that she'd been part of the sequence of events that had led to Jen's accident, but she'd stopped taking the blame for it, and now she could share in the joy of Jen's recovery. If only Massimo…

'You need to buy your wedding dress, we're leaving it awfully late,' she said, changing the subject before her mind dragged her off down that route.

'I know. There's a shop in town that does them to take away, so they don't need to be ordered. Will you come with me?'

She ignored the stab of pain, and hugged her sister. 'Of course I will.'

* * *

It was bittersweet.

They all went together—Lydia, Jen and their mother and she found a dress that laced up the back, with an inner elasticated corset that was perfect for giving her some extra back support.

'Oh, that's so comfy!' she said, and then looked in the mirror and her eyes filled.

'Oh...'

Lydia grabbed her mother's hand and hung on. It was definitely The Dress, and everybody's eyes were filling now.

'Oh, darling,' her mother said, and hugged her, laughing and crying at the same time, because it might never have come to this. They could have lost her, and yet here she was, standing on her own two feet, unaided, and in her wedding dress. Their tears were well and truly earned.

After she'd done another twirl and taken the dress off, the manageress of the little wedding shop poured them another glass of Prosecco to toast Jen's choice.

As the bubbles burst in her mouth, Lydia closed her eyes and thought of him.

Sitting on the terrace outside her bedroom, sipping Prosecco and talking into the night. They'd done it more than once, before the weather had turned. Pre-dinner drinks when Jen and Andy had come to visit. Sitting in the *trattoria* waiting for their food to come, the second time they'd made love.

'Lydia?'

She opened her eyes and dredged up a smile. 'You looked stunning in it, Jen. Absolutely beautiful. Andy'll be bowled over.'

'What about you?'

'I don't need a wedding dress!' she said abruptly, and then remembered she was supposed to be Jen's bridesmaid, and suddenly it was all too much.

'Can we do this another day?' she asked desperately, and Jen, seeing something in her eyes, nodded.

'Of course we can.'

She went back on her own a few days later, and flicked through the rails while she was waiting. And there, on a mannequin in the corner, was the most beautiful dress she'd ever seen.

The softest, heaviest silk crepe de Chine, cut on the cross and hanging beautifully, it was exquisite. So soft, she thought, fingering it with longing, such a far cry from the awful thing she'd worn for the competition, and she wondered, stupidly, if she'd worn it instead, would she have fallen? And if not, would she have known what it was to love him? Maybe, if he'd seen her wearing a dress like that...

'It's a beautiful dress, isn't it? Why don't you try it on?'

'I don't need a wedding dress,' she said bluntly, dropping her hand to her side. 'I'm here for a bridesmaid's dress.'

'You could still try it on. We're quiet today, and I'd love to see it on you. You've got just the figure for it.'

How on earth had she let herself be talked into it? Because, of course, it fitted like a dream on her hourglass figure, smoothing her hips, showing off her waist, emphasising her bust.

For a moment—just a moment—she let herself imagine his face as he saw her in it. She'd seen that look before, when he'd been making love to her—

'This is silly,' she said, desperate to take it off now. 'I'm not getting married.'

Not ever...

The awful wedding dress was still hanging on the back of his door.

He stared at it numbly. It still had her blood on it, a dark brown stain on the bodice where she'd wiped her fingers after she'd touched the graze on her head.

He missed her. The ache never left him, overlying the other ache, the ache that had been there since Angelina died.

Their wedding photo was still on his desk, and he picked it up and studied it. Was Lydia right? Was her wearing a metaphorical hair shirt, punishing himself for what was really not his fault?

Rationally, he knew that, but he couldn't let it go.

Because he hadn't forgiven himself? Or because he was a coward?

It's not just you you're torturing, you're torturing me, as well, and your children. And they don't deserve to be tortured just because you're too much of a coward to let yourself love again!

Getting up from the desk, he went and found Carlotta and told her he was going out. And then he did what he should have done a long time ago.

He went to the place where she was buried, and he said goodbye, and then he went home and took off his wedding ring. There was an inscription inside. It read *'Amor vincit omnia'*.

Love conquers everything.

Could it? Not unless you gave it a chance, he thought, and pressing the ring to his lips, he nestled it in Angelina's jewellery box, with the lock of her hair, the first letter she'd ever sent him, a rose from her bouquet.

And then he put the box away, and went outside into the garden and stood at the railings, looking out over the valley below. She'll be here soon, he thought, and then I'll know.

Jen and Andy saw her off at the airport.

She put on a bright face, but in truth she was dreading this part of the wedding.

She was going over early to finalise the menu and meet the people who were going to be helping her. Carlotta's nephew, the owner of the *trattoria*, had loaned her one of his chefs and sourced the ingredients, and the waiting staff were all from local families and had worked for Anita before, but the final responsibility for the menu and the food was hers.

None of that bothered her. She was confident about the menu, confident in the ability of the chef and the waiting staff, and the food she was sure would be fine.

It was seeing Massimo that filled her with dread.

Dread, and longing.

She was thinner.

Thinner, and her face was drawn. She looked as if she'd been working too hard, and he wondered how her business was going. Maybe she'd been too successful?

He hoped not—no! That was wrong. If it was going well, if it was what she wanted, then he must let her go.

Pain stabbed through him and he sucked in a breath. For the past few weeks he'd put thoughts of failure out of his mind, but now—now, seeing her there, they all came rushing to the fore.

He walked towards her, and as if she sensed him there she turned her head and met his eyes. All the breath seemed to be sucked out of his body, and he had to tell his feet how to move.

'*Ciao, bella,*' he said softly, and her face seemed to crumple slightly.

'*Ciao,*' she said, her voice uneven, and then he hugged her, because she looked as if she'd fall down if he didn't.

'Is this everything?'

She nodded, and he took the case from her and wheeled it out of the airport to his car.

He was looking well, she thought. A little thinner, perhaps, but not as bad as she'd thought from what Anita had said. Because he was over her?

She felt a sharp stab of pain, and sucked in her breath. Maybe he'd been right. Maybe he couldn't handle it, and he'd just needed to get back onto an even keel again.

And then he came round and opened the car door for her, and she noticed his wedding ring was missing, and her heart began to thump.

Was it significant?

She didn't know, and he said nothing, just smiled at her as he got into the car and talked about what the children had been up to and how the wedding preparations were going, all the way back to the *palazzo*.

It was like coming home, she thought.

The children were thrilled to see her, especially Francesca who wrapped her arms around her and hugged her so hard she thought her ribs might break.

'Goodness, you've all grown so tall!' she said, her eyes filling. Lavinia's arms were round her waist, and Antonino was hanging on her arm and jumping up and down. It made getting up the steps a bit of a challenge, but they managed it, and Massimo just chuckled softly and carried her luggage in.

'I've put you in the same room,' he said, and she felt a shiver of dread. The last time she'd been in here, he'd broken her heart. She wasn't sure she wanted to be there again, but it felt like her room now, and it would be odd to be anywhere else.

'So, what's the plan?' she asked as he put her case down.

He smiled wryly. 'Anita's coming over. I've told her to give you time to unwind, but she said there was too much to do. Do you want a cup of tea?'

'I'd love a cup of tea,' she said fervently. 'But don't worry. I'll make it.'

He nodded. 'In that case, I'll go and get on. You know my mobile number—ring me if you need me.'

She didn't have time to need him, which was perhaps just as well. The next few days were a whirlwind, and by the time the family arrived, she was exhausted.

Anita was brilliant. She organised everything, made sure everyone knew what they were to do and kept them all calm and focused, and the day of the wedding went without a hitch.

Lydia's involvement in the food was over. She'd prepared the starters and the deserts, the cold buffet was in the refrigerated van beside the marquee, and all she had to do was dress her sister and hold her bouquet.

And catch it, apparently, when it was all over.

Jen wasn't subtle. She stood just a few feet from her, with everyone standing round cheering, and threw it straight at Lydia.

It hit her in the chest and she nearly dropped it, but then she looked up and caught Massimo's eye, and her heart began to pound slowly.

He was smiling.

Smiling? Why? Because he was glad it was all over? Or because the significance of her catching it wasn't lost on him?

She didn't know. She was too tired to care, and after Andy scooped his glowing, blushing bride up in his arms and carried her off at the end of the reception in a shower of confetti and good wishes, she took the chance and slipped quietly away.

There was so much to do—a mountain of clearing up in the kitchen in the *palazzo*, never mind all the catering equipment which had been hired in and had to be cleaned and returned.

Plates, cutlery, glasses, table linen.

'I thought I might find you in here.'

She looked up.

'There's a lot to do.'

'I know.'

He wasn't smiling. Not now. He was thoughtful. Maybe a little tense?

He took off his suit jacket and rolled up his sleeves and pitched in alongside her, and for a while they worked in silence. He changed the washing up water three times, she used a handful of tea towels, but finally the table was groaning with clean utensils.

'Better. The guests are leaving. Do you want to say goodbye?'

She smiled slightly and shook her head. 'They're not my guests. Let my parents do it. I've got enough to do.'

'I'll go and clear up outside,' he said, and she nodded. There was still a lot to do in there, and she worked until she was ready to drop.

Her feet hurt, her shoes were long gone and she wanted to lie down. The rest, she decided, would keep, and turning off the light, she headed back to her room.

She passed her parents in the colonnaded walkway around the courtyard, on their way in with Massimo's parents.

They stopped to praise the food yet again, and Elisa hugged her. 'It was wonderful. I knew it would be. You have an amazing talent.'

'I know,' her mother said. 'We're very proud of her.'

She was hugged and kissed again, and then she excused herself and finally got to her room, pausing in surprise in the doorway.

The door was open, the bedside light was on, and the bed was sprinkled with rose petals.

Rose petals?

She picked one up, lifting it to her nose and smelling the delicately heady fragrance.

Who—?

'May I come in?'

She spun round, the rose petal falling from her fingers, and he was standing there with a bottle of sparkling water and two glasses. 'I thought you might be thirsty,' he said.

'I don't know what I am,' she said. 'Too tired to know.'

He laughed softly, and she wondered—just briefly, with the small part of her brain that was still functioning—how often he'd done that since she went away.

'Lie down before you fall.'

She didn't need telling twice. She didn't bother to take the dress off. It was probably ruined anyway, and realistically when would she wear it again? She didn't go to dressy events very often. She flopped onto the bed, and he went round the other side, kicked off his shoes and settled himself beside her, propped up against the headboard.

'Here, drink this,' he said, handing her a glass, and she drained the water and handed the glass back.

'More.'

He laughed—again?—and refilled it, then leant back and sighed.

'Good wedding.'

'It was. Thank you. Without you, it wouldn't have happened.'

'It might have been at the hotel.'

'No. Nobody was giving me a lift—well, only Nico, and we both know how that might have ended.'

'Don't.' He took the empty glass from her again, put them both down and slid down the bed so he was lying flat beside her. His hand reached out, and their fingers linked and held.

'How are you, really?' he asked softly.

He wasn't talking about tonight, she realised, and decided she might as well be honest. It was the only thing she had left.

'All right, I suppose. I've missed you.'

'I've missed you, too. I didn't know I could hurt as much as that, not any more. Apparently I can.'

She rolled to her side to face him, and he did the same, his smile gone now, his eyes serious.

'Massimo,' she said, cutting to the chase, 'where's your wedding ring?'

'Ah, *cara*. So observant. I took it off. I didn't need it any more. You were right, it was time to let the past go and move on with my life.'

'Without guilt?'

His smile was sad. 'Without guilt. With regret, perhaps. The knowledge that things probably wouldn't have been very different whatever I'd done. I'd lost sight of that. And you?' he added. 'Are you moving on with your life?'

She tried to laugh, but she was too tired and too hurt to make it believable. 'No. My business is going well, but I don't care. It's all meaningless without you.'

'Oh, *bella*,' he said softly, and reached for her. 'My life is the same. The only thing that's kept me going the last few weeks has been the knowledge that I'd see you again soon. Without that I would have gone insane. I nearly did go insane.'

'I know. Anita rang me. They were all worried about you.'

He eased her up against his chest, so that her face lay against the fine silk shirt, warm from his skin, the beat of his heart echoing in her ear, slow and steady.

'Stay with me,' he said. 'I have no right to ask you, after I sent you away like that, but I can't live without you. No. That's not true. I can. I just don't want to, because without you, I don't laugh. Lavinia was right. I don't laugh because there's nothing to laugh at when you're not here. Nothing seems funny, everything is cold and colourless and futile. The days are busy but monotonous, and the nights—the nights are so lonely.'

She swallowed a sob, and lifted her hand and cradled his stubbled jaw. 'I know. I've lain awake night after night and missed you. I can fill the days, but the nights…'

'The nights are endless. Cold and lonely and endless. I've tried working, but there comes a time when I have to sleep, and then every time I close my eyes, I see you.'

'Not Angelina?'

'No. Not Angelina. I said goodbye to her. I hadn't done it. I hadn't grieved for her properly, I'd buried myself in work and I thought I was all right, but then I met you and I couldn't love you as you deserved because I wasn't free. And instead of freeing myself, I sent you away.'

'I'm sorry. It must have been hard.'

His eyes softened, and he smiled and shook his head. 'No. It was surprisingly easy. I was ready to do it—more than ready. And I'm ready to move on. I just need to know that you're ready to come with me.'

She smiled and bit her lip. 'Where are we going?'

'Wherever life takes us. It will be here, because this is who I am and where I have to be, but what we do with that life is down to us.'

He took her hand from his cheek and held it, staring intently into her eyes. 'Marry me, Lydia. You've set me free, but that freedom is no use to me without you. I love you, *bella. Te amo*. If you still love me, if you haven't come to your senses in all this time, then marry me. Please.'

'Of course I'll marry you,' she breathed, her heart overflowing. 'Oh, you foolish, silly, wonderful man, of course I'll marry you! Just try and stop me. And I'll never, never stop loving you.'

'I've still got the dress,' he told her some time later, his eyes sparkling with mischief. 'It's hanging on my office door. I thought I'd keep it, just in case you said yes.'

Did the woman in the wedding dress shop have second sight? 'I think I might treat myself to a new one,' she said, and smiled at him.

They were married in June, in the town hall where Jen and Andy had been married.

It had been a rush—she'd had to pack up all her things in England and ship them over, and they'd moved, on his parents' insistence, into the main part of the *palazzo*.

A new start, a clean slate.

It would take some getting used to, but as Massimo said, it was a family home and it should have children in it. It was where he and his brothers and sisters had been brought up, and it was family tradition for the eldest son to take over the formal rooms of the *palazzo*. And hopefully, there would be other children to fill it.

She held onto that thought. She'd liked the simplicity of the other wing, but there was much more elbow room in the central part, essential if they were to have more children, and the views were, if anything, even more stunning. And maybe one day she'd grow into the grandeur.

But until their wedding night, she was still using the room she'd always had, and it was in there that Jen and her mother helped her put on the beautiful silk dress. It seemed woefully extravagant for such a small and simple occasion, but she was wearing it for him, only for him, and when she walked out to meet him, her heart was in her mouth.

He was waiting for her in the frescoed courtyard, and his eyes stroked slowly over her. He said nothing, and for an endless moment she thought he hated it. But then he lifted his eyes to hers, and the heat in them threatened to set her on fire.

She looked stunning.

He'd thought she was beautiful in the other wedding dress, much as he'd hated it. In this, she was spectacular. It hugged her curves like a lover, and just to look at her made him ache.

She wasn't wearing a veil, and the natural curls of her fine blonde hair fell softly to her shoulders. It was the way he liked it. Everything about her was the way he liked it, and at last he found a smile.

'*Mia bella ragazza,*' he said softly, and held out his hand to her.

It was a beautiful, simple ceremony.

Their vows, said by both of them in both English and Italian, were from the heart, and they were witnessed by their closest family and friends. Both sets of parents, his three sisters, Jen and Andy, Luca and Isabelle, Gio, Anita, Carlotta and Roberto, and of course the children.

Francesca and Lavinia were bridesmaids, and Antonino was the ring bearer. There was a tense moment when he wobbled and the rings started to slide, but it was all right, and with a smile of encouragement for his son, Massimo took her ring from the little cushion and slid it onto her finger, his eyes locked with hers.

He loved her. When he'd lost Angelina, he'd thought he could never love again, but Lydia had shown him the way. There was always room for love, he realised, always room for another person in your heart, and his heart had made room for her. How had he ever thought it could do otherwise?

She slid the other ring onto his finger, her fingers firm and confident, and he cupped her shoulders in his hands and bent his head and kissed her.

'*Te amo,*' he murmured, and then his words were drowned out by the clapping and cheering of their family.

* * *

Afterwards they went for lunch to the little *trattoria* owned by Carlotta's nephew. He did them proud. They drank Prosecco and ate simple, hearty food exquisitely cooked, and when it was over, they drove back to the *palazzo*. The others were going back to Luca and Isabelle's for the rest of the day, to give them a little privacy, and Massimo intended to take full advantage of it.

He drove up to the front door, scooped her up in his arms and carried her up the steps. The last time he'd done this she'd been bloodstained and battered. This time—this time she was his wife, and he felt like the luckiest man alive.

Pausing at the top he turned, staring out over the valley spread out below them. Home, he thought, his heart filled with joy, and Lydia rested her head on his shoulder and sighed.

'It's so beautiful.'

'Not as beautiful as you. And that dress...' He nuzzled her neck, making her arch against him. 'I've been wanting to take it off you all day.'

'Don't you like it? I wasn't sure myself. I thought maybe I should have stuck to the other one,' she teased, and he laughed, the sound carrying softly on the night air.

It was a sound she'd never tire of, she thought content-edly as he turned, still smiling, and carried his bride over the threshold.

* * * * *

Mills & Boon® is excited to present this
new family saga from award-winning author
Lucy Gordon

The Falcon Dynasty

Five successful brothers looking for brides!

Amos Falcon is a proud, self-made man who wants
his legacy to live on through his five sons. Each son is
different, for they have different mothers, but in one
aspect they are the same: he has raised them to be
ruthless in business and sensible in matters of the heart.

But one by one these high-achieving brothers will find
that when the right woman comes along love is the
greatest power of them all…

RESCUED BY THE BROODING TYCOON
August 2011

MISS PRIM AND THE BILLIONAIRE
February 2012

PLAIN JANE IN THE SPOTLIGHT
July 2012

Dear Reader,

With the third book of THE FALCON DYNASTY I found myself facing new challenges. Travis is unlike most other heroes, and certainly unlike the other Falcons. Amos's ruthless, demanding nature has descended to several of his sons. Darius, Marcel and Leonid have obvious traces of their father. Even Jackson is a Falcon, in his clear-eyed determination to do things his way.

But Travis is different: an actor in the glamorous city of Los Angeles, he's a gentle, sweet-natured man who makes his way through life with charm and humour. His greatest gift is for winning hearts, so his career flourishes and he can take his choice of beautiful women. Whatever he touches turns to gold, and he seems to have everything a man could wish for.

It takes a special woman to discover the truth. Charlene would call herself plain and dowdy, but she's the only one Travis trusts sufficiently to reveal the vulnerability he hides from the rest of the world.

Despised and half rejected by his domineering father, Travis has always felt on the outside of the Falcon family. Now Charlene's open arms offer comfort and safety, and he takes joyful refuge in them. But when suddenly he has the chance to win Amos's respect it could be at Charlene's expense.

What he does now will define his life, and his decision reveals him as a true Falcon: not to be deflected from his chosen path. But few men would have the strength to do what he does.

Travis is my favourite Falcon. I hope you love him as much as I do.

Best wishes,

Lucy Gordon

PLAIN JANE IN
THE SPOTLIGHT

BY
LUCY GORDON

MILLS & BOON

First published in Great Britain 2012
by Mills & Boon, an imprint of Harlequin (UK) Limited,
Eton House, 18-24 Paradise Road, Richmond, Surrey TW9 1SR

© Lucy Gordon 2012

ISBN: 978 0 263 89445 5
ebook ISBN: 978 1 408 97119 2

23-0712

Harlequin (UK) policy is to use papers that are natural, renewable and recyclable products and made from wood grown in sustainable forests. The logging and manufacturing processes conform to the legal environmental regulations of the country of origin.

Printed and bound in Spain
by Blackprint CPI, Barcelona

Lucy Gordon cut her writing teeth on magazine journalism, interviewing many of the world's most interesting men, including Warren Beatty, Charlton Heston and Sir Roger Moore. She also camped out with lions in Africa, and had many other unusual experiences, which have often provided the background for her books. Several years ago, while staying in Venice, she met a Venetian who proposed in two days. They have been married ever since. Naturally this has affected her writing, where romantic Italian men tend to feature strongly.

Two of her books have won a Romance Writers of America RITA® Award.

You can visit her website at www.lucy-gordon.com

CHAPTER ONE

'For pity's sake, Travis, why do you never listen? You've been warned a dozen times. *Stay out of sleazy nightclubs.*'

Denzil Raines, boss of the Sandora Studio in Los Angeles, snapped out the command and tried to control his temper. It was hard because Travis would try anyone's patience.

The studio produced several money-making television series, but none of them raked in the wealth as fast and gloriously as *The Man From Heaven*, starring Travis Falcon, and protecting that investment was a major operation.

The young man enduring the lecture seemed to sum up the whole of the investment in himself. Travis's body was lean and vigorous, his face was handsome, his air charming, his smile devastating. It spoke of eagerness to enjoy life to the full. Late nights, curiosity for new experiences, untiring energy for a vast range of pleasurable activities. They were all there in the quirk of his mouth, the gleam in his eye, and they caused much hair tearing among those who needed to keep him in check.

Denzil reflected that he'd picked the right word. Sleazy. That was it. Sleazy nightclubs, sleazy pleasures, sleazy Travis. But he knew it was precisely the hint of a 'bad boy' lurking in the shadows that hit the magic spot with the public. And it would go on doing so as long as it stayed in the safety of the shadows. If it was allowed to escape... Denzil groaned.

Travis was standing by the window, looking out over the view of Los Angeles. Clearly visible in the distance was the huge gleaming sign, HOLLYWOOD, that for ninety years had symbolised the city where glamour, entertainment and money united in brilliant supremacy. His gaze was fixed on the sign, as though to remind himself of the achievements he was fighting to keep. He stood, bathed in sunlight, apparently nonchalant, but actually alive to every threatening nuance.

'I didn't know it was sleazy,' he said with a shrug. 'My friend chose it for his stag night.'

'Stag night?' Denzil echoed in outrage. 'Then you might have guessed there'd be half-naked dolly birds prancing around. What else are stag nights for? You should have got out of the place instead of...*this*!'

He held out a newspaper, jamming his finger down on a picture of a man and a girl clinging to each other. He was sitting down, shirt ripped open, the half-naked girl on his lap, her arms about his neck, kissing him madly, which he showed every sign of enjoying.

'You had to lay yourself out for those girls,' Denzil groaned.

'I didn't lay myself out,' Travis protested. 'I was having a quiet drink when this lady...well...'

'Quiet? Hah! When did you last do anything quietly? And she was no lady. She'd been hired for the night to "entertain" the male guests. She entertained you all right.'

'I didn't ask her to sit on my lap.'

'You didn't push her off, either.'

'No, that would have been rude. I was just trying to be polite.'

'Oh, it was politeness that made you put your arms about her waist, draw her close, nuzzle her—'

'I'm only human,' Travis protested. 'When a half-naked girl drapes herself over a guy he's expected to show some appreciation.'

'You did that all right,' Denzil snapped. 'She's not the only one who's half-naked. Look at your shirt, open to the waist, so that she can dance her fingers over your bare chest. Did she pull it open? Did *you*? Or did you arrive like that, hoping something would happen?'

Travis groaned. 'Can we just leave this? I didn't know the press was there, OK?'

'The press is always there where you're concerned,' Denzil growled. 'You should know that by now. Ever since the show became a hit they've been watching you, trying to find out something that makes people's hair stand on end. And, let's face it, there are plenty of those!'

'I refuse to answer on the grounds that it may incriminate me,' Travis said with a touch of wry humour.

'Very wise. They just want to catch you out with something really damaging. It wouldn't be such a problem if you were playing a different character, but this one is full of danger.'

The TV series, *The Man From Heaven*, was the talk of the entertainment world. Superficially, it seemed a conventional hospital drama, centred around the young, handsome Dr Brad Harrison, played by Travis Falcon. But beneath it was another tale. The doctor lived a life of strict virtue that was wildly at odds with his flamboyant sexual presence, and there was just a hint that he wasn't a mortal man at all, but a spirit from another dimension.

It was the intriguing contrast between Dr Harrison's austere life and the sexual indulgence open to a man of his attractions that had sent the show to the top of all the popularity charts. The producers were determined to keep it there, if only they could rein in Travis's more lurid off-screen activities.

'Folk out there like nothing better than to discover "the heavenly being" acting on his lowest human instincts,' Denzil pointed out now.

'But I'm not a heavenly being,' Travis said firmly.

'You don't have to tell me that,' Denzil snapped. 'Look, the public's crazy about you, the money's pouring in. The next series is being planned. But that could all change if you step too much out of character in private. Look, I'm not unreasonable. Of course you want female company. Just not *that* sort.'

Travis studied the picture again and sighed. 'I know. I was careless. I'll be more careful.'

'It would help if you were in a relationship with a respectable girl. Don't pull that face. I know "respectable" is like the kiss of death to you, but we need the public to believe in you as one of the good guys, not a philanderer.'

'But I *am* a philanderer,' Travis pointed out.

'Then try to pretend you're not,' Denzil roared. 'You're an actor aren't you? So *act*!'

'Act what? Do I lie to the girl and pretend it's real? No way. That would be dishonest. Or do I tell her upfront that she's being made use of, then see her go straight to the press?'

Denzil groaned. 'Just get your life in order. There's a lot at stake, Travis. Think career. Think money.'

'All right. I'll think money.'

'And while we're on the subject—about tonight—'

'I'm not going to be at the dinner tonight,' Travis said firmly. 'There's been too much bad blood between Brenton and me.'

He escaped, breathing out hard in his exasperation and relief. As he headed down the corridor his cellphone shrilled. It was Pete, his agent.

'I suppose they've been onto you too?' Travis demanded.

'Denzil called me as soon as you'd gone,' Pete said. 'Apart from anything else, he's cross because you won't come to the dinner tonight.'

'And I told him the answer's still no,' Travis groaned.

There was to be a celebration dinner for Frank Brenton's sixtieth birthday. He was a studio big shot who'd invested a lot of money in the past and it was hoped he would put in more. Hence the big party.

'He can't stand me and I can't stand him,' Travis said. 'He pulled every string he could find to stop me being cast in the show, and he hates my guts because he failed. Best if we don't meet.'

'OK, OK. I told Denzil I'd raise it. But about the other thing, he just wants to be sure you understood the message.'

'But why have I got to be the only virtuous guy in Los Angeles?' Travis growled.

'Because it makes you different, and that difference puts a couple of extra noughts on the cheque. You haven't suddenly stopped caring for money and success, have you?'

'No way.'

'Then get a grip.'

'Am I supposed to live a totally moral life?' Travis demanded, aghast.

'No, I know you too well for that. But keep the fun stuff behind closed doors. In public, be seen only with ladies of impeccable morality. If they decided to replace you—well, there are several other actors just slavering to grab that part from you.'

He hung up, leaving Travis scowling at the dead phone.

'Grr!' he said.

He knew that both Pete and Denzil were right. Carelessly indulgent behaviour could imperil his career, and that was the last thing he wanted. He enjoyed the benefits of stardom too much. But what to do about it was a problem. The 're-spectable' road definitely did not attract him.

But he couldn't say that openly without risking everything that mattered to him: his career, his reputation, his pride, the money that was pouring in. That money told the tale of a successful man; not just to himself, but to others whose respect he cared for more than he wanted to admit.

'They think it's so easy,' he mused. 'If I *play* a guy who

can soar above human temptations then I can be like that in real life. As if! All right, I was a bit careless with that girl in the nightclub, and I very nearly... But I didn't! It took a lot of self-control, but I didn't.

'If I was really a heavenly being, I could solve the problem in an instant. I'd turn the next corner and find the perfect solution just waiting for me. But in real life that kind of miracle doesn't happen. Ah well! Time to get to work. With luck, I might even get in touch with my virtuous side.'

He gave a wry laugh.

'Whatever that means.'

Charlene took a deep breath as she neared the studio entrance. It was now or never. In another moment she would get through that door as a member of a party privileged to tour the studio. Or perhaps someone would spot that she was a fraud; that she was here to see Lee Anton, the man with whom she was secretly in love, who had once seemed to love her, and whose feelings she desperately hoped to revive.

A pause in the queue gave her the chance to regard herself in a wall mirror. She'd taken trouble over her appearance and knew she looked as good as possible. Which wasn't very good, she thought sadly. Nature hadn't made her a beauty. Not exactly plain, but not exactly pretty either. Lee had called her 'Nice-looking' and praised her eyes.

'I like dark eyes,' he'd said, 'especially when they sparkle like yours.'

She'd clung to such remarks, and the fact that he sought her company rather than the beauties in the amateur dramatic society where they'd met. He was a professional actor, but back then his engagements were scarce and he'd been on the verge of chucking it in.

To pass the time he'd joined the amateur society, which was where they had met and quickly become attracted to each other. With her, attraction had soon become love, and she reached out to him with nothing held back. He'd responded eagerly, and the nights spent in his arms were the most joyful experiences of her life.

The play had been a triumph. She'd looked forward to the moment when he would ask her to marry him, and thought it had come when he said excitedly, 'Guess what! The most incredible thing—'

'Yes?' she asked breathlessly. Out of sight, she crossed her fingers. Here it came. The proposal.

Lee was almost dancing with joy.

'It's so wonderful!' he squeaked. 'It just shows that if you wait for the right moment—'

'And? *And? And?*'

'There was an American agent in the audience.'

'Wh…what?'

'He wants to take me on. He reckons he could get me a part in *The Man From Heaven*. They're looking for an English actor. Isn't that great? Isn't that the best thing you ever heard?'

'Yes,' she mumbled. 'Oh, yes, great.'

Two days later he'd left for Los Angeles.

'I'll stay in touch,' he'd promised.

And he had—after a fashion. There were emails, texts, the odd phone call, but no invitation for her to follow him. He was slipping away from her, and she couldn't let that happen. She had something urgent to tell him, something that couldn't be told on the phone.

Charlene had arrived three days ago, called him, leaving a message but receiving no response. Texts and emails went unanswered, and now she realised that he'd never given her an address. In the end she'd booked a place on the tour as the only way of seeing him.

She'd looked up the show online and learned the background story, and the role Lee was playing.

Up-and-coming English actor Lee Anton will be mak-
ing his debut as Dr Franklin Baker, newly seconded
to work at the Mercyland Hospital, where he rapidly
becomes the friend and confidant of Brad Harrison,
(played by Travis Falcon) and the only one who sus-
pects his mysterious secret.

That morning she'd bought a newspaper, attracted by the
headline—*HEAVENLY ANTICS, the latest startling story*
from the show everyone's talking about.

But to her disappointment there was only the briefest mention of Lee. Most of the page was taken up by a photograph
of a man sitting with a girl on his lap, his shirt open to the
waist, her hand seductively caressing his bare chest. His face
was only half visible and for a fearful moment she checked
in case it was Lee. But it wasn't and she breathed again. It
was only Travis Falcon.

Whoever he was, she thought, uninterested.

She knew she must be careful. Exposed to the glamorous temptations of Los Angeles, Lee was bound to have indulged himself, and she wouldn't spoil things between them
by harsh judgements. That was in the past. When he'd heard
her news everything would be all right, and only the future
would matter.

But she was glad it wasn't Lee in the picture.

The queue was moving. Then she was inside, following
the others in the guided tour that would end in the special
privilege of being allowed to watch a scene being rehearsed.
She paid only the slightest attention, while all the time her
eyes wandered, seeking Lee.

Inside her head two voices were raging at each other.

He's dumped you. Why don't you face it?

And the other voice.

But he doesn't know about... When you tell him the news
it'll make all the difference.

And then she saw him.

He was down the far end of a corridor, reading something on the wall. She tried to call him but her emotion caused her to choke. Suddenly he turned away and vanished around a corner. She began to run, not looking where she was going until she collided with an obstacle, felt two arms tighten around her and heard a man's voice say, 'Hey, steady there.'

'Let me go. I must catch him.'

Charlene wrenched herself free and ran along the rest of the corridor, turning the corner, then stopping abruptly, backing off, hand to mouth to silence the joyful cry that had been about to burst from her.

Now she could see him again: Lee, half turned away from her, hailing someone just out of sight.

'Where have you been?' he called. 'I've been looking for you. Come here and kiss me.'

The next moment a girl appeared from nowhere, throwing herself into his wide open arms, kissing him again and again between squeals of laughter, crying, 'Oh, darling, it's such wonderful news!'

He was laughing too, kissing her back, saying breathlessly, 'Hey that's right, give me a kiss...and another...and another... Oh, I like that...oh, yes...oh, yes—'

He was lurching backwards under the girl's impact, until they both vanished around a corner. Charlene felt as though her heart had stopped dead. Not just her heart, but the whole world. That had been Lee. No—impossible. Yes—it had been Lee. No—yes—no—yes—*no*!

She turned wildly, knowing she had to get out of here. But her way was blocked by the man who'd been there before and who'd reappeared.

'I'm...I'm sorry—'

He put a friendly hand on her shoulder.

'Don't get upset. That guy's not worth it.'

'I—' She tried to speak normally, but only a choke would come.

'Don't cry,' he advised her.

'I'm not crying,' she said fiercely, although tears were streaming down her cheeks.

He didn't waste time arguing, just took out a clean handkerchief and dabbed her face gently.

'People kiss each other all the time,' he said. 'It doesn't mean anything, not in this place. Kissing is just like saying hello.'

She knew that what she'd seen was far more than that, but he was trying to be kind, and she forced herself to be calm.

'Yes—yes—thank you. I'll stop bothering you now—'

'You're not bothering me. I just don't like to see you upset. Do you know him?'

'I thought I did—I mean, yes—no—'

He nodded, as though fully comprehending her confusion.

'I can't say I like him much myself,' he admitted. 'Are you one of his fans? You sound English. Did you follow him here?'

'No!' she said fiercely. 'Of course I didn't. What a thing to say!'

'Sorry, sorry. No offence. So you haven't lost your heart to him?'

'*No!*' she said violently. 'That would be just silly—mooning over a pretty face just because he's an actor.'

'It has been known,' he murmured wryly. 'But if you haven't, that's good. This is no place for people with hearts. What's your name?'

'Charlene Wilkins. Who are you?'

She sensed, rather than saw, a tremor of surprise go through him. 'What did you say?'

'I just asked your name. Have I seen you before somewhere?'

'Evidently not. My name's Travis Falcon. I work here.'

'Oh, yes—you're in the show, aren't you?'

His lips twitched with something that might have been amusement. 'That's one way of putting it. Now, let's get out of here. We've got time for a coffee before I start work.'

'No, I'm fine…fine—honestly—'

It was a lie. Appalled, she could feel herself on the verge of hysterics as the truth crashed in on her.

'Come on,' he said firmly. 'I'm not leaving you on your own in a strange place. Not given the state you're in.'

But to be alone was what she needed in case the screams rising within her broke out. When he reached for her she flailed madly to fend him off, and the next moment she heard a loud crack as her hand made contact with his face.

The sound was shocking and the way he rubbed his cheek told its own story. Charlene backed away, hands over her mouth, eyes wide with horror. But, incredibly, he wasn't offended.

'Hey, it's not that bad,' Travis said. 'No big deal.'

'It is. Oh, heavens, I hit you really hard. I didn't mean to— I'm sorry—'

'You will be if you don't let me buy you a coffee. Come on, no more arguments or I'll get tough.'

His tone was light but he held her arm in a no-nonsense grip. Nor could she have defied him now. All the strength seemed to have drained out of her. The next thing she knew, she was sitting at a table in the corner of the studio canteen.

'I'm going to the counter,' he said. 'Don't even think of escaping while I'm gone, or I'll get mad.' He gave her a kindly smile. 'I can be very nasty when I'm mad.'

He left her and she sat there, without the strength to move. She felt herself sagging everywhere—body, mind and heart. How had she been such a fool as to let it come to this? Plain, sensible Charlene, famed for her common sense! And she'd gone down like a row of ninepins.

Travis Falcon. Now she recalled that he was the star of the show. He didn't act like a star, proud and pompous. He hadn't been offended when she'd failed to recognise him, or even when she'd accidentally struck him. More like a nice guy than a star.

She dived into her bag and pulled out the newspaper with the picture of the man in the nightclub. As she opened it another picture fell out. It had been taken on a stage and showed a young man and a girl in nineteenth-century costumes, fervently clinging to each other. She took it with her everywhere.

'Here we are.' Travis's voice made her jump as he appeared with coffee and rolls. 'It's good to see you calmer. I was getting worried.'

'I'm really sorry about your face,' she said. 'I didn't mean to hit you.'

'I know you didn't.'

'It's not swelling, is it?' she asked, searching his face. 'If I've damaged you the studio will probably sue me.'

'Hey, do you think I'm some sort of a wimp to be so easily hurt? You're not the first girl to— Yeah, well, never mind that. Anyway, we're only rehearsing today, not shooting, so if you've disfigured me it won't matter until tomorrow.'

His comic self-deprecation was attractive, and her nerves eased enough to manage a shaky laugh, which made him regard her with approval.

'That's better. Now, let's talk. How do you come to be here? I suppose you were looking for Lee?' She nodded and he said, 'Perhaps you should have warned him you were coming?'

'But I did, only…he doesn't seem to be getting his messages the last few days.'

Travis judged it best to maintain a tactful silence. He'd known Lee for only a few weeks and disliked him. Selfish, self-centred, indifferent to everyone else was how he would have described him. In the short time Lee had been in Los

Angeles he'd raised the roof with his 'girly antics' as they
had become known.

But he wouldn't say this to the young woman sitting beside him. There was no need. Clearly she was discovering
it for herself.

'Do you know him well?' he asked.

'We've acted together.'

'You're an actress?'

'Not professionally. I work in a bank, but I do a lot of amateur acting. That's how I met Lee.'

'Hey, now I remember. There was a story in the papers—
he hadn't had a job in a while, so he did some amateur stuff
and an agent saw him.'

'That's right.' Charlene showed him the photograph.
'That's us.'

'What was the play?'

'A Midsummer Night's Dream.'

He raised his eyebrows. 'Lee played Shakespeare?'

'He was very good,' she said defensively. 'He was
Demetrius, I was Helena.'

And Helena spent most of the play pursuing Demetrius,
begging to know why he no longer loved her. Travis studied
the picture, noticing the passionate adoration in her face and
the impatience in his. How much of it was acting? Not much,
he guessed, drawing on his knowledge of Lee.

He glanced at her. She was tall, with dark, straight hair,
flowing casually over her shoulders. Not a beauty. Not even
pretty in the strictest sense. Her features were regular but
there was a slight touch of severity about her face that might
warn people off, just at first, although it faded when she
smiled, brightening her large dark eyes.

Intriguing, he thought. She didn't flaunt everything on
the surface, but perhaps she might lure a man along a fascinating path of discovery. Or maybe not. Who could say?

But she was exactly the kind of woman he doubted that Lee bothered with for long.

He knew a twinge of pity. He had an uneasy feeling that she was facing heartbreak.

A shadow appeared in the doorway and a woman strode in, looking around frantically.

'Oh, goodness!' Charlene said. 'I got in as part of a studio tour, and that's the leader, looking for me.'

The woman bore down on them, uttering words of concern and disapproval.

'I'm afraid it's my fault,' Travis said at once. 'Charlene is an old friend of mine and when I saw her here I persuaded her to spend the day with me.' He smiled at Charlene. 'You should have told me you were coming and I'd have rolled out the red carpet.'

'I didn't want to be a trouble,' she said, falling into character.

'You're never a trouble to me.' He turned back to the leader. 'You can safely leave her in my care.'

He accompanied the words with his warmest look and the leader melted.

'Oh, well…in that case I'll leave you to it.' She departed, but not before giving him a mystified look over her shoulder.

'You see?' Travis said to Charlene. 'No problem.'

'That was an incredible performance,' she said. 'You really fooled her. Thank you so much. And I won't be a nuisance. I'll go now.'

'No way. You just heard me say you were spending the day with me, so that's what you have to do.' He dropped his voice to a theatrical undertone. 'If you flee my company it looks bad. People will think I'm losing my touch.'

'And we can't have them thinking that,' she agreed.

'Right. Now it's time we went to the rehearsal.'

'We? Am I allowed?'

'You were going to go with the group.'

'Yes, but will they let me in on my own?'

'You won't be on your own. You're my guest, and you can do anything I say.'

He drew her to her feet, then crooked his arm for her to take.

'Time for our entrance,' he said.

CHAPTER TWO

WHEN they entered the rehearsal room the director raised his eyebrows, but a smile from Travis and his arm around Charlene's shoulder evidently answered all questions.

He saw her comfortably seated and flicked open the script. 'Which scene is it this morning?'

'The one where you try to talk Myra out of being in love with Dr. Baker,' the director said, 'and Baker overhears you—if those two would only turn up—ah, Lee, Penny, there you are!'

Charlene stiffened as Lee appeared in the doorway, with the girl she'd seen him with earlier. She turned her head but not quickly enough.

Lee had seen her.

He'd recognised her.

She tried to interpret his stunned look as pleasure. Now he would hurry across the floor to greet her.

But he stayed where he was, confused, troubled. Not delighted.

'Right, Lee,' the director said, 'we'll have a camera on you, to get a reaction shot. Travis, start at, "You should forget Dr Baker."'

They took their places and Travis began.

'You should forget Dr Baker. I know he's incredibly handsome, but looks don't really matter. Try to believe me. A man's face is the least of him.'

'Oh, they do matter, Dr Harrison, truly they do.' Penny sighed. 'He's so attractive that I can't help loving him.'

'But is he generous, affectionate, honest? Will he always put you first?'

'You mean is he dull and reliable?' she challenged.

Dr Harrison took her hands in his and spoke with feeling. 'I promise you, when you come to marry, dull and reliable is the best.'

'Fine,' the director said. 'Lee, you should try to look as though you've just had a terrible shock.'

Which he has, Charlene thought sadly.

The actress called Penny gave Travis a look of laughing camaraderie. '"Dull and reliable is the best,"' she teased. 'You sounded like you believed that nonsense.'

'I'm an actor,' Travis protested. 'I'm supposed to talk nonsense convincingly.' He grinned. 'However little I believe it.'

'Well nobody ever accused you of being dull and reliable. That picture—'

'You didn't see it,' he said hastily. 'There's no picture.'

'If you say so.'

They rehearsed the scene several more times. Never once did Lee look in Charlene's direction, and perhaps Travis realised this too, because when there was a break he went over to him. Charlene couldn't hear what they said but she saw him take Lee's arm and draw him towards her. She noticed, too, the uneasy glance he gave Penny.

As Lee sat down next to her he managed a polite smile, but his words brought a chill to her heart.

'Fancy seeing you again.'

'Why do you sound surprised? I've been sending you texts—'

'My cellphone needs repair. Never mind. It's great to see you again. What are you doing here? Did you come to see Travis? I hear you're an old friend of his. *OK, I'm just coming!'*

The last words were called to Penny, who was standing by the door, signalling him and mouthing a word that looked like *Lunch.*

'Old friend and good friend,' came a voice above Charlene's head. It was Travis, who'd been shamelessly eavesdropping. 'It made my day when you turned up here, Charlene. Now, make it even better and have lunch with me.'

His hand on her arm brooked no resistance. Not that she wanted to resist. She was too grateful to him. Lee gave her a meaningless smile and vanished out of the door with Penny.

There was no doubt that Travis had saved her dignity. All eyes were on them as he escorted her out of the studio, into the corridor, into the elevator, finally the canteen. Heads turned, people stared at him in the company of a girl nobody had seen before.

Charlene struggled to collect her thoughts. Lee's blank manner had told her everything she needed to know. But would that change when he heard her news? She had a terrible fear that it wouldn't.

'Thank you,' she said when they were sitting at the table. 'You saved me from looking a complete fool.'

'Don't call yourself a fool. That's just playing his game. Presentation is all important.'

'It'll take more than presentation to stop me looking pathetic,' she said in a tone of self-contempt. 'I came all this way for a man who isn't interested.'

'But nobody has to know. Smile at me. Let them see us enjoying each other's company. Go on, smile. More. That's better.'

She was aware of the crowded canteen, and even more aware of Lee and Penny sitting together.

Good, she thought defiantly. Now he knew she wasn't desperate for him.

'So you're a financial genius,' he said.

She made a face. 'That's what I used to think, but it seems not.'

'Hey, if you're good with figures then I'm impressed. I'm rubbish at them.'

'But it's possible to be good with figures and rubbish at everything else,' she said quietly. 'It doesn't make you good with people. I thought being good at the job was all I needed to get promoted, but the promotion went to some little doll-face who'd learned the job from me in the first place. When I protested I was told that they relied on me to keep an eye on her.'

'So you'd do the work and she'd get the credit?' Travis said sympathetically.

'And the company car. And the increase in salary. So I told them to forget it.'

'Good for you!'

She gave a brief laugh. 'I wasn't very clever. They offered me a bonus if I'd stay there, look after her and promise to keep quiet about "everything".'

'Meaning your boss and the girl he was sleeping with?'

'Right. I could have had it made, but I lost my temper. I was really violent. They say the building shook when I slammed out.'

'You?' he queried. 'Violent?'

'Well, you've already found that out, haven't you?'

'No, you didn't hit me on purpose. Pure accident. You seem so sedate, I just can't imagine you slamming out.'

He might have added that her clothes, hair and make-up told the same story: austere, severe, sober, stern, unyielding. There was nothing fiery about her. Not on the surface, anyway. But inside he guessed there was something else.

Perhaps Lee had tempted it out into the open, which made it all the more strange that he was avoiding her.

'Well, I'm paying for it,' she said. 'If I'd been clever I'd have driven them to fire me, then claimed unfair dismissal and sued.'

'Admirable, but could you have driven them to fire you?'

'Maybe. People can be tricked into doing what you want.' She smiled. 'I expect you know that.'

'Sometimes,' he conceded. 'But I have a feeling I'm not as good at it as you.'

'Well, I wasn't good at it this time. First I lost my temper, then I realised I shouldn't have, and by then it was too late. I did everything by the virtuous book, but sometimes you can have too much virtue.'

'How true,' he murmured. 'So how did you find the cash to come here?'

'My grandparents paid. They brought me up since my parents died. They're lovely, adventurous people. Right now they're on holiday in Africa, looking for elephants. They said I could go with them but I chose to come here instead.'

'To find Lee?'

'Yes.'

'Where are you staying?'

'The Howley. Why do you shudder? Do you know it?'

'Not the hotel but that part of town. Depressing. I'd get out if I was you, find something better.'

He could have bitten his tongue out for his own tactlessness. Obviously she was making the money last, not knowing how long she would be here.

He took hold of her hand. 'Charlene, listen to me. Don't do anything crazy. It's not—'

'Well, this is nice!'

They both looked at the man who'd appeared just behind Travis. He was middle-aged, bulky, and his smile was a little too broad to be convincing.

'Hello, Denzil,' Travis said. 'Charlene, this is Denzil Raines, my boss.'

'None of that "boss" stuff,' Denzil said jovially. 'We're all friends here. So you're Charlene. I've been hearing about you. Nice to meet you. Hope you're having a good time. Travis, make sure you treat this lady well. All right, all right, I'll leave you two alone now.'

He took himself off, only turning at the last moment to give Travis a thumbs up sign and a beaming grin. Travis gave an inward groan.

'He seems nice,' Charlene observed. 'Is something the matter?'

'Everything's the matter. I'm sorry about that. Denzil is thinking how he can make use of you.'

'Of me? How?'

'The fact is—I've been a bit of an idiot, and if there's a disaster it'll be my own fault.' Caution made him stop there, but then he saw her face, kindly and understanding, as so few faces were in his world, and something drove him on to say, 'I went to a nightclub with some friends, and there was this girl—'

'The one that sat on your lap? Is that how they got the picture?'

He groaned. 'You've seen it? Yes, it was in the newspaper, wasn't it? I'm finished.'

'No, she's a bit blurred. You can sort of vaguely tell what she's up to, and the fact that she's hardly wearing anything, but the only face you can see is yours.'

'Yeah, me cuddling a nearly naked girl,' he groaned. 'Actually, I was fairly tipsy by then and I just sat there and let her…well… And I'm paying for it. I'm supposed to be virtuous in private as well as in front of the cameras.'

'And you're not,' she said sympathetically. 'Not below the waist, anyway.'

'Right,' he said, relieved to find her so mentally in tune.

'Well, I have the answer,' she said. 'The perfect solution to all your problems.'

'Tell me.'

'It's simple. All you have to do is take up residence in a monastery. There, your life will be unassailably righteous, your career will be protected, and the studio profits will be safe.'

He stared. 'You…you…' Then he saw the wicked glint in her eyes and joined in her laughter. 'You evil hussy!' he choked. 'I ought to…oh, but it was a good joke. You really had me scared for a moment.'

'Well, at least you're laughing,' she said.

'Yes, but it's no laughing matter. I could lose so much.'

Travis's phone rang. He answered quickly and seemed on edge.

'Mom, it's all right. Honestly. I can handle it. Stop worrying, I'll call you later.'

He hung up, looking harassed.

'She thinks I'm going to be brought down by scandal,' he said. 'When she was making films nobody could have survived what's happening now.'

'A film actress? Hey, that's it. I thought you reminded me of someone, and now I can see. Julia Franklin.'

Julia Franklin had been a promising film actress some thirty years ago. For a while she'd shone brightly, and her old films were still shown on television.

'That's right,' Travis said. 'She's my mother. You've seen her?'

'One of her films was on television last night, and they're often shown in England. Everyone thought she'd go on to be a big star, but for some reason it didn't happen.'

'That's because she had me. Total disaster.'

'Did your father make her give up acting to be a full-time wife?'

'They weren't married. My father's English, a businessman who's always travelled a lot. Thirty years ago he was in the States to make some deal, met my mother briefly, and I'm the result.

'He was already married to his second wife, his first having chucked him out for playing around. My mother's film career was just taking off but he wanted her to throw it all away and follow him to England. Not for marriage, just to live as his mistress, be there when it suited him and keep quiet when it didn't.'

'I hope she told him what he could do with himself,' Charlene said indignantly.

'I'm proud to say that she did. In fact she did more than say it. If you met him you'd see a tiny little scar on his chin where she…let's say, put her feelings into action.'

'Do you mean *Amos* Falcon?' Charlene said suddenly. 'Hey, you're one of the Falcon dynasty.'

'In a sense,' Travis said so quietly that she barely heard.

'Amos Falcon was in the papers last week,' she went on excitedly, 'and there was a picture with this little scar—'

Travis groaned. 'All right, yes, but please forget it. I shouldn't have told you.'

Charlene began to chuckle. 'The journalist went on about that scar, how the "heroic" Amos Falcon confronted a robber and drove him off, at the cost of injury to himself.'

Travis gave a shout of laughter. 'Robber, my foot! Mom chucked an ashtray at him. She must have been a bit like you, losing your temper and storming out of the bank. She's got her violent side too. I reckon you two would like each other. She really scared my father. Not that he'd ever admit it, but after that things tended to be at a distance.'

'Do you mean you don't see him?'

'We meet occasionally, but we're not close. His second wife booted him out as well and he married a third time. I told Mom once that he ought to have married her—I was very young and naive in those days. She said she'd sooner marry the devil himself, except that the devil wouldn't be nearly so interesting as Amos Falcon.'

'He sounds a colourful character.'

'I believe his business enemies say the same. A falcon is a bird of prey, and he's known for preying on people. But enough about him. I must tell Mom the nice things you said about her. She'll be so thrilled that someone remembers her. What was the film they were showing?'

'Dancing on the Edge,' Charlene remembered.

'That's her,' Travis said at once. 'How often have I heard her say, "If it isn't on the edge, it isn't fun"?'

'She played the hero's sister, the one who was always putting her foot in it, but everyone forgave her because she had that lovely cheeky grin.'

'True. And it's just how it is in real life. She blurts out all sorts of outrageous things, then says "Sorry, honey", and gives you such a smile that you have to forgive her.'

Charlene wondered if he realised that he had the same smile—mischievous, delightfully wicked. He was nice too, courteously paying her as much attention as if she'd been a raving beauty. Not like Lee Anton, she had to admit with an inner sigh.

As if reading her thoughts, Travis said suddenly, 'Why do you bother with him?'

'Maybe because I'm a fool,' she said lightly. 'We got close during the play—all those scenes we had together—'

'But they weren't love scenes,' Travis pointed out. 'Demetrius rejects Helena until the last minute—'

Charlene nodded. 'Saying things like, *I love thee not, therefore pursue me not.* But Helena won't get the message. She follows him saying, *Neglect me, lose me, only give me leave, unworthy as I am, to follow you.* What a twerp she is!'

She gave a grim laugh at herself. 'Listen to me, saying that. Follow him. That's exactly what I did.'

'But Helena won Demetrius in the end,' Travis pointed out.

'Only because someone cast a spell on him. It wasn't true love. It doesn't happen in real life. Oh, look, I'm sorry. I shouldn't be going on like this, making you listen. You've been really nice to me, although I can't think why, considering that I assaulted you.'

He'd been wondering that himself. He had a kind heart and often went out of his way to help people, but he didn't normally linger. Strangely, her clout across his face had been a turning point. Her horror and dismay had aroused his pity, making him want to defend her. He didn't fully understand it, but she ignited his protective instincts in a way that only one other person did. And that other person was his mother.

'I'll get out and stop bothering you—' she hastened to say.

'You're not bothering me.' He took her hand in both his and spoke gently. 'Look, I'll be honest. I have a selfish motive. I don't like Lee. I'm not sure why. There's just something about him that gets up my nose. It'll be a real pleasure to annoy him. You wouldn't be so hard-hearted as to deny me that pleasure, would you?'

It was a performance. The twinkle in his eyes revealed as much, and also the fact that he expected her to share the joke. And why not, she thought, since she gained from it?

'How could I be hard-hearted enough to deny you anything?' she said lightly, matching his theatrical fervour with her own.

He brushed his lips against her hand. 'That's good,' he murmured, 'because Lee's watching. No, don't turn your head. Just look at me. Try to seem entranced.'

She sighed, throwing back her head and giving him a glance of adoration, plus a brilliant smile.

'Well done,' Travis said. 'That'll teach him.'

'If he saw.'

'He did. He edged just closer enough to see everything. Trust me, I'm directing this production. Am I doing a good job?'

'They should give you an award,' she assured him, and he grinned. 'Is he still watching?' she asked.

'I'm afraid not. He's concentrating on Penny, which makes sense because she's the female star of the show.'

'And she can do him a lot of good,' Charlene mused.

So Lee's interest in Penny was mostly professional. She would cling to that thought.

Travis read her mind and burst out, 'Forget him. He can't matter that much.'

'He does,' she said softly. 'But I can't talk about it.'

'All right, I won't press you. We'll talk some more tonight, over dinner.'

'I can't promise that—'

'You mean you want to stay free for him. But he's engaged this evening. He's got to go to this ghastly dinner they're giving for Frank Brenton. He and I can't stand each other so I won't be— *Wait a minute!*' He slapped his hand to his forehead. 'What am I thinking of? It's been staring me in the face all the time.'

'What is?'

He didn't answer but grasped her hand, looking round and calling, *'Denzil!'*

Denzil had appeared in the doorway and Travis hailed him loudly. He came straight over. Charlene felt Travis tighten his grip on her hand, urging her to say nothing.

'What's up with you suddenly?' Denzil asked, sitting down.

'I've been thinking about tonight, and maybe I was a little unreasonable. I'd like to attend that dinner after all, if they can accommodate me at the last moment.'

Denzil beamed. 'I don't think there'll be any problem about that,' he said.

'Fine, I'll want a table for two. Charlene will be my guest.'

Denzil nodded slowly, as though something had just become clear to him.

'Leave it to me. I'll fix it.' He vanished.

'So that's settled,' Travis said. 'Lee will be there tonight, so dress up to the nines. Let him know what he's missing.'

Her head was in a spin. Travis was making everything happen so fast, it was like being taken over by a whirling dervish. But a kindly dervish.

'It's nice of you to take so much trouble for me—' she began.

But he shook his head firmly. 'Let's be clear about this. I'm not being nice. I'm doing it for myself. You'll make me look respectable and that'll get them off my back. That's why I strong-armed you into it without asking your opinion first. Sheer bullying to get what I want. So don't praise me. I'm just being selfish.'

She regarded him fondly. 'So you're being selfish?'

'Horribly selfish.' There was a twinkling devil in his eyes. 'I don't know how you can stand me for a moment.'

'Neither do I,' she agreed. 'In fact, all I can say is—' she paused for dramatic effect '—if that's your idea of being selfish, I wish there were more selfish people in the world.'

'So you'll come?'

'Just try to stop me.'

'Fine, then it's time for you to go back to your hotel and prepare for tonight. Rick, my driver, will take you.'

A quick phone call to summon the car, then he escorted her out to where it was waiting with Rick behind the wheel. He was an elderly man with a good-natured face.

'Rick, this is Miss Wilkins, who'll be coming to the Brenton dinner with me tonight.'

Rick was astounded. 'But you said—'

'Never mind that. Things have changed. I want you to take her to her hotel now, and return there for her tonight. See you both later.'

He waved and stepped back as the car headed out into the traffic.

'Did I hear him right?' Rick called over his shoulder. 'The Brenton dinner?'

'Yes, what's the big deal? I know he'd planned not to go—'

'You can say that again. Travis gets on well with most people, but not that one. Brenton tried to ruin his big chance.'

'How?'

'His son's an agent, and he had his own candidate for the role. Brenton did all he could to talk the studio bosses out of giving it to Travis. He failed, so then he set out to get him fired. Spreading rumours, bad stories in the press. Didn't work. Since then it's been armed truce. Nobody expected Travis to go tonight. But now he's going so that he can take you. Lady, you must be really something!'

The habit of years made her begin modestly, 'Oh, I don't think I'm—' But then her courage rose. 'As long as he thinks so, that's all that matters.'

'You said it!'

Charlene leaned back against the upholstery. Suddenly she was enjoying this, despite everything.

Rick delivered her to the hotel, waited while she collected her key, smiled and departed. She knew he'd regarded the surroundings with surprise. It was the kind of hotel described as 'budget', which meant that she had a dormitory room, shared with two other women. It wasn't ideal, but the place was clean and efficient, and she could connect her laptop to the Internet. This she did as soon as she arrived, looking up Travis Falcon, and growing more wide-eyed the more she learned of him.

The basics she already knew. He was the son of Julia Franklin and Amos Falcon of the international Falcon dynasty. But now she learned that he'd started his career on the stage, graduated to tiny roles in films before being pounced on by the studio and cast in the series.

There were hints that his private life was colourful. He was a playboy who never seemed to stay with one girlfriend for long. He indulged in flirtations, not love. But until now his liveliness had stayed within acceptable bounds. The night-club picture marked the start of a new phase, and Charlene could see why his bosses were concerned.

Studying the photographs, she had to admit that he was the handsomest man she'd ever seen. And the most charming. It wasn't a matter of looks. His face had a magical 'something' that spoke of a lust for life, a readiness to dive in anywhere and try anything. He was filled with humour, sometimes bawdy, sometimes cheeky.

Actually, she mused, *the man from heaven can be a bit of a devil. Good for him!*

She remembered how he'd treated her that afternoon— kindly, gently, with warmth and understanding, and she thought she could see those things in his face. Most people would have missed them, she reckoned, but she knew better.

All right, he was making use of her. But in a way she was making use of him. It was a fair bargain. Now it was time to prepare for the evening in such a way that she would be a credit both to herself and Travis.

I ought to be grateful, she thought. *Lee's turned his back on me—*

But the next moment she clasped her hand across her stomach, still slim despite her suspicions.

But things may change, she told herself. *I won't know anything until I've told him.*

She refused to believe that he could have dumped her completely after what they had shared. There was still hope.

CHAPTER THREE

A QUICK visit to a nearby hairdresser and her dark locks were transformed, becoming curled and lush. The blue satin dress was elegant, closely fitting a slender figure that many women would have envied.

And yet there was something missing. Honesty forced Charlene to admit that. Whatever the magical 'extra' was, she knew she didn't have it. She looked pleasant, but not special.

Nor could she recall ever being really special to anyone in her life. Even her mother.

Her father had been mostly absent, more absorbed by his work than his family. He'd died when she was five, and her mother had remarried a year later. She and Mark, her step-father, had been reasonably affectionate in an undemonstrative sort of way, but she'd sensed even then that they meant more to each other than she did to either of them. Mark had a son, James, by a previous marriage, who lived with his mother. Mark had been immensely proud of him, often speaking of him in a way that made Charlene feel that she herself didn't really exist. Even her mother, anxious to please her husband, had sometimes seemed to value James more than her own daughter.

Once she'd overheard them discussing the idea of another baby.

'It would be nice to have a daughter,' Mark had remarked.

'We've got Charlene,' her mother had pointed out.

'Yes, but—you know what I mean. A real daughter—ours.'

She had crept hastily away and never mentioned what she had heard. The casually unkind words, *a real daughter*, haunted her ever after.

When she was fifteen they had taken a holiday together. Just the two of them.

'Can't I come?' Charlene had pleaded.

'Darling, it's our anniversary,' her mother had said. 'Mark and I need to be alone. You can understand that, can't you?'

Of course she could understand. She'd always understood why she wasn't a priority.

So they had gone without her, and never returned. Everyone said how lucky it was that she hadn't been on the plane when it crashed, but haunting her grief was the knowledge that she hadn't been wanted.

Her mother's parents had taken her in. They had no other children or grandchildren, and they consoled themselves by lavishing affection on Charlene. In their warmth she blossomed, and much of the pain was eased. She had two people to love, and she knew that they loved her.

But the knowledge of having been second best never quite left her. Her stepbrother was never in touch, which made her sad because it would have been nice to have a big brother.

She'd come to understand that she was moderate in all things: moderate-looking, nothing special; moderately talented, with skills that were efficient rather than glamorous. Her bank employers praised her with the words, 'We need good back-room staff.' And she felt that this was where she belonged. In the back room—of work, of life, of love, of everything. The spotlight was for others.

She had boyfriends, but none seemed to last long. The one she'd cared for most had turned out to be using her to get close to her best friend. Charlene had been a bridesmaid at their wedding, which had seemed to her to be a gloomy portent for the future.

Always the bridesmaid, never the bride, she'd thought, gazing at her reflection on the day.

But on the stage it was different. In the spotlight another side of her came to life, and she revelled in it. Her scenes with Lee had inspired the producer to say, 'You two really make something fizz between you. Keep going.'

And something had happened, something that continued when they'd left the stage, that took them into each other's arms, then into the same bed. It was her first experience of passion, and she rejoiced.

Lee hadn't rejoiced. He'd been troubled.

'Look, I'm sorry,' he'd said hastily. 'I didn't know you weren't…that you hadn't…I mean…'

'I guess I was waiting for you,' she'd said softly, but that had seemed to trouble him even more.

She'd thought how nice he was to be concerned for her. The other thought, that he simply hated responsibility, was one she avoided.

But soon it would have to be faced. This afternoon he'd seen her at her dullest. Tonight she would present a face that reminded him of another time. And they would talk.

Her two room-mates, both pleasant young women, applauded her appearance.

'Got a decent guy escorting you?' one of them asked.

'Travis Falcon.'

They whistled, as though impressed. But in the mirror she caught the look they exchanged, which said plainly that she was fantasising. Nobody who had to stay in this run-down hotel could ever attract such a glamorous escort.

She didn't really blame them for not believing her. She barely believed it herself. Perhaps it really was a fantasy, and Travis would fail to turn up, leaving her abandoned.

In fact he was downstairs at that moment, looking around

with horrified eyes. It was as bad as Rick had warned him. He hastened upstairs and knocked on her door.

It was opened by a young woman whose face registered total astonishment at the sight of him.

'Is Charlene here?' he asked.

'Yes, she… Hey, Charlene—' She turned back to Travis. 'Are you really…really…?' She seemed about to faint.

'Yes, really,' he assured her, stepping into the room and offering Charlene his arm. 'Shall we go, my lady?'

To his delight, she slipped into the role easily, taking his arm and declaring, 'Thank you, kind sir.'

From the way the other two stared at them it was clear that Charlene's standing had rocketed. They came out into the corridor and followed the couple with longing eyes until they had vanished. Then they threw themselves into each other's arms and screamed.

Charlene tried, unsuccessfully, to control her mirth.

'Glad you find it funny,' Travis said as they settled into the back seats of the car.

'It's myself I'm laughing at, not you.' She chuckled. 'Did you see their faces? A woman who can claim Travis Falcon as an escort is a woman to be reckoned with.'

'Even if she's poor enough to stay in this neighbourhood,' he said. 'You should have something better. Bad characters hang out here, and they'll be very interested in that bracelet you're wearing. Did Lee give it to you? If so, I commend his taste.'

'No, it belongs to my grandmother.'

'Are you wearing anything from him?'

She shook her head. There had been no gifts from Lee.

'Then put this on,' he said, holding up a necklace.

Even in the dim light of the car she could see that it was a glorious, expensive piece. She felt in a daze as he fixed it around her neck, his fingers touching her softly. She was going to a glamorous occasion, escorted by the most handsome man she'd ever seen, and she was determined to enjoy it. Whatever the future held, she would make the most of tonight.

She had only the vaguest notion of their destination, and her eyes widened as they reached Sunset Boulevard, in the heart of the most glamorous part of a glamorous city.

'Where is this dinner being held?' she asked.

'At the Stollway Hotel.'

Her jaw dropped. The Stollway was among the most lush, lavish and expensive places in town. Next moment, they were nearing the entrance and she could see the flashing lights, the cars crowding in to disgorge gorgeously dressed men and women onto the broad red carpet.

'I had no idea it would be like this,' she gasped.

'The PR department has made the most of it,' Travis said.

'But I thought it would just be a restaurant. This place is so big and...that crowd...it's like a premier.'

'Good. So there'll be a lot of people to see the story we're trying to tell them. They'll know that you don't need Lee Anton, because you can have any guy you want, just by snapping your fingers. And they'll see that I only like nice girls.'

While she struggled for words, his face softened, his eyes became pleading.

'I guess I wasn't quite straight with you. I should have told you everything but I was afraid you'd say no, and I really need to do this. You can get me out of trouble as nobody else can.'

She remembered how he'd cast his protective mantle over her that afternoon. But for that, she'd be back in the hotel now, fighting back tears of rejection.

'But do you think I'm up to it?' she said. 'It's so scary.'

'We'll do it together. Don't be afraid. Just smile and make it look as though it was the most natural thing in the world to you, and you love every minute.'

He put his hands on either side of her face, looking deep into her eyes. 'Give the performance I know you can give.'

Suddenly she was inspired. There was a time for ducking out and a time for making the most of things, and this was definitely the second.

'As long as you're there, giving me directions,' she said. 'Let's do it.'

'That's the spirit. I knew I could rely on you. Now, here comes our grand entrance.'

The car stopped. Cheers erupted from the crowd as they saw Travis emerge, smiling, waving, then reaching in for her. She took his hand and he drew her out into the spotlight.

He was playing his part perfectly, leading her slowly along the carpet so that everyone could get a good view of her quiet, restrained appearance. A gentle tug on her hand and he drew her around to the other side, just in case there was anyone who hadn't seen how modest and ladylike she was.

Charlene smiled, turned to meet his eyes, and almost gasped at the adoring look he was giving her. If she hadn't known better, she could almost have believed him about to fall on his knees and worship her.

What an actor! she thought.

He drew her hand to his lips and the cheers rose around them. She lowered her eyes, apparently overcome, and felt him draw her close.

'Well done,' he murmured in her ear. 'Keep it up.'

As they approached the huge main doors there was a flicker of interest from behind them. Turning, they saw another car arrive, the door open and Lee emerge, accompanied by Penny. Their arrival caused a small commotion but nothing like the agitation that had greeted Travis. As they danced along the carpet three photographers dashed out to get closer shots.

Lee turned his head, laughing, preening in the spotlight. But his smile died as the photographers passed him by to surround Travis and Charlene. She had a brief glimpse of Lee's face, aghast, astounded, chagrined. Then Travis swept her into the building.

Inside, there was more of the same as they made their way to the huge restaurant at the back of the hotel. It was called Aladdin's Cave, and decorated with a magical theme. Brightly coloured lanterns hung from the ceiling, elaborate pictures decorated the walls and everywhere there was the glitter of gold.

They were escorted to a table for two, where he settled her with every attention and said, 'Let's have something to drink.'

'Orange juice for me, please.'

'This is an evening for champagne,' he protested.

'Orange juice,' she said firmly. 'Or sparkling water.'

He was silent a moment, but then nodded and made the order. He asked no further questions, but she had a sense that he understood why she wouldn't touch alcohol.

Denzil bustled over, rubbing his hands with delight, paid Charlene extravagant compliments and then bustled away. People were arriving slowly, waving at Travis, looking curiously at Charlene before flaunting themselves before each other, all putting on performances. For the moment it was still quiet enough to talk.

'You've saved my neck, you know that?' Travis said. 'All those pictures they took of us outside. I have a career again.'

'Just like that?'

'It can happen that way in this city. Here today, gone tomorrow, back again the day after.'

'Don't you ever find the life exhausting?'

'Well, I do end up living on edge a lot of the time, but it can feel worth it.'

'I suppose success is wonderful.'

'Yes. Not that I've been a success long enough to know very much. But it matters to me to achieve everything I can, just to stop my father disowning me.'

'But surely you don't need him? You're independent.'

'I meant disowning me in spirit.' Travis gave a brief laugh. 'It's odd isn't it? I disapprove of Amos, sometimes I even dislike him. But I still hate the feeling that I'm the one on the outside of the family. He despises me for not being like him, the way my brothers are.'

'All of them?'

'Mostly. Darius is a big man in finance, just like Amos. He's been hit by the credit crunch, and now he's living on Herringdean, an island off the south coast of England that one of his debtors used to pay him off. He started out hating it, but he came to love it. Falling in love with a local girl helped. I was at their wedding a few weeks ago and if ever two people were crazy about each other it's those two.'

'You sound as though you envy them.'

'In a way I do. It's nice to know your final destination, and be able to reach it. Darius has been married before and it didn't work out, but he's safe with Harriet. Plus his first wife likes her, even encouraged them to marry because their two children like her as well.'

Charlene recalled him talking about his father and all the children Amos had by different women. His brother's arrangement sounded so much happier that she began to understand the touch of wistfulness in his voice.

He can't really be jealous, she thought. *An ordinary domestic set-up. Many people would call it boring, but the great star actually wishes...no, that's just the sort of thing he'd say in interviews. I'm imagining things. Shut up, Charlie.*

'What did you say?' Travis asked, staring at her suddenly.

'Nothing.'

'I thought you whispered, "Shut up, Charlie".'

'Did I say that out loud? Oh, heck!'

'You actually call yourself Charlie?'

'When I'm trying to remember to be sensible. It's not easy in a place like LA. Common sense seems the last thing you can manage, and actually the last thing you want.'

'I know the feeling,' he said wryly.

'So your brother's settled for common sense?'

'That's not what Darius calls it. To him it's finding out what his life is really all about.'

'And it's not just about money?'

'Not any more. It was once but that was his "Amos" side. Now he's found something else and the Amos side is having to stand back.'

'I'll bet Amos doesn't like that.'

'Too right. He tried to stop their marriage, but failed. Mind you, Darius will climb to the financial top again. It's in the Falcon genes. Marcel is like Amos too, except for being half French. He makes his money from hotels. He's got a big, glamorous place in Paris and he's recently bought another one in London to "extend his empire". Amos loves that. To him, that's how a Falcon should think, in terms of empire.'

'Perhaps you need to play a Roman emperor,' Charlene mused. 'How about Julius Caesar?'

'Better still, Nero,' he said, catching her mood. 'Or Caligula.'

'But Nero was a tyrant,' Charlene objected.

'Great. That makes him a true Falcon.'

'And Caligula was mad. Wouldn't your father hate that?'

'Not if it made money.'

They laughed together.

'Haven't you got two other brothers?'

'Yes, there's Leonid, who's Russian and lives in Moscow. We don't know a lot about him, but he must be successful because Amos always speaks of him with respect. Jackson's different. He's a naturalist. He's written books and has a television series about wildlife all over the world.'

'That doesn't sound like it makes him a millionaire.'

'No, he's not. But Amos respects him, nonetheless, because the world knows him as a "serious man" doing a "serious job". I just "flaunt myself for the press", but Jackson "defends the environment" and that elevates the name Falcon, even if not in business.

'He actually told me once that I should change my name because he didn't want to be connected with someone "prancing around for the cameras".'

'Your father doesn't want you to be called after him?' she asked, aghast.

'He despises what I do. He was furious when I wouldn't take a different name.'

'No wonder you feel shut out,' she said sympathetically.

'Not by the others. I get on fine with my brothers, what little I see of them. But I think Amos is just hanging on in the hope that one day I'll change into a mini-Amos.'

'You could always act it,' she suggested.

'Not if I want to stay sane,' he said hastily. 'This way, at least I know who I am. Or I would, if people didn't keep wanting me to put on a performance in private as well as in front of the cameras.'

'You poor soul.' She sighed. 'The burdens of fame. Just think of all those unemployed actors out there who must be so grateful they don't have your problems.'

He scowled for a moment, but then relaxed and squeezed her hand, smiling ruefully.

'Yeah, right. I must be coming across as a bit of a wimp, eh? It's your fault. You're such a tempting, sympathetic shoulder to cry on that I gave in. But no more.' His voice deepened and he assumed a haughty mien. 'From now on, just macho authority and stern resolve.'

'Ouch, please, no!' she said. 'I can't stand men like that.'

'Neither can I,' he admitted. 'Perish the thought that I should ever be one of them.'

'Nothing could be less likely,' she reassured him.

He met her eyes in a look of total understanding, and suddenly she had the strangest feeling of having known him all her life. It made no sense but instinctively she was his friend, and she sensed him becoming her friend.

'You see right through me, don't you?' he said, amused.

'I guess I do. Do you mind?'

'Not a bit. Know what? I think we're going to get on really well.'

'Me too. Here's to a great evening.'

They raised their glasses, and were about to clink when a voice cut in between them like a knife.

'Well, well! Look who's here.'

Looking up, Charlene saw a tall, hard-faced, middle-aged man, regarding them coldly. She heard Travis groan, then say, 'Charlene, this is Frank Brenton. Brenton, this is Miss Charlene Wilkins.'

Brenton flickered cool, angry eyes over her, nodded, then spoke to Travis in a rough voice. 'Some people have a gift for escaping from awkward situations. I congratulate you. You got away with it this time, but there'll be others. That's guaranteed.'

'Nothing's guaranteed,' Travis said.

'I think you'll find you're wrong. You go about inviting trouble, Travis, and such an invitation always gets accepted.'

There was frank dislike in his eyes. His glance at Charlene was almost insulting, and an incredible suspicion came to her, making her temper flare.

She slipped her arm about Travis's neck, leaning her head against him.

'You never know what life holds next,' she said sweetly. 'Of course, some people think they do, but then they get taken by surprise.'

'Oh, I don't think I'm going to be surprised.'

She met his eyes. 'Nobody ever does until it happens.'

'Perhaps you'll be the one surprised.'

She shook her head. 'That won't happen, because I believe the worst of people.' She fixed him with a hard, steady gaze before saying, 'The very worst, more than most people would ever dream of, because I have a nasty, suspicious nature. But, like you say, we'll just have to wait and see.'

Brenton seemed on the verge of answering, but then he thought better of it, scowled and walked away.

Travis stared at her in astonishment. 'What the blue blazes was that all about?'

'You don't know? You haven't guessed?' she asked regarding him wryly.

'Did you just do what I thought you did? You drove the enemy off and now he's taking cover.'

'I think he might be more the enemy than you realised. That girl in the night club; did she really just appear out of nowhere?'

'Well, yes, it was a stag night and… Hey, what…are you saying—?'

'That he fixed it? I don't know. But it's possible, isn't it? He knew you'd be there, it would have been easy for him to arrange.'

'You mean he—?'

'First the girl, then the photographer. Was it just chance that they appeared? Didn't you ever wonder?'

He shook his head. 'I just thought it was one of those things,' he said.

'Travis, wake up! You live in the middle of this city, where people must be playing tricks on each other all the time. You're far too trusting. Now I've met him, I can see that he's exactly the kind of man who'd do that.'

'All in five minutes? You saw it and I didn't.' His shoulders sagged. 'And I think of myself as worldly wise.'

He sounded depressed and she smiled at him fondly. There was something about Travis that was the complete opposite of worldly wise, and which drew her towards him. He was, as he'd said, too trusting. In this sophisticated city, that part of him was dangerously vulnerable.

'Thank goodness for you,' he said. 'What would I do without you?'

'For the moment you don't have to. You've got a big sister keeping an eye out for you.'

He grinned and squeezed her hand. 'I'd offer to be your big brother, but I guess I'd keep tripping over things and making a mess of it.'

'Big brother sounds nice. I'll watch out to see you don't trip up too much. Hey, look at him now.'

Together they watched the long table at the head of the room. It was slightly raised, making it easy to see Brenton taking his place. People were waiting for him, including a man with a similar face.

'Travis, that man who's slapping Brenton on the shoulder—'

'His son.'

'You mean the agent? Rick told me about them.'

'That's right. And the guy with them is the actor Brenton wanted to see cast instead of me.'

'There's a faint likeness. He's not Brenton's son as well, is he?'

'Not officially, but there are rumours. I guess they're probably true.'

'So that's why they're so determined to discredit you. You watch out. He as good as said that he'll try something else. Just don't make it easy for them.'

'No, I won't—now I can see it—'

He rubbed his eyes, then looked at her again closely and spoke in a voice of awed discovery. 'I'm beginning to think meeting you was the best thing that's ever happened to me.'

CHAPTER FOUR

Travis rubbed his eyes again. 'I guess you just never know what's around the corner, and… Charlene?'

But he'd lost her attention. Her gaze was fixed on the far side of the room where Lee was entering with Penny on his arm. They were smiling at the world and at each other, looking around the room, then back to each other. A photographer positioned himself before them and they twisted and turned as expected, before making their way to their table.

Travis observed Charlene, noting how she never moved, but sat clasping the stem of her glass with tense fingers. At last she relaxed and looked away. He took her hand in his and squeezed it gently. She squeezed back. There was no need to say anything.

The evening began. A lavish banquet was served to the long table up high at the end of the room and the twenty smaller tables spread out around the room. As she ate the delicious food Charlene wondered what had possessed her to speak as she had done. She'd implied to Travis that she was here for him and only for him, to take care of him and be 'big sister' to his 'big brother'.

But that couldn't happen. She was here for Lee. Soon they would talk, she would tell him her news, they would become a couple and her usefulness to Travis would end.

She searched the room. Lee was sitting with Penny, not

far away but half obscured by other tables. She watched him, willing him to see her. Yes, now his glance had turned her way. But no, now it had turned away again.

'Charlene,' Travis said quietly. 'Are you all right?'

'I'm fine,' she said, smiling at him, giving the performance they had agreed. 'It's going to be a really wonderful evening.'

He'd seen what had happened. He understood what she was doing, and his admiration grew.

As the meal neared its end people rose and drifted from table to table.

'Come on,' Travis said, taking her hand and drawing her across the floor, calling, 'Lee, good to see you here. And Penny. You look lovely, darling.'

Penny received his kiss with delight, glad to give the show's star her whole attention, leaving Lee no choice but to talk to Charlene.

'Fancy seeing you again,' he said brightly as she sat beside him.

'You speak as though you never expected to see me again,' she said. 'But we weren't going to leave things there, were we?'

'I didn't mean to dash off the way I did. Things just happened suddenly.'

'I know. I'm glad for you. But I had to see you again because…after we were so fond of each other…'

'Yes, we were. I remember that well, but…life moves on. Things are so different now that it wouldn't have been fair for me to try to drag you in, and—'

'But you didn't drag me. I'm here because I wanted to see you.'

'That's sweet of you, but I hate to think how much it must be costing you. This town is so expensive.'

'Well, it is a bit, yes, but—'

Surely he would offer to help her with the cost? She waited for the words.

'Look, Charlene, perhaps—'

'*Yes?*'

'Perhaps you should go home. You can't afford it and I shall worry about you.'

'You don't need to worry about me.'

'Well, I know that really. You were always the strong one, weren't you? Nothing happens that you can't cope with.'

His smile was like a steel mask.

'Lee, I need to talk to you. There's something—'

'*Attention, everybody!*' The cry came from the top table. 'Can you all return to your seats, please? The best part of the evening is about to start.'

Charlene sat still, feeling as though dead weights were dragging her down, until Travis's gentle hands drew her to her feet. He paused to smile back at Penny, saying, 'I'll claim that dance later. Keep it for me.'

'Oh, lovely!' she cried.

Images flickered through Charlene's consciousness. Penny, thrilled by attention from Travis, Lee disgruntled because she was focusing on another man.

At their table, Travis drew out her seat and ushered her into it, as theatrically attentive as a servant. He was doing it for her, she knew. Just as he'd fixed it so that she could talk to Lee, he would fix it again by dancing with Penny. But it would all be for nothing. Lee was embarrassed to see her. He'd made that very plain.

She should never have come here.

Charlene laid her hand softly over her stomach, then moved it away quickly, unaware that Travis was watching her with kindly, troubled eyes.

The speeches began. Denzil Raines praised Brenton to the skies, wished him happy birthday and presented him with a costly gift. More gifts, more speeches. Brenton accepted it all with an evident sense of entitlement. Charlene reckoned this was a man used to getting his own way, who didn't easily give up.

It was time for the dancing. Travis claimed Penny at once, thus freeing Lee to talk to Charlene. But when she approached his table it was empty.

It offended her pride to go searching for him, but pride was something she couldn't afford right now, so she looked around until she saw him deep in conversation with Denzil. There was no way she could interrupt him now, as he must have known. Heavy-hearted, she began to return to her table.

'Got a few minutes to spare for me?'

Brenton was standing there, a grim smile on his face.

'So Travis has dumped you already, has he?' he asked. 'That's what you must expect. He's just making use of you. When you've served your purpose you'll be out.'

'And you know all about using people to serve a purpose, don't you, Mr Brenton. Who do you think you're fooling?'

'And just what does that mean?'

'It means exactly what you're afraid it means. I know what you did. You're not so on top of the situation as you think you are.'

'Everything all right?' That was Travis's voice. The dance had ended and Penny had already gone in search of Lee.

'Everything is wonderfully all right,' Charlene declared. 'Mr Brenton has just made his meaning plain to me, and I've made my meaning plain to him.'

Very deliberately, she stepped closer to Travis and slid her arm around his neck. Her message was plain. Brenton could do his worst. Travis was under her protection now and everyone had better remember that.

Travis reacted on cue, putting his arm around her waist, drawing her close, echoing her message. Brenton made a face and walked away.

'Let's go outside for a while,' Travis said.

'Oh, yes,' she said gratefully. 'Let's get away from here.'

The hotel garden was full of trees hung with lights. As they strolled beneath them, music reached them from a distance.

'I'm not sure exactly what I walked into,' Travis said, 'but I reckon you just sent the enemy packing for the second time tonight. Was he giving you trouble?'

'Not as much as I gave him. He warned me that you'd dump me when I'd served my purpose.'

'I won't get the chance. You'll dump me first. Did you fix things with Lee?'

He sensed her reluctance to answer. 'Not really,' she said. 'We need another meeting.'

'And will that be any different?' he asked ironically. 'No, no, I shouldn't have said that. I'm sorry, *I'm sorry!*'

'Probably not,' she admitted. 'I can't kid myself that he was glad to see me, but I can't leave things as they are.'

'Well, one thing will definitely change. You're not staying in the Howley. You must move in here.'

'I couldn't possibly afford this place,' she protested.

'But I can. You've helped me, and now I'm going to help you. You won't even ask me about the bill.'

'Won't I?'

'No. That's an order. You're moving in here and living like a star. It's the only way to be taken seriously in this town. We'll book your room now, then collect your things from the Howley. That's settled. No argument!'

She surveyed him tenderly. 'So you really can do macho?'

'Well, sometimes—if someone else writes the script. Come on, let's get this sorted.'

A hundred pairs of eyes watched as they left the restaurant, arms about each other's waists. At the reception desk there were more curious eyes to see Travis order the room.

'I want the best suite you have,' he said. 'Make sure it's ready in an hour. And please give this note to my driver, who's in the canteen at the back, so that he'll know I want the car.'

'Are you sure you should be leaving?' she asked as they headed out of the hotel. 'Perhaps you should stay for the rest of the celebration.'

'The things I'm celebrating have nothing to do with this place. And I'm not letting you out of my sight in case you vanish,' he said, looking alarmed. 'You saved me from disaster.'

As if to prove it, Denzil appeared, smiling to see them together, and waved them on their way.

'See what I mean?' Travis said. 'That was the official seal of approval. Ah, there's Rick!'

When they were settled in the car and moving off, Rick said over his shoulder, 'I watched the arrivals on TV. You sure looked good.'

Travis grinned and gave Charlene a thumbs up. She returned the gesture.

At the Howley, Travis accompanied her up to her room, waited while she packed, then picked up her luggage and headed downstairs.

'Oh, no!' she said, in dismay. 'The desk is closed. How can I pay my bill if there's nobody there?'

'You've already paid the bill,' Travis said.

'But how—?'

'Rick saw to it while we were upstairs.'

'But how did he know to—? That note you sent him. You told him to—'

'Let's get out of here,' he said hastily.

'You went behind my back.'

'I didn't want to waste time arguing, and I still don't. Come on, let's go.'

As they went out she said, 'Of course I'll pay it back. How much do I owe you?'

'Just get in the car.'

'How much?'

'Get in the car!'

On the journey back she tried to feel indignant, but it was

impossible. The feeling of being protected was like a draught of magic. Even her sadness about Lee faded before it.

'You know what you are, don't you?' she murmured.

'Something terrible, I guess.'

'A male chauvinist porker!'

He beamed. 'That's the nicest compliment anyone's ever paid me!'

Rick roared with laughter over his shoulder.

They reached the hotel to find that the revelries had ended and the place was quietening down for the night. Travis escorted her to her suite.

It had a luxurious bathroom, a huge bed and vast windows overlooking Sunset Boulevard. Charlene stared, trying, unsuccessfully, to imagine her ordinary self in these palatial surroundings. But she made no protest. Clearly Travis had a plan in mind, and now she must leave everything to him.

She knew that some people would say this was foolish. How could she draw Lee back to her by being seen with Travis?

But in her heart she knew that a few short hours had changed everything between herself and Lee. He hadn't missed her and didn't want her. Only a woman determined to delude herself could think otherwise. He was ambitious, which was one reason for escorting Penny, who was more established and could inspire the interest of the press.

But the really big star was Travis. It was he who made headlines, and the fact that Charlene had apparently secured his interest had made Lee gape with astonishment.

She didn't know what the future held, but having Travis as her champion saved her from humiliation and she would cling to him.

As though he'd read her thoughts, Travis said, 'Don't worry. If Lee comes knocking I'll fade into the background.'

'I wonder if he will,' she mused.

'And if he did, would that make you happy? Do you really want him?'

'Let's say I'm seeing him with new eyes, but…it might be complicated—'

He put his hands on her shoulders. 'Are you pregnant?' he asked quietly.

She looked up and the misery in her face made him catch his breath.

'I don't know for sure,' she said desperately. 'When I was late I did a pregnancy test, and it was positive. But then someone told me that shop-bought pregnancy tests aren't always one hundred per cent accurate so I did another one and that was negative. But I'm still late. Perhaps I should have waited until I was more certain before I came here, but I was so happy, and I thought he might be happy too.'

She choked off into silence. Travis wasted no more words. Instead he drew her close, his arms around her in a warm hug.

'I've got a doctor friend who'll help you,' he said. 'We'll get a definite yes or no. Don't worry. I'll take care of everything. Now, I'm going. Go to bed and get some sleep. I'll call you in the morning.'

He placed a gentle kiss on her cheek, and left.

She went to bed but couldn't sleep. Her thoughts seemed to be fighting each other. One saying that she'd expected better from Lee. The other asking if it was really such a surprise? Hadn't she, in her heart, known that he wouldn't welcome her?

She laid her hands over her stomach, wondering what she should tell him; wondering if there was anything to tell.

Her eyes were closing when a soft knock at the door made them open wide. Throwing on a robe, she hurried to answer, half expecting Travis.

But it was Lee who stood there, looking anxious.

'Are you alone?' he asked.

'Quite alone,' she said, standing back to let him in. 'What else did you expect?'

'Well…he might be with you.'

'He?'

'Travis. They say he never passes up a chance.'

'Well, you're wrong,' she said with a touch of anger. 'I came to Los Angeles to see you.'

'Yes, but after the way he's been haunting you tonight, I thought… Well, you've really got his attention.'

'Lee did you come here to insult me, because—?'

'I'm not insulting you. That guy lives in the spotlight, and if he's interested in you then you've got the spotlight as well. This is LA. These things matter.'

'And you wouldn't mind me sharing his spotlight?' she demanded. 'Even though you and I have some unfinished business?'

'I thought we sorted that out earlier.'

'Then you must think it was very easily sorted. We made love, Lee, and sometimes that can produce results. Have you thought of that?'

The sheer blank horror in his face answered every possible question.

'Are you saying…? You mean you're…? Are you sure?'

'No, I'm not sure. It isn't definite yet.'

'Phew! So things might still be all right.'

'That depends on what you mean by all right.'

'Charlene, I swear I didn't want to leave you in trouble. If the worst comes to the worst I'll help you fix it. There are places where these things can be arranged discreetly.'

'And that would make everything…all right?' she said slowly.

'You won't have any problems, I promise you. Just call me when you know for certain, and we'll do what's necessary. But let's hope for the best. It may be a false alarm.'

Suddenly she couldn't bear the sight of him. Every word he uttered seemed a blow to her heart.

'You'd better leave,' she said. 'Go!'

'Ah, you think he may still turn up? Right. You don't want him to find me here.'

'I didn't say that. I'm not expecting him.'

'Oh, come on! He was good to you. Don't tell me he doesn't want something in return.'

Her eyes blazed. 'Get out before I do something violent.'

He escaped. As the door closed behind him it took all of her self-control not to hurl something at it.

Could he be right? she wondered. Would Travis arrive and demand 'payment', thus proving himself as cynical and self-seeking as every other man?

As the night wore on she tensed at every sound outside her door, waiting for the knock. But it never came, and at last she realised that Travis was better than her fears, better than Lee's spiteful accusations.

Somehow after that it was easier to sleep.

Next morning she rose very early and ordered breakfast through room service. As she was finishing, the phone rang.

'It's me,' said Travis. 'Can I come up or will I be in the way?'

'I'm alone,' she said, correctly interpreting this. 'Do come.'

She was waiting for him with the door open, and shut it quickly behind him.

'I came up the back stairs,' he said. 'Nobody will know I'm here so if Lee…you know…'

'If Lee asks any jealous questions you won't have compromised me,' she said, bitterly amused. 'Don't worry, he won't. And he'd actually be glad you were here.'

'Why would he…? Oh, no, tell me I'm wrong.'

'You'd relieve him of a problem. He was here last night. Not for long. He escaped as soon as he could.'

'You told him about the baby?'

'I told him there might be one. He was horrified. He's probably calling abortion doctors this minute.'

Travis drew in a sharp breath. 'Would you—?'

'No, of course not!' she said passionately. 'Never, *never*! If I'm pregnant I'll have the child, and if its father isn't interested…I'll manage.'

She began to pace the room, clenching and unclenching her hands until he took gentle hold of her.

'Calm down,' he said. 'We've got to find out the truth. We can't do anything until we know one way or the other.'

'You're kind but it's me that's got to do something, not you. I won't drag you into this.'

'I'm already part of this. You "dragged me in" when you socked me on the cheek yesterday.'

'I didn't sock you. It was a light tap and there isn't the slightest mark—'

She stopped. His eyes were full of kindly humour, telling her that he was joking, and she should have realised.

'Just shut up and let me look after you, OK?' he said.

'I don't know what to do next. Perhaps I should go back to England.'

'Before you've established the facts? Surely not.'

'What difference will it make either way if Lee… I don't know… Wait, let me give you this now.'

She took out the expensive necklace he'd loaned her.

'I ought to have given it back to you last night, but there were so many things on my mind—'

'That's all right. I understand.'

'Take it, take it.' She was pushing the necklace into his hands as though desperate to get it out of her possession. It might have been some fearful thing, full of horrific memories, he thought, dismayed.

'All right,' he said, putting the jewels into his pocket. 'Now, let's talk this over calmly.' He drew her to the bed and sat beside her. 'Running away isn't a good idea. I'm not letting you out of my sight until we know what's going to happen. Is there anyone at home for you?'

'No, I live with my grandparents but they're away at the moment.'

'What about other family? Brothers, sisters?'

'Nobody, but that doesn't matter. I'm strong, I can cope. Please don't worry about me.'

He got up and strode to the window, standing with his back to her while he tried to get his head round what was happening. Before him stretched Sunset Boulevard, a glamorous place that seemed to typify the world he took for granted; a world in which presentation was all-important and most things had a price, even if it was often dressed up with tinsel.

Take whatever life offered, give as little as possible in return. That was the conventional wisdom. He'd gained much from Charlene's presence. Now she was obligingly offering to vanish, causing no trouble, asking no favours, even handing back jewellery that many women would have tried to claim. It couldn't be better and a shrewd man would seize what she'd given him, pack her onto the next plane, bless his luck and forget about her.

Travis made a slight turn, glancing over his shoulder at where she still sat on the bed. She wasn't looking at him, just staring blankly into space.

This was how she would cope, he thought; sitting alone in an empty house, looking into the distance. Abandoned by her lover, abandoned by the man who'd called himself her friend and brother.

Common sense demanded that he get rid of her while she was still doing him good and before she could become awkward.

But common sense had never been his strong suit, he thought wryly. Almost everyone who knew him agreed about that.

'So now we have to get moving,' he said, returning to sit beside her. 'Hurry up and pack.'

His businesslike tone sent a faint chill through her. He was dumping her, and she couldn't blame him. But somehow it wasn't what she'd expected.

But she should have expected it, she thought, depressed. Clearly he was as unreliable as Lee!

She pulled herself together. 'Time I was going.'

'No, you're not,' he said firmly. 'You're coming to stay with me.'

'With you—where?'

'In my apartment. Nobody will know you're there and you'll have privacy as long as you want it. And don't give me any more nonsense about how strong you are because every time you say it I believe it less and less. And if you really think I'm the kind of rotten friend who'd abandon you when you need a hand to hold, well—thanks for the insult.'

'I never meant to insult you. I just didn't want to be a burden. I have no claim on you.'

'Except the claim of gratitude. After last night I owe you big-time. Brenton's flaming mad, which is great. It means he knows he's losing the fight and it's due to you. You're my best defence, and there's no way I'm going to let you leave Los Angeles. I'm taking you prisoner. Get used to it. Do as you're told!'

Without warning, she was flooded by tears. Whatever he said, the truth was that he was protecting her out of kindness. The macho words were just a smokescreen.

'Hey, come on,' he said, taking her into a firm hug. 'No need to cry.'

'I'm not crying,' she wept.

'Of course you're not. You're much too strong for that, aren't you?'

In despair, she shook her head.

'I'm going downstairs,' he told her. 'I'll be back in a moment. Don't even think of locking me out, unless, of course, Lee appears, in which case I'll vanish.'

But that wouldn't happen, and they both knew it.

When he'd gone she packed her things, moving mechanically. What happened now was beyond her control. She was in Travis's hands, his dependant, even perhaps his victim.

The thought should have troubled her but it didn't. Stronger than anything was the feeling of having landed safely in the middle of a storm.

CHAPTER FIVE

WHEN Travis returned Charlene was ready with everything packed.

'We have to decide on the PR,' he said. 'It's part of living in Los Angeles. PR gets hard-wired into you. You decide what you're actually doing, and then decide what you want the world to think you're doing. They're not usually the same thing.'

'Right,' she said, in the voice of someone trying to hang in there. 'How do we decide?'

'We must consider whether we want to be seen together. Last night we were, and it was great, but your priority is still Lee, so let's be discreet until that situation is sorted. It's best if nobody sees us leave together, so we'll go down the back stairs.'

'But my bill—'

'That's sorted. Just take my hand.'

It felt inevitable to put her hand in his and feel him clasp it in a firm, comforting grip. Looking back afterwards, she had the feeling that this moment had shone a light on the path ahead. From now on she would go where he led.

Quietly they descended, to find Rick waiting halfway down. He seized her suitcase and hurried ahead. By the time they reached the door he was there with the car. Nobody saw them get inside and settle in the back as the car glided out of the hotel's rear car park into Sunset Boulevard.

It was still early in the day and the sun was rising high. Already the street was busy and she looked out at it with fascination.

'I looked it up online before I came out here,' she said in wonder, 'but nothing really prepares you.'

'That's true. I grew up here but it still makes me think—*get down*!'

Next moment he'd seized her, drawing her close so that her head was against his shoulder, everything about him radiating alarm.

'There was someone I knew,' he said from above her head. 'I don't think they saw your face, but let's keep it hidden and not take chances. Sorry to grab you like that. I hope I didn't hurt you.'

'No, I'm fine,' she managed to say.

She could feel one of his hands on her hair while the other lay gently over her face, just enough to conceal her features from anyone who happened to be close.

'Sorry about this,' he said. 'I'll release you as soon as it's safe.'

'Don't worry. I'm quite comfortable.'

She felt him move so that he leaned down over her, concealing his own face as much as possible.

'Get into the back streets as soon as possible, Rick,' he called.

The next moment the car swung wildly around a corner so that she had to move quickly to cling to Travis.

'OK?' he asked.

'Sure. No worries.'

'Charlene,' he said, as he sensed something amazing, *'are you laughing?'*

'I guess I am.' She chuckled. 'Don't ask me why. It's mad, crazy. Whatever I expected, it wasn't this.'

'Me neither,' he admitted. 'But that's life, isn't it?'

'I guess it's more fun that way.'

'Definitely. And at all costs, let life be fun.'

Now he too was laughing, enfolding her in his arms. She felt his body in her hands, against her own body, and she knew a flash of wisdom. It was lucky she was in no danger of falling in love with him, because otherwise this delicious moment could seriously threaten her common sense.

Luckily she was safe. Quite safe.

She repeated that again. Completely safe.

After a while he said, 'I think we could risk it now,' loosening his grip and easing her up from his shoulder.

'I've made a mess of your hair,' he said, brushing it back.

'And of course my hair is what I'm chiefly concerned about.'

'Well, some girls would be,' he said wryly. 'Never mind. When we get home you can spend the day looking after yourself.'

'Where do you live?'

'Beachwood Canyon, part of the Hollywood Hills.'

Soon she could see the land rising steeply above them, crowned by the famous HOLLYWOOD sign that defined this magical place. Much of Hollywood's activities had now drifted to other parts of the city, but this was where it had all begun. Humphrey Bogart had lived here, also Charlie Chaplin. In this place was enshrined much of the city's glamorous history, especially in the part known as Beachwood Canyon.

As they climbed higher and higher, Charlene gazed out of the window, riveted. Soon they were driving along a street lined with palm trees, until they came in sight of a three-storey block.

'I'm on the top floor,' he said.

His cellphone rang and he answered it impatiently. 'Yes, I'm on my way—something came up—I'll call you back.'

'Am I making you late for work?' she asked anxiously.

'Don't worry about it. I'll show you in and then dash off.'

Luck favoured them in the elevator ride to the top, and they entered his home without being seen.

'I've got to go now,' he said at once. 'The spare bedroom's over there. Make yourself at home. Raid the fridge. The place is yours. Here's my phone number. Call me if anything worries you.'

'I can't call you while you're working,' she said, aghast. 'What would your bosses say?'

'Nothing. The only thing that upsets them is if I damage my public image. But if I behave like a spoilt brat on-set it's just dismissed as part of my "great star" personality.'

The wicked gleam in his eyes robbed the words of conceit. To him it was all a joke, she realised, and if the joke was against himself he enjoyed that best of all.

'We're not filming today, just rehearsing again. So call me if you need to.'

'All right, I'll do whatever you think best.'

'Now that's wisdom talking. And don't worry. Everything's going to be fine.'

He vanished.

Yes, she thought. He could make her feel that all would be well as long as he was there. It was a rare gift.

The apartment was luxurious but in a down-to-earth way that pleasantly surprised her. Instinct told her that the man who lived here wasn't 'full of himself' as he might so easily have become. He just liked his own way. Which was fair enough, she reckoned.

Charlene spent the day as he'd said, making herself at home, eating a snack from the fridge, always alert for a call from Lee. But when the phone rang in the late morning it was Travis to ask how she was. Later he called again to say he was on his way home.

But from Lee, not a word.

When Travis arrived he gave her a searching look and said quietly, 'Nothing?'

'Nothing.'

'He just needs a little time to think about it. Now, let's have supper, if you can stand my cooking.'

He was no chef but his cooking was edible. As they devoured chicken he said, 'Lee kept giving me some odd looks today. He doesn't know whether he's coming or going.'

'I think he'd like to be going,' she said sadly. 'Then he could get away from me.'

'He's probably just confused. He might be a father, or he might not. He needs to know for sure before he can decide how he feels.'

'You talk as if you know,' she said curiously.

'It happened to me once. We'd known each other a while, then she said she was expecting but she didn't know if it was mine or not. In the end we found that it wasn't.'

'Did you mind?' she asked, struck by a new note in his voice.

'It might have been nice. A baby anchors you to reality, tells you where you belong.'

'But you have all those brothers.'

'Yes, but at a distance. I hear about them, and about my father, and it's like getting messages from another universe. If her baby had been mine nothing could have kept me away, and Lee will probably be the same when he knows.'

'Yes,' she said, knowing she didn't sound convinced.

'Are you really in love with him?'

'I don't know. We had that time together—and it was so sweet, so close. I really wanted that closeness.'

'I know the feeling,' he said quietly. 'And at least I had my brothers, even if they lived at a distance. But you have nobody except your grandparents, is that right?'

'I have a stepbrother, James, but we're not in contact. My mother and his father took a trip to celebrate their wedding anniversary, and never came back. Their plane crashed. The last time I saw James was at their funeral.'

'And your grandparents? Are they any comfort to you in this situation?'

'I haven't told them. They know I'm in Los Angeles but not why. If it works out badly I don't want to spoil their African holiday.'

'So you knew it might work out badly,' he said, 'right from the day you came out here?'

'Yes, well—you always hope for the best, don't you?'

'That's right. Keep on hoping.'

Travis squeezed her hand and they sat in silence for a moment.

'What do you think of this place?' he asked at last, rising to fetch more coffee.

'Fascinating. Especially your bookcase. All that Shakespeare.'

'You were naturally surprised to find that a TV actor is bright enough to understand Shakespeare.'

'No, I didn't mean that,' she said hurriedly.

He grinned. 'Didn't you? All right, I'll take your word for it. Actually, the only play I know well is *A Midsummer Night's Dream*. That's how I understood what you were saying about how you met Lee. I acted in it once, years ago.'

'Were you Lysander or Demetrius?' she asked, naming the two young male leads.

'Neither. I played Puck.'

Of course, she thought. Puck, the fiendish but delight-ful elf, described by one person as a 'shrewd and knavish sprite' and by himself as 'that merry wanderer of the night'. He spent the play performing roguish tricks and laughing at the chaos that resulted.

Strangely, Puck was the perfect role for Travis. His 'ro-mantic hero' looks might seem more suitable for one of the lovers but the sense of delightfully wicked mischief that per-vaded him suggested a different story. And something told Charlene that this was his true self.

'I'm just staggered by the window in my room,' she said.

'Enormous. Floor to ceiling. And that long view down to the city. It's the most beautiful thing I've ever seen.'

'The ones in my room are even better,' he said. 'Come and look. It's a sight you'll never forget.'

Taking her hand, he drew her into his room and made a gesture of revelation. Charlene gasped as she saw the two huge breathtaking walls of glass, angled to form a corner. It wasn't yet completely dark, but evening was closing in and the lights of Los Angeles gleamed against the shadows.

'I was wrong before,' she breathed. '*This* is the most beautiful thing I've ever seen. Nothing else could ever be like it. Oh, goodness!'

'That's how I feel,' Travis agreed. 'I look at the view every night before I go to bed.'

'And the HOLLYWOOD sign,' she said, pointing into the distance. 'Just to remind you what it's all about.'

'All about,' he murmured, his eyes fixed on the view. Briefly he glanced at her over his shoulder. 'Do we ever really know what it's all about?'

'Perhaps it's better not to,' she suggested.

'That could be the wisest thing you've ever said.'

He gazed at the view a moment longer, then pulled the huge curtains closed and led her out of the room.

'An early night for me. After this morning I was warned not to be late again.'

Charlene tidied away plates in the kitchen, then glanced briefly out of a small window that looked out over the front of the building. Suddenly she tensed. Beneath the lamp at the gate she'd just glimpsed a woman followed by a man.

And the woman had red hair.

Pictures raged through her mind. The lap dancer who'd set her sights on Travis in the club—she had red hair, didn't she?

It was impossible.

Was it?

Like the sound of approaching fate, she heard the elevator rise and come to a halt. The next moment Travis's bell rang.

She flew into the hall as he approached the front door, catching him just as he reached out to open it. By using all her weight, she was just able to stop him.

'Hey, what—?'

'That girl who sat on your lap. She had red hair, didn't she?'

'Yes, but—'

'It's her out there.'

'*What?* Are you sure?'

'I caught a glimpse of her hair as she went under the lamp. Don't you see what they're doing? If you open up, she'll grab you and the photographer will pounce. Frank Brenton warned us that he'd try something else.'

'Then it's time I hit back. Stand aside.'

He made a lunge for the front door. By using all her strength, she was just able to slam him back against the wall.

'Hey, what are you doing?'

'Stopping you making the biggest mistake of your life. Open that door and you're finished. But you're not going to, because I'm not going to let you.'

'Oh, you're not?'

'No, I'm not.'

'Look, I know you mean well, but it's time for action. I'm going to put a stop to their tricks.'

'But you won't. You'll simply hand them another weapon and there'll be no end to it. Your only hope is to play it cool. Let them hammer on the door as much as they like. It won't open.'

'Won't it?' he growled.

'No, because with your usual brilliance you've seen through their rotten little trick and you're one up on them. That'll teach Frank Brenton. He won't enjoy being made a fool of.'

Travis had been trying to free himself from her, but now he stopped, staring into her face as light dawned.

'It could work,' he said.

'It's *going* to work. Here's what we do. Make sure all the lights are off and go to bed. When you're in your room don't be tempted to pull open the curtains. You're not there. You're not here. You're not anywhere. And don't answer the phone.'

He gave her a stunned look. 'Remind me never to get on your wrong side.'

'That's a promise.'

The doorbell rang again. She felt Travis tense, and tightened her grip in case he yielded to temptation. But he stayed completely still, seemingly turned to stone while the bell rang and rang.

Then the knocking began. Fists thundered against the door, growing louder when they received no response.

'Let's leave them to it,' Charlene said softly, drawing him away.

'Will they never stop?'

'Probably not. So what? Let them go on all night. If you don't go to the door they'll gain nothing.'

'You think they really would keep that up all night?'

'Unless your neighbours lose patience and threaten them with the police.'

'Think what a story that would make,' Travis mused, beginning to laugh.

'Oh, yes.' She laughed with him and they stood together in the dim hallway, shaking, holding on to each other.

'Hey!' From outside the door came an angry yell. 'Stop that noise. Some of us want to get some sleep.'

Mumbles, arguments, exasperation. Finally silence.

But then came the sound of Travis's cellphone.

'Don't answer it,' Charlene said quickly.

'Don't worry, I'm not going to. I can see it's a number I don't recognise. Take no chances.'

'And you won't answer it if it rings again later?'

'I promise you can safely let me out of your sight. Play it cool. I'm learning a lot from you.'

Another noise from below.

'That sounded like the front door being slammed.' Travis went to the tiny window and peered through the crack. 'Yes, they're going. It's over.'

'Yippee! We beat them.'

'You beat them. I'd have walked right into the trap.' He regarded her with a touch of awe. 'What was that remark about my usual brilliance? Someone was brilliant, but it wasn't me.'

He hugged her, not briefly or lightly, but with both arms folded around her, holding her tight.

'Goodnight,' he said softly. 'Thanks for everything.'

He saw her to her door before going to his own room. There he lay awake for a while, enjoying a feeling of contentment. It was strange to feel that way, he thought, given how recently his nerves had been jangling, but all was well. Instinct, stronger than words, told him that.

Just once he got up and went out into the hall, lingering outside her door, wondering if by chance Lee was calling her. But there was only silence, and after a while he went back to bed. Smiling, he snuggled down and slept the sleep of the innocent.

When they met in the kitchen next morning Travis eyed her with an air of caution.

'Is everything OK?' she asked.

'I'm not sure. I'm becoming nervous of you.' He rubbed his shoulder where it had rammed against the wall in their tussle. 'Women are supposed to be the weaker sex, but I guess that's just a myth.'

'Just beware us when we're really determined.' She laughed.

'I learned that last night.' He rubbed his shoulder again. 'I'm getting used to you beating me up.'

Suddenly he dropped his joking manner.

'But I'm glad you did. You really saved me from disaster. Why I was crazy enough to argue with you—if I'd opened the door—'

'It did seem strange. I thought you were being cautious.'

'I was, but I lost my temper. It doesn't happen often, so when it does I don't tend to think straight.' He touched her face. 'Thank you. Thank you more than I can say.'

She placed her hand over his and held it against her cheek, moved by an emotion for which there were no words.

'I told you about my doctor friend,' he said. 'I'm going to send her to see you. She's a nice lady. She'll do that test, then you'll know and you can make decisions.'

Charlene nodded. 'Yes, that's the best way. Thank you.'

'Don't thank me. I'm in your debt, not the other way around. I'll call you. Bye.'

He kissed her cheek and departed.

Dr Grace Hanley arrived an hour later. She was in her forties with a mature, kindly face. Charlene tried not to feel too nervous. This was it. The final answer.

They got quickly down to business and soon Grace was studying the test cylinder with a face that revealed nothing.

'Were you hoping to be pregnant?' she asked.

'I'm not sure. Does that mean it's a negative?'

'Yes, I'm afraid so.'

'But at least…now I know. Thank you, Doctor. Can I make you some coffee?'

She was trying to sound normal and untroubled, but the doctor evidently understood her inner turmoil because she declined, patted her hand gently, and departed.

The walls of the apartment seemed to crush Charlene in bleak, hopeless silence. So that was that. It had all been for nothing. She'd made a fool of herself by pursuing a man who didn't want her.

She lay down, trying to control her flickering memories.

There was Lee, or was it Demetrius, smiling as they came offstage after a rehearsal, complimenting her.

'Hey, you really played that scene for all it was worth. Wow!'

And herself, dazzled to receive a compliment from such a knowledgeable source, gazing at him, starry-eyed.

She could see him now, warming to her, holding her in his arms, smiling as they made love.

Or was it love? Perhaps on her side, but whatever he'd been making it wasn't love. She should have faced that earlier.

Yet if there had been a baby, might his feelings not have warmed, flowering into family affection that would embrace her and their child?

Instead—nothing.

Nothing!

She was seized by a fierce longing for Travis to be there, wrapping her in his arms, offering brotherly comfort that would have made this bearable.

No!

The ferocity of her emotion made her sit up. Hell would freeze over before she became a pathetic, needy creature, clinging to Travis. He would be kind, she knew, but soon the kindness would become forced, as he strove to conceal his exasperation.

That mustn't happen. The moment she sensed him thinking, *How long must I put up with this?* was the moment she would inwardly die. Or run a mile. Or both.

When he came home she was waiting for him, calm and smiling.

'Everything all right?' he asked.

'Everything's fine.'

He didn't ask her for the test result. It would have been dishonest when he already knew. As promised, Grace had discreetly texted him one word: *No.* It might be a disgraceful violation of professional confidence, but friends did that for each other. So he waited for Charlene to speak, which at last she did.

'I'm not pregnant, so that's that.' She made a gesture of finality. 'I'll make some coffee.'

She turned away but he detained her. 'Wait a moment. "That's that"? Nothing more? You don't care?'

'Not really. This always seemed likely. And besides, something else has happened.' She laid her hand over her stomach.

'You mean you've finally—?'

'Yes. I don't know what made me late in the first place, but perhaps it was caused by tension because it started barely an hour after the doctor left. Anyway, it's the clincher. There's no baby. There never was, thank goodness.'

Her voice was bright and efficient, informing him that all was well.

But he didn't believe it. All was far from well with a woman who could wear such a dead smile.

'Well, I can see it solves one problem,' he said cautiously.

'It solves all the problems. Think of the catastrophe if I'd been pregnant while Lee... *Ugh!*' She shivered. 'It doesn't bear thinking about.'

Travis was troubled by an inner desire, as mysterious as it was illogical, to hear that she was saddened by the news. But she was bright, breezy, practical. And she froze his heart.

In the kitchen she made coffee, talking without stopping.

'I'm really sorry to have given you all this trouble. Just think of me making so much fuss about nothing. You must be good 'n' mad.'

'Not at all,' he said in an equally unrevealing voice. 'These things happen. You have to deal with matters as they come up. Sooner or later we all of us—'

Stop burbling, Travis told himself in disgust.

'I hope you don't mind but I have to vanish,' he told her. 'I've got a lot of lines to learn. Goodnight.'

He grabbed a sandwich and fled to his room.

So all was well. A potentially awkward situation had vanished. He could continue on his way, planning, calculating, arranging things for his own benefit, doing everything with an eye on his career.

It was absurd to be disappointed at her sensible reaction. What had he expected?

As the light failed he rose and drew the curtains across the great windows, shutting out the view. Just to the side was Charlene's window, already almost covered by curtain, with just a gap of a few inches left.

There she was, a shadow standing in the gap. Her light was off and in the near darkness it was hard to discern her. He switched off his own light so that he could watch, unobserved in the darkness.

She stood quite still, looking down at Los Angeles, then gazing up into the sky. Now he could see her face a little more clearly. It was sad, and there was a hint of tears on her cheeks. The mask had fallen away, revealing loneliness and despair.

Then she did something that broke his heart, leaning her head against the glass, clasping her arms about her body as though to protect herself from some unknown danger, and rocking back and forth.

That was the truth, he thought, cursing himself for stupidity. And she didn't trust him enough to let him see her grief. How had he been so easily fooled?

For a few minutes he paced the floor, then walked out into the hall, heading for her room. But at her door he stopped, aghast at what he could hear from the other side.

'What's the next flight to London?' came Charlene's voice. 'Midday tomorrow? Right, I'd like to book a ticket—'

The crash of her door being thrown open made her look up. '*Hey, what are you doing?* Give me that phone.'

'Like hell!' Travis said, shutting it down. 'What do you think *you're* doing?'

'Booking my flight home.'

'And no thought for anyone else,' he raged. 'Who cares about the damage you'll do to me? I put my neck on the line for you, Charlene. I've done everything I could to help you. And this is how you thank me. People saw us together, it gave them ideas. Just how do you think I'll look if they know you've fled the country without a backward glance? They'll laugh themselves sick. I can just hear them—*Guess he must be losing his touch! Ho, ho, ho!*

'I didn't make an issue of this when Lee was still in the picture, but now it's different. You can rescue me or make a fool of me, and you didn't give me a thought.'

'Travis, please, I didn't realise—'

'No, you didn't. I still have problems about that lap dancer. Brenton isn't giving up, and you're the only person who can help. So what do you do? Abandon me.'

'I'm sorry. You're right; I do owe you some help.'

'Yes, I think you do, but of course if you don't want to bother—' he retorted.

'I do, I do! I just didn't think—I'm really sorry—tell me what to do.'

'I want you to stay here, in this apartment. Let the world think we're a couple.'

'But will that help your image? If people believe we're living together—is that respectable?'

'It is these days. At one time it would have been a scandal, but now a lot of unmarried couples share a home, and as long as they're faithful to each other nobody thinks anything of it. It's lap dancers that get you into trouble. While you're here, you're my protection against Brenton and his nasty tricks.'

'All right; you give the orders.'

'That's what I like to hear.'

She was baffling, he thought. Nobody, seeing her now, could have suspected the agonised despair that had consumed her only a few minutes ago. She must be a better actress than he'd realised.

But then, his own performance had been admirable. Out-raged pride, indignation at her 'ingratitude'; these had been master strokes born of desperation. When he'd thought of her returning to England to sit alone in an empty house, he'd known that he had to stop her at all costs. So he'd assumed a new character, aggressive, self-centred, as different from the real Travis as it was possible to get.

If he said it himself, it had been an award-winner of a performance.

At her bedroom door he said, 'You'll still be here tomorrow?'

'Word of honour.'

'Goodnight. Sleep tight.'

He walked away without even the briefest backward glance. It took a lot of self-control, but he was getting good at that.

CHAPTER SIX

AT BREAKFAST next day Travis said, 'Has Lee called you?'

'No.'

Nor would he, Travis thought. He'd dive for cover and hope the storm would pass.

'Have you called him?' he asked.

'No.'

'You can't put it off for ever.' He added reluctantly, 'Would you like me to—?'

'Thanks, but no. There are some things I must do for myself.' Charlene gave a little laugh. 'Oh, Travis, if you could see your face. I've never seen a man so relieved.'

'Yes,' he admitted. 'But I'd have done it if you'd really wanted me to.'

How kind he was! she thought. How different from anyone else! Impulsively, she laid a fond hand on his cheek, and he put his own hand over it.

'Time to make our plans,' he said. 'I need to flaunt you a bit. I hope you don't mind.'

'Not at all.'

'We must announce ourselves to the world as a couple. An evening out together, in the spotlight, should do it. The Stollway Hotel is best because they already know you there.'

'Fine. What about the "stage directions"? You'll have to give me detailed instructions.'

'Good idea. Do you remember, when you go into the hotel there's a broad staircase leading up from Reception to a landing with a huge picture? Go up there to admire the picture. Stay there until I arrive.'

'And while you're looking for me you must turn around slowly a few times,' she said, 'so everyone can get a good view of you.'

'Right. Walk down the stairs very slowly. I'll be waiting at the bottom, looking up at you, riveted with admiration. Or should it be adoration?'

'Hmm, I don't think so,' she said, considering this seriously. 'Admiration will be enough for now. Adoration can come later.'

'Aren't I allowed to fall ecstatically at your feet, overcome with worship?'

'Not just yet, I think.'

'Very well, I'll control my ardour—for the moment. Later I'll turn up the heat and sigh yearningly at my goddess. Hey, do you mind? Women don't usually burst out laughing when I say things like that.'

'They would if they could listen to you now,' she choked, struggling to get her mirth under control. 'And just how often do you say "things like that"?'

'Let's leave it,' he said hastily. 'I'm glad you find it so funny.'

'You're not glad at all,' she teased.

He ground his teeth. 'Have you finished?'

'Yes.'

'Then I'll continue. You come down the stairs and when you reach me I'll take your hand and draw you close. With any luck, somebody will have a cellphone with a camera, so we'll give them a sight to enjoy.'

'What will you be wearing?'

'Dinner jacket and bow tie. What about you? I think you'll

need a new wardrobe while you're here, which gives us a bit of a problem.'

'What kind of a problem?'

'Since you're doing this for me, it's my responsibility to pay for the new clothes. But if I offer I suppose you'll come over all offended, and if our last meetings are anything to go by you'll thump the living daylights out of me. Ah, well, I guess I'll just have to get used to it. Here.' He pushed a credit card across the table.

'Go to—' He named a famous purveyor of fashionable clothes for both men and women. 'I'll call them and say you have my permission to use that. Get a whole wardrobe.'

'Just the dress for tonight. Restrained and *respectable*! They'll take one look and know that you've opted for a life of virtue.' She eyed him satirically. 'However unlikely that might seem!'

He grinned. 'I refuse to answer on the grounds that it may incriminate me.' He checked his watch. 'Hey, I've got to be going. I'm being interviewed by a journalist.'

'What will you tell them?'

'Nothing much. Just drop a few mysterious hints. Get them wondering. That's far more effective.'

'You really know how to make people dance to your tune, don't you? I suppose that's as big a talent as acting.'

'Yes, and I'm not the only one who has it,' he said, regarding her significantly.

Wanting to do him proud, Charlene concentrated fiercely on getting her appearance right for that evening. The gown she chose was dark red velvet with a neckline that came modestly up to the base of her throat, but which hugged her slender figure temptingly. She reckoned that was a good compromise.

She was pleased, too, with the way the hairdresser swept up her hair in an exquisite display of elegance, leaving just a few long curls drifting down over her neck.

It was important to be always ready to embrace new experiences. Tonight she was going to dine with the handsomest, most charming man she'd ever met, revelling in the attention he would pay her and the envy of other women. And that was quite definitely a new experience.

'Time for curtain up!' she murmured. 'Let the performance begin.'

At the agreed time, Travis entered the hotel lobby. There was an immediate rustle of interest as he went to stand at the foot of the stairs as she descended slowly, her eyes fixed on him, as his were on her. In a white tuxedo and bow tie, he was at his starry best.

If I was a dreamy teenager, she thought, amused, *I could fall for him. Lucky for both of us that I'm not.*

Following the stage directions, he reached out and took her hand, murmuring, 'Charlene.' Then he brushed his lips against her fingers, whispering her name again.

'Travis.' She sighed.

Holding her head high, she allowed him to draw her across the floor to the restaurant. A waiter showed them to the table and was about to pull out her chair when Travis stopped him, indicating that he alone would perform this service for his lady. Only when he was certain that she was at ease did he attend to his own comfort.

When the wine waiter appeared he asked her tenderly, 'Do you have a preference…my darling?'

'I'll let you choose.' She sighed.

He gave an order, adding, 'And a bottle of your very best champagne.' Leaning towards Charlene, he added, 'We need to celebrate.'

The waiter eyed them with new interest, ears alert for Charlene's reply. 'Isn't it a little soon to celebrate?' she asked.

'Not for us,' Travis assured her. When the waiter was out of earshot he murmured, 'That got him.'

'You're just a natural-born deceiver,' she murmured back.

'Thank you for the compliment. Of course I am. It's what acting's all about. He who deceives best gets top billing.'

'And the best pay?'

'Naturally. A wise old actor once told me, "When the crowds are cheering, the applause is deafening and they're fighting to hire you, never forget that you could be out of work tomorrow." And he was right.'

Which was why, she thought, he was so determined to protect what he had, using any method necessary.

The food was served. It was excellent, and they both tucked in with pleasure. As he ate, Travis was studying her appearance with approval.

'Superb,' he said. 'Modest but attractive. Give my congratulations to the wardrobe mistress.'

When they had finished eating and were alone again, Travis said, 'I think this is the right moment.'

'Right moment for what?'

'I stopped in a jeweller's shop and bought you a small gift.'

'That sounds like it would fit the script,' she said, nodding wisely.

'I thought so too.'

From his pocket he took a tiny box that looked as though it might have come from a jeweller's.

'This is for you, my darling,' he said fervently.

Earrings? she wondered. Or a bracelet?

She lingered to give him a dramatic smile of gratitude before opening the box.

Then she stared.

They were certainly earrings, but not diamonds, pearls or anything romantic. They depicted a cartoon character called Daft Doody, very popular with children just then.

'What is it?' he asked, seeing her astonished face. 'Don't you—? Oh, goodness, no! Put it away. It's the wrong box. How did I—?'

His self-reproach was drowned by a burst of laughter from Charlene.

'I'm sorry,' she choked, 'but you must admit it's hilarious.'

'Must I? These are a birthday gift for the little daughter of a friend who's very keen on Daft Doody. I bought them at the same time as your pearl earrings—the boxes are alike and I picked up the wrong one—*hell*!'

'I guess that wasn't in the script,' she said, still chuckling.

He opened his mouth to reply, but then gave up and grinned sheepishly.

'But I don't have your present with me. I brought this one and left yours behind.'

'Don't worry. Actually, I rather like these kiddy earrings. I think I'll keep them. It's all right, don't look like that. Here you are.'

'Thank you,' he groaned, taking the box from her. 'I'll give you yours when we get home.'

'No, no,' she said urgently. 'You can't give them to me privately. What would you gain by that?'

'Right. I'll present them next time we're out.'

'Unless you get confused and bring me a set of cufflinks instead,' she teased.

'I suppose I deserved that.'

'Hey, come on, it's not a tragedy.'

'No, but it's reality. That's the trouble with the life I live. You kind of lose touch with reality until it socks you on the jaw. This is the sort of careless mistake I make easily, and I get away with it because I'm surrounded by people whose job it is to tell me that everything's fine, I'm doing well.'

'They just want to boost your confidence so that you can give your all to the performance.'

'I know, but it can be dangerous if you hear it too often. You get conceited, start thinking that whatever you do is perfect, but in real life it isn't and you make an idiot of yourself.'

She was intrigued. Travis had opened a small window,

allowing her a glimpse of the confusions and complications deep inside him. She would have sought to know more but, as though suddenly alerted to danger, he closed the window and resumed a cheerful manner, raising his champagne glass.

'What are we celebrating?' she asked.

'You! Your genius and daring.'

She lifted her glass and they saluted each other.

'This is going to be fun,' he said. 'Here's to fraud, cheating and dishonesty.'

'What would life be without them?'

Charlene leaned back in her chair, taking a faintly incredulous look around the luxurious restaurant, trying to believe she was really here.

'What are you thinking?' he asked.

'I'm just surprised that I'm enjoying myself so much after all that's happened. It's so nice to sit and talk, and say what you really mean.'

He nodded. 'Yes, I find it's a rare pleasure too.'

'Talking to you is like having that big brother I dreamed of. Oh!' She covered her mouth with her hand as though concealing a guilty secret. 'No, sorry! I shouldn't have said that.'

'Said what?'

She gave a quick glance over her shoulder to make sure nobody was listening, then mouthed, 'Brother!'

'Ah, yes! I see. Brother's not the image we're trying to convey to the world, is it?' He assumed a tone of mock severity. 'Be more careful next time.'

She gave a brief salute. 'Aye, aye, sir!'

They laughed and he said warmly, 'But in private, brother and sister is ideal.'

'Right. Friends, allies, siblings.'

They shook on it.

She regarded him fondly, saying, 'And you'll always know that you're safe with me.'

'Safe in what sense? Safe because you're not going to knock me out, kick my shins, poison my coffee?'

'That too. But safe chiefly because I'm not going to lose my heart to you. I promise faithfully! You're not my type.'

'Hmm!' He frowned with comical emphasis. 'That's not what I'm used to hearing.'

'I know. You're used to females who swoon and yearn and say you're the handsomest man in the world. Sorry. No can do! But think how much you'll enjoy that. What a relaxing change it'll be!'

'Yes,' he said. 'I suppose it will. Perhaps it's time we were going.'

Charlene spent the next day on a shopping binge, justifying it with the need to acquire suitable costumes for the role she had to play. At last she returned home and collapsed flat out on the bed. Self-indulgence could be exhausting.

Travis called, apologising that something had come up and he wouldn't be home until late. She assured him that all was well, and he hung up hastily, leaving her wondering if the whole arrangement was about to come to an end. Perhaps she'd already served her purpose and was being cast off.

That would be sad. Not because her heart was engaged, for it wasn't. But Travis appealed to her as a nice man: sweet-natured, generous and not corrupted by his fame. If he turned out to be as cynically self-seeking as other men it would be a disappointment.

By chance one of the television channels was showing a whole evening of *The Man From Heaven*. Episodes from the first series were repeated, end to end, and she came to understand Dr Brad Harrison as never before.

Wearing a white coat and a calm expression, he strode through the corridors of Mercyland Hospital. Everyone revered him. His sweet smile calmed their fears. He achieved miraculous medical cures, but more miraculous still were the cures of the heart that followed his tender advice.

Her last view of him was gazing up into the sky, crying, 'That's what we must all remember. Seize the moment whenever it comes. Don't let the chance slip away, or we may regret it for ever.'

His face was illuminated with a mysterious smile. The camera panned away from him, the credits came up. It was over.

'Too handsome and perfect to be true,' she mused. 'But then, he isn't supposed to be true. He's a glorious fantasy. I pity any girl who forgets that.'

At eleven o'clock he telephoned, full of excitement.

'I need you to come to the studio tomorrow,' he said. 'There are a lot of people anxious to meet you. Lee will be there. Are you all right about meeting him?'

'I've got to see him some time,' she said. 'Let's do it.'

'Right, I'll set it up. Don't wait up. In the meantime, check out "Notes For You".'

This was a website made up of items taken mostly from the cellphones of private individuals, snapping what they saw in the street or in restaurants. Accessing it on her laptop, Charlene wasn't really surprised to discover shots of herself and Travis in the restaurant the previous evening.

'They didn't waste any time,' she murmured. 'But that's what we wanted when we flaunted ourselves.'

She studied herself on the screen. The picture was slightly blurred, but she reckoned that was an advantage.

'A definite improvement,' she decided. 'Elegant and not *too* dowdy. Let's just hope nobody gets a sharper lens.'

She wondered what was keeping Travis out so late. Work? Or was he 'enjoying himself' in a way that a kind sister would not ask about?

None of her business.

By the time he came in she'd already retired for the night.
She heard him close the door of his bedroom, and after that
she could go to sleep.

For her appearance at the studio next morning she chose a
plain dress and jacket, but let her hair hang about her shoulders to soften the effect. Travis nodded approval. They spoke
little on the journey, mindful that the driver could hear everything, but as they walked into the studio she said, 'I looked
up "Notes For You". What a start we've made!'

'You're doing a terrific job,' he said. 'I'm grateful. Look,
there's an audience waiting.'

The entrance was crowded with people who'd found an
excuse to be there when Travis arrived.

'You're a star,' he murmured.

'Help!' she squeaked.

His hand was around her waist, holding her close. 'Don't
worry. Everything will be fine. This guy approaching is
Vince, the director.'

Vince was about forty, vigorous, calculating but amiable.
He looked Charlene over quickly and seemed pleased.

'Glad to meet a lady I've heard so much about. Travis says
you're his guest of honour, so we'll have to make sure you
enjoy your visit.'

The day that followed was breathtaking. One by one, all
the big shots came to greet her, size her up and nod their approval. It was clear that they had guessed the true situation,
since Travis had been seen with her so soon after the scandal. Denzil Raines went so far as to give him the thumbs up
and say, 'Well done. Good move.'

Since she was protecting the studio's most valuable prop-
erty, she was assigned an 'assistant'. This was Vera, a back-
room girl who shadowed Charlene with instructions to take
care of her needs. At lunchtime Travis took her to the studio cafe.

'Sorry to have left you alone last night,' he said.

'Actually, I wasn't alone. One of the TV channels showed wall-to-wall episodes, and there you were, all the time.'

'You mean you couldn't get rid of me.' He laughed.

'Let's say it was useful for research. I noted the way you end every episode with some declaration about life.' She struck an attitude and recited, '"Seize the moment whenever it comes. Don't let the chance slip away, or we may regret it for ever." Why, what's the matter?'

Travis had groaned and covered his eyes.

'You couldn't have picked a worse example.' He sighed. 'Life imitating art and making a mess of it. I told you about going to the wedding of my brother Darius. While I was there they showed that episode, where I announced "Seize the moment". Unfortunately, my brother Marcel saw it, and it gave him a mad idea. At the reception he announced his engagement to *his* lady love, Cassie.'

'Why is that unfortunate?'

'Because he overlooked the little matter of asking her first.'

'Ouch!'

'Exactly!'

'Did she refuse him in front of everyone?'

'No, she played along in public but refused him when they were alone. I gather they've now separated.'

'But that's his fault, not yours.'

'I know, but it's depressing. I want to do my family good, not harm them, even indirectly. I'd like to get closer to them. I know we're in different countries but even so—'

'You can be emotionally close even from different countries,' she agreed.

'Yes, we might if things were better, but something always goes wrong. Darius's wedding was the first family celebration I'd managed to get to for ages. I had visions of a friendly reunion with my father. How stupid can you get?'

'Wouldn't he speak to you?'

'He wasn't there. He didn't want Darius to marry Harriet and did all he could to split them up. When he didn't succeed, he was furious and snubbed the wedding.'

'But you're all grown men. Who does he think he is?'

'One of those Roman emperors we were talking about. Probably Nero.'

'I promise never to tell him you said that.'

'Thanks, though I doubt you'll get the chance.'

There it was again, the hint of wry sadness beneath the cheerful mask. But it was gone in a moment. Something across the room had attracted his attention.

'Lee's here,' he said. 'In the doorway, watching us. But don't look round.'

'I wasn't going to. I don't want him to think I'm yearning after him. I must talk to him once, tell him he's got nothing to worry about—' She gave an ironical smile which made Travis put his hand over hers. 'When I've done that we'll draw a line under it and go our different ways, with no looking back.'

'Isn't there always some looking back?' he asked gently.

'A little, but we don't have to be sentimental. What's done is done.'

'That's very good. I just hope you can go on feeling like that. Yearning and regret for what can't be changed can waste your life. Now, I have to go; they're beckoning me.'

Left alone, she brooded. Travis's remarks about the wisdom of not indulging in regrets made her remember his absence the night before. Was he already looking ahead to the day when she would be surplus to his requirements? She guessed he wouldn't cruelly dump her. He would hand her gently into the arms of another suitor, thus preserving her feelings and her dignity.

She supposed she ought to be grateful to him. She couldn't imagine why she wasn't.

'Can I sit down?'

Looking up, she saw Lee, smiling at her in a way that had once made her heart turn over.

'Sure,' she said.

'I've been waiting for the chance, but I didn't want to disturb you when you were with the great man.'

'I tried to call you this morning but your phone was switched off.'

'Yes, it still isn't working properly,' he said with an uneasy laugh.

Suddenly she pitied him. Maybe it wasn't entirely his fault that he was a coward. Not every man could be brave and generous like Travis.

'Stop worrying,' she said. 'It was a false alarm.'

'You mean you're not—?'

'No, I'm not. It's over. *Finito. Kaput.* Nothing for you to worry about.'

He beamed. 'Oh, wow! That's wonderful. Then everything's all right.'

'I suppose if you look at it one way, yes.' It annoyed her that it didn't seem to cross his mind that she might be disappointed. She wondered if anyone else's feelings had ever crossed his mind in his entire life.

'You're quite sure, aren't you?' he asked anxiously. 'There's no chance of a mistake?'

'No chance at all. Stop worrying.'

His whole being was brilliant with joy. 'This is so wonderful.' He leaned forward, seized her face between his hands and planted a smacking kiss on her mouth. 'Bless you for being a great girl!'

He danced away. Charlene stared after him, confused. Where was the devastation she should be feeling? Where was the disappointed love?

Love! said a scathing voice in her mind. *Is that what you called it? More fool you!*

She'd longed to believe it was love, especially when she'd

thought she was to have his child. But the bleak emptiness showed her a cruel truth. Her 'love' had been as much an illusion as his; a fantasy created by a lonely girl who yearned for a feeling of belonging.

There was even an incredible sense of relief that nothing now tied her to this irresponsible boy. She was free. Alone, but free.

'Charlene, for pity's sake, what's the matter?'

Travis suddenly appeared in the seat beside her, seizing her, anxiously searching her face.

'You look so strange,' he said frantically. 'I came back for a moment, and when I saw him kiss you I thought...I don't know what I thought. But please, tell me you're all right.'

'I'm fine, thank you,' she said lightly. 'He kissed me from relief, that's all. He's got what he wanted.'

'What about what you want? Did he ever think of that?' he demanded, unconsciously echoing her own thoughts.

'That would only have confused him.'

'Do you want me to punch him?'

She shrugged. 'Whatever for? Everyone's happy.'

'Are they? *Are they?*' His eyes, fixed on hers, were angry and dark with meaning.

She was saved from having to answer by the arrival of Vera, offering to take Charlene to see some more of the studio.

'That sounds great,' Charlene said cheerfully. 'Let's go.'

Her mind seemed to have slipped into another dimension and she enjoyed the tour, especially the last part, where they crept into the rehearsal room just as Travis was confronting Lee in a scene.

'It's best to think a little before you speak,' 'Dr Harrison' was saying. 'Your patients will appreciate it.'

'I do try,' Lee was saying in character. 'But things can get very difficult.'

'Hey, what happened there?' called Vince. 'Travis, you're

supposed to simply stand there and look at him, not reach out as though you meant to hit him.'

'Sorry,' Travis said in a tight voice. 'Something made me jump.'

'OK, do it again,' Vince called. 'Travis, remember you're full of warm feeling and generosity.'

'Yeah, right!'

'Let's leave them to it,' Vera murmured, and they slipped away.

Charlene recalled Travis saying he rarely lost his temper and found it hard to cope when he did. But surely he hadn't lost his temper with Lee?

Yet the look on his face had surprised her, and possibly everyone else in the room. Anger coming out of nowhere.

At the end of the day she went out to wait for him in the car. There were nods and salutations from the others who were leaving, always with an edge of curiosity and respect.

I could get used to this, she thought. *OK, so it's all a con, but who says I can't enjoy a con while it lasts?*

After a few minutes Travis joined her and they relaxed in the back together.

'Do you ever have to drive yourself?' she asked.

'I'm not *allowed* to drive myself,' he said, grinning. 'The bosses say they want me free to think of nothing but my "art". The truth is that I'm not a brilliant driver and they're terrified I'll have an accident that will reflect badly on the show.'

As the car pulled away, Charlene saw Lee watching her from a distance. He waved and quickly stepped back into the shadows. She glanced at Travis, wondering if he'd noticed, but he was looking the other way.

CHAPTER SEVEN

THEY got out a few blocks from his home, and went to dine in a small restaurant.

As they relaxed over the main course, Charlene said, 'We need to talk about money. You give me too much.'

'You deserve every penny. I want you to take more and equip yourself with more clothes.'

'Then I'll buy them myself.'

'At LA prices? No way.'

'I mean it. I'm your useful piece of stage equipment, not your kept woman. This is an arrangement of equals or it's nothing.'

'Equals?' He looked comically alarmed. 'I don't do equals.'

'You've never heard of women's lib?'

'I've heard of it but I try to ignore it. I don't know! My girlfriend paying for herself. Whatever is the world coming to? Well, at least you have to accept this.'

From his pocket he produced a small jewel box. Inside she found the pearl earrings that he'd left behind on the first night.

'Sorry about that,' he said.

'And the press thinks you're the great romantic,' she teased.

He fixed the earrings for her. She had to admit they were beautiful. He thought so too, from the way he was smiling.

They strolled home, yawning, for it was very late. As they

got into the elevator a middle-aged man appeared, hurrying. Travis held the doors open for him, calling, 'It's all right, Sam, I've got it.'

'Thanks,' said the man. He smiled and nodded at Charlene.

'Charlene, this is my friend, Sam Barton. He and his wife live on the floor below us.'

'And you don't have to tell me who this is,' Sam said, shaking her hand. 'You're the talk of LA.'

The three of them exchanged pleasantries until the elevator stopped, and Sam bid them goodnight, departing with a curious look at Charlene.

'Nice guy,' Travis said as they finished the journey. 'We must have him and his wife to supper. You'll like Rita.'

'Are they in the business?' Charlene asked. She had fallen easily into the habit of referring to the entertainment world as 'the business' as though there was no other. In Los Angeles it was easy to believe that was true.

'In a way. He works in one of the studios, on the financial side. She used to be a model and a dancer.'

In her own room she prepared for bed, then went to stand by the window and look down on the gleaming city. Just below, she could see the garden, and Travis, sitting there. He was leaning back against a tree, his eyes closed, his lips moving.

It would be fascinating, she thought, to be a bird in the nearby bush, and hear what he was saying. But she doubted she would ever understand him. Today he'd puzzled her afresh—calm, agitated, unpredictable, but never less than the kind man she valued so dearly.

She drew the curtain and stepped back.

Down below, Travis opened his eyes, glancing up to the top of the building. Again he murmured the words that had struck a nerve.

'"Useful piece of stage equipment." Well, I've been warned.'

* * *

They settled into a comfortable pattern, treating each other with the cheerful friendliness of siblings. At her suggestion, he began calling her Charlie.

'She's the real me, sensible and practical. Charlene is the fantasy version.'

He nodded. 'Very clever.'

He had to be away for a few days, shooting outdoor scenes. Every night he called to ask how she was, and she reassured him. Neither of them ever mentioned Lee.

She was glad of a few free days free. It gave her some time alone, which she felt she needed. Now everything about her had changed. Heads turned in the street, people nudged as she went past. If she'd needed confirmation of Travis's fame, she was getting it.

Now some of it seemed to have rubbed off on her. Cameras appeared, voices called, 'Look this way.' She obliged, careful to look pleasant, but always escaped quickly.

'And they keep asking me to give them a quote,' she told him. 'I don't, of course, but they're getting pressing.'

'I'm sorry you're having a hard time.'

'I didn't say I was having a hard time.' She laughed. 'It's got its funny side, but I don't want to risk saying the wrong thing.'

'We'll sort it out, I promise. We need to arrange things so that they come out the way we want. I'll be home soon. I had hoped it might be tonight, but there's been a big delay. I'll see you tomorrow.'

In fact the delay was cleared up sooner than expected, and he managed to make it home at three in the morning. The apartment was dark and he entered quietly.

But as he crossed the hall he heard a burst of laughter from Charlene's room. He wondered what could make a woman shriek with laughter at this hour, and didn't like any of the answers he came up with.

The gentlemanly thing might have been to creep away,

without asking questions about something that was none of his business. But he wasn't feeling like a gentleman. If that was Lee, and he had a horrible feeling that it was, then the silly girl must be protected.

Then came her voice again.

'Oh, come on, you can't do that. No, really, you mustn't. Behave yourself!'

Travis didn't hesitate. In a flash he had the door open, seeking Charlene and whoever she was entertaining. But then he stopped on the threshold, taken aback by what met his eyes.

She was alone in the room, sitting at the dressing table, talking into a cellphone. She glanced up at him, and said, 'Travis has just walked in.' She looked up at him. 'It's my grandparents.'

'Your—?'

'I told you about them. They called me from Nairobi and I've been telling them all about you. Hello—Emma, yes, he's still here. You can talk to him.' She handed him the phone.

Even far away in Nairobi they had heard the news from Los Angeles and wanted to thank him for befriending her. Charlene switched the phone onto 'hands free' so that she could hear their voices and join in, and they all spent a very jolly ten minutes.

Afterwards he sat on the edge of the bed, trying to pull himself together.

'You look absolutely knocked out,' she said sympathetically. 'Can I get you something?'

'No, I'll go straight to bed, thank you. I just need to get some sleep and…goodnight.'

He got out, fast.

Over breakfast next morning he said, 'You really scared me last night, telling someone to stop what they were doing. I thought a man had broken in.'

'No, it was just Frank and Emma. It's incredible, at their age they're such a pair of clowns.'

'Yes, they sounded like good fun,' he agreed. 'I'll hope to meet them some day. When are they coming back?'

'Not for six weeks.'

'But you're not in a rush to leave me, are you?'

'No, I like it here, if it's all right with you.'

'It's a deal then.'

They shook hands and spent the rest of the meal making domestic arrangements. Travis had a cleaner who came in three times a week, but apart from that he managed for himself. When it came to food, he either ate on the way home, arranged a takeout or made himself a basic snack. Charlene made a list of his favourite meals, studied it and set herself to practise seriously.

'You're a great cook,' he said a week later. 'You get better every day.'

'I do my best.'

'Then congratulations. It's a fantastic best.'

'And there's something else.' She took out a large envelope, filled with pieces of paper. 'I found this by accident. It just fell out and I had to gather up the papers from the floor.'

He groaned. 'They're receipts I'm supposed to send to my accountant. I'm afraid I let them get into a mess.'

'I can see that. And where you've made notes and done sums—well, never mind. I've been through, trying to put them in some sort of order.'

She handed him the list she'd made, and his face brightened.

'Hey, they actually make sense. I could send this to my accountant without a load of apologies. That's great!'

'So you don't mind? You don't feel I violated your privacy?'

'Charlie, you can violate my privacy any time you like,' he said fervently. 'In fact there are several things—'

In a short time she was privy to all his financial details, including investments. His accountant was a big name but there were a hundred smaller matters that Travis needed to get organised before sending them to him. And among his many talents efficiency and good order found no place.

With delight he dumped everything on Charlene. Now she had access to all his computer accounts, including passwords, enabling her to access his bank account every morning. This she did, several times raising queries, one of which averted a minor disaster.

Travis rewarded her with a glittering gold pendant, but what really pleased her was his look of joy and relief, and his exclamation, 'However did I manage without you?'

'Your own private bank clerk!' She chuckled.

'Bank clerk,' he said softly. 'Is that what you call it?'

Both his eyes and his voice told her that he called it something entirely different. But just what that something might be he wasn't ready to say.

Charlene enjoyed life in Beachwood Canyon. Despite its glamorous location, it closely resembled a village, with a coffee shop, a market and a number of little boutiques where people could meet casually. She saw several faces that she recognised, famous actors and musicians. At first she was tempted to stare, then realised that she too was being stared at.

'How are you coping?' asked an elderly man who came to sit beside her in a coffee shop. After a moment she recognised him as a once famous star, known for his dynamic sexiness, but now in his eighties.

'It is you, isn't it?' she asked.

'Yes, it's me. I'm flattered to be remembered.'

'I saw you on television in…you know, the film that nearly won you the Best Actor award.'

'The operative word being "nearly". In those days they were practically the only awards. These days there's a whole host of them, especially for TV shows. The TopGo Television Drama Awards are coming up soon and they say your guy's going to scoop every prize going. There's five categories he can be nominated for and the big money says he'll win every one. You two will have a great time at the award ceremony.'

'If I'm still here.'

'Sure you'll be here. Everyone says he's crazy about you. Are you saying he isn't?'

'I'm saying it's private.' She chuckled.

'Good for you. If I hadn't given so many interviews about things that should have stayed private I'd still be married to my second wife, or perhaps my third.'

They settled into a happy discussion, after which Charlene finished the day with a visit to a boutique that was as fashionable as anything to be found in the city. By now she was a little short of time, but she had her eye on a pair of stretch jeans.

'The size looks about right for me,' she said. 'You close in five minutes, don't you? I'll take them.'

Back in the apartment, she pulled on the jeans and considered herself thoughtfully.

They're just a little tighter than I thought, she mused. *Too tight? Yes? No? If my rear was bigger I could be accused of flaunting it, but I'm so skinny I can get away with it.*

But 'skinny' wasn't the right word, she knew. While not voluptuous, her behind was nicely shaped, elegantly curved.

She found a floaty chiffon blouse that hung loosely down over the revealing trousers, concealing her rear from general sight.

From the front door came the sound of a knock and a cry, 'Is anyone there?'

'Coming,' she called.

Outside, she found a middle-aged woman with a tall, lithe figure.

'Hello,' she said. 'I'm Rita Barton, your neighbour from

the next floor down. I came to return something I borrowed from Travis.'

She had a bright, cheerful face and Charlene instinctively liked her.

'Come in,' she said.

She realised that this was the woman whose husband they had met in the elevator. She'd been a model and a dancer, and although she was no longer young her movements were still graceful.

As they shared coffee, she looked Charlene up and down and said frankly, 'Thank heavens the rumours are true. They say he's found a nice girl who'll do him a lot of good and no harm. Good for you!'

'Thank you,' Charlene said.

'Of course you know the story about the dancer who descended on him at that party. She did it on purpose. I never liked her.'

'You know her?'

'I used to give lessons to girls who were going to dance in front of the camera. At least it was called dancing, but mostly it was sexy wriggling. She was one of my pupils.' She added hastily, 'But don't tell Travis.'

'I promise.' Charlene laughed. 'But about those lessons, you mean you can teach that sort of thing?'

'There are certain tricks, depending on how provocative you want to be.' She noticed a definite look in Charlene's eyes and asked teasingly, 'Want to try?'

She was about to decline when the daring imp who seemed to pop up in her mind a lot these days said, *Go on. Be a devil.*

'Yes,' she said. 'I'd like to give it a try.'

'Like this,' Rita said, and went into a wriggling dance that still contained much of her old ability.

She laughed as she danced, obviously enjoying the joke, and Charlene laughed too as she imitated her.

'Put your hands up high over your head so that people can see your body moving,' Rita advised.

'Like that?'

'Fine. Now imagine that the man you're dancing for is sitting in that chair over there. Approach him slinkily—good, that's right, but move your bottom more. You have to twist and squirm a bit—more, more—you're getting the hang of it. Now try to twirl and writhe at the same time. *Well done!*'

Laughing, Charlene spun around, moving so fast that she lost track of the room whirling about her, and didn't see the door open, admitting Travis. Next moment she lost her balance and felt herself falling.

'Aaaah!' she cried.

'It's all right, I've got you.'

It was Travis's comforting voice, and Travis's steady arms enclosing her. But she'd collided with him so hard that he too lost his balance and fell into the chair with her in his lap.

'OK.' He laughed. 'The worst is over now.'

'Well,' Rita said, arms akimbo, 'that's one way of getting onto the guy's lap. Not one I've seen before, but I guess it works.'

'Hello, Rita,' Travis said. 'What are you two up to?'

'Rita was teaching me lap dancing,' Charlene said breathlessly.

'Really? Planning to take up a new career?'

'You never know,' she retorted. 'It's good to try anything once.'

'And she's got a real gift for it,' Rita added.

'Yeah, the gift of knocking a guy flying,' Travis said with a grin. 'I've come across it before.' He rubbed his back.

'I'm sorry,' Charlene said. 'Let me do that for you.'

She reached for him but he veered away. 'No need. I'll manage. You're a wicked woman. Rita, don't teach her any more dangerous tricks. She's beginning to scare me.'

'Nonsense, I've always scared you,' Charlene retorted, and the three of them shared a laugh.

'You know what you should do,' Rita said. 'Go back to that nightclub where *it* happened—'

'Not in a million years,' Travis said at once.

'No, wait. Take Charlene with you, and if those floozies start their nonsense again she'll show that she can do it even better than they can.'

'Hey, that's an idea,' Charlene said, fascinated.

'No,' Travis said quietly.

Rita beamed at Charlene. 'I'll need to teach you a bit more so that you're really expert—'

'I said no,' Travis snapped.

In the silence that followed they both looked at him, puzzled. That Travis, a man known for his sweet temper, should speak in that way was astonishing.

'I'm sorry,' he said, recovering himself quickly. 'It's been a long, hard day and I'm not at my best.'

'I'll be off now,' Rita said. 'I only came to return your book.'

She pushed it towards him, blew them both a kiss, and was gone.

'Did it go well today?' Charlene asked.

'Not too good. I've got a bad headache. I'll go straight to bed.'

'Let me get you something to eat.'

'No, thanks.' His words were tense and his smile forced. 'I just need to sleep. Goodnight.'

He vanished into his room, leaving Charlene staring at the closed door, frowning.

Why was Travis cross with her?

Ah, well, she thought at last. His headache must be worse than he'd said.

* * *

Travis lay awake for a long time. Something had happened that he needed to come to terms with, if he only knew how.

The moment when Charlene had landed in his lap was still with him. Her wriggling movements had been innocent, he knew. She'd been trying to steady herself, not inflame his senses, but she'd inflamed them nonetheless. The awareness of her body was burned into his flesh: searing, alarming, impossible to remove.

He'd never dreamed of this. Her plain looks had tricked him into thinking that the rest of her was the same. But now he knew otherwise, he thought, groaning as he remembered the enticing way she had moved against him, almost caressing him. Beneath her usually unrevealing clothes was a truly lovely body, one that he wanted to see as well as touch. The alarming discovery had been the reason he'd snapped at them, driven to distraction by the effort to keep himself under control while Rita joked about Charlene's sensual possibilities.

He groaned as he felt desire singing through his body, ignoring his attempts to silence it. He no longer knew the woman living in his home. She was a new, different Charlene, one he'd never imagined before.

One thing was clear. She must never know. His desire violated every promise he'd made to her. It also, he realised, broke her own promises about keeping everything sisterly. But in her innocence she had no idea about that. Nor would he allow her to suspect.

Over breakfast next morning his phone rang. As soon as he answered, his face brightened. '*Mom!* You're coming home? Great. Tomorrow. We'll be at the airport. Yes, both of us. You can meet Charlene and I can meet—what did you say his name was? Sure I'm cheeky. I always was.'

He hung up, saying, 'You probably gathered what that was about. I told you my mom leads a colourful life.'

'With plenty of "gentleman friends"?'

'Definitely. She's been on vacation in Paris with Eric, the latest, and they're returning tomorrow.'

They were there early next day. To pass the time Travis bought a magazine and flicked through it casually until he came to something that made him stare.

Glancing over his shoulder, Charlene saw a young woman, scantily dressed, stretched out on a sofa. Her figure was curvaceous and magnificent, but that wasn't her chief attraction. It was more the look in her eyes as they gazed into the camera, a look that said, *Why don't we get together and... see what happens?*

She felt mildly insulted. If Travis expected her to play the role of the faithful girlfriend it was hardly courteous of him to slaver over another female in public.

'Hmm,' she said.

Glancing up, he read her thoughts. 'No, no, it's not what you think. That's Cassie.'

'Cassie? The one who—?'

'The girl Marcel wants to marry, and who told him to take a running jump. I did hear a rumour that she'd once had a career as a glamour model—'

'She seems to have returned to it.'

'And how! Poor Marcel.' Travis sighed. 'I shouldn't think he'll get her back now.'

'I wonder how much they paid her for that,' Charlene mused. 'Enough to buy her a lot of independence.'

'Is that all you see?' he demanded, comically outraged. 'Money?'

'It matters. When we're finished, I think I'll buy myself a toy boy.'

'He wouldn't be called Lee, would he?' Travis asked lightly. He knew he shouldn't have asked the question, but since the other night something mysterious seemed to have happened to his self-control.

'Lee? No way. He's in the past. But of course—' she studied the picture again '—if I looked like her I wouldn't need to pay. The men would be clamouring to enjoy my charms.'

'It's not just voluptuous women who make men clamour,' he observed. 'There are other things that can be enchanting.'

'Nonsense!' she teased. 'That's just polite male talk. What all of you actually think is that real women are plump and luscious. The rest of us are too skinny to count.'

'Oh, that's what men think, is it?' he asked, raising his eyebrows.

'Sure is.'

'And who made you an expert in male thinking?'

'Women are born knowing it. And if they don't, they soon find out.'

He cocked his head on one side. 'So you're going to lecture me on the subject?'

'Why not? Since we're brother and sister, I can say what I like to you.'

'Brother and sister,' he murmured.

'It's what we agreed. That way, we're both safe.'

'Then, since we're speaking frankly, let me tell you that you don't know half what you think you do. Some men like to be taken by surprise.'

That made her gaze at him, wondering about his meaning and the slight edge in his voice. But then the loudspeaker shrieked, *'The flight from Paris has landed—'*

The moment collapsed and died. It was time to get back to real life.

Whatever that was.

Julia Franklin still looked much as Charlene remembered her from old films on television. Though well into her fifties, she could have passed for forty or less, the result, Charlene guessed, of much cosmetic surgery and sessions in the gym. It was the same with her charm, which was untouched by the years.

She greeted Travis with an eager cry of, *'Darling!'*

shrieked over a distance, and began to run. He did the same and they threw themselves into each other's arms, to the delight of the crowd, most of whom had recognised Travis.

Behind Julia came a man in his thirties, with a cherubic face and a good-natured air. This must be Eric, Charlene thought. Travis greeted him amiably, but with the caution of a man who'd met too many of his predecessors.

A cab took them to Bunker Hill, where Julia lived in a house that was defiantly colourful and un-modern. From the first moment Charlene felt herself under inspection. Julia had clearly heard the talk and was buzzing with curiosity.

'I haven't told her everything about us,' Travis had said earlier. 'Only that we met by accident in the studio, and found we could talk to each other easily. She doesn't know anything about Lee.'

During the meal, Julia dominated the conversation, talking about Paris and Rome, where she and Eric had spent their vacation. Eric sat looking at Julia with a little smile on his face.

Afterwards, Julia drew Charlene aside, saying, 'Come and have lunch here tomorrow. We'll do much better without the men.' Her voice became teasing. 'I think we always do better without men, don't you?'

'Sometimes.' Charlene laughed. 'But they come in handy now and then.'

'Good thinking,' Julia said triumphantly.

Later, Julia pulled her son into the kitchen and shut the door.

'So that's her. That's really her. I've been dying to meet her, although I've seen so many pictures of the two of you that I almost feel I know her. Look at that.'

She held up the snap taken in the hotel restaurant, showing Charlene convulsed with laughter.

'I'd bought her some pearl earrings,' Travis recalled, 'but I'd also bought some Daft Doody earrings for a friend, and I got muddled and gave her the wrong ones.'

'And she saw the funny side of that?' Julia asked, amazed.
'As you see.'

'Then she's a real jewel.' She eyed him with motherly suspicion. 'You do realise that, don't you?'

'Oh, yes,' he murmured. 'I realise that. Mom, can we talk about this later? I have a lot to tell you.'

'And I've got a lot to tell you. Paris was fantastic, and guess what! I bumped into your father. I was invited to some big reception, and there he was. Marcel was there too. Poor soul, he's so sad since he broke up with Cassie. He sent you his good wishes.'

'I'll bet my father didn't send me any good wishes.'

'Actually, he was on his best behaviour because Freya was there.'

'Freya? She's his stepdaughter by his new wife, isn't she?'

'Yes, and she's really very nice. Amos has set his heart on marrying her to one of his sons. He failed with Darius, so now he wants it to be Marcel. You should be careful. If he fails with Marcel he'll get you in his sights.'

'Hey, c'mon!'

'Really. "The Falcon" never gives up. That's what they say.'

'Then I'll have to set Charlene onto him. If that doesn't fill him with fear, nothing will.'

Which left Julia regarding him oddly and mulling over the conversation long into the night, so that Eric was roused to ask if anything was wrong.

'Nothing wrong,' she murmured. 'Just something I can't make up my mind about.'

'Would a cuddle help?'

Yes, please!

CHAPTER EIGHT

NEXT day Charlene paid Julia a visit. The two women liked each other. Julia was no actress. The cheeky kid she'd played as a starlet was simply her real self, and after thirty years she still existed. For much of the meal they swapped witticisms, but they both wanted to talk about Travis, and at last Julia said, 'He was always a lovely boy. So sweet-natured and full of feeling. I used to wish he didn't have so many feelings, so that his father couldn't hurt him so much.'

'He really minded about that, didn't he? He didn't say much but I could sense rivers running deep underneath.'

Julia nodded, then went to a cupboard and brought out a large book, which she opened, revealing a portrait photograph of Amos Falcon.

'I took this shot of him when we knew each other, years ago,' she said.

Amos had been an attractive man, not conventionally handsome, but with a fierce purpose in his face that proclaimed him one of life's winners. Many women would find that appealing, as the young Julia had done.

As she still did, Charlene thought, watching the other woman as she surveyed the photograph. After all this time, there was sadness and longing in her face as she flipped over the pages to find pictures of the two of them together. Amos and Julia, a young girl, her face full of love, happy in

the conviction that she had found her man and they would
be together for ever.

More pictures: Julia with baby Travis in her arms, but
never the three of them together.

'Are there any of Amos and Travis together?' she asked.

'None,' Julia said. 'That's one thing I can't forgive Amos
for. He paid maintenance for Travis, but he never took any
real interest in him. He'd visit, talk to him about how he was
doing at school, criticise him. But he wouldn't pose for a picture or become really involved with him. But look at these.'

At the back of the book were newspaper cuttings showing
Amos with some of his other sons.

'Darius, Jackson, Marcel,' Julia said bitterly. 'But not
Travis. I've seen him looking at these pictures with such
sadness. Just imagine what he must have been thinking.'

'That they were a complete family without him,' Charlene
whispered. 'How well I know that feeling.'

'Then you understand how it's been for him. I'm so glad.'

'It was much the same for me,' Charlene said.

Briefly she outlined the situation in her own family.

'I'm lucky in my grandparents. I get on with them wonderfully, and thank goodness I do because they're all I've got.'

'And I'm all Travis has got,' Julia said. 'I have no rela-
tives. I'm an orphan, raised in an institution.' She gave a grim
laugh. 'You wouldn't believe it, would you? The big star, the
world at his feet, women pursuing him, but it breaks his heart
that he's never felt really included in a family.

'I haven't been as good a mother as I meant to be,' she
added wryly. 'At one time I thought I'd marry and give him
a father, but none of my relationships ever quite worked out
and…well, it didn't increase stability, if you see what I mean.'

Charlene nodded, liking Julia even more for the honesty
with which she admitted her own failings.

'But he's got you,' Julia went on. 'He hasn't said much,
but I gather you're protecting him from the people who are

out to harm him. I can see that he's close to you, much closer than to women he sleeps with. Sometimes sex can actually form a barrier to closeness.'

She took Charlene's hand. 'Just be there for him,' she said. 'I know you will be, and I thank you with all my heart.'

'I'll be there,' Charlene promised.

Soon after that Travis arrived to collect her, looking from one to the other, smiling when he sensed the warmth and friendliness.

As soon as she could, Julia drew him aside, murmuring, 'Now I can have an easy mind about you. And I never thought I'd say that.'

'Mom, it's not like that. She's a friend.'

'A friend who happens to be living with you. A friend the whole world is talking about.'

'That's just it. We want the world to be talking about her so that they forget what happened in the nightclub. I couldn't face losing all I'd gained. Luckily Charlene agreed to help me.'

'How much does she know?'

'Everything. I didn't lie to her. That's the most wonderful thing about her. You can be completely honest and trust her to understand. It's such a relief.'

'Someone you can be completely open with. That's more luck than most people ever have. And you actually persuaded her to put on a big performance for the cameras?'

'Yes.'

'And the fact that you're living together isn't—?'

'No.'

'And you're not—?'

'No!'

'And you haven't even tried to—?'

'No!'

She surveyed him, half cynical, half amused.

'I don't think you're my son at all. You're an impostor. What have you done with the real Travis?'

He grinned. 'He decided to lie low for a while. He reckons he isn't so clever.'

She patted his hand. 'Well, getting Charlene to help you was really clever. She'll do you the world of good. You might start appreciating other things about women than the shape of their behinds. Why, darling, you're blushing!'

'Nonsense!' he said hurriedly. 'Can we leave it?'

'Of course. I'll just say this. I think she's the woman for you, and you should try to win her for life.'

'Mom, please. You just don't understand.'

She patted his face. 'No, my darling. It's you that doesn't understand.'

Life settled into a comfortable pattern. Sometimes they would go out together, always choosing a place where they would be seen and enjoying the public reaction, whether it appeared in the press or on the Internet.

'But don't overdo it,' Joe, the Press Officer, had warned. 'The public are quite sophisticated about this kind of thing these days, and if you live in each other's pockets they suspect a PR stunt.'

With one voice they exclaimed, *'Shocking!'*

Joe grinned. 'You two scare me sometimes. It's like the same brain working both of you!'

They shared a smile. Their instinctive mental harmony was a source of pleasure to them.

But they heeded Joe's words, and went out separately. She enjoyed the theatre, while he preferred to spend an evening with friends. She wondered if the friends included the kind of ladies he didn't dare be seen with, but if so he never mentioned it. When describing his evening he would finish with, 'I was boringly virtuous. You'd have been proud of me.'

'You could tell me if anything happened,' she said once. 'I wouldn't be jealous.'

'And I would tell you, if there was anything to tell. You'd need to be warned, for practical reasons.'

And since she had a deep belief in the trust between them, she accepted his word.

One evening Travis arrived home to find her about to leave.

'Going somewhere interesting?'

'To the theatre, with some of the girls from the TV studio. There's six of us going in total. It's an open air performance, so I'm just dressed casual.'

He noticed that by 'just casual' she meant the tight jeans she'd been wearing the day she sat on his lap, when he—

He shut off the thought.

From below came a beep from a horn.

'That's my taxi,' she said. 'Right, I'll be off.'

'Will you be late?'

'Very late, probably.' She added significantly, 'And I promise to come in quietly.'

He understood. She was saying that he was free to enjoy himself with another woman—or women.

'Charlene—'

'Got to dash. Bye!'

She blew him a kiss, and was gone.

From the window he watched her hop merrily into the taxi. As he turned back into the room he realised how empty it was. How silent and lonely.

Suddenly it was intolerable. He ran swiftly through a list of female names, seeking one that would do. The problem was that there were so many that would 'do'. Too many.

His choice fell on Susie. They were old friends and she liked nothing better than to have a good time, with nothing serious on either side, except a generous gift to finish the evening. He picked up the phone.

As soon as she heard his voice she cried, '*Darling!* It's been a long time.'

'How about we put that right? Are you free this evening?'

'I am for you. Where shall we meet?'

'Why don't you come over here?'

She gave a knowing laugh. 'That sounds lovely. Who needs other people?'

They understood each other perfectly.

Charlene's evening out was short-lived. The play was poor, the acting terrible. In the interval she and her friends poured out and headed into the nearest restaurant.

'Hey, look who's there!' exclaimed a young woman. 'Penny Danes. She's the TV star in *The Man From Heaven.* Who's that handsome guy snuggling up to her?'

'His name's Lee Anton,' Charlene said. 'He's just started in the series.'

Cameras were flashing on the theatrically loving couple. Penny stretched out her hand, flaunting a ring, then kissed Lee, waving the ring again.

'Looks like they've got engaged,' someone observed. 'Do you know him, Charlene?'

'No,' she said quietly. 'I don't know him.'

Soon after that she discovered that she was tired. Bidding goodnight to her companions, she slipped quietly away and went to stand outside the restaurant, looking in at Lee and his new lover.

It should have hurt, she thought wryly, but that was all over. Now she had a new life, thanks to Travis, with his gift of touching her emotions. Their relationship might only be friendly, but so few people had ever bothered with her emotions in the past that it could be dangerous if she wasn't careful.

But I am careful, she thought. *Careful is my middle name. He's my dear brother, and I won't let anything spoil it.*

She turned and went to hail a taxi. Nothing appeared and after a while she thought of going back inside. But when she turned, Lee was standing there.

'Fancy seeing you! Come in and meet my fiancée.'

'Thank you, no. But I wish you every happiness, Lee.'

'You don't blame me, then?'

'Why should I blame you? There was nothing really between us.'

She had the feeling that this didn't please him.

'Anyway, I hope Travis doesn't hurt you too much when your break-up comes. And it will. He's not known as a faithful guy. The girls love him, but he doesn't love them. Since he linked up with you they say he's a reformed character.' He eyed her hilariously. 'But I guess you'd know about that.'

'I see a taxi,' she said hurriedly. 'Goodnight, Lee.'

She couldn't get away from him fast enough.

It was dark when she reached home. She let herself in quietly, meaning to tiptoe to her room, unnoticed. But the door to Travis's bedroom was ajar, and from behind it she could hear a woman's voice.

'Oh, darling, you're so sweet. If only other people saw the real you—knew you as I do—'

Silence. Charlene was tense, waiting for his voice, wondering what he would say.

'It's better if they don't,' he said at last. 'Let's keep it our secret.'

'Oh, yes, of course you're right. This is special to us—'

Charlene flattened herself against the wall, her eyes darting frantically from side to side. There was no way to reach her own room without passing the open door, and the thought of being discovered like this made her quail.

But the alternative was to stay concealed, effectively spying on Travis.

Help! wailed a voice in her head. *I can't handle this.*

'I've really missed you,' came the female voice again. 'And you've missed me. I can tell. You have, haven't you?'

Heart pounding, Charlene waited for his answer, but instead of words there came only a *Mmm* sound, suggesting a prolonged kiss.

'Travis—'

'Wait.' That was his voice.

He was moving about the room. Charlene held her breath as she sensed him grow nearer. Even so, she wasn't prepared for the moment when he came into sight. The door was open just wide enough to show the whole of him, naked except for a pair of black briefs, so tiny they were almost non-existent.

She drew back into the shadows as far as she could go, unable to take her eyes off him. That a man so tall and lean should yet have such perfectly formed muscles, such a hint of restrained power, such beauty. She could hardly believe what her eyes were telling her.

He seemed preoccupied with troublesome thoughts, which was strange if he was on the verge of making love to his companion. He turned, showing his body from a new angle, the gentle swell of his rear, the length of his thighs.

At last he moved away behind the door, and she seized the chance to creep to her room. She didn't even put the light on. At all costs he mustn't suspect that she'd returned. She could feel her heart beating so fiercely that she feared he must be able to hear even at that distance.

She undressed quickly and got into bed, diving beneath the cover as though seeking shelter. The whole world seemed to have rocked. It was disgraceful to have seen his near nakedness while he was unaware, but she couldn't make herself regret it. Even now he walked through her thoughts, casually magnificent.

But he wasn't alone. A young woman was with him, lying in his bed, waiting for him to approach her. Obviously he'd called her as soon as she herself had gone out for the evening.

Lee's words came back to her. *The girls love him, but he doesn't love them.*

She had no right to complain. She'd promised to come in quietly in case he had a girl. But somehow she hadn't really believed it, and the reality came as a shock.

She rolled over, burying her face in the pillow.

'Don't you care for me any more?' Susie's soft voice was petulant.

'What do you mean?'

'Usually by this time you've tossed me on the bed and—' She finished with a significant little giggle.

'A man learns patience as he gets older,' he said with a touch of desperation.

'But don't I attract you?'

'Of course you do,' he said determinedly. 'You're as lovely as ever. It's just that—'

He fought for something to say. Anything would do, other than the truth, which was that inviting her here tonight had been the biggest mistake he'd ever made, and he was paying for it. He'd watched as she undressed, waiting for the moment when his excitement rose, but nothing had happened.

Nor had it happened when she removed his own clothes. Her touch, her voluptuous charms left him unmoved.

Disaster!

If only he could banish the cheeky ghost that lingered in the apartment, a ghost who teased him as a sister, who'd shown him a whole new side of life, even made him see himself in a new light. A ghost with a tempting body that she kept concealed from the world so that only the privileged were allowed to discover it.

And who was out tonight—doing what? And with whom?

'What is it?' Susie demanded. 'You suddenly jumped as though you'd seen a ghost.'

'I think I did,' he said, seizing inspiration quickly. 'It's Charlene—she could come back at any moment—'

'But you said she'd be gone a long time.'

'I could be wrong. I'm sorry, I'm not at my best. I think we should forget this.'

'Well, really! What a way to treat a lady!'

He'd never seen Susie in a temper before, and it wasn't a pretty sight. After spitting out a few curses, she declared significantly, 'I don't like wasting my time.'

'Of course you don't,' he placated her, 'but I have a present for you. Here.'

He took a bracelet from a drawer where he'd left it, awaiting the right moment to give it to Charlene. Mollified, Susie let him put it on her wrist.

'That's more like it,' she said. 'And next time maybe we'll have more luck.'

There wasn't going to be a next time but he was too wise to say so.

'Goodbye, Susie.'

She stalked out of the bedroom towards the front door, which he held open for her. There she turned to give him a beguiling smile, to remind him what he was missing. But, to her annoyance, he wasn't looking at her. His attention had been caught by something a few feet away, and it seemed to astound him.

'Goodbye,' she snapped.

He didn't reply, merely closing the door without taking his eyes from whatever had caught them. Susie flounced on her way.

Travis was too dazed to move. What he'd seen had stunned him with its implications. There, on a small table, was Charlene's purse.

She'd taken it with her. It shouldn't be here.

But it was.

Which meant that she was here too. She must have come

in while he was with Susie, and slipped quietly into her room, passing his bedroom door, which had been standing open.

And she'd seen—?

What?

After struggling with himself for what felt like ages, he tapped on her door.

'Hello?' came her voice.

'It's me.'

The door opened, revealing her in an all covering robe.

'You left your purse out here,' he said, holding it up.

'Oh, I…didn't notice…' She seemed as distracted as himself. 'Thank you.'

He waited for her to stand back and invite him in. But she didn't.

'I wasn't expecting you back as soon as this,' he said lamely.

'The play was a disaster. I came home early.'

So she was pretending not to know about Susie, he thought. But he wasn't fooled. There was no way she couldn't know.

'I had a friend over,' he said casually.

'Good. I hope it was fun. I expect you're worn out now.'

Clearly she thought he'd been making love to Susie, and equally clearly it didn't bother her.

That was good, he admonished himself. *Brother and sister. Don't forget.*

'No, I'm not worn out,' he said. 'It wasn't *that* much of a fun evening.'

After a brief pause, she asked, 'Really?'

'Really,' he said firmly.

She managed a faint smile. 'I'm disappointed in you.'

'So was the lady. I don't think I met her expectations. Suddenly I wasn't interested, and there are some things that… well, you just can't pretend.'

It hurt her to see the strain in his face.

'It'll be better next time,' she murmured. 'There are so many other girls.'

'When you're young and stupid perhaps. But in the end it has to be the right one.'

'But you are young. You aren't thirty yet.'

'Suddenly I don't feel young any more. Hey, guess what! Maybe I grew up. I wonder what made that happen.'

Travis was on the edge of a precipice, saying things he should never have dared say to her, but he didn't know how to stop.

'Don't listen to me; I'm talking nonsense,' he hurried to say.

'That's all right. You can say anything to your big sister.'

As often before, she reached out to lay a gentle hand against his cheek. Travis laid his own hand over it but didn't look up to meet her eyes. His gaze seemed fixed on his feet.

'It's late,' he said at last. 'Time we were getting some sleep. I'm sorry I disturbed you.'

'Yes, of course,' she said, disappointed. 'Goodnight.'

She closed the door. Whatever he'd been about to say would not now be said. What he might have done would be left undone. She sighed.

Travis stood in the dark hall for a moment, then backed away, knowing he must get as far from her as possible and silence the raging tremors that went through his body. What Susie's flaunting sexuality had failed to do, Charlene's lightest touch on his cheek had done with ease. For the second time that night his mind said *Disaster*, but for a different reason.

When he remembered how he'd admitted his own failure to her he wanted to vanish into thin air. Instead, he curled up in bed, pulled the covers over his head and tried to pretend he didn't exist.

In her own room, Charlene got slowly into bed, disturbed by a thousand conflicting instincts. But she couldn't cope with them. She must try to escape into sleep. She closed her eyes and headed for the safety of oblivion.

Looking back at what happened next, she supposed she should have seen it coming. It was as inevitable as the rising of the sun, but she didn't understand that at the time.

Her dreams were vague, just impressions floating through her mind, until suddenly Travis appeared.

Time had turned back and they were talking together in warmth and friendship. He touched her cheek, a sign of warmth that they frequently exchanged. It was the lightest gesture and she had responded to it happily—laughing, pleased but unruffled.

But now that touch was happening again in her dreams, and her flesh was reacting as it hadn't done before. Suddenly she was responding with all her heart, relishing their emotional closeness and understanding, but above all rejoicing in his touch.

It was there again, his hand moving softly against her skin, tempting her to reach up, clasp it, drawing it further down. His eyes were telling her that this was what he wanted, if only she—

Charlene awoke with a cry, finding herself sitting up in bed, staring into the darkness, appalled at herself. Everything she remembered, the urgency in his caress, the vibrancy of her response—*these things hadn't happened!*

Except perhaps deep inside, hidden out of sight in some remote place where neither her mind nor her feelings were in control.

Mysteriously, her body had stored up the memory, waiting until she was ready to confront it, then releasing it now, when her heart was suddenly open to him and she had no defences to protect her from its dangerous message.

No, she told herself, trying to be firm. *I'm imagining things. Just a pathetic fantasist telling herself what she wants to believe.*

Travis's voice came from behind the door. 'Charlene—Charlie—? What's happened?'

'Nothing, I'm fine,' she forced herself to call back.

'Are you sure? I thought I heard you cry out.'

'I was out of bed,' she stammered. 'I stubbed my toe.'

'Can I come in?'

'No,' she cried quickly. 'Goodnight.'

'Goodnight.' He sounded reluctant, but at last she heard him move away.

She lay there, breathing hard, trying to pull herself together, but with no success. Where was calm, sensible Charlie when she was needed? Nowhere to be found.

But she was strong. She wouldn't give in to her sudden fierce awareness of him as a man. That was her problem, not his, and he mustn't be allowed to suspect. She closed her eyes, trying to banish him.

Yet he was stubborn and awkward, lingering on the edge of her consciousness, demanding entry to remind her once more how her heart was eagerly opening to him, reproaching her for not feeling it before.

'No,' she cried desperately. 'You mustn't— *I* mustn't— No, *please*!''

'Charlie!'

'No—no—'

'Charlie—wake up!'

She could feel his hands, grasping her firmly until she opened her eyes and realised that Travis had come into the room. He was sitting on the bed, holding her shoulders and giving her a gentle shake.

'Wake up,' he said. 'Charlie, please wake up.'

'Oh—yes—yes—'

'Are you awake now?'

'Yes,' she choked.

'My poor dear. Such a terrible nightmare you must have had. You sounded in agony.'

'You could hear me?' she cried, aghast. Whatever had she said? What had she revealed?

'I could hear you in my room, through two closed doors. I know you sent me away before but I couldn't leave you to suffer alone like that. I heard you call, "I mustn't—no, please". What's so terrible that you mustn't do it? Come on, you can tell me. I'm your brother, remember?'

That was the one thing he would never be again, she thought desperately. He was a man, with all a man's attractions. She'd deluded herself about this before, but never again.

Now he was lying down on the bed, his arms about her in a hug that devastated her with its hint of things she might yearn for but could never claim. The blankets were between them and she clung to that thought for safety, because she so desperately wished that they weren't. Even so, she could feel the shape of his body, its warmth and power, its promise of delight for a woman he had chosen.

But she was not that woman. He hadn't chosen her. He'd turned to her in despair.

'What was the dream about?' he whispered.

'I'm...not sure. It was so vague—'

'But you sounded scared. You were pleading. Who were you pleading with?'

I was pleading with myself not to fall in love with you, pleading for strength and common sense to save me from what I want so much.

'Nobody,' she said. 'Nothing.'

'You're lying. Why? What is it that you can't tell me?'

I can never tell you anything again.

'I can't remember,' she forced herself to say. 'It's over now. I can go back to sleep.'

'You want me to go?'

'You've got a long day tomorrow,' she said with an attempt at brightness. 'You must think of that.'

'I see. All right, I'll go.'

There was a faintly forlorn note in his voice, almost as though he felt snubbed. But she barely heard it through her own feeling of rejection. She waited until he'd gone, then rolled over and curled up in a ball, as though trying to shut out the whole world. She stayed like that, wide awake and fretting, for the rest of the night.

CHAPTER NINE

Next morning she told him about Lee and Penny's engagement.

'Oh, Charlie, I'm sorry. Was it very painful for you?'

'Not at all. Over and done with.'

'The one I'm sorry for is Penny,' he mused. 'Her contract has just been renewed for next season's show. So far, his hasn't. But with her to fight his corner—' He shrugged.

'Let's hope things work out well for them both,' she said.

It was strange to recall how this would once have broken her heart, but that was before her new awareness of Travis as a man. While it was only his kind friendship that had touched her it had been easy to keep a sense of proportion. But since she'd seen him nearly naked everything had been different.

'What is it?' he asked suddenly.

'What's what?'

'That look on your face, as though you'd discovered a secret joke. What have I said that's funny?'

'Nothing. It's not you that's funny. It's me.'

'So tell me.'

'No…no, I can't,' she insisted.

'All right, I don't want to pry. By the way, I'm sorry about last night.'

'But what is there to be sorry about?'

'Getting all miserable and emotional. I went too far. You do know you've got nothing to fear from me, don't you?'

'Yes,' she said with a touch of sadness. 'I do know.'

'I promised you that when you moved in here—' he gave a self-conscious laugh '—when I more or less forced you to move in.'

'You didn't force me.'

'Manipulated you, then. I seized the chance to make you do what suited me. I'm good at that, I'm afraid, and I don't blame you if you don't trust me. I wouldn't trust me. I'm a bad character. But you know that.'

'Travis, there's no need for this, honestly.'

'All right, I'll shut up in a minute. I talk too much as well.'

That was true. If she hadn't been distracted by her own nerves she might have noticed that he was gabbling like a man holding on for dear life.

'You're probably planning to make a run for it,' he went on, 'but there's no need. I give you my word. Don't leave me, Charlie.'

'I won't leave. I know you can't manage without your big sister.'

'Funny how you always say *big* sister, although I'm older than you.'

'No, you're not. Compared to me, you're about five years old.'

He gave a rueful grin. 'I guess that's true. What would I do without you to keep me on the straight and narrow?'

'You'd pick someone else from the crowds who'd apply.'

'But there aren't crowds because nobody else knows that much about me. I'd never let them. Only you.'

'Well, be careful how many of your dark secrets you tell me. When this is over I'll probably blackmail you.'

They both laughed, but then he said, 'Why should it be over? Why can't we stay in touch for the rest of our lives? You're the best friend I ever had, and I'm not going to let my best friend go.'

Best friend. Once the words would have pleased her. Now they were like the crack of doom.

The phone rang. He answered it and a moment later she heard him cry, *'Yes!'* in a voice full of delight. 'That's wonderful! I don't know what took you so long—yes, yes, all right. Of course I'm coming. I wouldn't miss it for the world. Give Cassie my love.'

He hung up, seized Charlene and waltzed her around the room.

'What's happened?' she asked, laughing.

'That was my brother, Marcel.'

'The one who made a mess of his proposal and she went back to modelling?'

'That's the one. But he's got her back. You remember that picture we saw, and you said she must be making a lot of money? Well, she was, enough to invest in his business. Then she marched in, told him she was a fellow shareholder.'

'So he had to treat her as an equal instead of walking all over her,' Charlene said. 'Excellent.'

'Somehow they've managed to get it together, and they're marrying in Paris next month. It'll be a big celebration. We'll have a great time, and you can meet my family.'

'Am I invited?'

'Are you—? Listen, everyone's crazy to meet you. I wouldn't dare go without you. Hang it! Who's that?' The phone had rung again. 'Yes? Hi, Joe. Yes, I'm on my way—glad you're pleased—well, I guess we could do some more—wait, she's here. I'll ask her.'

He turned to Charlene. 'It's Joe. He's pleased with the story so far, but he wants to "direct strategy" as he puts it. Can you come into the studio with me this morning?'

'Sure.'

'Joe, we're on our way.'

Joe cornered them as soon as they arrived and swept them down to the studio canteen. By now Charlene was used to being surveyed, and wasn't offended by the way he looked her up and down, then nodded.

'Yup. Going well.'

'Thank you,' she said ironically.

'No, really, you're doing a fantastic job.'

'What about me?' Travis demanded comically.

'Oh, sure, you too.'

Travis put his arm around Charlene's shoulder, hugging her and saying, 'You see how it is. Now you're here nobody notices me any more. I could get insulted.'

'Yeah, right.' She aimed a shadow punch at him. He delighted her in this jokey mood.

'Can we be serious?' Joe demanded. 'I know the press are in pursuit but we need to stage something where we're in control. I've arranged a theatre attendance for you so that they can see you entering the box, standing there for all to see. And I think a couple of shopping expeditions. Travis, you should buy her some jewellery so that'll start them speculating.'

'Do we want them to speculate?' Charlene asked. 'What happens when it comes to nothing?'

'Who says it comes to nothing?' Joe asked.

'That's enough,' Travis said firmly. 'Don't go too far. Charlene's helping us out of the goodness of her heart.'

'And she'll gain. You can give her a lot of jewellery, all paid for by the studio, and if you eventually quarrel and she chucks it back at you, I'll make sure it's returned to her quietly.'

'Oh, we quarrel and I chuck it back at him?' she said hilariously.

'Yeah, but be careful how you do that. Don't hit his face. The studio has a lot of money invested in that face.'

'Fine, I'll just punch him in the stomach.'

'You're enjoying this, aren't you?' Travis asked wildly.

'I don't know how I'm keeping a straight face,' she told him.

'Yeah, it's got its funny side,' Joe conceded with a grin,

'but it's serious too. I shouldn't be telling you this quite so soon but—' he lowered his voice '—it's just possible that the series will be turned into a film.'

They both stared at him, dumbstruck.

'A film?' Travis whispered.

'Right. And you're the leading candidate for the part.'

'He should be the only candidate,' Charlene said indignantly. 'He made it what it is.'

'And that's why we're backing him all the way,' Joe said. 'But Alaric Lanley is interested.'

The other two drew sharp breaths. Lanley was a major film star.

'If he wants it they'll give it to him,' Travis said.

'Not necessarily. Like Charlene says, it's you that's associated with the part, and that's worth money. Have you ever met Alaric, by the way?'

'Yes, once at a party,' Travis said. 'I thought he seemed a nice guy.'

'Well, don't let anyone hear you say that,' Joe said, scandalised. 'You're enemies. This is a fight to the death. Give a few interviews saying he'll steal your role at his peril. Nothing specific. Just some vague showbizzy threats.'

'Forget it,' Travis said at once.

'Look—'

'I said forget it. Excuse me.' He leaned sideways to attract the attention of a waitress.

While he was talking to her, Joe growled to Charlene, 'What can you do with this guy? There are things he just doesn't understand.'

'Yes,' she agreed, 'being nasty is something he definitely doesn't understand. Kicking people in the teeth, treating them badly because they've treated him badly. Don't try to change it. It makes him what he is.'

He gave her a look of appreciation. 'Guess you're right. Fine,' he resumed as Travis turned back to them, 'we've got to do some urgent PR work to keep you in front of the public at all times.

'It helps that we've got this big story about the two of you. So far it's been great. People have seen you in the street, in restaurants. But now we need to direct the public to what we want them to see.'

Charlene knew a moment's doubt. This almost military planning wasn't what she had agreed to. But then she saw Travis watching her uneasily, and knew that she had no choice. This was his big chance, and she'd promised to be here for him.

'Are you up for it?' Joe asked.

'Yes,' she said firmly.

'Yes,' Travis said, giving her a look of gratitude.

'Great. Then let's make plans.'

'What about a beach party?' Travis said. 'We gather on Venice Beach, swim, romp, dance around.'

'Great!' Joe exclaimed. 'I'll set it up and let you know.'

So that was that, Travis thought, mentally reclining with a sense of satisfaction. What he knew of Charlene's body came from sensations. He desperately needed to see the whole of her and marry the feelings up with visions. He'd been racking his brain for a way, and now one had been presented to him. A beach. Charlene in a bathing costume, everything laid out for his delighted inspection.

He knew a faint twinge of guilt. To trick her into displaying her body wasn't the act of a gentleman.

'Are you all right with this?' he asked her anxiously. 'I know you said yes to help me, but I wouldn't want to force you into anything.'

A picture swam into Charlene's vision: Travis as she'd seen him last night, naked but for the tiny trunks, just as he would be again on the beach.

'I think I can just about endure it,' she said.

* * *

Joe pursued his plans determinedly, announcing that their theatre seats had been booked for the following night.

'What's the show?' Travis asked.

'Um…hang on, I'll check.'

He scanned a newspaper, prompting Travis to ask in an appalled tone, 'You booked the play without knowing what it was?'

'It's a great theatre with a huge box where everyone will see you. What does the play matter? Here we are. *Seek the Nightmare.*'

They both jumped at the sound of the play that was notorious for being learned and mysterious.

'It was a big success in the West End of London,' Joe said. 'Charlene saw it there and loved it.'

'I did not,' she said indignantly. 'Not my sort of thing at all.'

'You loved it,' Joe said firmly. 'And Travis is taking you to it here as a special treat.'

'I'm glad you told me,' Travis said in a faint voice. 'I don't have to pretend to like it, do I?'

'You'll have to decide whether you're the gallant chevalier enduring it for the sake of his lady, or the dark-browed intellectual sunk in thought,' Joe told him.

Travis gave him a look. Charlene covered her quivering lips.

'And during the interval,' Joe continued, gathering his things, 'remember to talk. The press love that because they can imagine what you're saying, and write the script for themselves. "Has he asked her yet?" That kind of thing. All right, I'm off.'

He left them before either could speculate about what 'asking her' might mean.

On the night they wore evening clothes. Around her neck Charlene sported a diamond necklace, bought by the studio and glamorous enough to inspire questions. She didn't care.

The actress in her was enjoying the game. And on her wrist she wore a bracelet, given to her by Travis with the words, 'I bought you a gift a few days ago but things have been so hectic I didn't give it until now.'

He reckoned that explanation would have to do, since he could hardly tell the truth, that it was a replacement for the one he'd had to give Susie to cover his embarrassment.

At the theatre they were applauded in the foyer and again when they made their entrance into the box. The play was officially 'intellectual', a dark, soul-searching work that made Charlene want to laugh derisively at its self-indulgence. But Joe was delighted with the reports he'd received from his spy in the stalls.

'You looked great and you talked to each other, so people could see you interacting,' he whooped.

'It's as well they couldn't hear the conversation.' She chuckled when they were alone.

'Yes, me threatening to leave if it got any more boring, and you promising to wake me up when it was over. That would have given Joe a heart attack.'

'Never mind. He won't find out. We're a team.'

'Yes,' he murmured, holding her hand. 'We are.'

The arrangements for the party on Venice Beach had been made with detailed precision.

'It's a day out for everyone,' Joe had explained. 'The whole cast, crew, director, we all decided to treat ourselves to a rest day, and the press just happened to find out. They'll be watching you two, walking, swimming, eating—whatever.'

'Are you sure you're all right with this?' Travis asked her again as they got ready to leave in the morning. 'You had an odd look on your face when Joe was describing it.'

'I was only worried in case I couldn't measure up.'

'You'll measure up. You're going to be wonderful, because you always are.'

Charlene spoke seriously. 'I hope I'm everything you want me to be, because I know how much this matters to you. I saw the look on your face too, only it wasn't a funny look. This was a man full of excitement because he could see the big chance coming up. But he was also just a little afraid in case he couldn't make the most of it.'

'How well you understand me.' Travis sighed. 'All the shields and defences that fool other people—you just see right through them as though they weren't there.' He took both her hands in his and kissed each one lightly. 'With anyone else that would scare me, but with you I know it's all right.' He added wryly, 'You only got one thing wrong.'

'What was that?'

'I'm not "just a little afraid". I'm scared stiff. To lose this chance—' he gave a brief laugh '—if I get that film part, it could lead to so much.'

'Yes, it would. There'd be a second film, and then a third, and studios would be falling over themselves to hire you.'

'I'd be so much bigger than I am now, and then perhaps—'

'Then even your father would have to give you some respect,' she said. 'Yes, he'll be proud of you, and boast about you. "Hey, my son is Travis Falcon."'

'Yup! That's it. It's stupid, isn't it? I'm a grown man, well, at least I pretend to be. I fool the others, but not you.'

'Maybe I have my own ideas of what constitutes a grown man,' she said.

'Lucky for me.'

'If he's kind and gentle, generous and caring, that's all I care about. You can stuff the macho business.'

'You don't think I'm making too much of today, do you?' he asked. 'It's only a few hours spent fooling for the camera—'

'It's not going to win the victory on its own,' she agreed. 'But it's a step on the road. Then you'll take another step, and another, until you're running so fast that nobody can catch you.'

'*We'll* be running,' he corrected.

'No, this is about you. I'm just backup. You'll be a big, *big* star and you'll make so much money that your father and your brothers will want to borrow from you.'

He grinned. 'In my dreams. But yes, that's where the road leads. I'll become obsessed with money, and then they'll know that I'm a real Falcon after all.' He added quietly, 'But do I want to travel that road?'

'You won't become obsessed with money,' she told him. 'Not you. What you make of it is up to you. It'll be *your* road. *Your* decisions.'

'What about yours?'

'Yours,' she said firmly. 'Nobody else's.'

He looked at her for a moment, then drew her close, wrapping his arms right around her and holding her against him.

'What would I do without you?' he murmured against her hair. 'Don't leave me, because I couldn't bear that. I… You see, if I could only… Just don't leave me.'

She stroked his hair, deeply touched by what she'd seen inside him. Travis might say what he liked about money and stardom, but that was a front. Inside him there still lived a little boy, longing for his father's attention and the feeling that he belonged in the family that always seemed to exclude him. She tightened her arms, instinctively seeking to protect that little boy.

'Don't worry,' she said. 'I'm here as long as you need me.'

'Charlie—'

The doorbell rang.

'That'll be Rick, come to collect us,' Travis said reluctantly.

She raised a clenched first. 'Forward into battle.'

He mimicked the gesture. 'Victory awaits.'

They were to travel in an open car, the better to be seen.

When they were seated in the back, Rick drove them down to where Joe was waiting with several of the others.

'Most of them have gone on ahead,' he told them. 'It looks more natural if we don't all arrive together. Let's get started.' But when he saw Travis's arm about Charlene's shoulders he looked doubtful. 'I'm not sure that's enough. Maybe you should be leaning close so that your head is resting on Travis's shoulder.'

'Occasionally,' Charlene agreed. 'But this journey is new to me, so I think he'd be pointing things out. I'd say, "Oh how wonderful!" and we'd interact.'

'Great! You've got a real talent for giving directions.'

'You're telling me,' Travis said with feeling. 'You should see how hen-pecked I am at home.'

Everybody laughed and they set off down the Santa Monica Freeway. It was a merry start to the day.

After an hour's drive they reached the roads that led to the beach, and the car slowed down so that passers-by could see them. Now Charlene rested her head on his shoulder, as per instructions, and he laid his own head against her hair. Joe, overtaking, gave a thumbs up sign. Perfect!

About twenty of the crowd from the show had arrived before them and had taken over a small section of the beach, entertaining photographers with their antics while everyone awaited the star.

Vera, who'd looked after Charlene on the first day, approached, saying, 'Your changing huts are over here.'

They each vanished into a hut, emerging a few moments later to stand in the sun, breathing in the fresh air with expressions of ecstasy, while secretly sizing each other up.

Now Charlene knew she'd been right to come on this trip. Not for anything would she have missed the sight of Travis in tight black swimming trunks, reminiscent of the other night. He was everything she remembered, lightly tanned, smooth chested, the perfect combination of lean and muscular.

But he seemed less pleased, frowning a little at her modest one piece. 'I thought you'd have chosen a bikini.'

'Tut, tut!' she murmured. 'Your respectable girlfriend doesn't flaunt herself like that. Besides,' she added in a tone of coming down to earth, 'I'm too skinny for a bikini.'

'You're not skinny,' he said. 'Just beautifully slim. There are models who'd give their eye-teeth for your figure.'

'Thank you, kind sir, but I'd still like to be more curvaceous where it matters. Like here.' She wriggled her behind to give him a better view. 'Wouldn't that bit be improved by a little more oomph?'

'No,' he said with feeling. 'It wouldn't.'

'Oh, come on, take a proper look.'

'I am taking a proper look,' he said in a strained voice. 'It's perfect as it is.'

'Well, that's very kind but I suppose you've got to say it, haven't you? We both know I need a bit more there. Perhaps I should try to put on some weight.'

'I warn you, do that and you'll be sorry.'

'Ooh, the dominant male,' she teased. 'I thought you didn't do macho.'

'Maybe it's time I tried.'

By now they had reached the water. She hopped in front of him, dancing backwards through the tiny waves.

'C'mon,' she taunted. 'Make me sorry.'

'Whatever could I do that would make you sorry?'

The thought, *You could send me away from you, and I'd be sorry for ever* flashed through her mind, but was banished. Nothing was going to spoil today.

'You'll never find out,' she said, moving faster.

But that was a mistake. She lost her balance and rocked wildly until he seized her and drew her against himself to steady her. She had a wild sensation of his bare chest against her and clung to him, wishing the rest of the world would just vanish.

Joe appeared beside them.

'Nice stuff, but go back to shore. Charlene, I don't want you swimming just yet because of your hair. Travis, why don't you carry her?'

'Happy to oblige,' he said, grinning and sweeping her up into his arms.

True to her role, she clung to him, shaking her head so that her hair could float in the sun. As they emerged from the water the rest of the cast was there, playing games, tossing balls about, cheering them.

Then Travis saw something that soured his mood.

'What the devil is he doing here?'

'Who?'

'Him.' He jerked his head in the direction of a young man capering by the water's edge.

'Oh, it's Lee,' Charlene said. 'Well, nearly everyone's here, so I suppose he was bound to be included. And look, there's Penny.'

Penny was laying firm claim to her fiancé, which should have eased Travis's mind, but didn't.

How did she feel about him? Travis wondered. She said it was over but now he knew that she was an accomplished actress. That was fine for presenting a mask to others, but he hated to think that she might be presenting a mask to him.

'Shouldn't you put me down now?' she said.

'Not until I have Joe's permission,' he said firmly, marching away up the beach.

She chuckled and buried her face in his shoulder. He only wished he could be sure she wasn't looking back at Lee.

Vera was waiting with a large white towel spread out on the sand. Travis dropped to his knees and laid her out so that she showed to best advantage. Then he lay down beside her, propping his head up on one hand and gazing down adoringly.

She gazed back up, trying to match his expression. It was easy. Too easy, she thought with a flicker of alarm.

He's only acting, said the warning voice in her mind. *Don't forget that.*

And I'm acting too, replied her sensible self. *I'm not falling in love with him. I'm not! I'm not! I'm not.*

'Let's do this later,' she said. 'It's too soon to lie down.' She rose hurriedly, needing to get further away from Travis. This was dangerous.

Someone had brought beach balls, which were tossed high in the air. Much chasing and jumping followed, showing off several figures to advantage. But none were quite as fine as Travis's figure, Charlene thought with appreciation.

Following the 'stage directions', they held hands to walk along the water's edge, chased each other, laughed into each other's faces and generally gave an expert performance.

His arm about her was strong and delightful and she was emboldened to raise her hand and lay it against his chest. She could feel the faint beat of his heart against her fingers and knew there had never been a moment as sweet as this in her life. Perhaps there never would be again, so she would remember and treasure this for ever.

'How are you managing?' he asked, leaning down so that he could speak quietly.

'I'm enjoying it. I said I'd do anything and I meant it.'

For a moment something flickered in his eyes. 'Anything at all?'

'What do you think?'

'I wish I knew what to think.'

From nearby, Joe, always keeping watch, complained, 'You both look too serious. Say something to each other.'

'You're treading on my foot,' Charlene told Travis fervently.

'Something nice,' Joe corrected.

'You're the most handsome man in the world,' she declared.

'Now you're just making him laugh,' Joe protested.

'What do you expect?' Travis demanded, grinning. 'How can anyone keep a straight face like this?'

Some journalists and photographers appeared.

'Hey, Travis, tell us about your lady. All Los Angeles is talking about her.'

'Then you don't need me to tell you,' he said in a voice that sounded slightly uneasy.

She wondered if he feared to offend her by saying too much and was sure of it when he patted her hand, murmuring, 'Don't worry.'

'Aw, c'mon. Just a quote. How did you meet?'

'We bumped into each other in the studio,' she said. 'I'd lost my way and he...he found it for me.' She gave a mysterious smile. 'Maybe. Now, I think that's all, don't you?'

As they resumed their walk she said, 'I hope you don't think I said too much.'

'That was brilliant!' Joe spluttered. 'The perfect story. You're really good at this, isn't she, Travis?'

'Yes,' he said quietly. 'She is.' He glanced over his shoulder at the paparazzi still in pursuit and said in a harassed voice, 'Don't they ever give up?'

'They're waiting for you to kiss her,' Joe informed him. 'Get on with it.'

He slid quickly away lest he be caught in the picture.

'He's right,' Travis said.

'Of course he is.'

'I'm sorry.'

'We have to be professional,' she assured him.

The sun was beginning to set, throwing a golden glow over the sand and making the water glitter. As if united by the same thought, they strolled a little way into the sea and paused, gazing into each other's faces.

Gently he pushed the hair back from her face.

'Time to be professional,' he said, and lowered his mouth. She'd thought herself braced against the impact but knew instantly that nothing could have guarded her from the feel of his lips. Gentle, hesitant, then firm, pleading, enticing, commanding.

It was all an act, she reminded herself wildly—mostly on the surface to fool the cameramen, and just a little between them to provoke her into the right reaction. Nothing for real.

Remember that!

But it was hard to remember while she was held so strongly against his chest, his bare legs against hers, his arm behind her head, holding her close.

Feelings chased each other through her in confusing whirls. Pleasure, excitement, a feeling that life had opened up new possibilities. But also fear, because she knew she was on the verge of losing control. She wanted him more—and more—and any moment now—

'That's it, gentlemen,' came Joe's voice out of the mists. 'Mr Falcon just wanted a pleasant day, without you invading his privacy. Time you went.'

Nobody was fooled but they had what they wanted, and they began to drift away.

'Are you all right?' Travis asked softly.

'Yes, I…I'm all right.'

'I'm sorry about this. It's not what you signed up for.'

'Everything's fine. I'm not going to make trouble, I promise you. Sensible and level headed. That's what we agreed, and that's what I'm giving you.'

He hesitated a moment, as though something had taken him by surprise. But then he gently released her, saying, 'Of course. I know you always keep your word. It's time we were going home.'

Now they would be alone and something more might happen between them, she thought happily. But Joe intervened like an awkward demon, announcing that he'd booked a table for them at one of the city's most glamorous restaurants.

So the performance continued that evening under glittering chandeliers. They talked but it meant nothing. Charlene had a sense that he was keeping slightly distant, as though wary after the day's events. She could be patient. Perhaps when they got home he would speak more freely.

But at last he closed his eyes and said, 'I think I've had too much to drink. We should get home before I have an embarrassing collapse.'

He left with his arm around her shoulders, murmuring, 'You don't mind propping me up, do you?'

She patted his hand. 'It's what I'm here for,' she said tenderly.

Charlene looked forward to taking him home, seeing him warm and comfortable, even perhaps happy. That was really all she asked. That he should be happy.

There was no hint then of what was to come, and how it would devastate him.

CHAPTER TEN

As soon as they reached home Travis put on the television, as he always did, to catch up with the news. Almost at once he tensed, staring at the screen.

'Isn't that—?' Charlene gasped.

'That's my father,' he confirmed, turning up the sound.

'...people who remember Amos Falcon from the old days are intrigued to see him in action again, and this conference in New York...'

Dazed, Travis sat down on the sofa, his eyes fixed on the screen. Charlene sat beside him, trying to imagine how this would be affecting him.

It seemed that Amos Falcon had been in New York for three days, during which time he had attended meetings and socialised with men as wealthy as himself. The only thing he hadn't done was contact his son in Los Angeles.

Suddenly she felt Travis grow even more tense. Another man had appeared on the screen. He was in his thirties, had a facial resemblance to Amos and seemed on the best of terms with him.

'...his son, Darius Falcon, who once seemed to have withdrawn from the world of finance, but who'll be joining his father in this new opportunity...'

The item ended. Travis sat frozen.

'He's in New York,' he murmured. 'What time is it there?'

'Three hours ahead of us,' Charlene said. 'He should be in bed by now.'

'A good time to call him, then. No, wait.'

He began clicking buttons on his cellphone, looking for a message, Charlene thought. But there was nothing.

'They didn't say where he was staying,' she said. 'So where could you call him? Perhaps someone in his home would know. If you called—'

'*No!*' Travis interrupted her violently. 'Never.'

Of course he wasn't going to advertise that his father had ignored him, Charlene thought, blaming herself for thoughtlessness.

Travis named a hotel. 'He's always stayed there in the past.'

He dialled a number. Charlene moved quietly away. She had a horrible fear of what was about to happen, and knew he would hate anyone to see it.

But she left her bedroom door open and heard him say, 'Fine, when he comes in would you give him a message? I'll give you my home number and my cellphone. Any time will do, night or day.'

He hung up and turned to see her standing in the door.

'Goodnight,' he said. 'You've had a long, tiring day.'

His message was plain. He'd spoken often of their closeness and his reliance on her, yet she could not help him now.

Quietly she closed the door.

Twice more during the night she rose and looked out discreetly. He was still there, silent and motionless. Never once did the phone ring.

There could be a simple answer. Amos might have stayed out overnight, or returned late and noted the message for later. The call would come. Surely it must.

Over breakfast she asked for the latest news, not revealing how much she knew.

'I fell asleep,' Travis said indifferently. 'If the phone rang I might not have heard it.'

Her heart was heavy as she saw him off to work. Instinct warned her to fear the worst. She knew of Travis's feeling of isolation, of being shut out from the heart of the family. He was obsessively aware of his father's indifference to him, bordering on contempt. Now she saw the reality.

Amos had come to the country where his son lived but hadn't contacted him, or even told him in advance. When Travis reached out he'd made no response. And Travis had been forced to watch him with brother Darius, the favoured son, as he himself would never be.

But Amos would call. He must. He would probably use the cellphone and contact Travis at the studio. But just in case he dialled the landline she would stay in all day.

Hours went past in silence. In the early afternoon the phone rang and she seized it up.

'It's me,' said Travis's voice. 'Have there been any phone calls?'

'No.'

'I see. All right. I'll see you tonight.'

He came home early, questioned her with a look, and shrugged when she shook her head. He settled on the sofa, watching television news, seeking further information about Amos. But there was nothing.

She brought him some coffee. 'You look tired—'

The phone rang.

Their eyes met, sharing the same brilliant hope. He grabbed the phone.

'Hello? *Father!* Good to hear from you. I heard you were over here. Maybe we could meet. I can get a couple of days off to fly to New York—what's that? Oh, I see. Well, in that case—'

Curse Amos Falcon, she thought wildly. Curse him for daring to hurt Travis.

It broke her heart to see Travis's face as hope died from it, leaving behind a dismal nothing.

The phone call ended. He stayed sitting on the sofa as though too weary ever to move again.

'What happened?' she asked, going to sit beside him.

'He's on his way back to Monte Carlo,' Travis said in a blank voice. 'He called me from the airport.'

'Damn him!'

He shrugged. 'I mean nothing to him. Why should he pretend otherwise? Right, that's it. Time to be realistic. I think I'll go out. Don't wait up!'

'Can't I come with you?'

'No, it won't be the sort of evening that you'd enjoy.'

'Hey, stop there! Be careful. If you end up in a nightclub with a floozie it'll do you more damage than you could cope with.'

'No women, I promise, just—'

'Just too much to drink, huh?'

'Maybe just a little.'

She had a vision of the evening ahead if she left him unprotected. It wouldn't be like last night when he'd got faintly tipsy before going quietly home with her. This time there would be a little indulgence, then a lot, more and more. The word would go around, people would text and his enemies would be alerted. Suddenly everyone who wanted to damage him would converge.

'No way,' she said, taking hold of him. 'Don't even think of leaving.'

But he eased away from her.

'I'm going,' he said. 'I know you mean it kindly, but I can't shelter behind you for ever.'

'Travis, don't do this. It's dangerous.'

'That's for me to say. A man's entitled to behave badly sometimes.'

'Sure he is. And you behave as badly as you want, but do it here, with me. No witnesses. And if anyone asks if you behaved badly I'll lie my head off.'

'But that's just another way of sheltering behind you. Don't try to control me, Charlene.'

In despair she stayed where she was on the sofa, leaning forward with her head in her hands. This was what it had come to. She couldn't really help him at all.

'Come on, don't make so much of it,' he said, sitting beside her. 'I won't be long, but maybe it's time I let go of your apron strings. Hey, are you crying?'

'No,' she said huskily.

'Yes, you are. It'll be all right, I promise.'

She looked at him, defenceless, tears pouring down her cheeks. 'Please,' she choked. 'Please don't do this. They'll be waiting for you. They always are.'

'Don't you think that sounds a bit paranoid?'

'Yes. I am paranoid. Sometimes paranoid is the right thing to be. Please, Travis, don't go. I'm not trying to control you. I'm trying to stop you losing everything.'

'I won't—'

'You will, you will. Oh, goodness, how can you throw it all away? Please—*please*—'

She was swamped by a sense of helplessness. His father's behaviour had had an unnerving effect on Travis, seeming to imbue him with a sense of self-destruction, so that only rebellion would calm his spirit. He would pay a heavy price for it, and she, who'd vowed to protect him, could do nothing. Her weeping became more desperate.

'Don't cry,' he said, brushing his fingers against her cheek. 'Please, Charlene, don't cry. I can't bear it. Look…look I—' There was a long silence.

She looked up, her eyes meeting his as she raised a tentative hand to touch his face.

'Don't go,' she whispered. 'Please don't go.'

'Charlene, what—?'

'Don't go.'

Now her fingertips were touching his mouth, drifting back and forth so that tremors went through him. Suddenly he seized her hand, kissing the palm fiercely, looking up with a question in his eyes.

'Please,' she murmured.

He gave a sudden groan. 'All right, I give in. I'll do whatever you want. You're the boss lady.'

She looked at him, unable to believe it. The feelings that had risen and swamped her made the tears flow more than ever.

'Don't,' he begged. 'Don't... Look...come here.'

His arms tightened about her, his lips brushed her wet cheeks.

'It's all right,' he said fiercely, '*it's all right*. I'll do anything you want. Just tell me and I'll do it.'

'I just want you to be safe,' she whispered.

'And I will be safe, as long as I have you.'

'You'll always have me.'

'Look at me,' he murmured, lifting her chin with his fingers.

There was a dark light in his eyes, not the anger that had been there before, but one that seemed to open a new door. If only she knew—

Their mouths were close and she could feel the warmth of his breath against her lips. Scarcely knowing what she did, she moved until they brushed softly against each other. It was the faintest touch, yet it was enough to bring back the moment on the beach when he had kissed her. She was shaking now as she had been then, and so was he. Now she sensed in him the same mixture of reactions—joy, disbelief, wonder, confusion—as she sensed in herself.

He lowered his mouth to touch hers more completely. Even then he was hesitant, but only for a moment, until he read the message of tender willingness in her lips, her hands touching his face. The wild excitement that had taken them by storm on the beach was there, but still lurking in the shadows, tempting them on with the promise of sweet discoveries, when they should have the courage to make them.

'Charlene—' He drew back a fraction. 'Do you think—?'

'Hush. What I think is…that this is no time for thinking.'

He hesitated only a moment, as if needing to be quite sure. Then he rose slowly, taking her hand for the short journey to his room. The huge windows, looking down over the lights of the city, were uncovered. But they didn't draw the curtains across. There was no need. Up here, in the dark, nobody could see them as their clothes fell away.

For a while, lying on the bed, they were strangely still, silently asking each other questions, seeking answers, happy when they found them. Then the first movements, tentative, discovering each other, realising that all was well.

His touch was gentle, fingers drifting across her naked skin, pausing, exploring slowly as though ready to retreat, but never doing so. She was glad of that. If he had stopped now she would have been devastated. She tried to convey her feelings through her own fingertips, caressing him softly, letting him know that this was right, perfect. The moment when she became his was the sweetest of her life.

Afterwards there was peace, the joyous satisfaction of lying back with his head on her chest, both of them totally still. In a few moments she was asleep.

She awoke in the early hours to find Travis restless, moving here and there as though desperately seeking something. His eyes were closed and his breathing deep. He still slept, but even in the depths of sleep something was disturbing him.

She touched him gently and at once he grew still. After a moment he moved again, reaching out until his hands encountered her, touched her face, her eyes, her lips.

'I'm here,' she whispered. 'I'm here beside you.'

Slowly she felt the tension drain from him. A long sigh came softly from his lips. He turned so that his head was resting on her shoulder, and after that he never moved again until they awoke together in the early morning.

He rested on his elbows to look down at her.

'Is everything all right?' he asked.

'Everything's fine with me. Did you have a good night's sleep?'

'I did in the end. I don't know what happened. I was restless for a while. I wanted to wake up but I couldn't make it happen. But then suddenly all the trouble vanished and everything was peaceful.'

'Dreams can be like that,' she whispered.

He stroked her face. 'Was it just a dream? Charlene, I don't know how to say this, but—'

'Then don't say it,' she whispered, her finger over his lips. 'Not now.'

He rose from the bed, divided by two conflicting desires, to be close to her, feeling her warmth and comfort enfold him again, and to be alone with his confused thoughts.

Which of them, he wondered, had led the other into the bedroom? He'd been the first to rise to his feet, take her hand and draw her after him. But he knew he would never have done so if he hadn't felt her willingness, sensed that she was urging him to take action and would be disappointed if he didn't.

So who had led who?

But there was another question, more urgent, more worrying.

Last night she had rescued him, as so often before. But who was the woman who had come into his bed? Charlene, the lover who had touched his heart? Or Charlie, the sister and protector who pandered to his needs like a nursemaid?

And if it was the second, might there not be a tiny hint of contempt in her kindness?

That thought made him shiver.

Over the next few days Charlene had the feeling that Travis had changed towards her. He never spoke of the passion they had shared, nor did his manner invite her to speak of it. He seemed uneasy in her company, as though he felt they'd come too close and was trying to step back. Several times he took her out to dinner, but always with other friends present. It was as though he didn't want to be alone with her.

She waited, hoping that he would open his arms to her and take her again into his bed, where they could rediscover the tenderness that had been so special. Then she would know what it had really meant.

But she waited in vain. Travis seemed to have put their lovemaking behind them as completely as if it had never happened. Sometimes she would look up to find him regarding her with a strange questioning expression. But when he saw her glance he would immediately begin to talk about something unimportant.

With pain and dismay, she realised that he'd turned to her, not in love but in need. She could give him something he'd found nowhere else, but he wasn't ready for the next step. Perhaps he never would be.

But she refused to give up hope yet. It would take time for them to find each other, but she would be patient. There was everything to gain.

A location shoot caused him to be away in Washington for several nights. His calls home were cheerful, but left her wondering if he was glad to be away from her. Perhaps she would know everything when she saw him again.

But when she met him and Joe at the airport there had been a development that briefly blotted out everything else.

'I've had a call from Marcel,' he said. 'His wedding is next week.'

'Next week?'

'Yes, it's got to be fitted in with some money-making project.'

'How does the bride feel about that?'

Travis grinned. 'I should have mentioned; it's her money-making project. So next week we're off to Paris.'

'Can you get time off?' she asked.

Travis looked over his shoulder to Joe, walking just behind them. 'You said there'd be no problem, didn't you?'

'Sure thing,' announced Joe. 'Great PR stuff. You're a Falcon among Falcons. Big names. Lots of spotlight. Go to Paris, have a great time and do your stuff, both of you.'

The next few days were hectic. Travis devoted himself to filming while Charlene went on a shopping binge, accompanied by Julia, whose advice was expert.

She remembered their first evening in Los Angeles, discussing Shakespeare and the time she'd played the role of Helena.

Another unwanted female, she thought. *She spends most of the play trailing after her lover, begging him not to reject her. He comes back to her in the end, but only because someone has cast a magic spell on him. That's not the same as the real thing. Strange how I always got that sort of part.*

But was it really strange? she wondered. The plain one. The girl chosen as a last resort. The one with whom the hero would 'make do'. That had been her on the stage, and was it now, perhaps, coming true in her life?

Travis might one day come to love her a little, but not as she loved him. If there was one thing certain in the universe, it was that. He might make do with her. Children, stability, the feeling of being wanted for himself and not for his fame.

These things were what he yearned for, and to win them he could decide to do without romantic love.

One of Helena's lines came back to her.

Love looks not with the eyes but with the mind.

Travis's eyes must have told him that she was plain, despite his kind remarks about her figure. His mind had told him that she had qualities of sympathy and understanding that he needed. But could that substitute for love?

Her own love had looked not with eyes that could be distracted by his handsome appearance, but with a mind and heart that saw the man who concealed himself from others, yet reached out to her. There was no way she could not have loved him.

On the day of departure he did a final session at the studio and she went with him, to be ready as soon as he'd finished. While he worked, Joe took her to the canteen. The two of them got on well, and he missed no chance to express his admiration for the service she was doing the studio.

'Thank heavens for you,' he said now. 'You're going to help him get that film part. The only reason Alaric Lanley is in the running is because he's better known. You help to keep Travis in the headlines, and that's good.

'This wedding is another chance. The Falcon dynasty, the great Amos—well, OK, maybe not great. People say he's the biggest bastard in creation, so how did he father a lovely guy like Travis? When you meet him, sweet-talk him, OK? Try to get a picture of the three of you together.'

There was serious doubt whether Amos would be there, but Charlene judged it more tactful not to mention this and slipped hastily away to powder her nose.

Returning a few minutes later, she could see that Joe was on the phone and was about to retreat when she heard him say, 'Look, Travis, why don't you just marry the girl? All right, all right, no need to blast my ear off—yes, I know but—Travis, will you listen to me? Charlene's good for you. I can see how well you get on and she'll keep you safe—there's no need to say that—I didn't mean to offend you. We'll say no more.'

Now she backed away hastily. She desperately needed to be alone to come to terms with the devastating conversation.

She hadn't heard Travis's end, but she didn't need to. At the thought of marrying her he'd exploded. The mere idea of it offended him. Joe had spoken of safety and 'getting on well'. He was promoting a convenient marriage, and clearly Travis wanted none of it.

How ridiculous her dreams appeared now! All the signs had been there when they'd swapped jokes about their un-romantic friendship.

'You're safe with me,' she'd said. 'You're not my type.'

He'd pretended to be insulted, but actually he was relieved. Marry her? How he must be laughing at the thought!

When she was finally calm enough to return, she found the call finished and Joe cheerful.

'Travis called to say work's finished and we need to get over there fast. He's all ready to go and the photographers are in place.'

'Oh…yes,' she said uneasily.

'What's the matter? Why do you suddenly look like that? Not getting cold feet, are you?'

'No, of course not.'

'Too late for that. Travis needs you.'

'I'm ready,' she said at once.

She couldn't back out now without explaining why, and there was no way she could reveal what she'd just learned.

So she became an actress again, smiling for the camera, smiling for Travis, embracing him, letting him usher her into the car, waving to the little crowd that had gathered.

'I really need this!' he exclaimed, squeezing her hand. 'Time off in Paris, and you all to myself.'

'You're always with me,' she said lightly. 'You need to be with your family while you have the chance.'

'The family, yes.' His sudden beaming look touched her heart. 'As many of them as we can get together. Maybe all of them, I don't know—'

She gave a theatrically blissful sigh. 'Oh, I'm looking forward to this trip. I've always wanted to see Paris. And look, I can go exploring on my own if you want to spend time with your brothers with no womenfolk around.'

He eyed her ironically. 'Nice try, but I'm keeping my eye on you at all times.'

Charlene shook her head. 'That's one thing you don't need to do and you know it. Now, wave at the crowd. They're calling to you.'

As always, he did as required, performing perfectly, while wondering exactly what she'd meant by 'and you know it'.

CHAPTER ELEVEN

THE flight from Los Angeles to Paris was thirteen hours. Charlene dozed as much as she could manage, sometimes awakening to find him holding her hand. After many hours had passed they found themselves over the Atlantic.

'Is anything more boring than flying?' she murmured.

'Not much,' he agreed. 'You just end up staring at clouds that go on endlessly.'

'At least we've got this to read,' she said, taking out the brochure of La Couronne, the magnificent hotel that was the heart of Marcel Falcon's empire, which was where they were to stay for the next few days. The gloriously coloured pictures showed a building that was several hundred years old, originally built as a palace, home of the nobility, whose portraits were also included.

'They were executed in the Revolution,' Travis said. 'The house changed hands a few times until Marcel bought it and turned it into a hotel. Last year he bought up a London hotel with the idea of duplicating La Couronne as The Crown. That's how he met Mrs Henshaw, who turned out to be Cassie, a girl he'd been in love with eight years ago.'

'Eight years,' she marvelled. 'And they found each other again after so long?'

'It's incredible, isn't it? But I guess if love is real it can overcome time.'

'That's not all it had to overcome,' she reminded him. 'His clumsy proposal—without asking her first.'

Travis grinned. 'That'll teach him not to take any notice of me.'

'Anyway, they got it right in the end.'

'So much so that Marcel has created a wedding chapel in the hotel, something he always refused to do before.'

'What about your father? Will he be there?'

'It isn't settled. He's not pleased about this wedding either. He wants one of us to marry Freya, his stepdaughter, but she actually helped Cassie raise the money to buy into the business.'

'I thought you said she raised it modelling.'

'Some of it, yes. But Freya topped it up with a loan of money that Amos had given her to provide a dowry. He hoped she'd use it to entice Marcel. Instead, she used it to see him married to someone else. According to Marcel, Amos is still seething.'

'Did you never talk to him again after he called from the airport?'

'No. I might as well not exist as far as he's concerned. The last time I saw him was almost a year ago, in Monte Carlo, where he lives for tax reasons. He had a heart attack and we all went there to be with him, in case it was the last time.'

'But he recovered, and you had the chance to talk to him.'

'Yes,' Travis said wryly. 'The chief thing I remember is him grunting, "Don't give up. You can still do better."'

'I suppose that's a kind of encouragement.'

'He didn't want to encourage me. Quite the reverse. He wanted me to get a "serious job". He's not going to change now. I just hope he's there and we can meet cordially.'

They started the descent. She looked down with fascination as Paris came into view below them. Whatever else happened, there were things about this trip that she was going to enjoy.

When they had reclaimed their bags Travis looked around. Suddenly his face lit up.

'*Marcel!*'

There at the barrier a tall man in his thirties was waving eagerly. Beside him was a truly beautiful young woman, whom Charlene recognised as the glamour model in the magazine.

Their meeting was joyful. Marcel thumped his brother's shoulders and was thumped in return before everyone calmed down for the introductions.

Charlene never forgot her first sight of Paris. It was a glorious day, with the city showing at its glamorous best as they made their way to La Couronne. From the outside, the hotel still looked like a palace. Inside, it presented a traditional appearance, but beneath the surface was every modern convenience.

A man with a faint resemblance to Marcel was waiting on the huge stone stairway that led up to the hotel entrance. This must be Darius, Charlene thought, watching him greet Travis.

'Let's leave the three of them to talk,' Cassie said. 'I'll show you to your suite.'

Of course they had put them together, Charlene realised. To have asked for separate rooms when they were known to be living together would have invited suspicion.

'You're all on the same floor,' Cassie explained. 'Darius and Harriet have rooms just along the corridor, Jackson's around the corner, then Leonid, and over here is for Amos and his wife, and Freya.'

'If they come,' Charlene said wryly.

'I'm crossing my fingers. It will make Marcel very sad if Amos snubs him.'

They were accommodated in a grandiose suite, dominated by a double bed so huge that the occupants could hardly be described as sleeping together. Cassie showed her out onto

the balcony, from where they could see a cab drawing up to
the entrance and a young woman descend.

'That's Freya,' Cassie said. 'And she's alone. Freya! Up
here!'

But no Amos, Charlene thought with sinking heart. She
knew a spurt of anger at the thought of Travis's disappointment.

I'm being absurd, she reproved herself. *It's Marcel who's
being rejected, not Travis.*

But she knew that he would feel it the most.

Freya and Cassie greeted each other as old friends, reminding Charlene that Freya had helped raise the money for the
hotel investment. She was a brisk, efficient young woman,
attractive without being glamorous. She and Charlene took
to each other at once.

'Why are you here alone?' Cassie asked. 'Aren't Amos
and your mother coming?'

'I hope so. I left them arguing about it. Amos is still dis-
pleased with me for helping Marcel to marry you, but he
doesn't rule my life, and so I told him.'

'Good for you,' Cassie said at once, adding wickedly to
Charlene, 'You want to watch out. He'll be trying to marry
Freya to Travis next.'

Freya winked. 'Don't worry. Travis doesn't interest me.'

'It wouldn't bother me if he did,' Charlene said, laughing.
'Be my guest. He's all yours.'

'Excuse me,' said a voice from the door. 'Did I hear that
right?'

Travis was standing there, clearly enjoying the joke. Freya
threw herself into his arms with a delighted cry.

'Trust you to come in at the wrong moment,' Cassie observed.

He gave a melodramatic sigh. 'Don't worry, I'm used to
rejection. Freya, it's lovely to see you.'

There came a noise from the corridor outside. Cassie and

Freya dashed out, crying, 'Leonid, Jackson!' followed by Travis.

Charlene followed more slowly and received a surprise at the sight of the two men. One she recognised as Jackson Falcon, whom she'd often seen on television, fronting nature programmes. The other man bore such a strong resemblance to Travis that it was startling. He had the same lean features, generous mouth and dark eyes. The difference lay in the atmosphere that clung to him. Travis's air was light-hearted and charming. Leonid Falcon carried a brooding melancholy that seemed to come from a darker world.

He greeted everyone with quiet courtesy, speaking in a heavily accented voice, but then seemed to stand back, watching with cautious eyes.

Now Marcel and Darius were there, revving up spirits for the evening ahead.

'We're going to have a great party,' Marcel announced. 'It's too long since we all saw each other, and we're going to make the most of it.'

A cheer went up. The fun had started.

The family dined together. Charlene got on especially well with Harriet, Darius's bride from the island of Herringdean.

'Everyone wants to meet you,' she said, plumping down beside her and offering a glass of wine. 'The girl who's won Travis's heart.'

Charlene made a laughing reply, but the words, *If only,* flitted through her brain.

'You know, of course, how Marcel nearly ruined his own chances when Darius and I got married,' Harriet added.

'By taking my cue from my daft brother,' Marcel put in, joining them.

'Don't blame me,' Travis protested, appearing behind him. 'It was the character, a virtuous, magical being, not me. Some people can't tell the difference.'

'Nonsense. I could tell the difference between you and a

virtuous being without any trouble,' Marcel declared, and a cheer went up from the others.

This was what Travis had secretly yearned for all his life, Charlene thought; the support and cheerful companionship of people who were linked to him by unbreakable ties. She felt a glow of pleasure in the happiness he must be feeling.

La Couronne prided itself on being international. English and American newspapers were on sale, and the guests could receive television channels in several languages. So it wasn't a surprise when a pile of papers on a low table turned out to contain a showbiz publication, sporting the headline *Who Will Be The Man From Heaven?*

'Why, that's my brother, of course,' Darius declared with mock indignation. 'Nobody else need apply.'

Amid laughter, he read out a highly coloured piece about the rivalry between Travis Falcon and Alaric Lanley, phrased to make it sound as though the two were at each other's throats.

'"Both great stars,"' Darius read, '"both poised to seize the next huge chance and brook no opposition, both ready to explode in the firmament. The entertainment world watches breathless as these two giants fight it out."'

Cheers, laughter. Then sudden silence. Everyone looked up to see a man and woman standing in the doorway.

The man was in his seventies, tall, white-haired, with features that were stern and uncompromising. He stood looking around at the gathering, as though their silence was a tribute that he accepted as natural.

Amos Falcon.

'Good evening,' he said.

Charlene had seen his picture in newspapers, but in the flesh he was different, more vibrant, more—she fought for the words—more menacing.

It was easy to believe that he'd made enemies, fought them, crushed them, seldom been defeated. Formidable as a foe, perhaps formidable as a friend, certainly formidable as a father.

At the sight of Travis he nodded, speaking gruffly but cordially. 'Glad to see you. Wasn't sure you'd make the journey, such a distance.'

'You don't think I'd let Marcel tie the knot without being there to chuck things at him, do you?' Travis grinned.

Then Amos did something that took everyone by surprise. Laying a hand on his son's shoulder, he said, 'Just make sure your aim is good.'

The others looked at each other, startled. Amos had actually made a joke, and with his least favourite son. Whatever was the world coming to?

To cap it all, when he made his way to a seat it was Travis he urged to come with him.

'Haven't seen you in a long time, except on television, of course. Can't get away from you there.'

'Sorry if that bothers you,' Travis said, knowing Amos had never been a fan of his career.

But his father surprised him again.

'Doesn't bother me. Good to see you doing well. Show business is like anything else. If you climb high you become somebody. There's profit to be had.'

'I think I'm beginning to understand this,' Harriet murmured. 'Somebody's told Poppa Falcon that Travis's career prospects have suddenly leapt up to the heights.'

'Right,' Cassie agreed. 'It's one thing to have a TV series, but quite another to be a big film star.'

'But does he know anything about film stars?' Charlene asked. 'I wouldn't think he acknowledged their existence.'

'I think I may be responsible for that,' Freya said with a laugh. 'I've always been a big fan of Alaric Lanley.'

'I'm not surprised. He's gorgeous.' Harriet sighed.

Darius glanced up. 'Did you say something?'

'Not a thing,' she told him cheekily. 'Never mind me. Go back to making money.'

'Yes, dear.'

For a moment his severe aspect faded and he exchanged a conspiratorial smile with his wife that revealed a hidden world beneath their conventional exteriors.

How lucky they are, Charlene thought. Would it ever be the same for herself and Travis? They exchanged many smiles, even spoke with affection, but there was still a barrier that they hadn't brought down.

'Amos saw me reading stuff about Lanley,' Freya continued, 'and he started looking through it. That's how he discovered how big he is, how much money he's making, how he can take his pick of the roles.'

'Ah, I see,' Harriet murmured. 'So when he discovered that Travis was challenging him and was expected to win, suddenly Travis looked different.'

'Someone he might actually be proud of,' Charlene added. 'Even boast about.'

'And who'd make an amount of money that even Amos would have to take seriously,' Cassie added.

The three women nodded solemnly.

At last Travis drew his father in Charlene's direction.

'Father, there's someone I'd like you to meet.'

Amos knew her at once, she realised. Clearly he'd been following the press reports and needed nobody to tell him who she was or what part she played in Travis's public persona. He looked her up and down, nodding in a satisfied way. After that he spared her few words. If she'd been concerned for herself she might have been offended, but she cared only how this affected Travis, so she said what was necessary and retreated to leave him with his father.

The other women did the same, drifting to the far end of the room for a final coffee before bed.

'They'll probably talk all night,' Harriet muttered. 'I need a good sleep to get ready for tomorrow, and I'm sure Cassie does.'

'What about poor Charlene?' Cassie said. 'She must be so jet-lagged after that long flight.'

Yet, far from being jet-lagged, she felt vibrantly alive. At this moment she badly wanted to be with Travis, but she knew he would probably be a long time. At least, she hoped so. The longer Amos kept him there the better.

They were joined by Janine, Amos's current wife and Freya's mother. Charlene liked her at once, especially when she gave a humorous account of how she'd persuaded her husband to attend the wedding.

'He snubbed Darius's wedding. If he'd snubbed this one too he'd have looked ridiculous. Amos couldn't bear that.'

'He can't snub them all just because they don't marry me.' Freya chuckled. 'He'll run out of sons to snub. Silly man.'

'Don't let him hear you say that,' her mother warned. 'He's very fond of you. That's why he wants you in the family. But there's only Jackson and Leonid left, so you'd better make a choice soon.'

Freya glanced over to the corner, where Jackson and Leonid could both be seen.

'Perhaps I've already made it,' she said mysteriously.

They began to drift away. Charlene gave Travis a wave, then flapped her hand, indicating for him to go back to his father. He smiled.

She was feeling good as she went up to their suite. There she had a shower, donned a nightdress and settled down to watch television. By mysterious luck one channel had just begun to show *The Man From Heaven* with French subtitles, which she enjoyed enormously.

'Something funny?' Travis asked, coming in a couple of hours later and finding her laughing.

'You,' she said, pointing at the screen. 'There's no getting away from you, is there?'

He grinned. 'My father said something like that, but he actually seemed to think it might be a good thing.'

'It's really going well, isn't it?'

'Well, he's listening to what I say, which makes a change.'

'I'm so happy for you.' She threw herself back on the bed. 'Oh, it was a great night, even before he came. A real family occasion!'

'You mean with my brothers sending me up something rotten?' he said, grinning.

'Yes, exactly. That's what families do, send each other up rotten, but still be there for each other.' She was helping him undress and hanging up his clothes.

'Isn't it lovely that your father's here?' she remarked.

'It's good for Marcel that he didn't snub him,' Travis conceded slowly.

'And you?'

'And me, yes. But—' he dropped down beside her and gently brushed the hair back from her forehead '—right this minute—'

'You know I'm here if you need me.'

'I do need you. You know that. You point the way for me, and somehow it always turns out to be the right way. I'm only afraid—' he stopped uneasily '—I'm afraid you've got the wrong idea now.'

'How have I done that?'

'This suite. I should have asked you first but I didn't tell them to put us together, they just assumed. Everyone thinks… I'm sorry if I've put you in an awkward position.'

She had hoped for much from this night, but now she sensed that emotionally he was backing away again, reminding her how shocked he'd been at the suggestion of marriage. But she concealed her disappointment.

'How have you put me in an awkward position?' she demanded. 'Everyone knows we're living under the same roof in Los Angeles. This was bound to happen. Now stop talking

like a Victorian parson and come to bed, because the jet lag
has caught up with me and I'm about to zonk out.'

'Me too,' he said, getting in beside her. 'As long as you're
not offended.'

'Go to sleep!'

Next morning they were up early to prepare for the wedding.
All around them they could hear the family in the other suites
and sometimes outside in the corridor, where Freya was having a lively argument with her mother.

'If you really want to please your father, the answer's simple,' Charlene said as lightly as she could manage. 'Just marry
Freya.'

He was sitting on the bed. Now he put his head on one
side, seeming to consider.

'Really?' he mused. 'I don't think so. The fact is—I'd
rather marry you.'

She hoped he didn't hear the little gasp that burst from
her. She knew he didn't really want to marry her. She'd been
prepared for rejection, polite excuses as to why their relationship could go no further. This sudden reversal sent a
jolt through her like a burst of lightning, but she controlled
herself, assumed a smile, then her most cheerful tone to say,
'I'm serious.'

'So am I,' he said.

'No, you're not. It's one of your daft jokes. I blame Jackson.
The pair of you are like a couple of school kids.'

'Then obviously I need a good teacher to keep me in line.
But I take it you don't fancy the job.'

'I don't think I'd be up to it. It would take more than me
to keep you in line.'

'No, just you. You're the only one who's ever come close.
Even Mom admits that.'

'Oh, she wants to hand over the job of being your mother,
does she? Thus freeing her for a succession of toy boys.'

His smile almost made her heart turn over. 'Something like that.'

She could hardly breathe. Beneath the teasing atmosphere, something serious was happening.

'Well?' he murmured.

'Well…the fact is…I'm not sure I'm up to the job.'

'You mean you don't think you could put up with me?'

'Maybe yes, maybe no. I never rush big decisions.'

'Then take your time.' He kissed her cheek. 'We'll talk again later.'

He vanished into the shower, leaving her stunned, not only by him but by herself.

Why hadn't she leapt at his offer of marriage? She loved him deeply. She wanted nothing more than to be with him for the rest of her life.

But his own feelings fell short of hers. That was the fact that she must face. He'd asked her because he'd decided to take Joe's advice. His career was going well. His relationship with Amos was going well, and he wanted to consolidate everything by making a sensible marriage to a woman who could care for him as no other woman could.

The temptation was fierce. *Seize the chance. Make the best of it. What else does life offer?*

If possible, she would have dismissed her sensible side, but it hammered on her brain for admittance, reminding her how devastating was the decision she must make.

To marry him, knowing that her feelings were far greater than his, and his merely practical affection could never reach the heights of her passionate adoration. Or refuse him, walk away, knowing she had left this vulnerable man at the mercy of what life would do to him.

Nonsense! This is a grown man. He doesn't need you to protect him.

But he does.

OK, so he marries you and you give him the children he

*wants. He's grateful and affectionate, and for a while every-
thing is lovely. But then he gets infatuated with some sexy
little bimbo. Maybe he won't leave you, but will he be faithful to you?*

I don't know.

Yes, you do. Admit it.

I don't know!

CHAPTER TWELVE

Like everything else in La Couronne, the wedding area was magnificent. Chandeliers hung from the ceiling, gilt decoration adorned the walls.

'It's glorious,' Harriet said to Charlene, 'but I still prefer the ceremony Darius and I had on the beach at Herringdean.'

'That sounds lovely,' Charlene agreed.

'It was lovely,' Travis said. 'Especially with the dog there. How is Phantom, Harry? I know everyone was afraid he wouldn't live much longer.'

'He's managing to hold on. Every day is precious.'

'I'm longing to see what Cassie looks like in her wedding dress,' Freya said. 'She's so beautiful that I could hate her if I didn't like her so much.'

The room was packed. Marcel had few friends but many business acquaintances who appreciated the invitation, and much the same could be said for Cassie.

At last Jackson and Leonid entered, then Amos and Janine. Amos looked proud and magnificent. Nobody, Charlene thought, would have dreamt that he'd come to this wedding against his will.

Now Marcel appeared, taking his place at the front, with Darius, his best man. At last everything was in place for the bride's arrival.

As Freya had predicted, she was astonishingly beautiful.

Charlene knew a pang. It wasn't fair that one woman could be like that and another... She looked down disparagingly at herself.

Marcel turned to watch his bride approach, and Charlene drew a sharp breath at his expression. It was possessive, adoring and slightly incredulous, as though he couldn't quite understand how such good fortune was his. That was how a man ought to regard his bride, she thought. It was how Travis would never regard her.

The voice of common sense echoed in her mind.

Time to face facts. Yes, I know you hate the thought, but listen. He doesn't really love you. Not as you love him. And he's never going to, you know that, don't you?

I guess I do.

So be sensible. Get out now.

But that means abandoning him when he needs me.

That won't be your problem.

Loving Travis will always be my problem. I can either love him at a distance, wondering how he is. Or I can love him close up, doing everything I can to make him happy.

And being hurt yourself. Think about it.

The same look was on Marcel's face when he finally led his new wife back along the aisle, followed by applause from the congregation.

Then the photographs, a dozen different combinations of family members. In one, Amos stood with all five of his sons. This was followed by pictures of Amos with Darius and Marcel, then Jackson and Leonid.

'Wait,' Amos called. 'We haven't finished. Travis, get over here.'

And so it came about that Travis was the only one of Amos's sons to be photographed alone with him.

'Yes,' Charlene murmured happily. 'Yes, *yes, yes.*'

The reception was a riot of speeches and champagne. Watching the bride and groom, Charlene saw the same look she'd seen on Marcel's face earlier. Darius too looked the same whenever his eyes fell on Harriet.

Would he look at you like that, at your wedding? demanded the sensible voice.

Probably. He's a very good actor.

At last the guests began to leave. The goodbyes were said, and the rest of the evening became an extension of the family reunion. Cassie and Marcel were staying in Paris that night, leaving for their honeymoon next day, when the rest of the family departed. Travis, Charlene was glad to notice, was deep in conversation with Leonid, whose grim air had vanished in the pleasure of his brother's company. As she passed by, both men reached out to catch her hand and drew her to sit with them.

'I was saying how glad I am to meet my brother again,' Leonid said, 'and how sad that tomorrow we must say goodbye, and not know when next we meet.'

Charlene was inspired.

'But that's easy,' she said. 'The show filmed an episode in London, so why not an episode in Moscow?'

'That's brilliant!' Travis exclaimed.

'But you are going to do the film,' Leonid protested. 'Will you have time?'

'I haven't got the film yet, and even if I do there are TV episodes to shoot first. I'll talk to them about this as soon as we get back to LA.'

'And they will say yes because you are a very big man and they do as you wish,' Leonid said triumphantly. 'Just wait until you get to Moscow and I can boast that this is my brother.'

He seized Charlene's hand and kissed it.

'Thank you for your idea. You are a genius. Travis, your lady is a genius.'

'I know that,' he said, regarding her with fond gratitude.

'Come on, I only suggested it.' She laughed. 'If they do this it will be to please Travis.'

'True,' Leonid agreed. 'Travis is the great man. But a great man needs a great lady beside him all the time.'

'He certainly does,' Travis said firmly. 'Damn! Why does the phone have to ring now? Hello, Joe!…What's that?' Suddenly his face brightened. 'Are you sure? It's not a mistake? That's great. Yes, I'll make a note of the date. Next month. Right.'

'What is it?' she asked.

'It's the nominations for the TopGo Television Drama Awards. Joe's had some advance notice.'

'And you've got a nomination?' Darius demanded. The family were gathering around them.

'More than one, apparently. Joe, how many? *How many?*' He looked around frantically. 'Paper—paper—'

Jackson produced a scrap of paper. Leonid shoved a pen into Travis's hands. Now everyone was riveted as he began to scribble.

'That's four!' Marcel exclaimed, reading over his shoulder as Travis hung up. '*Four* nominations?'

'Let's see,' squeaked Harriet. Seizing the paper, she began to read aloud. '"Award for the best performance by a leading actor in a television series. Award for the best comedy performance by an actor in a television series."'

'It's a con,' Travis groaned. 'There was one episode that was played for laughs, so someone's been pulling strings to get me this nomination. It doesn't mean a thing.'

'Stop being modest,' Jackson ordered. 'It doesn't suit you. What else is there?'

'"Award for the best dramatic performance by an actor in a television play,"' Harriet read. 'You do one-off plays as well?'

'I did one last year. Just one.'

'And "best contribution to an educational feature,"' Harriet read.

Travis's brothers roared with laughter. 'Education?' Darius echoed. 'You?'

'Very funny.' Travis grinned. 'I made an appearance in a couple of documentaries. I told you, it's a con. Somebody's fixed this.'

'Of course,' Marcel declared. 'Nobody could ever think you were "somebody" just because you've got more nominations than the rest.'

Everyone cheered and applauded, raising their glasses in salute, while Travis looked modestly embarrassed even through his laughter.

Amos took the paper from Harriet and studied it.

'It's a fix,' Travis repeated. 'Nobody gets as many as that unless someone's pulling strings.'

'Of course,' Amos agreed. 'Obviously this is about boosting you for the film part. You will win everything. Your incredible achievement will be in the papers, and the part will be yours. Excellent.'

'You think that's good?' Travis queried.

'If you want something to happen, you have to arrange for it to happen,' Amos told him. 'Clearly you are supported by big, important people.'

It was clear that Travis had gone up in his estimation. In Amos Falcon's world this was how things were done.

'You mentioned a date next month,' Amos said.

Travis nodded. 'The award ceremony is on the fifteenth, in Los Angeles.'

'Splendid. I shall be there.'

'And me,' Marcel said at once. 'And Cassie.'

'And me,' Darius added. 'And Harriet.'

Jackson and Leonid joined in, and with dizzying speed it was set up. All Travis's family, even Amos, would be there for his great event. Both professionally and personally, this would be his night of glory.

On the way up to their suite he was incandescent, whooping, 'You did it! You did it!'

'No, you did it,' she protested.

'Don't argue with me. You did it. Come here!'

He pulled her hard against him, kissing her with a fierce eagerness that brought her own desire rioting to the surface, overwhelming her despite her good resolutions. Only the sound of the elevator doors opening brought them back to earth.

'Come on,' he said, heading for their suite.

Once inside, he held her face between his hands, smiling into her eyes.

'Leonid's right,' he said. 'I need you beside me, so now you definitely have to marry me.'

'But—'

'No buts. I won't take no for an answer. Say you'll marry me.'

'Travis—'

'Say yes. Say it.'

Overjoyed but bewildered, she searched his face, desperately trying to understand something that could never be understood.

'Say it!'

'Yes,' she whispered. 'Yes.'

'You mean it? You won't change your mind?'

'I mean it.'

'Prove it to me.'

No need to ask what he meant. Even as he spoke, he was drawing her down onto the bed, and she went eagerly.

In the days after their first loving they'd been wary of each other, making her wonder if it would ever happen again. Now she understood how terrible that would have been. Never to have touched him again, or feel him touch her, never again to know the sweet thrill of being close to him, then closer until finally they were each other's with a completeness that made her dizzy with delight.

He loved slowly, even hesitantly, as though the first loving had left him still in doubt. But that was his way, she thought, trying to think clearly through a haze of pleasure. It was hard for him to be truly confident, even now, but surely it was in her power to find the way for him. With her arms firmly around him she gave herself up to the sensations and emotions that were like a new world: the world they would find together.

When he was asleep she rose and went to sit by the window, watching his still form on the bed. Common sense was still raging at her, and she knew she must tell it to stop its nonsense once and for all.

You did it. You gave in, settled for second best.

Travis could never be second best.

But what he's offering you is second best, and you know it. Is it coincidence that it happened tonight? You proved your usefulness again with that Moscow suggestion, and now he's definitely not going to let you go.

I don't want him to let me go.

But what's he offering? Love?

I don't know.

Yes, you do. He's not in love with you, not the way you are with him.

But he needs me, and I'll be there for him. And if…if one day it's over, I'll still be glad of the time we had together.

This is the twenty-first century. What happened to liberated woman?

I guess I'm not very liberated where Travis is concerned. And that's fine by me. I'll love him and cherish him, and give him whatever I can. And if he's happy, that's all I ask. Now go away and don't come bothering me again.

Silence!

* * *

Back in Los Angeles, everything was humming as preparations were made for the big night. Rumours had gone around about what was to happen, and the announcement about the film that was expected afterwards. Everyone who was anyone was determined to be there.

One disappointment was that her grandparents couldn't make it. Their holiday would be over just two days before the award ceremony, and they would be too tired from the long flight home to embark on another to Los Angeles.

'Could they change the flight?' Travis suggested. 'Come straight here from Africa, then stay with us for a while to get their strength back before returning to London?'

But when Charlene suggested this to Frank on the phone, he thanked her but refused.

'Emma's worn out. She needs to get home. We'll watch it on television. You'll hear us cheering.'

'What a shame,' Travis said. 'It would have made everything perfect to have them there, especially when we tell everyone our news.'

He planned to cap the evening by announcing their engagement.

'I'd better do it when I receive the first award,' he mused, 'in case there aren't any others.'

'You know how many there are going to be,' she said. 'This is going to be your night.'

His night in every way. Two days before the event, his family began to arrive. Amos, Janine and Freya dined with them and Charlene was struck by the look of pride and satisfaction on Amos's face.

He's got what he wanted from his father at last, she thought. *At least, he's nearly got it. Don't let anything happen to spoil it now.*

Her dress for the evening was a magnificent dark blue velvet with a tight waist and long flowing skirt. Travis helped her on with it, and zipped it up.

'I like that blue,' he said. 'It goes well with this.' He showed her a ring of diamonds and sapphires.

'Let me wear it now,' she begged.

'No, we agreed I'd give it to you when I make the announcement.' His eyes were teasing. 'Until then, you'll have to be patient.' He kissed her.

'I'll try. Oh, Travis, I hope tonight is everything you hoped for.'

'If you're there, it will be. Hell! What's that?'

'My phone. Hang on, I'll get rid of them quickly.'

'Charlie?' It was her grandfather's voice. 'Something terrible's happened.'

'What?' she asked, but she knew the answer before he spoke.

'Emma's had a heart attack, a big one. Oh, darling, they say she might not last the night.'

'Sweet heaven,' she whispered.

'Can you come? It could be for the last time. She said I wasn't to call you because you had this other thing happening but—'

'Of course you were right to call me,' she said, almost violently. 'I'll be on the next plane. Which hospital?'

She wrote it down and said, 'Tell her I'm coming. Tell her I love her.'

'Emma?' Travis asked as soon as she hung up. He'd been watching and listening, motionless.

'She's had a heart attack. She's dying.'

'Then we've got to get over there fast. There's a flight this afternoon.'

'We—? No, Travis, you can't come. You've got the awards ceremony and those people will be there—your family—'

He stared at her. 'Are you seriously saying that you think I'll put all that stuff first? Before you?'

'You must. You can't miss tonight when there's so much hanging on it. I know you'd come with me if you could, and I'll treasure that. But you *can't*. Surely you can see that you can't?'

'What I can see—' he said slowly '—is something I never saw before. I didn't understand—but I do now.'

'You know I'm right,' she said. 'This is your big moment. I won't let you lose it because of me.'

He moved away from her. 'You'd better get ready while I make the arrangements,' he said. And walked out.

While she threw some things together in a small bag she concentrated fiercely on the task in hand. If she let her thoughts get out of control she feared she would break down. Travis had said the right things about wanting to come with her, but he'd let her talk him out of it more easily than she could have dreamed.

And that was how things were between them. She'd told herself that she was willing to settle for second best, but she hadn't expected the reality to become so brutally clear so soon.

She changed into sensible clothes, taking just enough to manage. When she emerged, Travis was sitting at the table hurriedly writing something.

'It's all settled,' he said, folding the paper into his pocket. 'I've called the airport and fixed your ticket. Rick will take us.'

'Us?'

'I'm just coming to see you off.'

He opened the door, ushering her out before she could protest. She was struck by how cool and businesslike his manner had become. This was a practical man who'd dealt with the emotion, brushed it aside and was ready to get on with the important things in life. She felt a chill run through her.

The car was waiting, with Rick at the wheel. Once inside,

she dropped her head in her hands and sat motionless. Travis put his arms around her, drawing her close. She reached out slightly, trying to respond, but she felt abandoned in another world, one that he wasn't part of, no matter how much he pretended.

'We're nearly there,' he said.

She pulled herself together. In a few moments they would part. She would return to her world, he would return to his, and who could say if they would ever meet again? At this moment she doubted it.

Now the rest of her life stretched ahead, empty because she would lose him, but even emptier because he would no longer be the man she loved and believed in.

As he helped her out of the car he called to Rick, 'Wait for me in the car park. I won't be long.'

'Perhaps you should go back now,' Charlene said.

'No, I've got time to see you into the Departure Lounge. Sit over there while I collect your ticket.'

He returned a few minutes later, handing her the ticket.

'Luckily you've only got hand luggage,' he said. 'So we can go straight to Check In.'

Closer and closer, the final moment approached. At the Check In desk she showed her ticket, received a boarding card and turned to say goodbye. But Travis wasn't looking at her. He was leaning over the desk, showing another ticket, receiving a boarding card.

'Travis, what—?'

'You didn't really think I'd let you go alone, did you?' he said.

'But you can't— The awards—'

'They'll have to do them without me.'

Joy and horror warred in her: joy at his generosity, horror at his sacrifice, rendering her speechless. While she floundered he urged her forward, brooking no resistance, and by the time she could think clearly they were in the Departure Lounge.

'Travis, how did you—?'

'A little bit of stage management. When I booked your ticket I booked one for me as well. Then I called Rick, told him what I was doing. He'll be halfway back to town by now.'

'But you told him to—'

'To wait in the car park, yes. But he knew I didn't mean it. It was just to fool you, so that you wouldn't suspect until it was too late.'

'Travis, please, be sensible. The studio bosses will be furious—'

'Let them.'

'Your family—'

'I called Darius. He said I was doing the right thing and he's going to explain things to the others.'

'And your father?'

'I'll have to call him separately. In fact I'll do it now.'

But he was saved the effort by the ring of his phone. It was Amos, speaking in a voice so sharp and loud that Charlene could hear it from several inches away.

'Have you gone mad?' Amos raged.

'Father, I'm sorry to let everyone down like this, but I had no choice.'

'Of course you had a choice. You've risked everything you've worked for, you've insulted me. What kind of a fool do I look now, turning up to see you win prizes and you can't be bothered to be there?'

'I never meant to insult you. I hoped you'd understand.'

'I understand that you're doing something criminally stupid. That any son of mine—'

'Right this minute I don't feel like your son,' Travis interrupted him. 'And that makes me glad.'

'Stop talking like that and get back here at once. I'm telling you, no woman is worth it—'

His voice stopped suddenly. Travis had hung up.

'You cut him off,' Charlene said, aghast. 'He'll never forgive you.'

'And I will never forgive him for insulting you.'

'But listen—' she seized him '—it's wonderful of you to be prepared to do this for me, but you mustn't do it. Go back. It's not too late.'

'Haven't you understood yet? It was too late from the moment I met you. I didn't realise it then. It took me too long to see it, but now I know that you're the only woman I could ever love.

'I've never been able to speak of love before because I wasn't sure of you. First there was Lee. I thought you wanted him, but then you seemed to let him go easily, and I began to hope. But you see—' he made a helpless gesture '—I don't just love you. I need you. I depend on you. We've always made jokes about that but I began to be afraid in case you just saw me as some clinging juvenile. Suddenly it wasn't a joke any more.'

One day she would try to explain that she rejoiced in his need of her. Being needed was almost as beautiful as being loved. But there would be time for that later.

With shining eyes, she gazed at him.

'But think of all you might be giving up—'

'All I can think of is what I'll gain. If I'd let you go alone it would always be between us, that I wasn't there for you when you needed me. You'd have been nice about it, but we would always have known. And something would never have been right for us.'

'But do you really understand what you might be losing?'

'Yes, I know what I might lose. I might lose *you*. I might lose the woman I love more than anyone in the world. With you would go all my chance of happiness, of a future that meant anything. I'd lose my hope of children, for if you aren't my children's mother, nobody else ever will be. I'd lose all purpose in life. I'd lose everything.'

Now she was beyond speech, gazing at him, trying to understand the glimpse of his heart and soul he'd given her, and which was so unlike anything she'd imagined. She'd thought she understood Travis so well. Now she saw that she'd never understood the first thing about him.

'You didn't know I felt like that about you, did you?' he asked gently.

She shook her head. 'I thought the love was mostly on my side. I love you so much it scares me.'

'But you always kept so cool. Even when you agreed to marry me it was as though you were being cautious—'

'I was. I thought you only half wanted to. I heard Joe talking to you on the phone. He suggested that you should marry me, and you lost your temper at the other end.'

He groaned. 'Of course I lost my temper. I was mad at him for daring to think I'd marry you as a PR stunt. I loved you. I was trying every way I knew to win your love, and I felt he'd insulted you. That's why I got mad. And you thought— Oh, good grief!' He pulled her against him. 'How did we ever find each other when we've taken so many wrong turnings?'

'But we found the right road in the end,' she said.

'You thought I asked you to marry me as a career move? That's why you didn't want me to come to London with you?'

'I don't want you to risk losing everything.'

He shook his head. 'If I don't lose you, I haven't lost anything. If I do lose you, I've lost everything. Promise to stay with me, and that's all I ask.'

'I'll stay as long as you want me.'

He kissed her, and would have said more but for the loudspeaker. It was time to board.

They said little on the journey. Everything that mattered had already been said, and they sat resting against each other, sometimes dozing, sometimes basking in their mutual contentment and joy.

In London a cab took them to the hospital. As they arrived they exchanged a fearful glance. In a moment they would know—

Frank looked up as they entered the little ward.

'Thank goodness!' he said fervently. 'Emma, darling, look who's here!'

Her eyes were open, and even in her dreadfully weakened state she could recognise them.

'Charlene—I knew you'd come.'

'And look who I've brought to meet you,' she said.

'But he's— This is—'

'This is your future grandson-in-law,' Travis said. 'And now you've got to get well fast, because we want to see you in Los Angeles for our wedding.'

'Oh, darlings! How wonderful!'

'Don't get agitated,' the doctor warned.

'I'm not agitated. I'm happy. I'm going to be there.'

She closed her eyes, smiling.

They stayed in the hospital for the rest of the day and all night. Now and then Emma would awaken, always a little stronger than before.

'The doctor says her chances are improving by the minute,' Frank told them. 'It means the world to her that you gave up so much to come here. Thank you with all my heart. But were you wise to do it?'

'It was the wisest thing I ever did,' Travis said with a tender glance at Charlene.

They left the hospital that evening and spent the night in a nearby hotel, ready to return if there was an emergency call. But no call came.

As they snuggled down in each other's arms Charlene's thoughts were far away in Los Angeles, where the crowds would be gathering for the award ceremony, and people would be exclaiming in surprise, and perhaps annoyance, because the star of the evening wasn't there. She wondered how Travis felt now that the moment had come. But when she looked at him his eyes were closed. He might almost have been asleep, except that he turned and pressed his lips against her forehead.

Was he regretting his decision? Would he tell her if he did?

At last she fell asleep. In the early hours she awoke to find him just hanging up the phone.

'Any news?' she asked tensely.

'Yes, I called Joe. The awards ceremony was a success. I won the dramatic actor in a series award.'

'Not the other three?'

'No, but one is enough for me. Joe said they told the audience where I'd gone and why, and they applauded. We'll start work again as soon as I return. So you see, I've suffered no harm.'

'What about the film part?'

'Well—'

'Oh, no!'

'That's gone to the other guy. But who cares? I still have the series. And I have you. There'll be other film parts. But there won't be another you. My darling, try to understand. I've made my choice and I won't regret it. At least, I won't regret it as long as you stay with me, and love me.'

'Do you doubt that?' she whispered.

There was a strange look in his eyes, a mixture of teasing and adoration.

'What is it?' she asked.

'I was thinking that if Joe was here, he'd want you to say something nice to me. You wouldn't like to do that, would you?'

She considered. 'I might. I could say that I love you, that I've never loved anyone in my life as I love you, and I know that I never will. You *are* my life. I can have no other, and

I want no other. I'll stay with you for ever, loving only you. And when the end comes I hope we'll still be together.'

She reached up to touch his cheek. 'Do you think that will do?'

He smiled, taking her hand and brushing it with his lips. 'That will do perfectly,' he said.

* * * * *